Not So Sincerely, Yours

A.M. JOHNSON

Cover Design: Murphy Rae
Cover Illustrarion: Ashley Quick
Editing: Elaine York, Allusion Publishing
www.allusionpublishing.com
Proofreading: Kathleen, Payne Proofing
Formatting: Elaine York, Allusion Publishing
www.allusionpublishing.com

Not So Sincerely, Yours

To all the bookish folx, introverts,
and word junkies, you are my tribe.

For the Matchmakers
Jodi and Beth
The boys send their gratitude.

"What is that you express in your eyes?
It seems to me more than all the print
I have read in my life."
Walt Whitman~

Anders

Then

The quiet, tinny voice of Billie Holiday crooned from the speakers, and I adjusted my tie as a tight, cold pinch invaded my chest. Why I'd offered Wilder my house for his pre-wedding rehearsal dinner party was yet another example of how, even now, after all this time, he could get me to bend over backward for him. I'd only moved in a few months ago, and between the long hours I'd put in for some of my newer clients in Atlanta, and the time I'd spent in New York, I could count on one hand how many times I'd actually slept here. Scanning the living room, the smell of fresh paint lingered in the air. Everything seemed to be in its place. Staged. I'd left the curtains open on the tall, wide windows. The pink sky a perfect backdrop. But this place, this huge, three-bedroom, three-bathroom house, with its high ceilings,

1

and warm, brick-covered walls was wasted on me. A house for the modern family. But I was a family of one.

I chuckled at the sappy train of thought. Wilder getting married shouldn't have me fucked up like this. I'd been around him and Jax enough to get over what I'd once had with Wilder. Which wasn't much, if I was truthful with myself. We'd been friends with benefits, except I'd made the fatal error of falling in love with him. I'd thought time would help. Wasn't that the cliché? Time healed all wounds. Complete bullshit. It had taken me three years to fall in love with him. How was eighteen months supposed to be enough time to move on?

"What're you doing, baby?" Chloe draped her arms around my waist. "You okay?"

Big blue eyes framed between thick black lashes blinked up at me.

"Just thinking," I managed to say as I took her hands and held out her arms. "You look stunning."

Her red-stained lips split into a vivid smile. "I clean up nice."

A real laugh rumbled in my chest as she flipped her long brown hair over one shoulder. "You look good in anything." I ran my finger under the thin strap of her black dress, and she shivered. "Though, I think you look best in nothing at all."

She laughed and shoved my chest. "You're such a guy."

I shrugged and kissed her neck. "And how is that a bad thing?"

She tilted her head, exposing more of her smooth, pale skin. "Anders... we have maybe ten minutes before people start showing up... don't start something you don't have time to finish."

"Is that a challenge?"

Chloe sighed, and as she pulled away, a cute wrinkle popped up between her brows. "That was supposed to be a compliment."

"Well, in that case..."

She backed away, grinning from ear to ear. "Stay." She held up her hand and I laughed. "You know I never get this fancy. It took me forever to straighten my hair. I promise you can make me a mess later."

"You can't say something that hot and walk away."

"I'll make you a drink," she said over her shoulder.

"Tease," I hollered, and she laughed.

Chloe was sweet and sexy as hell. When I'd met her at a climbing gym six months ago, I hadn't been looking for anything serious, but she was laid back and didn't mind my crazy hours, or that I'd liked men too. Being bi-sexual sometimes freaked women out. It was nice to find one who didn't seem to care. Especially since I hadn't been able to get serious with another man after Wilder. I'd tried. Fucked a few guys. But it was difficult not to compare. Chloe was different. She was funny, and in truth, it was easy being with her. For one, my mother didn't harp as much about children and starting a family. When I was with her no one stared at us or dropped slurs. I couldn't say I'd ever cared what people thought of me. I should be able to love who I want without some asshole's opinion on the matter. And my parents' approval didn't define my success or who I was as a man. But it was hard not to notice the world's effortless support of my relationship with Chloe. No questions or dirty looks. Just blind acceptance.

I was about to head to the kitchen when the doorbell rang. My light mood shifted as a knot grew in my throat. I shook my head, irritated with myself. This was nothing new. Wilder and Jax were getting married. Today was a good day, I thought as the doorbell chimed again.

"Patience is a virtue," I said as I opened the door.

"Patience?" Wilder raised a brow. "Isn't that for boring people?"

"It's for adults. You should try it." I smirked when he pushed past me.

Jax gave me his shy smile as he reached out his hand. His grip was firm, and despite the way he never held my gaze for more than a few seconds, he was always kind to me. "Thanks for doing this for us."

"Of course," I said and stepped back. "Come on in."

Wilder had already made himself comfortable, leaning against the kitchen counter laughing at something Chloe had said as he popped a grape into his mouth. Jax kissed his cheek, setting the small grocery bag he'd had in his hand on the counter, and that same uncomfortable pinch from earlier returned.

"Hey, Chloe, where's that drink you made?" I asked.

She handed me a glass filled with clear liquid. I didn't taste it as I gulped it down.

"Thirsty?" Wilder asked, his sarcasm wasn't something I missed.

"Long day."

"I'd say so," Jax said. "Look at all of this food. You didn't have to—"

"It was catered," I said, and Chloe gave me a look. "What?"

"What Anders meant to say was…. he's just tickled to have the honor of hosting this party for y'all."

My laugh caught in my throat. "Yes… that… what she said."

I poured myself a little more vodka and plopped a lime in the glass. If I wanted to make it through this night, I'd need about five more of these. Maybe six.

Chloe put the cap on the bottle. "Maybe you should eat something."

Every pair of eyes was trained on me. I usually had my shit together. I was supposed to be the calm one. The guy who organized every minute detail. Not the lovesick lush who can't let go of the past. I cleared my throat and worked to smile.

"Probably a good idea," I conceded and pressed my lips to hers.

Chloe searched my face as I pulled away. She didn't know about my past relationship with Wilder. She only knew I was his literary agent. Chloe had no idea how hard this night would be for me. How I'd rather be anywhere else tomorrow when Wilder and Jax became official. And wasn't I the most pathetic person in the world. Wilder pissed me off half the time. I hated his drama and his me-centric energy. But he'd always been my pain in the ass. It's hard knowing I wasn't ever enough for him. It made me wonder if I'd ever be enough for anyone.

Chloe handed me a strawberry when the doorbell rang again. I set it down but Jax waved me off. "I'll get it, it's probably my mom. She left the hotel not too long ago."

Wilder followed Jax to the front door as Chloe kissed my cheek. "Something I should know?"

She was more perceptive than I'd given her credit for, or I was simply that obvious.

"Wilder... We used to be a thing once." Exhaling, I pulled her into my side. "Sometimes it's hard to forget how much I cared about him."

"Do you still care about him?"

"I do. But it's not the same. I just want him to be happy."

"Are you happy?" she asked.

The smile I gave her was practiced and easy. The same smile I gave my clients, strangers. She deserved more. But tonight, it was all I had to give.

I lifted her chin and met her eyes. "I am."

Laughter pulled my gaze to the living room. Jax had a huge grin on his face. More relaxed than I'd ever seen him, he hugged who I assumed was his mom. Wilder took her coat, and Chloe scrambled out of my arms to help.

"Let me take that," she said and Wilder handed it to her.

"Mom this is Chloe, Anders's girlfriend." Jax's smile held as I approached them.

"Nice to meet you, Mrs. Stettler."

"Call me Barb," she said and gave Chloe a hug.

She was tall for an older woman. Solid like her sons.

"Is this your house?" A younger version of Jax asked and I nodded.

"You must be Jason?" I held out my hand and he hesitated, his eyes wandering the big room.

When he finally took my hand, it was brief. "I'm Jaxon's brother."

"I figured. You guys look a lot alike."

"Jax has green eyes, mine are blue."

Chloe laughed and Jason's smile dimmed.

"But yeah... we're brothers... we look alike."

"Are you hungry, Jay?" Wilder asked, sending Chloe an icy glare before steering the Stettler family toward the kitchen.

"Shit..." she said "What just happened?"

"I forgot to tell you ... Jaxon's brother has some cognitive disabilities."

"Oh my God, I wasn't laughing at him. I thought he was being funny."

I placed my hand on the small of her back and leaned down to brush my lips across her pink cheeks. "You didn't know. I'll tell Wilder. It's my fault... don't worry alright?"

We both stared into the kitchen. Wilder's eyes were filled with mirth as he smacked Jax on the arm, his brother laughed full and uninhibited. The dynamic screamed family, and for the first time tonight I didn't feel that sharp pain of loss. Wilder had found his family. And that's all I'd ever wanted for him.

"What happened? Was he born—"

"It was a car accident. Jaxon said Jason was sixteen when it happened. Their dad had taken Jason fishing and, on the way home it started raining. He lost control of the car."

Chloe gasped and lifted her hand to her chest. "Oh no... that's awful."

"Their dad died, and Jason was under water for a long time. Wilder said Jason had quite the future planned. I don't know the whole story. But I know he won't ever be able to be on his own."

"God... how sad." She linked her fingers through mine.

"I know. I guess he's sort of stuck, like a little kid. I don't know if I'd want to live like that."

"What's the alternative?" A gruff voice I didn't recognize asked. I turned and was greeted by a pair of unfamiliar, caramel-colored eyes. "To be left for dead in a river?"

"That's not what I meant."

"It's not?" His lips in a stern line, he cocked his brow. "By all means, explain it to me then."

"I'm sorry, who are you?" I asked and Chloe squeezed my hand.

I had a couple of inches on the guy, but he squared his shoulders and didn't back down. "Ethan."

"Ethan, I—"

He brushed past me and Jason barreled into him. "When did you get here?"

"Just now, Jay." A smile softened his face, and when he wasn't scowling, I might've thought he was handsome. His arms were cut with lean muscle, and I liked the way his sandy brown hair fell over his forehead with a slight wave. It was casual, like the fitted, torn jeans he wore. "I missed the heck out of you."

Jason pulled away and yelled for Jaxon. "Ethan made it, Jax."

"I can see that." Jax pulled Ethan into a hug. "How's Colorado?"

"Cold as fuck."

"Language, boys." Barb winked and Ethan winced.

"Sorry, Mrs. Stettler."

When I laughed, he sent me another glare before heading into the kitchen.

"That went well," Chloe said and gave me a sympathetic look. "He's a little... intense."

Guilt wedged itself in the space between my diaphragm and stomach. Wilder had mentioned Ethan a few times. He was good friends with Jax and Jason, and I'd just stuck my foot in my mouth.

"I shouldn't have said that."

"You didn't say anything bad."

I'd basically said Jason's life was worse than death.

"I'm an asshole."

"Oh Lord..." June, Wilder's best friend, spoke from behind me, and when I turned, I found her with a hand on a hip and wide smile. "What did you do now?"

"Doesn't anyone use the doorbell anymore?" I asked as I wrapped her into a hug.

"Doorbells ruin the element of surprise." Tugging on my tie, she whispered, "How you holding up?"

"Surviving. I think I pissed off Ethan."

June laughed. "How in the world did you manage that? He's like the nicest guy ever."

"Ever? I see your flare for drama continues to rival Wilder's."

She hummed under her breath. "And I see you're as rude as ever. Who is this?"

Chloe held out her hand. "I'm the girlfriend."

"You can call her Chloe," I said and chuckled when June gave her a once-over.

"Be nice to this one, Anders, she's cute."

Chloe blushed. "He's always nice to me."

"I bet."

"Where's your better half?" I asked June. "Still at work?"

"Gwen's on her way."

"Come on." I nodded my chin toward the kitchen. "I'll make you a drink."

"I won't say no to that."

People slowly trickled in throughout the night, and I'd held Chloe's hand in mine the whole time. The heat of her skin steadied me as I maneuvered my way through smile after smile. The majority of the guests were from Bartley Press, Wilder's publisher, but there were a few people I didn't recognize, most I assumed were Jax's friends. Ethan's boyfriend Chance had shown up an hour ago, straight from the airport in dirty cargo shorts and muddy boots, looking like he hadn't seen a bottle of shampoo in over a week. I didn't give a shit if the guy had volunteered in Costa Rica for the last three weeks, he could have at least showered. The guilt I'd had about what I'd said earlier paled under the weight of my vodka-induced fog. And maybe it had something to do with how

I'd overheard Ethan in his ridiculous southern drawl comment on the size of my house, and how I must've been compensating for something.

Unfortunately, there was a ring of truth to what Ethan had said, and it had nothing to do with the size of my dick. This house should have been the next step in a well-plotted life, but I'd held out for too long, and now I owned a house with pictures on the walls that held no real meaning, and furniture I wasn't even sure I liked. It was as if I were the guest, and this place, this reflection of what I should have been no longer belonged to me. It belonged to them. Everyone around me. Jax and Wild.

Chloe let go of my hand and it shook me from my personal pity party.

"I'll be right back, Kris just got here."

She disappeared into the crowd, and I lifted my glass to my lips only to find it empty. I set it on the kitchen counter with a plan to fill it later. The sound of the party faded as I made my way to the back of the house to use the bathroom in my own bedroom, the break in the noise would offer me some much-needed clarity. It irritated me I'd let what Ethan said get under my skin. He'd pegged me as some rich, insensitive prick. He didn't know me. He didn't know how hard I'd worked for everything I had.

I tripped and hit the wall with my shoulder, realizing I might have been more drunk than I originally thought. Laughing at myself, I dragged my palm over my face and leaned against the wall outside of my bedroom. "Shit, Anders, get it together." I exhaled and closed my eyes.

I was thirty-six years old. I was a successful literary agent with a gorgeous girlfriend. I wasn't going to let some hillbilly kid, who had no problem drinking my top-shelf liquor, make me feel insignificant. I wasn't compensating for anything. Not one damn thing.

I shoved off the wall and opened my bedroom door. The grunts alone should have clued me in, but like a drunk idiot, I followed the sound to my bathroom. The door was partially opened, and I saw the reflection first. Ethan's face frozen in that perfect line between pleasure and pain. His neck stretched, his tendons straining under the open collar of his shirt. His head fell forward as Chance fucked into him, half-dressed, his filthy cargo shorts around his ankles. I should have said something, should have told them to get the hell out of my bedroom. But this weird rush of jealousy coursed through me, and I had no idea what to do with that revelation. I backed away, pissed there were strangers fucking in my bathroom and I wasn't going to do a thing about it.

In the hallway, I shut the door to my bedroom and pressed my forehead against the cool wood.

"How drunk are you?" Wilder asked, startling me and I lifted my head.

"Scale of one to ten?"

He nodded, his lopsided smile didn't cut me in two like it used to.

"Twenty."

"You look like shit."

"I always loved your honesty."

"Thank you for tonight," he said, his dark eyes holding a spark of sympathy.

I chuckled. "I'm fine."

I tried, unsuccessfully, to scrub the image of Ethan's face, strung out and about to come, from my brain. I'd tried to convince myself the jealousy I'd felt when I'd looked into that mirror was actually anger disguised by my over-consumption of alcohol. But the truth, I missed being with a man like that, missed feeling that powerful.

A man.

Not Wilder.

Not anymore.

"You're fine?" He didn't sound convinced.

"I am... truly." The smile on my face was real for once.

"Okay, then." He nervously picked at the hem of his button down.

"Could you do me a favor, though?" I asked.

"Absolutely."

"Tell Ethan... it doesn't matter how long it's been since he's seen his boyfriend, it's rude to fuck in another man's bathroom."

Ethan

Ten Months Later

A nagging, beep, beep, beep droned over and over again. Rolling to my side, I reached for my phone and almost fell out of the bed. Confused, I sat up, the room much too bright, and squinted at the pale blue walls. The unfamiliar color a reminder I wasn't in Denver anymore. Nope that was definitely Atlanta sunshine. How the hell was it already eight in the morning? I scratched the scruff on my jaw, my head swimming, my mouth sour with a fat tongue. Memories from last night slowly rolled in as I grabbed my phone from the pillow beside me.

"Jesus Christ," I groaned as I struggled to silence the damn alarm.

I needed to remember the next time Wilder offered me whiskey I should definitely not say yes. Ever. Again. With half-opened eyes, I noticed a text message from

Chance, and my stomach rebelled. For a good sixty seconds, I stared at it, wondering if I should delete it, debating whether or not I wanted to start my day depressed or pissed off. Who was I kidding? I was already fucking pissed off.

> Chance: Did you get there okay? Was hoping to hear from you.

I huffed and scrolled to the next text. He'd sent it an hour ago.

Five A.M. Mountain Standard Time.

> Chance: About to board my flight. I'll email when I can.

> Chance: I'll miss you. Miss us.

I pinched the bridge of my nose and threw my phone to the foot of the bed. He'd chosen this. He'd ruined it. I slid out of bed, my back aching from the overly soft mattress, and pulled out a pair of sweats and a t-shirt from one of the boxes piled near the window. Six boxes, to be exact. My entire life. It was sort of sad to think about how little I'd accumulated in all of my twenty-eight years. Everything about my entire situation was sort of sad. Before I could start feeling too sorry for myself, I trudged out of my room to the bathroom to take a piss. I finished my business, washed my face, and brushed my teeth. Feeling a little better, I figured I'd go investigate the kitchen and see what I could scrounge up for breakfast. Hopefully, they had coffee.

"You look like death, my friend." Wilder was spread out on the couch, half dressed in only a pair of pajama pants with a crooked grin on his face.

Feeling awkward, I averted my eyes to the fireplace. Wilder was married to my best friend Jax. A friend I used to crush on big time. A friend I might've kissed once. Before he got back with Wilder, of course. I was lucky they'd let me stay here on such short notice. But I'd been living with Chance for so long, it was weird being in other peoples' space.

"Completely your fault."

He laughed and set his book on the arm of the sofa. "Nobody made you drink... how many was it..." He tapped his finger on his lips.

"Three shots?" I asked.

"Six, I believe..."

"No..." I hung my head. "It was seven."

"That's right." He grinned. "Jax was worried you were going to throw up and choke to death in your sleep."

"I'm glad the possibility of my death amuses you so much," I teased. "Maybe you can use my misery as a muse for your next best seller."

"Never." Wilder smirked and ran his fingers through his dark, disheveled curls. "There's coffee if you want."

"Yeah?"

"Help yourself. I should warn you, though... Jax made it before he left for work."

"Warn me?"

He bit his bottom lip. "Let's just say he likes it strong, and not in a good way."

"Noted." I grimaced as I made my way to the kitchen.

The house wasn't huge but was perfect if you asked me. The kitchen was just off the living room, the long, granite breakfast bar separated the two rooms, giving the smaller space an open feeling. The main bedroom was upstairs with an attached office, offering Jax and Wilder their privacy from the other two bedrooms downstairs. Jax had built this place on his own with a little help from his contracting buddies. He'd made a nice life here. I'd wanted something like this with Chance one day. But settling down wasn't on his agenda.

"If you want, I'm heading to Cup and Quill in an hour to write. You can tag along... your stomach will thank you."

I chuckled as I poured the hot, very black liquid into a mug. "That's okay I have to look for a job today."

Wilder eyed me from the couch. "You just got here last night."

"If I want to start school in January, that gives me less than two months to get my shit together, and I'm not a freeloader." I took a sip of the coffee and tried, unsuccessfully, not to gag.

"I told you." He laughed. "That shit is lethal."

"No doubt." I dumped it into the sink.

Wilder set down his book and made his way into the kitchen. "Come with me. They have amazing crepes."

I didn't know what the hell a crepe was, but by the way Wilder drew out the word, *amazing*, like he was about to come, I figured it was something good.

"Alright."

He leaned lazily against the counter, a triumphant smile on his face. "You're not allowed to mope, Ethan. New city. New life. Remember?"

"Did I say that?"

"After shot number four... you said," he dropped his voice in an apparent attempt to mimic me, "'*Fuck Chance.*'"

"I do not sound like that."

"You totally sound like that."

I scrubbed my hand over my face, embarrassed. "God, I was drunk."

"Ethan, your boyfriend of two years, who you moved across the country for, just left to volunteer in Africa for at least a year. I'd be drunk as fuck too."

"Ex-boyfriend."

"Sure." He shrugged. "Whatever. Don't be too hard on yourself. And if it makes you feel any better, Jason is freaking out that you're here. He couldn't stop talking about it yesterday. He was mad his mom made him go home before you landed."

I'd gone to high school with Jax's brother Jason down in Florida, but we hadn't become friends until much later. It took ten years and a tragedy to eventually bring us all together. Jax's dad had gotten drunk and driven him and Jay into the Bell River one night. Jay had been under water too long. And now, his mind was on the level of an elementary student. But sometimes it was easy to see the man trapped inside of him. Jay and I were only sixteen when everything had happened. Jax had still been in college. He'd ended up dropping out to help take care of Jay and his momma. Thinking about it made me feel guilty. Here I was feeling sorry for myself over a guy, while Jay may never get to experience a relationship at all.

"Maybe I should go see him instead of—"

"No way... go shower. You need a good cup of coffee and powdered sugar bliss. It's the hangover cure. Trust me, you don't want to show up to Mrs. Stettler's house with your raggedy ass. I can smell the whiskey seeping from your pores, Ethan. She'll never let you see Jason ever again."

"I forgot how over the top you are sometimes."

Wilder placed his hand on his cocked hip. "You know there's this lovely little motel a few miles north. It has color television and everything. I hear they rent by the hour if you'd like to stay there."

"But do they have black tar heroin..."

"Is that a thing?"

"I think so."

"Then, yes, they have loads of it."

I smiled so wide it hurt my cheeks. "Well... shit. Why am I staying here again?"

Wilder shoved my shoulder and rolled his eyes. "Go get ready before I rescind the invitation."

"Thank you," I said, my tone serious. "For letting me crash here until I can get on my feet."

"Stay here as long as you want."

"Thanks." I gave him a smile and headed to my room to shower.

My room.

New city.

New life.

And maybe this time it might actually work out.

"Magic, right?" Wilder asked, laughing as I moaned.

With a mouthful of sugar and butter and strawberries, I mumbled, "Orgasmic."

"I'm always right, Ethan. You'll learn." He sipped from his cup of coffee.

I took another bite, feeling one hundred times better than I had thirty minutes ago. With the sugar overpowering the remnants of whiskey flowing through my blood, I was almost human again.

"You come here to write?" I asked and he nodded.

"Most days. The house feels... empty sometimes. Too quiet. The white noise here distracts me from getting too deep in my head. Sometimes I write at night, though, after Jax falls asleep. I used to have insomnia, but Jax was kind of the cure."

I thought about my last month in Denver. How I hadn't slept for more than an hour at a time, too worried about what to do with my life. I'd waited for Chance, put everything on hold, moved to fucking Denver, for Christ's sake. It was always about Chance. Always about his dreams.

"Ethan?"

I shook my head. "Sorry... just thinking."

He wrinkled his nose. "About Chance?"

"Unfortunately."

Wilder set his cup on the table and straightened his shoulders. "I'm here... if you want to talk about it."

I didn't want to talk about it. But maybe I needed to. I wasn't the type of person who wallowed. I'd always been positive, and I hated Chance a little for stealing some of that light.

"I guess I thought I was more important."

"You're important."

I huffed out a laugh. "Thanks... I mean, I know that... and it's a great opportunity for him. And I'd feel like shit if he'd turned it down for me. It's what he does, right? He likes to rebuild other peoples' lives. He's always known what he wanted to do, it's my own fault. I put myself second. I can't blame him for the choices I made for myself."

"He could've compromised. There's plenty of people in America who are homeless and need homes. He could have worked for a non-profit here, built houses in the states." Wilder shrugged. "Don't give him an easy out."

I pushed the last few pieces of food around my plate with my fork. "He acted like a year was no big deal. Like I should wait."

"Screw that."

"You waited for Jax for ten years."

"I didn't. I lived my life. I might've been a miserable human, but I tried my best. Second chances are rare, Ethan. Jax and I were lucky."

"You don't think I should wait?"

"I can't answer that."

I leaned back in my chair. "He was never around, always traveling. Costa Rica, Colombia, Panama, and before that Venezuela. Now it's Africa for a year. He says it's only a year, but what about next time."

"What about next time?" Wilder raised his brows. "What about what you want?"

"I want to be a nurse, help people like Jay." My heart thumped hard at the thought. My head light, I smiled.

"Then be a nurse. I happen to know a couple of nurses who would be willing to help you achieve that goal."

"June and Gwen just had a baby. They don't have time to help my ass."

"They would help you regardless. You applied to University of Georgia, right?"

"Georgia State."

"That's where Gwen went," he said, the excitement in his voice palpable. "See, it's kismet."

"Yeah," I said, suppressing my laugh. "Maybe it is."

"Speaking of fate and babies..."

"That sounds ominous."

Wilder sighed and pulled out his phone. "My friend has a job opening, his secretary is going on maternity leave next week."

"Next week?"

"I know you've mostly worked as a cashier, but if you know how to use spreadsheets and answer phones, you're basically hired."

"You asked him already?"

"Oh... no... but he's desperate. Trust me. He'll say yes."

"Maybe Jax will hire me."

"How are you supposed to work on a construction site and do homework?" he asked, his eyes on his phone as he eagerly tapped at the screen. I hated that he was right. "This job will be cush. It's perfect."

Taking my cell out of my pocket, I pulled up the web browser. "Is the application online?"

He scowled, distracted by something on his phone. "I don't think so."

"I'll look, what's the name of the company?"

"Lowe Literary."

"What?" I snapped, dropping my phone onto the table. "As in Anders Lowe."

Wilder glanced up from the screen, his expression bored. "Yeah... is that a problem?"

"That guy fucking hates me."

Not to mention, he's a judgmental prick with a stick up his ass.

"He does not."

"Wilder."

"Ethan."

"Did you forget about the incident?"

"Is that what we're calling it now?" he asked.

"You're not funny."

"I'm hysterical." He was barely able to contain his smile.

"He caught me fucking Chance in his bathroom, he's not going to hire me."

"I thought you were the one getting fucked." Wilder's grin was evil as he lifted his mug to his lips.

"I hate you." Heat spread up my neck to my cheeks. "I was drunk, and I hadn't seen Chance in weeks."

"There were other bathrooms you know... a guest room... a back porch."

"We were drunk. We weren't paying attention," I hissed. When Wilder barked out a laugh, I couldn't stop myself from laughing too. "He's an asshole anyway."

"Anders can be a bit of an elitist, but he's nice once you get to know him."

"You're only saying that because he's your agent." I sat back and looked around the room. The place was busy and bright. Sure, it would be hard to get homework done, but I bet the shifts were flexible. "Maybe there's a job opening here."

"Listen... the publishing world practically shuts down from Thanksgiving until after New Year's. You'll have plenty of time to settle in. It's an easy job, amazing pay. It'll be great for school."

"Hard pass."

Wilder's phone pinged and he cringed. "Too late."

"He did *not* say yes."

"You start next Monday."

My aversion to Anders wasn't necessarily about my embarrassment of being caught with my pants down. The guy had talked shit about Jason. Said Jason was essentially better off dead.

He was an ableist.

A privileged snob.

And... apparently my new boss.

Anders

"Would it kill you to answer your phone?" Wilder asked as he stormed into my office.

His hair flopped over his forehead, the curls obscuring his dark brown eyes as he sank down onto one of my office chairs, sulking like a teenager. The baby blue t-shirt he wore made his pale skin seem flawless. Young, like the first day I'd met him at Bartley Press when he'd worked as a copy editor. I closed my laptop and leaned my elbows on the cool wood of the desk.

"I already told you my answer," I said. "And I have a meeting scheduled soon, you should have knocked."

"What if my call was important? What if I'd been hit by a car?" he droned on, his drama, usually humorous, irritated me today.

"If you were dying, I assume you'd call your husband, or I don't know…" I leaned back in my chair. "Nine-one-one?"

Another long and aggravated sigh escaped his lips as he shoved his hair out of his eyes. "You have to hire him."

"I don't *have* to do anything, Wilder." I stifled my smile at his annoyance. Had it always been this easy to rile him up? "Afterall, I own the company."

His jaw clenched as he crossed his arms. "You're arrogant."

"We've already established that."

"Infuriating."

"Are we working on our adjectives today?"

"Just hire him," he said, voice raised. "He needs the job, and it would mean a lot to Jax."

"Not happening." I shook my head. "Why on Earth would I hire Ethan? Forgetting the fact, he has no respect for personal boundaries, he's not exactly well-versed in the world of publishing."

"Like Kris knew fuck all when you hired her?" He lifted a brow, a victorious grin spreading across his pretty face.

"This isn't a debate."

"Anders…" Wilder's dark eyes widened, the challenge in his posture melted. "Please do this one thing…"

He wanted this.

Shit.

"Don't look at me like that."

"Please," he asked again, and I could hear my coming defeat in his tone.

He had no idea how wrapped around his finger I truly was. I exhaled and raked my fingers through my hair.

"Part-time?" I asked.

He gave me a smile, leaning forward he said, "Part-time is exactly what he needs. Ethan starts school in January."

I tapped my fingers on the desk, dreading the words I was about to utter. "Part-time. Monday, Wednesday, and Friday." Wilder beamed. "Temporary. If he can't pull his weight, he's—"

"Thank you. You won't regret it."

I doubted that.

"Don't be too pleased with yourself. I doubt he'll last long." I opened one of the desk drawers and pulled out the contract I'd looked over earlier. "This is for you."

"What is it?" he asked.

Wilder slowly took the folder from my hand like he was afraid it would bite him.

"Working Pictures wants to create a series based on Abel."

"You're fucking with me?" Shock registered across his face as he skimmed the pages in front of him.

"I'm not. *The Street Vendor's Son* won a National Book Award. That book..." A smile worked its way across my lips. Wilder could exasperate the hell out of me, but in truth, he was hands down the most talented writer I'd ever worked with. "Wilder, it was a privilege to read it."

He dropped his eyes to the contract, his cheeks pink. "I pay you to stroke my ego."

"And you pay me well." I smirked. "But I mean it. You deserve this."

Wilder didn't look up from the contract, his hands trembling as he turned the pages. "This amount can't be right."

"It's accurate, I assure you."

"Anders... it's too much."

"It's not enough." I smiled at his skepticism. "I asked for more, but you're still an unknown in some circles."

He rolled his eyes. "Meaning I'm not pop culture enough?"

"Too high brow," I teased, and he scowled.

"Twelve episodes, sixty-grand plus two-point-five percent of the royalties, and you get final say on the script."

"Wow."

"You're welcome."

He snorted. "It's only one season."

I loved how he always tried to put me in my place.

"For now."

Wilder set the contract on the desk. "I don't think I've ever been speechless."

"I can attest to that."

"Don't ruin this moment with your mouth." The surly toddler was back.

"You ruined it by asking me to hire Ethan."

"Thank you," he said in a rare moment of humility. "He's been through a lot, and who knows, maybe you'll make a friend."

"I have enough friends." I handed him a pen. "Sign the last two pages and I'll fax it over today."

The pen scratched across the paper as he spoke. "Your clients do not count as friends, Anders. When was the last time you did anything for yourself?"

"I broke up with Chloe last month."

He exhaled, and I hated the sad way his lips pressed together. I didn't want his pity. "She was nice."

"If nice is a synonym for dull then, yes, she was very nice."

I had to admit, in the beginning Chloe had a certain appeal. Great in bed. Didn't care that I liked men, but the longer we'd stayed together, the more she'd started planning. She'd painted a picture of what my life *should* look like based on social standards. What my mom begged me for practically every day. House. Wife. Kids. Dog. I didn't want picture-perfect. At least not with her. I wanted someone I couldn't get out of my system no matter how hard I tried.

"You were always afraid of commitment," he said and handed me the contract.

"Says the man who pined for almost ten years and never had a serious relationship."

"We were—"

"Don't." I laughed. "We had a good time together, Wilder, but let's not pretend either one of us was ready for something serious." The lie was stale on my tongue.

"That doesn't mean you're not a commitment-phobe."

"Commitment shouldn't be obligatory... a next step. I guess I'm holding out for something a little more irrational..." I groaned. "Why are we talking about this?"

"Because... when *The Street Vendor's Son* wins an Emmy, you're not going to want to bring just anyone to the party." His grin was ridiculous.

"Your ego knows no bounds."

"Thanks to you."

Before I had a chance to reply, my office door opened.

"Oh, sorry, Mr. Lowe, I didn't realize—"

"It's alright, Nora. I'll be finished in a few minutes."

She gave me an apologetic smile and nodded. "I'll be in my office."

The door clicked shut and Wilder pursed his lips. "Who's Nora?"

"An agent," I said and stood. "She's new."

"She's pretty."

"And has a boyfriend."

"Really?" he said, looking far more put out than reasonable.

"Stop worrying about my sex life."

"Love life," he corrected. "You're getting too old for random hook-ups."

"Don't you have a book to write?" I asked as he pulled his bag over his shoulder.

"What time should Ethan be here on Monday?"

I exhaled, my earlier irritation back in full force. "How about never-thirty?"

"Eight o'clock then?" Wilder grinned as he opened the door.

"Seven. If he's late, he's fired. I'm serious, Wilder... this isn't a charity organization."

"I'll have him call you for the details just in case."

"What? No... I literally just told you—"

He shut the door, in true Wilder fashion, before I could finish my sentence, leaving me to wonder why I'd ever put up with his bullshit in the first place.

The Sunday morning sun hid behind the clouds as I sipped my coffee. Light rain and gray skies enhanced the deep green color of the trees and foliage visible through the large kitchen window at my parents' house. Morningside was known for its lush setting and cottage-like appeal. The home I grew up in was no different. The historic two-story, vine-covered, red brick, with an A-line roof framing its wooden front door, was like something out of a fairytale. Inside it was decked out with modern appliances and furniture only two lawyers could afford. The place I'd purchased in the city seemed insignificant compared to this estate. I'd done well for myself, started a successful literary agency with an office in Atlanta and Manhattan, but the wealth my parents had, at times felt like a heavy leash.

"What are you moping about, Anders, honey? Sit down, have something to eat. I started the batter for the pancakes you like." Her smile was anxious. "The pumpkin ones."

I chuckled and leaned in for a hug. My mother's arms were small and thin but warmed me all the same.

"Thanks. You didn't have to go to the trouble."

She pulled back and tapped me on the nose like I was five and not thirty-six. "You're my only child, and I have no grandchildren to speak of. Who else would I make them for?"

She usually waited until after I ate to drop the guilt trips.

"Mom..."

She waved her hands. "I know... I'm sorry, I worry and—"

"I know, Mom... trust me... I know."

She frowned as she pulled the batter from the giant, stainless-steel fridge. "We liked Chloe."

I leaned against the long island that cut through the center of the kitchen. Delicate glass lights hung from the tall ceiling on long wires, illuminating the dark granite, and I stared at the silver specks glittered along the top of the counter. "Dad liked Chloe."

She tutted and gave me a dirty look. "I liked her just fine."

Mom's Midwest accent leaked through and I smiled. She'd been raised on a dairy farm in Minnesota. She always preached about hard work, and how success was something you made for yourself. She'd worked her ass off to get into law school, that's where she'd met my dad. She could've quit school, been a southern socialite with all of Dad's family's money, but she'd made her own way. I respected that.

"You thought she was too prissy."

"I never said that." She busied herself with the stove, pouring batter onto the heated griddle.

The sizzling sound brought me back to when I was eight years old and reminded me of *Star Wars* pajama pants and Saturday morning cartoons.

"I distinctly remember the word prissy and maybe something about never working a hard day in her life."

"Well..." She glanced over shoulder. "I don't recall..."

"I thought lawyers were good with details."

"Alright. Maybe I did say something about her being a little delicate. But she was charming, and you seemed to like her."

"She wasn't man enough for me."

"Anders," she chided, and a familiar lump formed in the back of my throat.

I'd come out as bi to my parents in college. They'd acted supportive. Said they'd loved me no matter what gender I was attracted to, and for the most part, they'd seemed fine with everything. But when I'd brought home my first boyfriend, things hadn't felt all that fine. My dad, to my surprise, hadn't cared as much as my mom. He'd told me he wanted me to be happy, and originally my mom had said the same. But she had a vision for my life. One she never got to have for herself. She and my father weren't able to conceive. They'd tried for five years before they'd decided on adoption. I was eighteen months old when they'd adopted me. Mom wanted me to get married and make the babies she never had.

"Why do you do that?" I asked, trying to keep the hurt and anger, bottled up. "You know I like men, Mom."

"And women." She flipped a pancake onto a plate.

"Every time you do this..." I swallowed. "It's like you're saying I'm not good enough as I am."

"Honey." She poured more batter onto the griddle, ignoring me. "That's not true."

"Isn't it... What if I married a man and adopted like you and Dad did? That child would be your family too."

She set down the spatula and turned to look at me. Her eyes glassy she said, "Yes... but you could have—"

"A real child?" I stood, the stool grinding against the hardwood floor. "I can't believe—"

"Damn it, Anders, that's not what I was going to say." Tears spilled over her lashes and down her cheeks. "*You* are my real child, always have been and you know it. But yes, you have a chance at having biological children and I don't want to see you throw that away. I wouldn't trade anything for you. You are my son, and I love you regardless of whether or not I birthed you, but I can't deny I don't wish I could've held a pregnancy longer than eight weeks. I can't stop myself from being sad about all the miscarriages we had. The children we lost. But none of that means I don't love you just the same as I would a biological child."

Smoke billowed behind her and she swore. I watched in silence as she scooped the burnt pancake into the trash.

"I think I've lost my appetite," I said and picked up my car keys. "Thanks for the coffee."

"Honey... come on."

"You can rationalize it any way you want, Mom. But when you say I want you to have the life I didn't, or don't throw away your chance... you're saying I wasn't enough. You're saying you wish you had more." She wiped at her eyes and took a step toward me. "I've got to go. Tell Dad I'm sorry I had to leave."

She called out my name before I slammed the front door behind me. I didn't give in. Not this time. The rain soaked through my cotton t-shirt and jeans as I made my way to my car. The wet denim squeaked against the leather seat as I slid inside. I pulled my phone from my pocket to make sure it wasn't damaged by the moisture, and if I thought my morning couldn't get any worse, the missed text sitting in my inbox proved otherwise.

> Hey, this is Ethan Calloway. Wilder's friend. He gave me your number. He told me you weren't clear on what time you'd like me to be there tomorrow morning. I wanted to check in with you to make sure I arrive when you need me to.

My jaw pulsed and two knots formed in my back as my shoulders stiffened. I didn't need Wilder's shit attempt at humor right now.

> Me: Seven sharp.

Just as I finished reluctantly adding him to my contacts he texted back.

> Ethan: I'll be there. Thanks.

> Me: Try to keep your dick in your pants this time.

> Ethan: I'll try my best.

Ethan

The asphalt was slick with rain as we turned off the main road. The break in the weather faded into heavy, dark gray clouds that threatened to open up again, and I worried this fishing trip might not last as long as I needed it to. I'd been in Georgia a little over a week, and this was the first time I'd had to get outside with Jason and Jax. I wasn't a professional fisherman or anything of the sort. Most of the time I didn't give a damn if I caught anything at all. I loved the water, loved sitting in the fresh air with nothing between me and the flat surface of a lake, or the rapid of a river, except a line and a lure. My mind was the quietest then, when the sky watched, and the trees hovered. Not much else in the world gave me that much peace.

"One of the guys I work with said Allatoona has some of the best bass fishing around. Maybe next time we can rent a boat or something." Jax smiled as the truck rolled to a stop.

"Or we could just buy one," Jason muttered.

"I almost forgot you were here, buddy," Jax flashed his brother a smile as he cut the engine.

Jay had been unusually quiet on the forty-minute drive, or at least I thought it was unusual. But in all honesty, I hadn't seen him since the wedding, and for all I knew this could be his new norm.

"I expected you to talk my ear off," I said and turned in my seat.

He scowled. "I'm just tired."

"And mad... Might as well tell him, get it out of the way." Jax opened the driver side door. "I'll grab the poles from the back and meet y'all at the dock."

"Mad?" I asked as Jax shut the door. "What'd I do?"

Jay wouldn't look at me. He picked at the hole in his cargo shorts pocket with his fingernails. "Sure did take you forever to come see me."

"Aw, Jay... I wanted to. You were the first person I wanted to see."

"But," he said, his brows furrowed and angry.

"I had to get settled, and you had school. And I had a meeting with an advisor to go over my classes for next semester. But we're here now."

"Jax said you're gonna be busy." Big blue eyes stole my breath.

I loved this guy like he was my own brother, and the way he looked at me, like I'd ruined his damn life, almost killed me.

"Not too busy for you... ever. We can go fishing every Sunday if you want. Like today. It'll be our day."

"Sunday is God's day, Ethan. It can't be yours."

"I think He's willing to share," I said. "If it makes you happy."

His lips twitched, and ever so slowly he smiled. "It would... make me happy."

"Well, then, it's settled. Sundays are for God and fishing."

I laughed, thinking the quote belonged on a redneck cut-off, sleeveless t-shirt with a picture of Jesus holding a beer and a fishing pole.

"I don't think Momma would agree," he said but smiled.

"Your momma loves me, I bet I could convince her." I leaned over and messed up his hair with the palm of my hand.

He swatted my hand and grumbled under his breath. "I'm not a kid, you know."

"I know."

"Ms. Wilson said I'm a grown up... said I shouldn't let anyone make me feel small."

"Ms. Wilson?"

"My teacher, I like her." Jason's cheeks flushed. "She treats me like she treats Jax or any other person. She doesn't call me buddy or mess up my hair."

Guilt skittered inside my chest as his brows furled. "You doing good at this new school then?" I asked.

"It's alright, I guess. I'm reading high school books now."

"You like it better than Benchmark?"

He shrugged and looked out the window. "I miss Florida sometimes. I made some friends there. But I like Ms. Wilson better."

"She pretty?" I teased, and that got his attention.

He turned to scowl at me. "Like you'd care, you like boys."

"Hey, I can appreciate a good-looking woman."

"Yeah, she's pretty." He chewed the side of his lip. "And smart."

"Sounds like a nice lady. When do I get to meet her?"

"Anytime you want," he said, his excitement sparkling in his blue eyes. "I can show you around my school... it's small, so it won't take long. Maybe you can pick me up one day this week."

"I'd like that."

I was well aware Jax was at the dock probably waiting on us. But I missed this, missed shooting the shit with Jason. Learning about his life. Hoping he was happy. It seemed like he was. Jay had come into his own after he'd started the same day program Chance's sister attended when we'd all lived down in Bell River. She'd been there for a while, and it had been Chance's suggestion Jay had started in the first place. The thought of Chance and how we'd met at Harley's, the old hardware store where I'd used to work, made my heart squeeze inside my chest. The late nights I'd spend with him stocking the shelves and... other things. A weight settled on my shoulders as I thought about all the time I'd given him. I'd thought he'd been it for me. But I was tired of waiting for him. Tired of sacrificing myself over and over again.

"It might rain," Jay said, breaking me from my memories.

"Yeah." I smiled. "But that never stopped us before."

And twenty minutes later, the clouds opened up like he'd thought they would. The rain wasn't heavy, more of a drizzle, but the cool November temperature nipped at my skin. Jax and Jason had thought ahead and worn rain jackets. I was in a short sleeve and boardshorts. I shivered as the breeze picked up, skating across the water and into my bones.

"Shit, it's cold," I said, my teeth chattering.

"Got a sweatshirt in my truck if you want to borrow it." Jax's easy laugh made me smile. I guess I missed that too. "How in the hell did you survive a Denver winter?"

"It wasn't that bad. It's a dry cold, none of this humidity bullshit."

It wasn't a total lie, the snow was nice for the most part, the below-freezing temps, however, could fuck right the hell off.

Jason reeled in his line and gave me a dirty look. "I forgot how much you swear."

Jax and I both busted up laughing. "Jay... come on... I'm not that bad."

He cast his line again, not meeting my eyes he said, "Momma said you swear like a sailor. I don't know what sailors sound like, but I'm guessing they use bad words... a lot... like you."

My side ached with how hard he had me laughing. Jax wasn't much better off either. He grabbed a soda from the cooler and cracked it open, the grin on his face a mile wide. "This feels right. Having you back."

"He's gonna come pick me up from school, Jax," Jay glanced over his shoulder, the dimples in his cheeks popping as he smiled. "Meet Ms. Wilson."

Jaxon's brows raised. "Ahh… the infamous Ms. Jenni Wilson. You're in for a treat then."

"Ms. Wilson doesn't like fishing." Jason's smile fell. "But she loves basketball."

"She's a Hawks fan," Jax said, giving me a knowing look. He leaned in and whispered, "I think he has a crush on her."

"You think?" I asked, the sarcasm in my voice unmistakable. "That's weird, right?"

"She's only thirty, and cute as hell if I were into chicks."

"Okay…" I dragged out the word. "But she's his teacher. That's gross, man. He might be twenty-eight, but like… come on now… don't make me say it."

Jax's green eyes dimmed. "I know… but there's no harm in it, though, him liking her. He's been working out with me at least four nights a week, playing ball again. I don't know… maybe his mind is expanding, and if him having a crush makes him want to work harder at things, then I'm all for it."

I stared at Jason, noticing he'd filled out a bit. Stood taller. Jax was massive, all muscle and long limbs and big, broad shoulders. And it was easy to envision Jason being built the same way as his brother if things hadn't changed drastically for him the night his dad crashed into the river. But this Jenni chick was his teacher. And that didn't sit right with me.

"She's like... I don't know. She could take advantage of him."

Jax's jaw clenched. "He's come a long way, Ethan... cut him some slack. He's not stupid. And hell... what's the harm in it. It's not like she's thinking the same shit."

"But how do you know that?" I whispered, my frustration making me speak louder than I had intended.

"I guess I don't know." He smiled and it threw me off guard. "You worry too much. He's changed a lot... you'll see."

"Y'all can stop whispering about me like I'm not right here," Jason said, and when I glanced back at him, his eyes were on the fish he'd just reeled in.

Jax squeezed my shoulder. "I know you mean well... but Jason's been trapped for too long inside his own head, and I'm more inclined to let him feel what he wants, even if he gets hurt. It's better than being numb."

"I don't know," I said. "Numb sounds good to me."

"I'm sorry about Chance."

I reached into the tackle box, avoiding Jax's eyes. Settling on a curl tail grub, I gave in and met his worried gaze.

"I'll be fine. I'll be too busy with school and work. I won't have time to wallow."

"And before you know it, a year will be gone and he'll be back," Jax said, sounding way too optimistic.

"Too bad I'm not waiting on him." Jax followed me to the end of the dock where I gave Jason a smile. "I'm gonna try for a bass."

Jason snorted. "Good luck."

I knocked my shoulder into his and he laughed. I loved the sound of it. Jax was right. Jay did seem lighter.

"You really aren't gonna wait?" Jax asked and I sighed.

"Nah, man. I've waited long enough. I need to focus on me for now."

"You do," he agreed and cast his line. "But don't close yourself off to the possibility... I mean, look at me and Wild."

Possibility.

I couldn't think like that or I'd never get over him.

"Our relationship is different. This is who he is. Chance wants to travel the world doing humanitarian work, and that's great and admirable. But I like roots, Jax. Stability."

"Traveling all over the place sounds awful," Jason agreed. "I don't know why people don't like their homes. Why they always want to go, go, go. I'd be happy to stay in one place forever."

"See... Jay gets me," I teased, and Jax shook his head with a small smile.

"It's good to have you back," Jax gave my shoulder another squeeze. "Hopefully, Anders won't run you off."

I winced. "Ugh, don't remind me."

"I don't know what Wild was thinking, setting you up working for him. After what happened at—"

"I know," I said, cutting him off with a quick glance at Jay. "But I have to think it's water under the bridge if he hired me, right?"

Jax's chuckle did nothing to reassure me. "I guess we'll find out."

"If it sucks, I can work for you?"

"Of course."

I exhaled and cast my line into the water.

The city was awake with foot traffic and blaring car horns. People in business attire with cups of coffee buzzed by me as I leaned against the locked door of Lowe Literary. It was forty-five minutes after seven, and I'd been standing here since six-thirty, thinking it would be smart to arrive early. I'd been worried about parking, or worse, getting lost in the city. I didn't drive much around Denver, and growing up in small-town backcountry Florida, I could admit I wasn't adequately equipped for the big city. My hands were cold, even stuffed in my pockets, and my temper bordered on irate. I'd texted Anders about twenty minutes ago and he hadn't answered. I was seconds from saying fuck it and walking back to my car when he finally rounded the corner. Anders was all confidence in a steel-colored suit with a deep blue button down underneath. His golden blond hair was artfully disheveled, giving him a casual appearance, but I'd bet my left kidney it'd taken him an hour to get ready this morning. Maybe that's why he was late.

"You're early," he said, his voice smooth and bored.

He didn't spare me a glance as he pulled keys from his pocket and opened the door.

My jaw ached as I gritted my teeth. "Early? You told me to be here at seven."

"Did I?" he asked, and I could hear the fucking humor in his voice.

"Yeah..." Asshole. "You did."

I followed him into the office, the lights automatically illuminating as we stepped inside. The place was nice, not as cold as I assumed it would be. Instead of glass and metal, everything was warm wood and earth tones.

"Office hours are nine to four. Kris used to show up around eight-thirty," he said, leaning against the only desk in the lobby. "This is your workspace. I'll get your log-in information when you get back."

I took a calming breath. "Back from where?"

"The Starbucks two blocks west from here." His lips lifted more on the right side of his mouth, his grin crooked. He was enjoying himself at my expense. "Americano for me, and you can get whatever you want within reason. Here..." He reached into his bag while I seethed. No apology for making me sit in the damn cold for over an hour, nope, right to business. "This is the company card. I expect a receipt for any purchases you make for me or Lowe Literary."

I took the card from his hand. "Receipts. Got it."

His blue eyes traveled over my body slow and disapproving. I had on the best pair of jeans I owned and borrowed one of Jax's polo shirts. I didn't have the money for bullshit designer suits, but I cleaned up okay.

"You're the face of Lowe Literary, Mr. Calloway. I expect you to dress like you give a shit."

I huffed out a laugh. "Well, I expect a boss who shows up on time."

"I was on time." Arrogant as hell, he slipped his hand into his slacks.

"Why did you tell me seven if we don't open until nine?" I asked, ignoring his confident glare.

He hesitated, and I wondered what bullshit excuse he was about to give me when he surprised me with the truth. "Initiation. Payback. Perhaps a bit of both."

I understood the payback part. I'd be pissed if I caught strangers fucking in my house too. But initiation? Like what? Hazing?

"Look, I'm sorry about—"

He raised his hand, silencing me. "You're here because Wilder asked me to help out his friend. Apologies are unnecessary. This isn't about you. It's best if you remember that. Show up. Do your job. And there won't be a problem."

Before I had a chance to reply, he walked away and disappeared down the hall. Furious, and feeling smaller than I ever had in my entire life, I contemplated quitting. I didn't need to put up with his shit. I could be on site with Jax in an hour if I wanted. I slammed my eyes shut and tried to push down my anger and pride. This job would allow me the time I needed to do my schoolwork. And according to the nursing program advisor I'd spoken with last week, I had a shit ton of prerequisites I had to complete before I could even apply to the RN program. If it weren't for Mr. Superiority Complex, this would be the chillest job I could find. And I'd never find a gig that paid me as well as this did. I groaned and pocketed the business credit card, hating the way Anders had me by the balls.

The coffee shop was busting at the seams with people when I walked in. No one paid attention to anyone else, more fixated on their smartphones. The line was ridiculous, and to make matters worse, there were only two baristas. By the time I actually had my order in hand, thirty minutes had passed. It was after nine when I arrived back at the office. A woman in a black blouse and gray pencil skirt hovered in one of the office doors, chatting with someone I couldn't see. The office was awake and buzzing, and as I set the coffee down on my desk, the woman turned and looked at me.

She smiled, but like Anders, gave me a once over. By the crinkle in her nose, she'd found me wanting. "You must be new... I'm Claire."

"Ethan," I said and held out my hand.

She took my offered hand in hers, her grip too soft. "Charming. You're the new secretary?"

"I'm Anders's assistant," I corrected, and she grinned.

"Temporary, I assume?"

Ugh. I didn't know who I disliked more. Her or Anders. Was everyone here going to be a complete douchebag?

"Until Kris comes back, yeah."

She let go of my hand, her smile as fake as the bleached color of her hair. "Welcome... You'll fit right in."

I rolled my eyes when she turned to leave, grabbing Anders's coffee in my hand and headed down the hallway. There were only four offices, and I couldn't be sure which one belonged to Anders. I passed by Claire's office and

47

was grateful when she closed the door. The office she'd been standing in front of earlier was occupied with another woman who was busy on a call. She had kind brown eyes that silently said hello as I walked by. The third office was empty, and I assumed the last one was Anders. The door was cracked open and I knocked once and pushed it open.

"Most people wait for a confirmation before entering," he said, not looking up from his laptop.

"I figured since it was open…" The rest of my sentence fell away as I took in the room.

The sound of soft guitars hung in the air, spilling from the speakers of his laptop, the music reminded me of the folk stuff I listened to sometimes. His office was bigger than the others, but nothing too ostentatious like I figured it would be. He had shelves and shelves overflowing with books. There were three small paintings hanging on the wall behind his desk, the colors dark and gritty. A few framed pictures dotted a smaller shelf just below the artwork. This space, this office, it was a complete one-eighty from the house I'd visited for Jax's rehearsal. This room was dusty and comfortable, nothing like the man staring at me now.

"Have a seat," he said, and I handed him his coffee. Anders took a deep sip, and I swallowed as his Adam's apple moved slowly in his throat. "It's lukewarm."

"It's forty degrees outside."

The muscles in his jaw feathered and I internally smiled. I'd gotten under his skin.

He lifted a piece of paper and reached across his desk. "Take this. It's your log-in info. If you have any problems, the number for tech support is at the bottom of the page."

I lifted the paper from his hands and scanned over it. "Thanks."

"I leave for the Manhattan office on Thursday. I'll need a full report for the acquisition editor by then."

"Um... I'm sorry... I have no idea what that means."

He let out a long, aggravated breath. "This is going to be a nightmare."

"I'm not an idiot, alright... but isn't it customary to train new employees?"

He lifted his cell from the desk and tapped his thumb on the screen. After a second, the phone rang through the speaker.

"Hey, Anders, new guy making you crazy already?" A woman's voice floated from the phone.

The smile that graced his lips was real and softened the hard lines of his jaw. His perfect mask slipped, and if I didn't want to punch him in the face, I'd actually think he was kind of beautiful.

"Kris, if I said you could bring your baby to work would—"

"No way." She laughed. "What do you need, Anders? Cesar and I are putting together the crib."

A wistful look wrinkled around his eyes as he smiled. "Can you email Ethan a to-do list that explains the appointment spreadsheet and the acquisition emails? And while you're at it, give him your passcodes, it'll be good for him to look at some of your correspondences for examples. I'll have some of the other agents go over the queries until he knows what to look for."

"Is there some reason you're incapable—"

He quickly glanced at me, disconnected from the speaker, and brought the phone to his ear. "I'm busy and you're... you."

I coughed to hide my laugh, and his ice blue gaze narrowed. He finished up his call, his civility to his former assistant gave me hope, but when he spoke again, that hope died a hard and fast death.

"Kris will send you everything you need," he said with a dismissive wave at the door. I slowly stood, staring at him as he ignored me, tapping away on his laptop again.

"Thanks," I grumbled, and when he didn't respond I walked to my desk.

I booted up the computer, logged in with the email address and password Anders had given me, and waited for Kris's instructions. True to her word, she sent what I needed. I went over everything, opening up the programs I needed. Basically, I was in charge of Anders's calendar, sending the manuscripts he'd signed off on to the acquisitions editor, and eventually I'd get to field literary queries authors sent in looking for representation. That sounded a bit too over my head and was glad I wasn't expected to do that right out of the gate. I opened the calendar and noticed he had a meeting in the next thirty minutes. I clicked on the author's name and it brought me to another file. I opened it and found the contract and manuscript Anders planned on "shopping" like Kris had mentioned in her email. Without anything better to do, I started to read the first few paragraphs of the book. It was a nonfiction piece on the Stonewall riots back in the late sixties. I was about ten pages deep when an email notification popped up on my screen.

FROM: AndersLowe@LoweLitFic.com

TO: EthanCalloway@LoweLitFic.com

DATE: Nov 9 10:03 AM

SUBJECT: Professionalism

Mr. Calloway,

I'm sorry for the delay, my accountant has forwarded the necessary paperwork. I've attached the NDA you are required to sign, and the new employee paperwork, including your income tax worksheet, as well as a copy of the dress code. Please note that jeans are prohibited. If you have any questions or concerns, let me know.

Anders Lowe

Manager

Lowe Literary, LLC

NDA? I searched the Internet for clarification, not wanting him to realize I had no idea what the hell that meant. He already thought I was a total dumbass. Not that I cared what he thought about me. Not at all. It was more I didn't want him to have the satisfaction of being right, that indeed I was in a little over my head with this job. I printed the Non-Disclosure Agreement, some of the tax forms, and signed them. After a few failed attempts, I had this shit totally handled, I scanned the documents to my computer.

FROM: EthanCalloway@LoweLitFic.com

TO: AndersLowe@LoweLitFic.com

DATE: Nov 9 10:29 AM

SUBJECT: RE: Professionalism

Anders,

I have signed and attached the documents you required. In regard to said dress code, I, unlike some, have better things to do with my money than throw it away on showy suits. School, food, gasoline, and housing. You know, life stuff. But I'm sure I can procure a tie and a pair of slacks by eight not seven Wednesday morning.

Thanks for your concern,

Ethan Calloway

The Face of Lowe Literary

Anders

Lukewarm coffee dripped onto my tie as I lifted the cup to my lips. I sighed, grabbing an old takeout napkin from one of my desk drawers, pleased I'd had the foresight to save some in the first place. I dabbed at the spreading stain, cursing under my breath. I made it worse. I shoved out of my chair, with more ferocity than necessary, and undid my tie. My mood this morning left much to be desired, and my new assistant was partly to blame. Admittedly, I was more irritated with Wilder for putting me in this position. I thought about Ethan's email and my aggravation spiked again. Nervy asshole. I inhaled a deep breath and pinched the bridge of my nose, reminding myself I hadn't been the most welcoming either. I stared down at the stain, at the overly priced tie in my hand, and an uneasy pang tightened my chest.

School, food, gasoline, and housing. You know, life stuff.

Though completely rude and unprofessional, he had guilt swimming inside my chest. I didn't like it. I didn't like him. Annoyed at myself, at him, and this fucking tie, I swung open my office door and made my way to the bathroom. With the door locked behind me, I turned the faucet to cold and scrubbed at the stain, wondering why the hell I should bother anyway. I had about twenty more gray ties sitting in my closet at home. It seemed excessive, maybe, but I'd worked hard for everything I had. My parents were wealthy, but my money was my own. It was something I prided myself on. My parents had chosen to take me in. A strange child. It was the biggest handout I'd ever receive. And I wanted to prove to them they'd chosen wisely. That I was the son they should've picked. Even if I disappointed them sometimes. Even if I'd been a last resort.

My blue eyes looked back at me through the mirror. I popped open the top two buttons of my shirt, leaving the tie in the sink, and ran my damp hand through my hair. I'd let Ethan get inside my head. He'd made a baseless correlation between my money and who I was as a person. I might have accumulated wealth, but that didn't mean I was automatically entitled. He'd assumed a lot about me, and it pissed me off. This was my office. He had no right to come in here and judge me. For what? For accomplishing my goals? For being successful? "Fuck him," I whispered and threw my hundred-dollar tie in the trash.

I opened the bathroom door, ready to give Ethan a piece of my mind, and slammed right into a brick wall of muscle.

"Shit, I'm—" He looked up at me, his caramel eyes hardening. "You should probably watch where you're going."

"You ran into me," I argued, hating the childish sound of my own voice.

"Can I use the bathroom now." Ethan exhaled, frustrated and impatient. "Please."

It gave me some consolation that he disliked me as much as I disliked him.

"May I," I corrected and almost smiled at the confusion blooming across his face.

"May you what?"

"May I use the bathroom," I said, mustering as much indifference as humanly possible. "When you ask *Can I* it implies you're unsure of whether you're able to complete the task at hand... Can you use the bathroom? I don't know, can you?"

"Are you always this condescending?" he asked, even and unruffled.

"Not usually, no... and you?" I was prickly when I wanted to be, and today I was in top form. "Are you usually this judgmental?"

He grit his teeth. "I'm not the judgmental one in this scenario."

"If you say so." I stepped to the side, allowing him space to enter the bathroom, but he didn't move. "The bathroom's all yours."

He took a step toward me, his shoulder bumping mine as his scent, wood and soap and rain, filled my lungs. It made me think of early mornings and thunder. Confused by the nostalgia thrumming through me, I turned, only to have the door slammed in my face. I shook my head as I walked into my office, his smell trapped in my lungs. Maybe I was tired, I thought. I hadn't slept well last night, the disagreement with my mother had kept me up later than I would have liked. It didn't help matters much when my father had called me an hour after I'd left their house.

"Your mother's a mess," he'd said.

"She's a goddamn mess," he'd said.

Guilt seemed to be the word of the day.

I sank into my chair and opened my emails. I read over the one I'd sent Ethan. Cold. Distant. Impersonal.

"Professional," I said, an attempt to convince myself.

Ethan didn't want to be here. It was obvious. And as much as Wilder thought this would work out, I had my doubts Ethan would even show up Wednesday morning. Without thinking it over, I replied.

FROM: AndersLowe@LoweLitFic.com

TO: EthanCalloway@LoweLitFic.com

DATE: Nov 9 11:40 AM

SUBJECT: RE: Professionalism

Ethan,

You are under no obligation to work here. If you find this type of work unsuitable, you are free to give your resignation. The literary world is not for everyone. I'm sure there are many part-time options out there for students, opportunities that fit your needs more appropriately. That being said, you are more than welcome to stay. My request for professional attire is not unreasonable or meant to offend. If you worked at Starbucks, you'd have to wear their apron. I expect my team to dress for a business environment. In your case, slacks, dress shirt, and a tie would be the Lowe Literary apron if you will. Expensive clothes are not required. The only thing required is respect for the company, for me, and the position in which you hold.

Anders~

P.S.

Word of the day: Judgmental - an overly critical assessment or point of view

"I, unlike some, have better things to do with my money than throw it away on showy suits."

FROM: EthanCalloway@LoweLitFic.com

TO: AndersLowe@LoweLitFic.com

DATE: Nov 9 12:03 PM

SUBJECT: RE: Professionalism

Anders,

As much as I feel like a fish out of water here, I can assure you I will adapt. Slacks, tie, and dress shirt. Got it. I'll be here Wednesday. Can't get rid of me that easily.

Ethan~

P.S.

Word of the day: Condescending - superior attitude, patronizing.

"The literary world is not for everyone. I'm sure there are many part-time options out there for students, opportunities that fit your needs more appropriately."

Despite myself, I laughed. "Touché."

Ethan had some serious balls. I would have fired him by now if he were anyone else. But Wilder would never let me live it down. He'd bitch and pester me until I hired the jackass again. I was stuck with this guy unless he chose to leave of his own free will. Might as well come to terms with it and move on. I didn't have to like Ethan to work with him. I was used to this. There were authors, agents, publishers I couldn't stand, but I put on a smile and did my job. This was no different. As long as he *adapted* and did what he was here to do, I didn't give a shit what he thought about me.

I was about to respond to him and say as much when a soft knock on the door interrupted me.

Nora poked her head in. "Hungry?"

"I could definitely eat," I said, closing my laptop. "What did you have in mind?"

"Burgers and fries... but I know I shouldn't." A friendly smile appeared on her lips as she leaned her small, five-foot-four frame against the door jamb.

"I know a place a few blocks from here, best burgers in Atlanta."

"Yeah?" she asked as I stood.

"You deserve a burger." I grabbed my wallet and phone, slipping them into my back pocket. "You've barely been here three months, and you've already got quite the list of clients."

"I'm not as picky as you," she said, pushing her long, dark hair over her shoulder. "Maybe I should be though."

"Why do you say that?"

"Bartley passed on my last client." She sighed as we walked down the hall. "This author, Anders, is beyond talented. But if Bartley passed then... you know how it is. No one will pick it up." She held out her hands and shrugged. "I don't know what to do. Maybe she should self-publish?"

"God, no... Bartley is not the end all be all, grab your purse. We'll talk about it at lunch."

"Food always helps me make good decisions," she said as we made our way to the front lobby.

Ethan's eyes were fixed on the computer screen in front of him, his lips barely moving, whispering words as he read. His sandy brown hair fell over his forehead, almost obscuring his vision. His face was all shadows and angles. The softness of his cheeks balanced the wide, strict line of his jaw. I wasn't close enough to catch his scent again, but for some reason I could smell it. I stared at him for longer than I should have, and he noticed.

"Need something?" he asked, not lifting his eyes from the screen.

"I'm going to lunch."

He glanced up from whatever he'd been reading. "You have a meeting at two."

"I'm aware."

"You should come with us," Nora said, and my stomach flipped. That would make for the most awkward lunch of all time. "Anders promised me the best burger in Atlanta."

Ethan looked at her, then at me. His smile reached his eyes when he gave Nora his full attention. It was breathtaking. Unnerved, I dropped my eyes to my watch. "We better get going if I want to make it back on time... are you joining us?"

A scowl sat on his handsome face when I raised my eyes.

"Nah, I'm good. I probably couldn't afford it anyway."

I wasn't sure if that was a jab at me, or the truth. Either way, that bastard guilt found its way back inside my chest.

"Nonsense," Nora said. "It'd be a first-day celebration treat. On us."

His smile reappeared, lopsided and easy-going.

Ethan rubbed the back of his neck. "Maybe next time."

"Are you sure?" I asked, my indifference slipping for the briefest of seconds.

His eyes landed on mine. "Yeah... I'm good."

Once we were outside, Nora asked, "Did you know Ethan's going to school to be a nurse?"

"Wilder told me when he asked me to hire him."

"I think he's sweet."

I tried not to scoff. "I don't know if he'll stay with us long."

"He said he wants to work with kids who have disabilities."

We stopped at the crosswalk and waited for the light to change. "He did?"

Of course, he did. The insensitive comment I'd made about Jason that night at the party rattled me all over again.

"Yeah, it's why he didn't go to Africa with his boyfriend... well, ex-boyfriend."

The light changed and I stared at her.

"What?"

"And you know all of this how?" I asked.

She stepped out into the street with a laugh. I followed behind her a bit dazed. He'd been at the office for less than half the day and she already knew his story. And there was a part of me that wanted to know his story too. Ten months ago, I'd caught him with Chance, fucking like they were on a honeymoon. It was natural to be curious about how that had ended less than a year later.

"Don't look so surprised," she said. "You know me, I can sniff out a story a mile away."

She could. She read people well. I wondered if she could read how much I disliked him. As if she plucked the thought out of my head, she said, "Give him a chance, Anders, don't be such a hard ass."

"I'm not a hard ass."

"Okay," she said, pinning me with a placating look.

"He's not a saint, you know."

Oh God, why was I rationalizing? I had every right to be a hard ass. I'd built my business from the ground up. From copy editor to agent.

"Oh?" she asked, already constructing some sort of story in her head. "Do tell."

"The restaurant is around the corner on the next block." I had no intention of answering her question.

"You suck," she pouted, and I couldn't help the laugh that rumbled in my chest.

"There's nothing to tell."

"You're a terrible liar."

"You're terribly nosy, has anyone ever told you that?" I asked.

"On multiple occasions." She grinned. "It's part of my allure."

"This is it," I said, nodding toward the door with a burger and fall leaves painted on the glass.

"Sal's?" Nora laughed as I opened the door. "The place with those amazing cookies you always bring?"

"The one and only." I'd successfully distracted her from her line of questions. The wedding rehearsal party, Ethan and Chance, it wasn't my place to say anything. Office gossip wasn't my thing. "You'll never get a better burger anyplace else."

Ethan wasn't at his desk when we arrived back at the office. I placed a to-go container in front of his computer, grabbed the file he'd set out for my next meeting, and tucked it under my arm. Claire and Robbie were huddled over her desk as I walked by, flipping through a couple of hardbacks.

"I got cookies from Sal's Place."

Robbie grinned and took the container from my hand. "You're the best, boss."

"Glad to see you made it back," I said. "Did you have a good flight?" I asked.

"Sorry I was late," he said in his thick Brooklyn accent. "The flight was delayed."

"The morning meeting went well without you. I think Burgess will sign."

Claire smirked. "Of course, he will."

Robbie took a bite of a cookie and didn't bother waiting to speak. "Non-fiction, though... you think it will sell?"

"I do. It's important what happened at the Stonewall Inn. His voice should be heard." I gave them both a half smile. "Enjoy the cookies, I've got a meeting to—"

"Yeah, yeah... always so chatty." Robbie took another bite of his cookie, smiling like an idiot.

"You're lucky you have the connections you do," I joked.

"Or what?" he hollered as I walked down the hall. "You'd fire me?"

"In a heartbeat."

I chuckled as I shut my office door. Robbie gave me more shit than I needed in my life. But he was good at managing messes. His willingness to run the New York office practically on his own meant I could stay here in Atlanta. I loved New York, but it wasn't home. Robbie could give me as much shit as he liked as long as it meant I could be where I wanted to be. Sinking down into my chair, I opened my laptop. I skimmed through some emails and went over a few of the notes I'd prepared for my next meeting. Unlike this morning, this client had been with me for a few years. His manuscript was good, young adult fiction, but if he wanted to sell it, he'd have to tone down some of the sexual content. Telling authors to kill their darlings had to be the worst part of this job. Sometimes I toyed with the idea of starting my own publishing company. I'd take on the grit and truth and display it on the shelves. The world was fiction. Reality could be found on the pages of a well-written manuscript. It's why some of the best authors would be denied the chance to ever publish their words. Lies would always be more profitable.

I shut the folder, and let out a long breath, ready for this never-ending day to be over. Picking up the phone, I was about to call Ethan and tell him to send Jack in when he arrived when an email notification pinged through my laptop speakers.

FROM: EthanCalloway@LoweLitFic.com

TO: AndersLowe@LoweLitFic.com

DATE: Nov 9 1:47 PM

SUBJECT: Pity Cookies

I'm allergic to peanuts. Your pity cookies could have killed me.

Ethan~

FROM: AndersLowe@LoweLitFic.com

TO: EthanCalloway@LoweLitFic.com

DATE: Nov 9 1:51 PM

SUBJECT: RE: Pity Cookies

Ethan,

I apologize. Obviously, I was unaware. Shouldn't you have an EpiPen?

And for the record, they were not pity cookies. I always bring back cookies from Sal's.

Anders~

FROM: EthanCalloway@LoweLitFic.com

TO: AndersLowe@LoweLitFic.com

DATE: Nov 9 2:06 PM

SUBJECT: RE: Pity Cookies

I actually don't have a peanut allergy. But your concern was heartwarming. Also, your client is here.

Ethan~

P.S.

Word of the day: Joke - a trick for amusement.

FROM: AndersLowe@LoweLitFic.com

TO: EthanCalloway@LoweLitFic.com

DATE: Nov 9 2:05 PM

SUBJECT: RE: Pity Cookies

Ethan,

How about Infuriating - annoying someone enough to commit murder by peanut.

Anders~

P.S. Send him in.

Ethan

Oregano and garlic hung in the air as I pushed my way into the house. The bags in my hand, heavy and awkward, banged against the foyer wall as I stumbled inside. I kicked the door shut, grateful this damn day was almost over. Once I was in my room, I set the bags down on my bed, their familiar red logo staring back at me, mocking me. Definitely not designer, I thought, and if I could, I'd kick my own ass for caring. Before I let myself fall down the rabbit hole that was Anders Lowe, I toed off my shoes and headed into the empty kitchen. Figuring Wilder and Jax were around here somewhere, I helped myself to one of Jax's beers from the fridge. I cracked open the bottle, the bittersweet taste of citrus and barley exploded over my taste buds. The day from hell was officially over. Or so I'd thought. An unmistakable sound echoed through the silent house and down the stairs. A deep growl and then a grunt and oh my hell, they were fucking. I heard Wilder's voice, mumbling something, moaning, and I almost dropped my beer. I set it on the counter as a loud bang sounded over my head. They hadn't shut their bedroom door. Steam billowed from a pot of boiling water. Red sauce simmered on the stove. All of it, forgotten. Shocked, I hesitated longer than I'd meant to until I heard Jax call out his husband's name.

"Jesus Christ," I whispered, and hauled my ass back to my room.

I might've slammed the door. Not out of anger, but more like a *hey fuckers, I'm home*, and *hey, maybe you should shut the damn door*. But this was their house. They could fuck wherever and whenever they wanted. Leaning against the wall, I squeezed my eyes shut, trying to replace the images in my head with something less pornographic. Lures and fishing and miles of beach. A laugh crept up my chest, and once it escaped, I couldn't stop. Breathless, I rubbed my palm over my face and found Gandalf, Jax and Wilder's cat, perched on my pillow.

"Hiding out, too?" I asked and scratched behind his ear and he purred. "I'll take that as a yes."

Opening up the music app on my phone, I pressed play. Gandalf stared at me as I turned up the volume and set my cell on the bedside table. It was obnoxiously loud, but Jax and Wilder would get the point. This was my attempt at giving them some privacy. It was about three songs later, while I attempted to remove a tag from one of the dress shirts I'd purchased, a quiet knock sounded on my door.

"Come in," I said, lowering the music.

Jax walked in and Gandalf ran out of my room like a bat out of hell. Jax's cheeks were flushed, his hair messy as he rubbed at the back of his neck. "When did you get home?"

I pressed my lips together to hide my smile. His fingers fidgeted with the hem of his shirt, which I noticed was inside out.

"About fifteen, twenty minutes ago. You?" I asked and grinned when he averted his eyes.

Jax stared at the mess of clothes strewn across my bed and said, "Not too long ago."

"Good day?" I asked and almost choked on my laugh.

"You heard," he said, more of a statement than a question.

I chuckled and his cheeks flamed red all the way to the tips of his ears. "Y'all should've shut the door."

"I kind of want to die right now," he said, refusing to meet my eyes. "I'm sorry, man."

"You shouldn't be... this is your house, Jax. With me living here... it was bound to happen, glad to have gotten it out of the way. At least I didn't walk in on it."

"Thank Christ for that."

"Nah, he's got nothing to do with it."

Jax laughed and shoved his hands into the pockets of his sweats. "Wilder made dinner... if you're hungry."

"I'm always hungry."

"Someone went shopping." Wilder stood inside the doorway, shirtless in a pair of sleep pants. "I'm offended you didn't invite me along on your little spree."

Jax smiled, his eyes only for Wilder. It was innocent and whole, and as he bent down to kiss him, I turned away. Affection didn't bother me necessarily but watching them made what I'd lost that much harder to bear.

"Apparently, I need a new wardrobe for work," I said, focusing on something besides my pathetic thoughts. "Anders is an entitled asshole, by the way."

"Oh no... what happened?" Wilder plopped down on my bed, and I didn't stare at the reddish-purple mark on his neck as he said, "He can be bossy, but you have to put him in his place."

I laughed without humor. "Easy for you to say, you're his client, Wilder. I'm his *employee*. He made that very clear today. I'm expendable."

"I'll go check on the pasta," Jax said, giving me a sympathetic smile.

"Anders is harmless, he can be controlling and... abrasive, but he's as loyal as they come."

"I don't know. We're like oil and water. He's all big city pretentious, and I'm..." I waved a hand over my hand-me-down polo and worn-out jeans. "Me. I don't give a crap about money and all of that."

I pulled a pair of gray slacks from one of the bags. "Oh... I like those." Wilder practically clapped. "Show me what else you got."

I glared at him. "You're like the annoying little sister I never had."

"I'll take that as a compliment," he said, snooping through one of the bags. I grabbed it out of his hand, and he sighed. "That green shirt will look great with your eyes."

"Can you focus for a second? We're talking about how you suck for making me work for Anders."

"First of all, I did not *make* you do anything. And second, how can you expect me to focus with all these bags? Did you buy shoes?"

My frustration evaporated into a laugh, his grin ear to ear as I handed him the bag with the shoes inside. "They're cheap shit from Target, Wilder. Don't get too excited."

He looked downright offended as he opened the box. "Lord, next time you go shopping, please take me with you."

"There won't be a next time, this is ridiculous as it is. I should've applied for a job at the Cup and Quill and saved myself two-hundred-and-fifty bucks."

"Think about it this way, you'll need nice clothes for job interviews and... dates."

"Dates?" I asked, my brows rising to my hairline. "If I ever wear any of this crap on a date, you have my permission to kick me in the ass."

"Dinner's ready," Jax hollered from the kitchen.

Wilder stood and placed his hand on my shoulder. "It's not my place to say anything, but trust me when I say Anders is deeper than the surface he provides. No one's life is perfect, Ethan."

"I know that," I said. I thought how Anders had accused me of being judgmental and wished he hadn't hit the nail on the fucking head. "I'll try to give him a chance."

"Good." He gave me a smile. "I apologize in advance. I think the sauce might've burnt a little."

I huffed out a quiet laugh. "I'm sure it'll taste just fine."

After dinner, I'd finished putting away the clothes I'd purchased and had taken a shower. I ran a towel through my wet hair as I flipped on the bedside lamp and shut the door. Mentally exhausted, I fell into bed, too tired to throw on a pair of briefs. I was used to sleeping naked anyway, and I doubted Wilder or Jax would barge in without knocking. I picked up my phone with the intent to turn on some chill music when I saw I had a text message from Chance. I should've deleted it. I should've deleted it and not given a fuck. But that was my problem, I still cared.

Chance: Checking in.

He used to do this when we were together. When he would volunteer in places without cell service. He'd send me a text that always said, *checking in*, whenever he could. It'd been his own personal proof of life. I stared at my phone, a mix of anger and hurt pounding inside my chest.

Me: Where are you?

His response was immediate.

Chance: Lagos, Nigeria.

Chance: I didn't think you'd respond.

I didn't think you'd leave. I'd given him an ultimatum. Choose us, I'd said. He'd chosen Africa.

Me: I didn't want to.

I could imagine the sound of his voice. He'd say my name. *Ethan.* In that tone he'd perfected over the two years we'd been together. I'd feel selfish and apologize. He'd come home, built bigger than when he'd left, his thick beard untamed. We'd fuck away the time he'd given to other people, and I'd forget how lonely I'd been the entire time he'd been gone.

He'd chosen Africa... and I'd chosen me.

Me: I'm glad you're safe. Take care, Chance.

Three dots appeared and vanished a few times.

Chance: You're walking away then? After everything.

Anger overpowered the hurt.

Me: You walked away. Not me.

Me: I'm not doing this again. I told you what I wanted, and now you're in Nigeria. I need to do what makes me happy for once.

Chance: And I'm supposed to drop everything?

Me: No. What we had, it's run its course. We don't want the same things. I can't keep following your dreams. I have to follow my own.

This was typical, Chance. I was always wrong. I was always at fault. I was tired. The kind of tired that buried itself inside your bones and turned them to dust. A few minutes passed, and I wondered if he'd lost service, or if that was the end of it. I typed out one last message just in case.

Me: Stay safe.

He hadn't lost service; his response was immediate, which hurt almost as much as him leaving had.

Chance: I will, goodbye, Ethan.

Goodbye.

I could hear Wilder laughing in the kitchen, and I thought about getting dressed. Maybe he'd be down for whiskey again. Something to distract me from all the bullshit running through my head. But it was late and waking up hungover again would not be in my best interest. I deleted the messages from Chance and closed out of my messaging app. I didn't need any more reminders. He was gone and I had to move on. How was I supposed to accomplish that goal? I had no fucking idea. I could do what Nora had suggested today. She was a cool chick, and maybe it was because she'd been the only one at the office who'd been nice to me, but for some reason I opened up to her. I'd told her my entire stupid sob story this morning and she'd listened. She'd told me to get back out there as soon as possible. That it was the only way. At first, I'd thought she was nuts. I wasn't ready. Commitment. Relationships. No, thanks. But getting laid? It could be the distraction I needed.

I downloaded the Pegasus dating app and typed in my old username and password. I cringed at the cheesy shot of me on the beach. I'd taken the picture over two years ago when I'd been single and living in Bell River.

"Shit, I was skinny."

I got rid of the picture and updated my bio, changing the location to Atlanta, Georgia. My thumb hovered over the save button. Did I want this? I couldn't say I wasn't a casual sex fan. I'd hooked up some when I'd figured out girls weren't it for me. But I'd been young, and things had been different. But I was almost thirty, for Christ's sake, and part of me thought fucking around with random guys was kind of sad. *Wasn't it?* I leaned back and took a quick snapshot of my abs and uploaded it before I could talk myself out of it. I pressed save and tried not to regret it. New city. New life. Right? Curious, I flipped through a few bios, but nothing snagged my attention. I wasn't into twinks, and bears were out, thanks to Chance. A guy in a suit popped up on my screen and I paused. He had dark hair and nice-looking hazel eyes. He was more clean-cut than I preferred, but something about him had my dick saying how do you do.

Garrett. Thirty. Stockbroker. Into daddy kink.

And... that was a hell no.

"Jesus."

Flipping through his pictures, like a bad accident, I couldn't look away. Each shot more domineering than the last. He reminded me of Anders.

Anders.

Why was I thinking about Anders? The guy was a tool. I wasn't into men like him. Men who cared more about appearances than anything else. Hell, half the time I'd have to remind Chance to wash his damn clothes. Carbon footprint be damned. Anders was sleek lines, with a high-end smile. Sure, he smelled amazing, like chocolate and spice. But it was all surface. He was hot. But looks didn't mean anything when your personality was as dry as saltine and peanut butter sandwiches. I glanced down at the guy in the suit, and thoughts I shouldn't have had about my boss started to crack like fireworks in my head. Was he into shit like daddy kink? Was he on this app? I definitely shouldn't check. But of course, I one-hundred-fucking-percent did. I tried different variations of his name and came up with nothing, until I changed the city to New York.

He was there.

Anders Lowe.

"Holy shit," I whispered, glancing up from my screen, guilty, like I'd been caught watching porn.

All he had in his bio was his name, no interests, and a couple of pictures. One black and white with his face obscured a little by light, and his profile picture. But even that wasn't typical. Instead of abs and a smile, he'd posted a quote. I clicked on it, enlarging it enough that I could read it.

"Beauty is terror."

I didn't want to like how the three words encompassed his persona so perfectly. I didn't want to search the Internet for its origin, a book called *The Secret History* written by a woman named Donna Tart, and I certainly didn't want to buy the book. But goddammit, I did. I could tell myself I was merely intrigued by the quote itself and not the man, but I'd always been a shitty liar.

Anders

The office had been quiet and empty when I'd shown up this morning. The sun hadn't yet risen, and I had the opportunity to lose myself in words. It was a rare thing for me. I hardly ever allowed it. After all, my job was to propel others, not myself. But as my fingers stilled over the keyboard of my laptop, I found that I'd lost two hours and gained four-thousand words. Bright light streamed through the blinds, and I could hear voices murmuring out in the hallway. Writing was an out-of-body experience. It was normal for me to lose time like I had today. Words didn't bow down to me like they had for Wilder, or for any of my clients. I'd write and shape and delete. Over and over until something made sense. Half the time it didn't. I'd pluck sentences and phrases and force them together. It wasn't a talent, but more of a need, an itch reading alone could never scratch. I'd never actually do anything with it.

I highlighted the four-thousand words I'd written this morning and pressed delete. The blank document stared back at me and I exhaled, my mood low. I turned down the music I'd been listening to as my office door creaked open.

Ethan.

Leaning back in my chair, I took in his appearance as he shoved his hands into the pockets of his gray slacks. His hair was damp, a few stray pieces falling over his forehead, dusting his brow line. The sleeves of his blue button down were rolled to his elbows, exposing the lean muscle of his forearms. His pants hugged his thighs as he walked into the room. He even had on a tie. I'd be lying if I said he didn't look fantastic.

His usual cocky demeanor faded as I met his eyes. "You showed up."

Ethan's scowl was comical. "On time."

I checked my watch, knowing it would piss him off. I couldn't explain my need to rile him like I did. Our last few email exchanges had made me laugh as much as they'd infuriated me. He was flippant in a way I envied. It made me want to pick at him even more. It was too easy.

As predicted, Ethan's shoulders stiffened, and he sighed. "I'm running for coffee with Nora," he said, the strain in his voice evident. "Did you want us to grab you anything?"

"That's thoughtful of you," I said and meant it, despite my sarcastic tone.

He'd made an effort today, showing up dressed to kill. It pleased me.

"Thoughtful?" Ethan's lip twitched, holding back a smile. "I figured it was part of my job."

"Oh... well..." I dropped his gaze and opened up the files I needed for my morning meeting. "In that case, I'll have an Americano."

"Do you always get the same thing?"

"Yes... Why? Is that a problem?"

"It's boring. You should try new things, Anders. You might be surprised."

I raised my eyes and found his smug smile had returned. Was he mocking me or flirting? Both were inappropriate.

"I don't like surprises. They leave too much room for disappointment."

"You're depressing before you've had coffee."

"Usually," I said as sardonic as ever.

He laughed, soft and husky, unflappable.

"I'll make sure they give you an extra shot of espresso then."

Nora walked in before I could reply. Which was probably for the best. Anything I had to say would have only perpetuated this unhealthy need I harbored to have the last word when it came to Ethan. In most circumstances, I wouldn't have even cared. But evidently, he made me irrational. Maybe *I* was the easy mark.

She waved her fingers at me. "Hey, Anders. Early start?"

"Had a few things I needed to work on," I said and mustered a smile for her.

"Always working," she said and shook her head. "I wish I had half your drive."

"Says the woman who doesn't leave the office until nine at night sometimes." I chuckled. "Some of us are just morning people."

Ethan made a face, his mouth turning down into a frown. "Morning people are the worst."

Nora's eyes widened. "We better get going," she said, grabbing Ethan by the arm. "My client will be here in thirty." As she shut the door behind them, I heard her whisper, "Are you trying to get yourself fired?"

I had to laugh at that, at least I wasn't the only one who thought Ethan was wildly unprofessional. Letting out a long breath, I leaned into work, forgetting about Ethan and his smart mouth, and the simmering feeling under my skin every time I looked at him. I poured over the manuscript I'd pulled up earlier. This author was only twenty, but his words read like they'd been penned by an old soul, like he'd been writing for decades. He was young, too young, to have mastered himself like he had. I hadn't been this excited to meet a client in ages. I pulled a few quotes from the manuscript and added them to the pitch I'd been working on yesterday. I would've had this finished yesterday, but I'd spent most of the day looking for shit Kris had stored away on her files instead of doing my actual job. Names and numbers and emails of people she'd dealt with for me on a daily basis. As much as Ethan was a thorn in my side, it would've been more effective to have him here every day. *Or hire someone else.* The thought was appealing.

After a few finishing touches the pitch was complete. I printed it along with the contract, leaving me a little bit of time before my appointment. I stood on stiff legs and grabbed the warm paper off the top of the printer and set it on my desk. Taking advantage of a few more free minutes, I opened up the email app on my phone.

FROM: AndersLowe@LoweLitFic.com

TO: EthanCalloway@LoweLitFic.com

DATE: Nov 11 9:45 AM

SUBJECT: New York

Ethan,

Please see that the acquisition files are ready before I leave for my flight this evening. Also, confirm the reservation for tomorrow night at Emilio's. I've attached my hotel confirmation, please forward to Robbie and Mr. Kassen. Kris should have all this information stored somewhere on the desktop, most likely the address book.

Anders~

Right as I pressed send, Ethan walked into my office with coffee in hand.

"That place is a shit show," he said. "It's fast becoming my least favorite place in Atlanta."

His finger brushed against mine as I took the cup from his hand. The heat of his skin traveled up my arm and his cheeks flushed. The pale pink color reminded me of that night, of his reflection in my bathroom mirror. He'd been lost in the moment, in the feeling of getting fucked. My cock thickened behind my zipper, the image too vivid. I swallowed and quickly turned to my desk.

"I'll order delivery next time," I muttered without much conviction, sidetracked by the growing bulge in my pants.

I was too busy analyzing my physical reaction to my new assistant. Two men together, regardless of who they were, I rationalized, would be enough to make any man, gay or bisexual, hard. It didn't help matters it'd been over a month since I'd broken up with Chloe, since I'd been with anyone sexually. Maybe I needed to. I could easily find someone to hook up with while I was away. New York was best for hookups because the chances of having a do-over were slim to none.

"Anders?" Ethan's signature scowl was in full affect. "Are you hearing me?"

"Not really, no," I admitted.

"Your client is waiting in the lobby," he said, staring at me like I was an idiot.

A hypocrite, more likely. I spouted bullshit about professionalism, and here I was, with a semi, thinking about Ethan's pink goddamn cheeks. I adjusted myself as discreetly as possible under the desk.

"Send him in."

Ethan mumbled something under his breath as he left my office, but I kept my mouth shut, thankful my client had arrived, and all thoughts of fucking and hookups would be shelved away for the moment, or for forever. Forever worked for me.

"What do you think?" I asked Clay fifteen minutes later.

"I think it sounds too fucking good to be true."

I laughed and slid the contract across the desk. "Believe it. Best debut book I've ever read."

He ran longer fingers through his short blond curls. "You say that, but I don't believe it. Isn't Wilder Welles one of your clients?"

"He is. But your voice is different."

"'*Comparison is the death of joy*' and all that."

"See... anyone who can quote Mark Twain is a talent in my book."

"No one's as talented as Welles, man."

I wanted to tell him he was right, but of course I didn't.

I plastered on my winning smile and handed him a pen. "I'll agree to disagree."

"Yeah?" he asked, and his innocence killed me.

"This is the beginning of your journey. Your craft will only get better."

Clay stared at the contract, the grin on his face wistful as he dragged the tip on the pen over the signature line. "This is happening," he said.

"Indeed... it is."

With a copy of the contract rolled up in his back pocket, Clay shook my hand.

"When I get back from New York, I'll send out the pitch," I promised.

"I still can't wrap my head around it."

Entitlement seemed to be the practice when it came to younger authors. I was glad to be proven wrong.

I clapped him on the shoulder as I opened the office door. "Get used to it... it's all up from here on out."

"Thanks, man. I'll be in touch."

Leaning against the doorframe, I watched as he walked down the hall toward the lobby.

"Went well?" Robbie asked as he came out of the bathroom.

"It did."

"Bring some of that luck to New York tonight. Kassen has two agents chasing his tail."

"We don't need luck," I said. "We have experience and connections. That's all that matters."

"If you say so."

Robbie's eyes drifted to Claire's office.

"How's that going?" I asked and laughed when he narrowed his eyes.

"She's banging that asshole from Bartley Press."

Robbie and Claire were the definition of dysfunctional. Whenever he was in town, they'd hook up. But for the most part, she treated him like shit. To be fair, Claire treated everyone like shit. She was good at her job, though. Robbie too. They didn't let their drama affect their work, which was why I never reminded them how interoffice relationships were never a good idea.

"Which asshole?"

"I don't know..." he said, distracted. "I heard her talking about it with Nora."

My head fell back as I laughed. "You're ridiculous."

"What?" he asked, finally giving me his full attention.

"Tell her how you feel."

He choked on a laugh. "Have you met Claire? Women like her... they don't like that shit. Feelings... no way, man. She'd eat me alive."

"Sounds like a blast."

Robbie's lip curled into a smirk. "You have no idea."

"On that note..."

He elbowed me in the rib. "So sensitive, maybe you need to get laid."

"Maybe you shouldn't talk to your boss about your sex life?"

"You used to be fun," he said, grinning like a moron.

"I have work to do, if we want to leave here on time."

"We're heading to the airport together?" he asked.

"Yeah... Meet me at my place around five."

"Sounds good."

Robbie's eyes wandered to Claire's office again and I smiled as I shut my door. I picked up my coffee and took a sip, cringing as the cold, bitter liquid hit my tongue. Throwing it in the trash under my desk, I sat down. I had half a mind to tell Ethan to make another coffee run, but I needed to make sure he'd started working on everything I'd asked him to do first. I opened my emails and clicked on his reply.

FROM: EthanCalloway@LoweLitFic.com

TO: AndersLowe@LoweLitFic.com

DATE: Nov 11 10:30 AM

SUBJECT: RE: New York

Anders,

Acquisition files are attached. Reservation for Emilio's is at eight and hotel info is sent.

Are you aware you never say thank you... like ever?

Thanks,

Ethan~

FROM: AndersLowe@LoweLitFic.com

TO: EthanCalloway@LoweLitFic.com

DATE: Nov 11 11:03 AM

SUBJECT: RE: New York

Ethan,

Thank you.

Anders~

P.S. Word of the day: Coddle - indulge, pamper, spoil.

FROM: EthanCalloway@LoweLitFic.com

TO: AndersLowe@LoweLitFic.com

DATE: Nov 11 11:16 AM

SUBJECT: RE: New York

Anders,

Cute.

While you're indulging me, maybe you could buy my lunch?

Not so sincerely, Ethan.

P.S. Word of the day: Petty - childish and obstinate.

Jesus Christ, this guy. I couldn't decide if I wanted to laugh or snap my pen in two. I bit back my smile, mulling over what my response would be. He wanted to play. So be it. I couldn't fire him, but I could definitely ruffle those feathers of his enough he'd leave of his own volition.

FROM: AndersLowe@LoweLitFic.com

TO: EthanCalloway@LoweLitFic.com

DATE: Nov 11 11:26 AM

SUBJECT: RE: New York

Ethan,

Childish sounds about right. Maybe a McDonald's happy meal? Do you want the boy toy or the girl toy, or both? Unless gender roles are not your thing?

Anders~

FROM: EthanCalloway@LoweLitFic.com

TO: AndersLowe@LoweLitFic.com

DATE: Nov 11 11:38 AM

SUBJECT: RE: New York

Always the boy toy, and that has nothing to do with my gender identity.

P.S. Word of the day: Cheap - offering McDonald's when you can afford a room for four nights at the Greenwich Hotel.

I swiped my thumb over the screen on my cell and tapped out a quick text to Nora.

Me: Buying lunch.

She responded immediately.

Nora: What are you ordering?

Me: McDonald's

Nora: For real?

Yes, I was that fucking stubborn.

Me: Sometimes it sounds good.

Nora: I'll pass. But thanks!

It took me about five minutes to download the delivery app and order the food. I was perfectly aware of the absurd lengths I'd gone to in my attempt to piss Ethan off, but for some reason, I couldn't wipe the grin off my face. The last few days had been stressful. I'd ignored my mother's attempts to get in touch with me. With this trip to New York, I didn't want to delve too deep into feelings she wasn't ready to face. I needed a taste of absurdity—a moment to simply fuck off and eat a damn Happy Meal like the seven-year-old I apparently was.

Twenty minutes later, Ethan strolled into my office, without knocking. Surprise. Surprise. "Did you order the nuggets or the burger?"

"Burger," I said and somehow maintained a straight face.

He dropped one of the red and yellow boxes on the desk and I expected him to leave. Instead, he reached into his box and pulled out the toy. He gave it a curious once over. "What did you get?"

I opened the Happy Meal and pulled out a small football wrapped in plastic.

"Huh," he said, the corner of his lip tugging up on one side. "Me too." Ethan pocketed the small ball and set his box next to mine on the desk. I had a feeling I was about to lose this round of the game. "I'm meeting Jax and Wilder at Sal's for lunch. Thanks though, I feel so... what was the word? Loved? Pampered? Or was it spoiled?"

"I think the word for you is petty."

Ethan walked backward, his smile rising to his eyes. It was the same breathtaking smile he'd given Nora the other day. But this time he'd wielded it as a weapon. "Enjoy your lunch, Anders. I'll make sure to bring back some pity cookies."

Ethan

Friday couldn't have come any sooner, but unfortunately it was only one-thirty and I still had a little less than three hours to go. Earlier, I'd actually contemplated emailing Anders as a way to entertain myself. I'd started to enjoy pestering him. I'd kept the stupid toy from McDonald's as somewhat of a prize. I'd driven the man to record level pettiness. A guy who walked around like the world couldn't touch him. It was addictive, getting reactions from him. Like Wilder had said, there was more to him, and I was bound and determined to figure him out. Even if we both ended up murdering each other in the end. I had to admit, though, with him in New York, and Claire left behind to boss me around, the office was less palatable. Boring and slightly terrifying. Claire scared the shit out of me. I glanced over my shoulder. Thank hell her door was shut. I could never tell if she wanted to rip my head off or simply ask me to make her some copies.

Nora's soft laugh made me jump. "The snake is in her hidey hole?"

I grabbed my chest and exhaled. "Trying to give me a heart attack."

She rolled her eyes and handed me a small paper bag. "No, but this will."

The scent of peaches and cinnamon assaulted me as I opened the bag. "Cobbler?"

"Only the best cobbler ever." She reached into the bag and pulled out the clear plastic container. "It's better with ice cream, but I figured it'd melt before I could get here."

"Good thinking," I said and grabbed a fork out of the bag. "Sal's?"

"No way, there is only one place in Atlanta to get cobbler, and that's The Tea Room. I went there for lunch with Alex." She grabbed a fork as well as I opened the container. "They make the cobbler with biscuits."

"Alex is the boyfriend, right?"

"For now." She smiled around a forkful of peaches.

"Damn," I mumbled, my mouth too full to speak without being disgusting.

The flavor wasn't overly sweet. The warmth of it hit my belly and made me think about home and summer and the starched white feel of my father's Sunday button down shirt. When I was little my mom would make cobbler for most of our Sunday dinners. I'd sit on my dad's lap at the table with whipped cream on my face while he'd read us the scriptures. Times had changed since then. When I'd started openly dating Chance, my family hadn't totally been on board. But I'd gotten used to living without their approval. Originally, my dad had thrown me out when I'd told him I was gay. Eventually, he came around and let me come home. But my relationship with my parents had been irrevocably changed. They'd gone quiet. I'd almost wished for strained or angry. Quiet was suffocating. Quiet was for strangers. I hadn't been back home since I'd left for Denver.

"Well? What do you think?" she asked.

"I think you're gonna make me fat with all these fucking cookies and cobbler."

She leaned over the desk and shoved my shoulder. "Sweets are survival."

"Are we eating our feelings?" I asked before spooning another bite of cobbler and whipped cream into my mouth.

"I'm fine, it's you I'm worried about."

"Me?"

"You're mopey today. Are we missing a certain arrogant asshole?"

"I don't know what you're talking about," I lied and set my fork down into the container.

"No?" She quirked a brow. "You realize that's his favorite book?"

I glanced at the copy of *The Secret History* laying on my desk.

"And you stared at that little baby football on Wednesday like a kid on Christmas." She batted her eyelashes and I snorted.

"You should be a writer and not an agent with these stories you conjure up in your head," I said. "I didn't know it was his favorite book."

"Sure."

"I didn't."

She laughed and shrugged. "Denial is a powerful drug, my friend."

"Don't you have things you should be doing, not sitting here harassing the new guy?" I grabbed the damn book off the desk and shoved it into my laptop bag. "You better go away, or Claire will come out here. I can't handle another one of her fake smiles."

"I bring you cobbler, and this is how you treat me?" she asked in mock offense. Nora smiled when I gave her the finger. "I'm glad you work here, Ethan, it's much less dull with you around."

"I can imagine," I said, ready to deny any more accusations hurled my way about Anders, when the lobby door opened.

A petite woman, with more gray than black hair, dressed in a deep blue pant suit smiled at me and Nora. "Sorry to interrupt your lunch, I'm looking for Anders."

"We were just finishing up." I pushed the cobbler toward Nora and stood. "Anders isn't here though, I'm afraid."

"He isn't... I can just..." She took a deep breath, her smile trembling as she looked toward the hallway. "If he's with a client, I can wait."

"No, ma'am," I said, confused. "He's not here."

"He's not?" she asked, and Nora shook her head. "Or is that what he told you to tell me. You're new... Kris would never—"

"Ma'am, he's in New York until Monday."

"Oh..." she said, soft and fragile. "He usually tells me these things."

"Sandra," Claire said from behind me and walked over to the woman, kissing her right cheek and then her left. "It's been a while. How are you? How's Harlan? Anders said he was sick a few months ago."

"Yes, just a cold, nothing serious."

Claire's concern was about as fake as her smile. Nora turned to me and pretended to gag. Eyes wide, I tried not to laugh. Nora was worse than a teenager sometimes.

"Anders said as much. I hope he's doing better?" Claire asked.

"Much." The woman pinned me with her sad eyes. "Tell him I stopped by. That I need to speak with him when he has a minute." She plastered on a smile that rivaled Claire's. "He's impossible to get a hold of these days."

"I'll make sure his assistant tells him you stopped by. It's good to see you. Give Harlan my best."

"I will."

"Anders will want to know she stopped by," Claire said to me after the woman left. "Immediately."

"It would help if I knew who *she* was."

I flinched when she stepped toward me. I'd gotten through the day with my balls intact, I'd like to keep them that way.

"Sandra Lowe, his mother."

"Mother?" Nora and I asked at the same time.

"Yes." Claire glared at us. "Why do you both look shocked?"

She looked nothing like him. "She was nice," I said instead.

Nora laughed. "She was... and short. He must get his height from his dad."

Claire gave us a blank expression. "He's adopted."

"Anders's dad?" I asked.

"No, moron. Anders." She flipped a long strand of her hair over her shoulder. "Just let him know she stopped by."

Claire disappeared into her office and shut the door, leaving me and Nora a little dazed.

"Adopted... you didn't know?"

"Um, no... It's Anders. He's not an open book," she said. "Plus, I'm new, not as new as you but... Does it bug you that Claire knew though?"

"It shouldn't, but it does."

Laughing, she picked up the container of half-eaten cobbler. "Are you going to finish this?"

"Nah, you can have it." I smacked my stomach. "Cobbler and abs don't go together."

"Abs are overrated."

"If you say so." My phone pinged in my pocket. "I better get that. It's probably Claire reminding me to text Anders. Just in case I forgot in the last two minutes."

Nora held up the container in her hand. "If you change your mind, you know where to find me."

Adopted.

It was a piece to his puzzle. A lock opened. Distracted, I pulled my phone out of my pocket as I sat down.

Jax: Hey, any way you could pick up Jay this afternoon. My mom has a doctor's appointment and I'm stuck on site.

Me: Where's Wilder?

Jax: He's in a meeting with his publisher.

Me: What time?

Jax: Two thirty?

Shit. I had no idea if I could get out of work—or the city—that fast.

Me: Let me ask. Text you as soon as I can.

Jax: Thanks, man.

I thought about asking Claire, but that sounded about as fun as swimming in the Ichetucknee River during alligator mating season.

Me: Hey, boss, anyway I can cut out of work a little early? Jax needs a favor.

I didn't think he'd respond right away, but three dots popped up on the bottom of my screen.

Anders: How early?

Me: Now would work the best for me.

Anders: For you? And what about the rest of the office?

Me: I'm sure they'll survive.

Anders: Ask Claire.

Fuck. No way.

Me: Claire will say no.

Me: She's been on a power trip.

Anders: She's always on a power trip.

Me: Stop. Did we just agree on something?

Anders: Ask Claire. Power trip or not. I have no way of knowing what needs to be done before you leave.

Of course, he did. Not a damn thing. I was his assistant. I'd sent him everything he needed, making sure he could relax in his seven-hundred-dollar-a-night hotel room and scroll through his options on Pegasus. The thought pissed me off, but I ignored the twinge in my stomach and texted him back anyway.

Me: It's Jay. I need to pick him up from school. Jax is stuck on site, and Wilder is at his publisher's office. Jax's mom is at the doctor. I'm a last resort.

Anders: That's fine, you can go.

Anders: Next time, maybe lead with it's a family emergency and save us both the headache.

He knew Jay was family to me. I smiled, liking that way more than I should.

Me: Thanks. I appreciate it.

Me: Speaking of family. Your mom stopped by five minutes ago.

Anders: Make sure to check your email this weekend. I might need to get in touch with you.

Had he ignored the message about his mom, or did it not go through? And fuck that. I'm off on the weekends.

Me: Did you get the message about your mom?

Anders: I did.

Me: And about this weekend. Unless you're paying me... I won't be checking my work email on the weekends.

Anders: I'll remember that next time you ask for another favor.

God, I hated him.

Me: Here's my personal email. I'm more likely to check that over the weekend.

Me: hook_and_reelife@bellinx.mail.com if you need to send me anything. Otherwise, text me.

Anders: I'll be in touch.

I stared at my phone wishing those four words didn't excite me. Denial and stupidity seemed to be my drug of choice.

Jay's classroom was near empty by the time I got there, twenty minutes late. My guilt, as heavy as it was, lightened a bit when I found him talking to a woman who looked about our age, laughing and smiling like I'd never seen him before.

"Sorry I'm late," I said, and when he turned to look at me, his smile got wider than the horizon.

"I didn't know you were coming to get me." Jay hugged me. "This is Ms. Wilson."

"I've heard a lot about you," I said, holding out my hand and she shook it.

"This is Ethan," he said, his joy bouncing from the inside out.

Ms. Wilson smiled. "I feel like I'm meeting a famous person."

My face heated wondering about all the things Jason might've said about me. "I'm not that exciting. I promise."

"Yes, you are," he argued. "Don't believe him, Ms. Wilson."

"Call me Jenni," she said and let go of my hand.

"Can I show him around?" Jay asked and she nodded. "I don't see why not."

Jason looked at her like I used to look at Chance, and it made my stomach ache. Did Jenni know how he felt? She had to. Did she encourage it?

"Jay, can I talk to Ms. Wilson for a second. I want to ask her a question about the program."

"Why don't you go on and find Mabel, I'm sure she'd loved to meet Ethan too."

"Mabel?" I asked and Jay's cheeks flushed to a deep shade of red.

He rubbed the back of his neck, the muscles in his arms bunching like they had in high school. It was hard, sometimes, to reconcile this version of Jay with the one I'd known down in Bell River.

"Alright," he said, and wandered off toward the door.

"This may seem... out of left field," I started once he was out of the room. "But I'm concerned about... Well, to be honest, I think Jay has a crush on you."

Jenni's heart-shaped face broke into a wide smile. "A crush?"

"Yeah... I mean, you're not much older than him and—"

"Has he not told you?"

My stomach dropped. Told me what?

"Mabel is his girlfriend."

"Mabel is his—wait, what?"

Her smile softened, and the light wrinkles around her eyes deepened. "I've encouraged him to talk about her with Jax and Wilder. But he's very private about his feelings, I suppose."

Private? Not with me.

"Is Mabel a student?" I asked, trying to wrap my head around the word girlfriend.

"She is. Her situation is similar to Jason's." Jenni sat on the edge of her desk. "Mabel was hit by a car when she was seventeen and sustained a severe traumatic brain injury."

"God... that's awful." My shoulders sank. "Is she like Jason... I mean, is she on his level?"

"She is, but she's progressed further. Like Jason, with extensive work, and therapy, she's advanced. She's been here longer than he has, though. He's smart. He's moving a lot faster along than any of us originally thought he'd be capable. She helps him a lot."

"I thought he liked you." I laughed.

"I might've had a thought like that about you when he first got here. He talked about you non-stop. Still does. I think it makes Mabel jealous."

Jason walked back into the room, holding hands with a girl I assumed was Mabel. He wouldn't meet my eyes. "This is my... uh... my friend... Mabel."

Mabel kept her eyes on my mouth, silent as I spoke. "Nice to meet you."

She let go of Jay's hand and waved.

Mabel was cute, with constellations of freckles all over her face. Her auburn hair hung in long, heavy waves over her slim shoulders. She was shorter than Jay, but not by much. She looked up at him and started to move her hands in a way I recognized but didn't understand. Mabel was deaf.

"She said it's nice to meet you too." Jay gave her a private smile, and if I wasn't standing in a room with people I didn't know, I might've fucking cried.

My throat was thick, my voice raw as I tried to speak. "It's real good to meet you, Mabel."

"You two show Ethan around before I lock up, alright?"

Jason took her hand in his again and nodded toward the door. "Come on, I want to show you the music room. Mabel taught me how to play a few songs on the guitar."

Jason and Mabel showed me every square inch of the school, making sure to explain, in detail, how everything worked. Jay told me about his classes, the books he'd read, and how much better at math he'd gotten. Mabel chimed in a few times, with Jason's help interpreting, to tell me about how good he was at basketball, and how he'd promised to teach her how to fish. It wasn't until we'd made our way back to the main classroom that he asked her to come fishing with us next weekend.

"We can pick you up, or you can meet us at Jax's house?" I offered.

She signed something to Jason, and he nodded. I was impressed with how well he was able to communicate with her, and I wondered when the hell he'd learned sign language.

"You ready to head home, buddy?"

"Yeah," he grumbled, and I remembered I wasn't supposed to call him buddy anymore.

Shit.

"I'm grateful I had the opportunity to finally meet you," Jenni said, shaking my hand again.

"You too."

Jason and Mabel said their goodbyes to their teacher and followed me outside. When Jason leaned down to kiss Mabel on the cheek, I stared at the cracks in the sidewalk, giving them privacy. My mind spun a million miles an hour, worried how this would turn out for him, for them. Lust and love were such massive and scary concepts, at times, I didn't even understand fully. Jason was smart, and Mabel seemed so too. But mentally were they capable of a relationship like this? A car pulled up to the curb and Mabel waved back at me, with rosy cheeks, as she opened the door and got inside.

"That's her mom," Jay said, giving them a wave and a smile.

"How old is Mabel?" I asked.

"Twenty-five." He looked at me when the car pulled away. "I want to tell Jax about her."

"Okay."

"And my mom."

"Okay."

"What if she doesn't like fishing?"

"She will." I held in my chuckle when his brows furrowed.

"You think so?"

"Either way, I think she'll like it because you like it."

I wanted to ask him if he'd learned sign language for her, or if it was part of the program at school. I wanted to ask him if he was scared, and why he hadn't told his family.

"I like her," he said. "She has soft hands."

"Soft hands are good."

I squeezed his shoulder, and this time, I didn't fight the burn in my eyes.

Anders

The city lights glittered, obscuring the stars in the night sky as the last swallow of bourbon warmed my throat and stomach. I didn't usually drink bourbon, preferring gin or vodka over the sweet and heavy flavor of whiskey. But there was something about The Greenwich Hotel and its boozy mood with its red brick, marble floors and brown leather that made me want to indulge in something different. I tugged open my tie as I set the glass down on the table, leaving the large-paned glass window and view behind. I pushed open the pocket doors to the bedroom and laid my tie on the small bench in front of the bed. Last night had been a success. Robbie and I had spent most of the evening on our knees, figuratively speaking, trying to get Arthur Kassen to sign with Lowe Literary. We'd closed down Emilio's, drank entirely too much, but in the end, we'd gotten what we wanted. Mr. Kassen had signed at dinner tonight. Renowned in every venture he attempted in the publishing world, having him on my client list would not only bring in money, but respect as well. I was respected. I'd worked too damn hard not to be. But this, Arthur Kassen, this was next level. This meant more time in New York. More publishers. More everything.

I stared at the empty bed, it's bright white sheets, not a wrinkle in sight, and couldn't muster the faintest of smiles. The heat of the bourbon had faded. The levity of tonight's celebration had faded too. Did I want to spend more time in New York? Maybe move here? It would be easy enough. Most of the big publishers were here, it made sense. My connections to Bartley Press would remain even if I didn't live in Atlanta. Did I want to sell my house? Hadn't I wanted to build a home for myself? I could build one here. This could be a fresh start. A place where memories were made instead of avoided. My head hurt. All the questions and thoughts poking around, their barbed tongues taking advantage of the fact I didn't usually drink as much as I had tonight.

"Maybe you didn't drink enough," I said and chuckled at myself.

Most people were fun when they drank. I, on the other hand, turned into an introspective and melancholic drunk.

I stripped out of my shirt and slacks and walked into the bathroom. The walls, floor, and huge bathtub were all covered in marble, but the brass fixtures gave it an old-world feel I loved. I splashed some water on my face, debating on whether or not I wanted to take a shower or go to bed. Deciding on the latter, I brushed my teeth and practically fell into the overly soft mattress. Of course, as soon as my head hit the pillow, I was wide awake. Sleep eluded me more often than not and traveling sure as hell didn't help. I grabbed the novel I'd brought with me and flipped around, reading a few of my favorite passages. The phenomenal writing was what had originally drawn me into the book, but it was the darkness of the characters, the vulnerability, that made me want to read it over and over again. Imperfection was truth. There weren't enough books that embraced that side of humanity. I was half asleep with heavy eyes when my phone vibrated on the nightstand. Groggy, I grabbed it and unlocked the screen, immediately wishing I'd ignored it.

Mom: You can't shut me out forever. It'll be Thanksgiving soon.

I shook my head, exhaling a long breath as I sank back against the headboard. My mom and I had been fighting this battle, in one way or another, for years. Since I'd come out back in college. She wanted me to be happy, but on her terms. Her standard. Get a good job, a wife, a house, have a kid. Emphasis on have.

I'd had too much to drink, and having a conversation right now wasn't ideal, but I was fed up with her guilt trips.

Me: Why are you awake?

Mom: You're alive. Now I can sleep.

I dialed her number and the phone barely rang once.

"I'm sorry," I said.

"I'm supposed to apologize, not you."

"I didn't mean to make you worry... I needed space." I closed my eyes. "Mom, I don't think you understand."

"I understand," she said, and I could hear the quiet sound of her breath as she sighed. "Times have changed. And I have to adapt. I don't care about the bisexual thing, I—"

"The bisexual thing. Mom, it's not a thing. It's who I am. It's not something I can just put on a shelf and say well, that was fun. What's next? I can't help who I'm attracted to."

"I know."

"Okay," I said and scrubbed my palm down my face.

"I do. I get it... I've always wanted you to have a family and—"

"I can have a family." I raised my voice and sat up. "You know what, I think I'll be in New York for Thanksgiving."

"Anders Michael Lowe stop interrupting me," she shouted, and I was sixteen all over again, caught sneaking back through the patio door after making out with the neighbor's son who'd just come home for spring break. Obviously, she hadn't known about the son part at the time. "What I'm trying to say, if you would let me get a word in. You get that from your father, by the way."

I looked up at the ceiling, begging a god I didn't believe existed for patience, or the balls to hang up.

"Focus, Mom."

"I want you to have what me and your father had. Adopt. Get a surrogate... hell, don't have kids at all if that's what you want. I want you to be happy, Anders. Whether that's with a man or a woman. I don't care."

"You don't care?" I asked, not missing the scripted way she'd spoken. As if she'd had to practice, remind herself the right things to say.

"I don't. All I ever wanted, all any parent wants, is for their child to have a better life than they had. I want more for you. More than what I had."

And there it was again.

More.

A better life.

A life with a biological child.

"Mom... I have to get some sleep. You should too."

"What did I say now?"

My anger flared, everything I wanted to say but couldn't burned inside my throat.

"Anders?"

"I have to go."

I ended the call and threw the phone. It bounced off the bed and fell to the floor, shattering the screen and busting into two pieces.

"Fuck," I said and fell back into the pillows, too exhausted to care.

FROM: AndersLowe@LoweLitFic.com

TO: hook_and_reelife@bellinx.mail.com

DATE: Nov 14 8:30 AM

SUBJECT: Unfortunate Events

Ethan,

My phone broke last night, and I'm working on getting another one. All of my contacts are either on my phone, or the desktop address book, which, because today keeps getting better, won't grant me access for some unknown reason. Any insights would be appreciated.

Anders~

FROM: hook_and_reelife@bellinx.mail.com

TO: AndersLowe@LoweLitFic.com

DATE: Nov 14 8:53 AM

SUBJECT: RE: Unfortunate Events

Anders,

Karma is a bitch?

Ethan~

FROM: AndersLowe@LoweLitFic.com

TO: hook_and_reelife@bellinx.mail.com

DATE: Nov 14 8:56 AM

SUBJECT: RE: Unfortunate Events

Ethan,

As true as that statement is, especially this morning, that's not the type of insight I was looking for. Something that would actually get the contacts I need to do my job would be great.

Anders~

FROM: hook_and_reelife@bellinx.mail.com

TO: AndersLowe@LoweLitFic.com

DATE: Nov 14 9:06 AM

SUBJECT: RE: Unfortunate Events

Anders,

Robbie should have access to the desktop. I'm sure his phone is in working condition, filled with all the contacts your heart desires. Unless you both broke your phones during some drunken debauchery, which I'm all ears for. Otherwise, I'm off the clock.

Good luck,

Ethan~

P.S. It's too early. Remember. Morning people suck.

The cab stopped abruptly, and my laptop almost took a tumble to the floor.

"Shit."

"Sorry," the driver said with a smile that implied he wasn't sorry at all, but I couldn't be too pissed since he'd allowed me to use the hotspot on his cell phone.

I hadn't slept well last night, the drum in my head pounded, in no mood for Ethan's bullshit. I took a slow, calm breath. It wasn't Ethan's fault I'd thrown a tantrum and destroyed my phone. That was all on me. And thinking about the phone call last night pissed me off all over again.

FROM: AndersLowe@LoweLitFic.com

TO: hook_and_reelife@bellinx.mail.com

DATE: Nov 14 9:18 AM

SUBJECT: RE: Unfortunate Events

Ethan,

Robbie's phone I assume is in working order; however, I don't have any way to call him to be sure, and he's not responding to my emails. And no, debauchery was not on the menu last night. I should probably tell you that's inappropriate in the first place, but I have a headache. And yes, it's your day off, but I'm desperate. Give Robbie a call and tell him to meet me at the Apple Store on Fifth Avenue.

Anders~

P.S. Thank you.

FROM: hook_and_reelife@bellinx.mail.com

TO: AndersLowe@LoweLitFic.com

DATE: Nov 14 9:26 AM

SUBJECT: RE: Unfortunate Events

Anders,

Leave it to you to be boring AF in the city that never sleeps. Or is that Paris?

Anyway... I called Robbie, he said he'll get there as soon as he can.

Ethan~

P.S. Desperate enough to actually say thank you? Wow. Maybe I should have waited to call Robbie... see what else I could've persuaded you to do.

Sirens and car horns blared, and the cab came to another quick stop. The driver slammed on his brakes, waving his hands, and swearing at the guy in the cab next to us. Distracted, I read Ethan's email again. I smiled in spite of my shitty morning and all the chaos going on around me. I would've thought the last sentence was an attempt at flirting. But this was Ethan. He'd probably use my desperation as a way to get a rise out of me.

FROM: AndersLowe@LoweLitFic.com

TO: hook_and_reelife@bellinx.mail.com

DATE: Nov 14 9:33AM

SUBJECT: RE: Unfortunate Events

Ethan,

Paris is the City of Lights.

Thanks for calling Robbie.

Word of the Day: Maturity - the ability to think and act as an adult, or the state of being "boring as fuck" or as the kids like to say AF.

Anders~

P.S. You should've held out… With my morning, you could've probably persuaded me to do a lot of things. Why do I feel like public humiliation would have been your first choice?

I pressed send and closed my laptop, shoving it into my bag. The car still hadn't moved, and I decided walking would've been faster.

"I'm getting out here," I said, and he scowled.

"Suit yourself."

I paid the fare using the business card and gathered my things, handing him a cash tip. "Thanks."

The frigid fall air seized in my lungs as I stepped out of the cab. I adjusted my scarf, and tucked the ends into my peacoat, covering up as much skin as possible. The heavy wool worked as well as it could as the wind whipped down the sidewalk and around the buildings. I pulled my bag over my shoulder and pushed my hands into my pockets. People buzzed by, packed together on concrete, yet no one looked at anyone else. A sea of eyes, all pointed down, or out but never up. It was depressing. By the time I made it to the store, my knees were stiff. Tourists stood outside, snapping pictures of themselves in front of the large, glass square entrance, making sure to include the trademark Apple icon. I spotted Robbie by the door and called out his name.

"Jesus, fuck, it's cold," he said. "You had to pick this damn location."

"I didn't realize it was a tourist attraction."

"Everything in fucking Manhattan is a tourist attraction," he said. "Come on, let's get this shit over with."

To Robbie's surprise, the entire endeavor hadn't taken more than two hours, and after a much less bumpy cab ride, we were back at my hotel having lunch.

"What are your plans tonight?" Robbie asked. "Hopefully not destroying another phone."

"I dropped it. I didn't destroy it."

"The thing was in pieces," he said before taking a bite of his pasta.

"Shit happens."

I didn't want to think about the argument I'd had with my mom. I'd overreacted. Or maybe I hadn't. I didn't get how she couldn't wrap her head around how I felt. Her point was easy enough to understand. She loved me and wanted the best for me. That's great. But it was her definition of what "best" meant that had me twisted up inside. She hadn't reached out to me today that I knew of. No text messages, at least, and I was glad for it. I meant it when I'd told her I needed space.

"I was thinking of hitting up a club with a couple of buddies." Robbie wiped his mouth with his napkin. "You're more than welcome to come with us."

"That sounds terrible, actually."

"That's right... I forgot. Once you're on the darker side of thirty, you automatically become a tiresome asshole."

I laughed and nodded my chin. "You're not too far off from the dark side yourself."

"Come on, it'll be fun."

"I'll pass. I have plans anyway," I lied.

If I wanted to have plans I could. There were a wide variety of things and people to do in the city. But after last night, and the whole phone fiasco, I wanted to sleep until my meeting with Arthur Kassen tomorrow morning.

"Well, if your plans fall through, text me." Robbie's phone rang and his lips parted into a wide grin. "It's Claire."

"She's probably calling to bitch about something."

He flicked me off and answered the call. "Hey, babe."

Not wanting to eavesdrop, I dinked around with my phone, making sure everything was how it should be, and noticed I had an email I'd missed from Ethan.

FROM: hook_and_reelife@bellinx.mail.com

TO: AndersLowe@LoweLitFic.com

DATE: Nov 14 10:02 AM

SUBJECT: Gone Fishing

Anders,

Word of the day: Adventurous - living outside the box, aka not boring AF.

I'll be out fishing all day tomorrow with Jay and Jax, so I won't be at your beck and call.

Ethan~

*P.S. I might've made you try… wait for it *gasp* a cappuccino.*

P.P.S. If humiliation is your kink, I'm not the guy for you. But I bet you could find someone on Pegasus.

My pulse tripped.

Pegasus.

Most people dated via apps these days. Was he on there? Shit, did he know I was? Robbie was busy tearing the label off his beer, the crease between his brows deepening as he listened to whatever Claire had to say. I had a few minutes. I should email Ethan back, tell him he couldn't say shit like that in an email to his boss, for Christ's sake. But my curiosity had always been a thorn in my side. I swiped my thumb over the screen until I found what I was looking for. Opening the Pegasus app was like opening Pandora's box every time. But this time I couldn't fool myself into thinking this was a good idea. Ethan was my employee. I had no rationale for why I typed his name and city into the search bar. My thumb hovered over the screen. If I pressed enter, I'd cross a line. I'd invade his privacy. But, wait? Had he already invaded mine?

"Can I get you anything else?" the waiter asked, and I quickly closed out of the app. "Coffee, or dessert?"

"Just a cappuccino and the check."

Robbie finally hung up the phone as the waiter walked away.

"She's impossible," he complained.

"Why do you bother?"

"It's cliché, but there's that whole line between love and hate." He shrugged and drained his beer. "It's sexy as hell, man. Brutal. But sexy as hell."

"Brutal is the perfect adjective for Claire."

"I gotta take off," he said, laughter in his eyes. "Thanks for lunch."

"Of course."

"I'll meet you at the office in the morning. Kassen said he can be there by nine."

The waiter brought me my coffee as Robbie stood and pulled on his coat.

"Here you go, sir." He reached into the pocket of his apron and pulled out a small leather binder. "I took the liberty of charging it to your room, but here's a receipt if you need it."

"Thanks."

The man's eyes lingered over my smile. "Thank you."

Once the waiter was out of earshot, Robbie said, "I think you just found your plans for tonight."

"Not my type."

He was totally my type. Long and lean muscles. High cheekbones. Pretty lips. I was too predictable.

"Liar," Robbie teased. "Text me, though, if you change your mind about going out."

"I will." I wouldn't.

After he left, I stared down at the cup in front of me. A small heart made out of cream decorated the caramel-colored surface. The shade reminded me of Ethan's eyes. Before I took a sip, I snapped a quick picture and texted it to Ethan.

He didn't wait long to respond.

Ethan: You got a new phone?

Me: I did. I'm trying all kinds of new things it would seem.

Ethan: And how do you like it?

I lifted the cup to my lips, the scent of vanilla and nutmeg filling my lungs. The flavor made me think of Christmas mornings. Warm and sweet.

Me: More than I should.

Ethan

The bell on the toaster startled me as I leaned against the kitchen counter with my eyes half closed and a cup of coffee in my hand. Yawning, I set my mug down and grabbed a dish from the cabinet. Jax hadn't come downstairs yet. We had about thirty minutes before we had to pick up Jason, but I wasn't concerned. I'd let him sleep in, and if he didn't come down, I'd take Jay myself. I missed spending time with him without anyone else around. He was different without the weight of his brother's worry hovering over his head. Not that Jax was wrong for worrying about his little brother, but I supposed it could feel suffocating having people fuss over you all the time. I'd wager there was a side of Jason only Mabel saw. Smiling at the thought, I scraped some butter over the bread with a knife and took a bite. I was on my second piece of toast when my phone buzzed.

FROM: AndersLowe@LoweLitFic.com

TO: hook_and_reelife@bellinx.mail.com

DATE: Nov 15 7:51 AM

SUBJECT: RE: Gone Fishing

Ethan,

For the record, I don't expect you to ever be at my beck and call. And again, thank you for yesterday. I don't like to make a habit out of contacting people on their days off for work-related purposes. If I may ask, where are you fishing today?

Anders~

P.S. I'm trying a caramel macchiato today. See what you started.

FROM: hook_and_reelife@bellinx.mail.com

TO: AndersLowe@LoweLitFic.com

DATE: Nov 15 7:59 AM

SUBJECT: RE: Gone Fishing

Anders,

It depends on why you're asking. Are you going to hop out of a bush and give me more work to do? If it's merely curiosity then sure, you can ask all you like. I think we're hitting up a spot Jax likes along the Chattahoochee River.

Ethan~

P.S. Screw the macchiato. If you're stepping out of the box, you might as well try a coffee tonic. Or, if you're feeling a fall vibe walking through the city, try a dirty chai latte. I'm happy to feed this new addiction as long as you like.

FROM: AndersLowe@LoweLitFic.com

TO: hook_and_reelife@bellinx.mail.com

DATE: Nov 15 8:06 AM

SUBJECT: RE: Gone Fishing

Ethan,

If I had something for you to do, I'd tell you to do it. When it comes to work, I have no qualms asking for what I want. For example, I sent Robbie to get us both coffee tonics while I wait for Mr. Kassen to show up. In regard to my inquiry, I asked mostly out of curiosity. There's this great spot in Lullwater Preserve. My father used to take me there to fish when I was younger, and I would meet him there sometimes when I was in school at Emory. The park is quite picturesque. If you're looking to bring home dinner, Chattahoochee is a better bet, Lullwater is catch and release only. You should check it out sometime, Jason might like it.

Anders~

P.S. As stated above I decided on the tonic. I don't usually walk around the city when I'm here. Too busy for tourist attractions and fall vibes.

I stared at the screen, processing everything Anders had said. He was into fishing? It didn't compute. Anders was a high-priced suit with a stick up his ass. There was no universe in which I could picture him standing on a riverbank, in shorts and a t-shirt, chilling with a fishing pole. Maybe a yacht? I mean, the man's skin was impeccable. Not a sunspot to be seen on his perfect nose. And the bit about his dad. It was like he'd given me this intimate piece of thread to unravel. This was worse than snooping his profile on Pegasus. He was way too human to me now.

"What's wrong?" Jax asked, scratching his bare stomach as he walked into the kitchen.

"Huh?"

"You look confused." He shrugged and poured himself a cup of coffee. "Thanks for making this."

"Not sure if it'll be strong enough for you." I slipped my phone into my back pocket.

"I'll drink anything at this point."

"Late night?" I asked and he blushed.

"The drive isn't too far to the river," he said, changing the subject about as subtle as a fire ant trapped in a shoe.

I let him get away with it. After what happened this week, I didn't want Jax to be uncomfortable in his own home. "Have you ever taken Jay to Lullwater Preserve?"

He stole the half-eaten piece of toast off my plate and took a bite.

"What the hell?" I laughed and snatched the small piece of bread from his fingertips. "Make your own damn toast."

Wilder walked into the kitchen, hair pointing every which way and groaned as he snuggled under Jax's arm. "I need coffee, stat. I don't understand why anyone likes fishing. You have to get up early. Bugs. Snakes. Worms. It's like Hell on Earth." He eyed the bread in my hand. "You made toast?"

"Yeah... for me..." I finished off the last bite and took a swig of my coffee. "You're coming with us?"

Wilder's eyes widened. "God, no, why? Do I have to?"

"Nah, babe." Jax placed a chaste kiss on his lips. "You don't have to go if you don't want to."

They stared at each other for a few seconds, having one of those silent couple's conversations. The same kind I used to have with Chance. The kind where it only took one look to know they owned you. One look to know forever was his to have. Fuck, I didn't want to think about Chance. I'd done enough of that last night, lying in bed, wide awake, wondering about every life choice I'd ever made.

Wilder lowered the arm he had around Jax's waist and opened the bag of bread, sliding two pieces into the toaster. "Where are you guys going anyway? Back to Allatoona?"

"Anders said Lullwater had some good spots."

Jax and Wilder gave each other another silent look.

"Anders said?" Wilder asked, his lips rising at each corner. "What the hell does he know about fishing?"

"He told me his dad used to take him fishing there."

Wilder's hand froze, his coffee cup not yet touching his lips. "He did?"

Jax flicked his gaze to mine and then back to his husband.

"Yeah, in an email this morning." Why was Wilder looking at me like I'd grown a third damn eye. "What?"

"Anders has never mentioned that to me," he said, waving his hand in the air, far more worked up over this than he needed to be. "In all the years I've known him. Not once did he mention he was a closet fisherman."

He'd said the last sentence with an almost accusatory tone.

"Jesus, why are you looking at me like that?" I asked and Wilder's smile spread across his cheeks. "Jax, tell your husband to stop staring at me, he's making it weird."

Jax smirked. "Anders emailed you this morning?"

"And?" I drew out the word. "He responded to an email I sent yesterday." I sighed. "Now you're both pissing me off. Spit it out and stop looking at me like I'm stupid."

"Anders doesn't tell people personal shit, Ethan." Wilder pulled his toast out of the toaster and onto his plate. "And the last I checked, he wasn't your favorite person. Having a sudden change of heart?" I flicked him on the shoulder. "Ow, what was that for."

"I see what you're doing. Maybe he isn't completely on my shit list anymore, but that doesn't mean I want to bang the guy."

"For what it's worth, he's totally bangable."

"Um..." Jax chuckled. "Standing right here."

"And wouldn't you know, Ethan is too... the guy you kissed after you broke my heart and—"

"Point made." Jax bit back his smile as heat flamed in my cheeks.

"Y'all make everything fucking awkward." I huffed out a laugh. "Is this your way of getting me to move out sooner than later?"

Wilder ignored me and pressed on with his insane theories. "You and Anders would make an interesting pair if you were ready for another relationship."

"Have you met me? I don't think I'm his type." I poured what was left of the pot of coffee into my Thermos. "I'm not pretty enough."

"And he's his boss, Wild. That's complicated."

"That's an understatement," I said. "We don't even like each other."

Wilder hummed under his breath. "Keep telling yourself that."

"Would you quit it," I said and playfully shoved him in the chest. "Or I'll make you come with us today."

He lifted his hand to his heart, and I smiled at his theatrics. "And to think, you used to be my favorite."

"Stop picking on Ethan before he runs out of here and never looks back." Jax wrapped his arms around his husband's hips and pulled him into his chest. "I kind of like having my fishing buddy back, seeing how my husband can't be bothered."

"You didn't marry me for my fishing abilities."

"No, I didn't." Jax leaned down and kissed Wilder in a way that had me clearing my throat.

I smiled when neither of them paid me any mind and grabbed the Thermos off the counter. "I'll pack the truck while you get ready," I said and heard Jax grunt *okay* as I turned away.

FROM: hook_and_reelife@bellinx.mail.com

TO: AndersLowe@LoweLitFic.com

DATE: Nov 15 8:21 AM

SUBJECT: RE: Gone Fishing

Anders,

Thanks for the tip. I'll have to check it out. Not sure if we'll go today though. If we even go at all. It's weird living with a married couple. I swear, Jax and Wilder are attached at the mouth half the time. I probably shouldn't have told you that. Not because of your history with Wilder, but because that's their private business, and now I'm rambling, sitting in the truck freezing my ass off. Maybe I shouldn't have mentioned the history thing either. Shit. This is what happens when I spend too much time around Wilder. I lose my damn filter. I should erase all of this because as you love to say, it's unprofessional, but Jax is finally gracing me with his presence and we're going to head out.

Lullwater.

We'll try it out.

Thanks,

Ethan~

P.S. How was the tonic? Pretty amazing, right?

P.P.S. Too busy to walk around one of the greatest cities in America? I'd kill to be in New York during the fall. You've got the rest of the day off after your meeting. I should know. I run your calendar. Stop being a rich snob and leave your gilded palace. Hang with us peasants, aka the real everyday people who don't mind wearing jeans to work. I bet you'll like it as much as you liked that cappuccino.

Anders's suggestion had paid off. Jay loved the park. We'd walked around at first, checking out the waterfalls and trails until we found a quiet spot under the shade of a few ancient trees. It was chilly without the direct sunlight, but it reminded me of Bell River. Jax had brought up Thanksgiving earlier, and after being out here for most of the day, thinking about home, I no longer regretted my decision to head down for the holiday. My mom hadn't called me and officially invited me. Not that I thought she would have in the first place. But I hoped maybe if I showed up, there wouldn't be any expectations. It was probably a shit idea, Jaxon had said as much, but I had to try. I had to see if my relationship with my parents was worth the effort to be in their lives at all.

"This is such a great place, Ethan." Jason cast his line, the smile on his face priceless. "I wonder if Mabel's been here before?"

"Who's Mabel?" Jax asked and Jason's entire body went rigid.

"Uh... umm." Jason toed the mud with the tip of his Converse. "A girl from school."

"A girl?" Jax asked. Worry formed creases around his eyes and on his forehead. "Got something you want to tell me?"

Jason didn't look up.

"I met her," I blurted, my need to protect Jay uncontrollable at times. "Sweet girl. I met a few of his other friends too."

"No, you didn't. You only met Mabel." Jason corrected me and I ran a hand down my face.

"I met Ms. Wilson."

"She's my teacher, not my friend."

"And Mabel? She's a friend?" Jax asked and Jason finally looked him in the eyes.

"She's my girlfriend."

A flash of pity crossed Jax's eyes and his shoulders sank. "You mean, she's a friend who's a girl, Jay. Girlfriend means—"

"I know what it means, Jax." His voice took me by surprise. It was strong and deep, and for a split second he sounded like his big brother. "I know what it means," he repeated, this time his confidence wavered.

"Does she think that... I mean, does she know you think she's your girlfriend?"

"She's not stupid," he said, and I coughed in an attempt to cover my laugh.

Jax shot me a look and I cringed. "You met her?"

"Yeah, she's cute."

He narrowed his eyes. "And you didn't tell me because..."

"Because I wanted to tell you, Jax. It's... it's my life. I get to tell people things when I want. Just like you got to."

Jax's expression sobered. "Okay."

Jay nodded and Jax waited him out. "Mom doesn't know. I want to tell her tonight at dinner."

"About your girlfriend."

"Yeah. Mabel." Jason exhaled, more relaxed than he'd been a few minutes ago. "My girlfriend."

"Okay."

Jay reeled in his line and cast it a bit farther into the water. "She's got red hair, and soft hands, and a line of freckles on her cheek that goes all the way to her ear."

Jax smiled, his eyes a little wet. "I like freckles."

"On boys," Jay said, and Jax stuttered with laughter.

"Boys with freckles are hot." I smirked when Jason wrinkled his nose.

"Hey, what's that face?" Jax teased.

Jason's ears turned red. "I don't think a boy with freckles would be as pretty as Mabel."

"Probably not," I said and smiled at Jax. "She's teaching him sign language."

"She is?"

"She's deaf," Jason clarified. "She was born that way."

"That's gotta be hard," Jax said and took a sip from his bottle of water.

"Mabel said she never cared about hearing until she got hit by the car. She told me she wishes sometimes... that her ears would have worked on the day she got hit, that maybe she wouldn't be like how she is now."

"How is she?" Jax asked.

Jason looked up at me, his smile small. "I think she's great."

"Hit by a car," Jax whispered and I nodded. "Jesus Christ."

"She's so smart, Jax. I want her to come fishing with us next Sunday. Ethan said yes."

"I would love to meet her."

Jason's smile for his big brother was about a mile wide.

"I'm gonna grab a sandwich from the cooler, y'all want anything?" I asked, wanting to give them some one-on-one time as brothers.

"I'm good. Jay, you ready for lunch?"

"No, thanks."

"Alright, don't catch anything without me," I said and headed toward the truck.

I opened the tailgate and reached for the cooler. We hadn't packed much besides water and peanut butter and jelly sandwiches. Grape was Jay's favorite. I didn't think the flavor of the jelly mattered as long as it filled my stomach. I lifted myself onto the tailgate and opened up the plastic bag. The bread had flattened some, but it tasted good all the same. I took another bite and pulled my phone from my pocket, wondering if Anders had responded to my last email. On our way to the park this morning, I decided I liked unraveling his pieces. Rattling him. Unlike Wilder, I wasn't going to make this into something more than it needed to be. Messing with Anders made me feel something more than the flat line I'd been stuck in since I'd left Colorado. Plain and simple, our interactions were between us and I liked having a person, not necessarily a friend, outside the bubble of the Stettler house. Nora was great, and I thought of her as a friend already. But she was coupled up too. Maybe Anders was my misery loves company guy. All I knew was a week's worth of interactions wasn't enough. Pushing his buttons kept my mind here, in the present. And I'd like to think he enjoyed pushing my buttons too.

Sure enough, he'd replied.

FROM: AndersLowe@LoweLitFic.com

TO: hook_and_reelife@bellinx.mail.com

DATE: Nov 15 11:49 AM

SUBJECT: The Real New York

Ethan,

It seems I was able to escape my gilded cage, or palace. I like the word cage. It adds a bit more angst and grit. I'm currently sitting on a mushroom by the Alice in Wonderland statue, with a warm chai tea latte in my hand. Hold the espresso. Apparently, rich snobs like myself can't handle their coffee tonics that early in the morning. I think I might be awake for days. Thanks for that. It's cloudy today, but I like it. It mutes all the colors and makes the people stand out more. Downside... People never make eye contact here. It's why I don't like to "experience" the city. It's lonely. I'm sure you've heard the phrase money doesn't buy happiness. Rich or poor, isolation stings all the same. Now I'm the one rambling and being unprofessional. It's a side effect of you.

Anders Lowe

Newly Appointed Prince of Peasants

P.S. If you only had one day in the city, what would you choose to do?

FROM: hook_and_reelife@bellinx.mail.com

TO: AndersLowe@LoweLitFic.com

DATE: Nov 15 12:16 PM

SUBJECT: RE: The Real New York

Are you still Anders, or do I need to address you as Your Highness?

About the tonic... I forgot to mention it can give you a pretty heavy caffeine buzz. Bonus, you'll have energy to traipse around Manhattan. Speaking of which, pictures or it never happened. And not to sound too complimentary, but you paint a damn nice picture with words. Don't let it go to your head, though, God knows you don't need any more ego. Were you being metaphorical (is that a word) about loneliness? Is that inappropriate to ask? Well, you'll say it is, but you think everything is inappropriate. Except for Robbie and Claire being an item. Nora told me. Isn't fraternizing like the worst sin in the Lowe Bible of Sins? I'm still learning the ropes. New kid and all.

Your loyal servant,

Ethan~

P.S. One isn't enough. I want to say something less obvious, like go to The Cloisters or The Strand, but honestly, I've never been to the city, and I think I'd just want to stand in the middle of Times Square at night.

I pressed send and glanced over my shoulder. Jason and Jay were huddled close talking. Jay had a smile on his face, and I assumed that was a good sign. I took a second to finish my sandwich and reread Anders's email, I was halfway through when he sent me a text. It was a picture of his side profile, not much unlike the one I'd found on the dating app. He had on a mustard yellow beanie with chunks of his blond hair sticking out the side. The tip of his cheek was pink, and by the color of the sky I assumed it was cold outside. I could see the famous statue of Alice behind him, and I laughed at the kid, bundled in a coat and scarf, in the background photobombing him. He was a different person today. He wasn't that asshole I'd met in

January at the party, or the arrogant boss sitting behind the desk. I had to admit, I liked this version of Anders.

Me: Nice hat.

Anders: I stole it from that kid in the picture.

I barked out a laugh.

Me: Who are you and what have you done with my boss?

Anders: It's his day off.

Me: Tell him to take an extended holiday.

Me: I've only known him a week and he's a pain in the ass.

Anders: I can still fire you.

I smirked and tapped my fingers across the screen.

Me: But then you'd have no one to share your Happy Meals with.

Anders: Sharing Happy Meals falls under sin number 237 of the no fraternization policy.

Me: Which Claire and Robbie are exempt?

Anders: You try telling Claire no.

Me: Fair.

Anders: Word of the day: Metaphorical - in relation to a metaphor. Figurative language.

Me: It's a real word?

Anders: Indeed, it is. And yes... I was feeling a bit allegorical.

Me: Is that a metaphor about alligators?

Anders: And this is why I didn't want to hire you.

Anders: Shall I buy you a dictionary while I'm at the Strand?

Me: And he's back... that was a short vacation.

Anders: It was fun while it lasted.

It really was.

Anders: Did you go to Lullwater?

Me: Still here. I should probably get back to fishing.

A minute went by and I watched the dots at the bottom of my screen reappear and disappear four times.

Anders: I've never been to Times Square at night.

Me: You should go.

Anders: I think I might.

Me: Pictures or it didn't happen.

Me: Enjoy the day off, Your Highness.

Anders

I remembered why I never wanted to come to Times Square. I was a dot in a sea of fish, of street performers and blinking Broadway signs. Waves of people moved past me, like one of those videos where the camera honed in on a single person as the rest of the world streaked by, leaving only color in their wake. Surrounded again, yet the loneliness crept deeper under my skin. Robbie had texted me earlier, asking if I wanted to come over to his place for dinner and watch the football game. I almost said yes. But I was too deep in this Real New York venture and it had put me in a strange mood. Rules and standards. Two constants in my life. Two things I could control, at least most of the time. Today I'd veered off my usual path completely. I'd dropped my walls and broken more rules than I was comfortable with.

The Lowe Bible of Sins.

My laugh was soft as I tipped my head back. The barrage of people disappeared, leaving only a starless sky and the buildings that swallowed me whole. The noise of the lights sang over the girl on the corner with her guitar and country twang. The city was beautiful like this. In parts and fragments. It wasn't lonely, it was alive. I reached into my pocket and took out my phone to snap a few pictures. A street vendor. A human robot. The street packed with cars. I took a video and made a small circle, making sure to grab as much of the atmosphere as I could before I attached everything to a text and sent it to Ethan. He pushed me, and fuck if I didn't like it. He held no regard for my position as his boss and said whatever the hell he wanted. He was too honest at times, and nosy. He thought I was arrogant even though he was the one who'd made judgmental assumptions about me. Everything about him screamed stay away.

Not for you.

Will make you crazy.

But I was drawn to him nevertheless, and not like a moth to a flame or anything else ridiculously cliché. I was drawn to him because he was the exact opposite of what I thought was good for me. I was ancient in my skin. Traveling and never seeing. Reading but working. Breathing but slowly dying. I was thirty-six going on seventy-five, looking for the perfect ending to a life I hadn't yet lived.

My gilded palace was a cage, but one I'd created for myself. Why had it taken a walk through a city, a city

I'd been to a hundred times, to open my eyes? And how had Ethan, a guy I hardly knew, been able to figure out this was precisely what I'd needed? After Wilder it had become too easy to lose myself in my job, in the image I'd created. Perhaps it was time to shake things up.

The girl with the guitar started to sing one of my favorite songs right as my phone buzzed in my hand. I waited until she finished the chorus before I checked my messages, remembering the whole point of this experiment tonight was to step out of the box and breathe. Expecting it to be Ethan, I swiped my thumb across the screen and was disappointed to see a text notification from the airline reminding me to check in for my flight in the morning. I slipped my cell into my pocket and listened to the girl sing about falling in and out of love. The cold night air bit at my fingertips, and after about thirty minutes I decided to grab a cab and head to the hotel to thaw.

Back in my room, I ordered room service and showered. It was eleven and I hadn't heard back from Ethan. Why that bothered me as much as it did, I had a few ideas I chose not to entertain. Ideas about dropping a few more walls and allowing someone in even if it was against my better judgment. Today had been a weird and existential day, and as much as it thrilled me, I was exhausted. Ethan not texting back was probably a good thing in the long run. I pulled my t-shirt over my head and set it in my bag before I climbed into bed. I picked up my phone from the nightstand and was about to set my alarm when a text came through. I hated the relief that washed through me.

Ethan: I can't stop watching this video you sent. How freaking cool is Times Square?

Me: It's overrated.

Ethan: You can admit you liked it. I won't tell anyone.

Ethan: Unless you truly are a pretentious ass.

I was equally offended and amused.

Me: I'm not pretentious. I don't like large crowds.

Ethan: Then why'd you go?

Me: I don't like you either, but here I am texting when I should be sleeping.

Ethan: You like me....

Ethan: Your pretentious ass just won't admit it.

Me: That mouth of yours is going to get you into trouble.

Ethan: And now you're flirting with me.

Me: Definitely NOT flirting.

At least it hadn't been my intention. Apparently, my body hadn't gotten the memo. I was half hard thinking about my assistant's mouth. God, what the hell was wrong with me?

Ethan: That's right... sin number 232. Fraternization.

Me: I thought it was 237.

Ethan: Semantics.

I needed to get this conversation back on track, or end it, before I said something I'd regret the minute I saw him in the office tomorrow.

Me: Did you catch anything today?

Ethan: Nah... Jay did though.

Ethan: Speaking of fishing... I can't picture it.

Me: Picture what?

Ethan: You.

Ethan: I imagine it would be uncomfortable to fish while wearing a three-piece suit.

I rolled my eyes.

Me: I do own a few pairs of jeans.

Ethan: But do you own cargo shorts or cargo pants? Answer carefully, or all fishermen cred will be lost.

I laughed and sent my response, bracing for the shit he was about to throw at me.

Me: Alas, I'm not classy enough for cargo.

Ethan: Why am I not surprised?

Ethan: I bet you don't even know the difference between a fly and a lure.

Me: There you go with your assumptions again.

Ethan: If the shoe fits...

Once again, I found myself wanting to show him he was wrong about me. Prove to him I wasn't someone he could so easily categorize.

Me: Word of the day: Stereotypes - unfair and oversimplified ideas about certain people or groups of people.

Me: I am more than the suit I put on every day. Just as I assume you are more than the shorts you wear to fish.

I pressed send and exhaled. My irritation ebbing as I watched the dots dance across the bottom of the phone. He must have been writing a dissertation because three minutes had passed without a reply. I was about to set my phone down when his name popped up on my screen.

Ethan: You're right, I don't know you. But I want to.

I stared at the message, my heart in overdrive as my tendency to overthink kicked in. He wanted to know me. That simple sentence could change everything. Ruin it too.

Me: I don't know how to interpret that.

Ethan: Interpret it however you want.

I needed to shut this down. To close off whatever I'd started today when I'd sent that damn picture in Central Park. But I didn't want to. Today had been the first day in a long while where I'd actually felt like myself. And he had been partially responsible for that, no matter how much I wanted to resist it. I was friends with Nora and Robbie, but they were my peers. Agents like me. The power dynamic between me and Ethan complicated things. Especially since, much to my chagrin, I was attracted to him.

I typed out a response, hoping to lighten the conversation.

Me: I'm still not sharing my Happy Meals with you.

Ethan: All friendships have their quirks.

Me: Goodnight, Ethan.

Ethan: You're no fun.

Me: But you already knew that.

I pressed my lips together and typed out another text.

Me: Today was nice.

Ethan: It was the coffee, wasn't it?

Me: Ha ha

Ethan: I should sleep. My boss is a real prick if I'm late.

Me: He sounds like my kind of guy.

Ethan: Shut up, I'm sleeping.

Laughing, I switched off the lamp and set my phone to wake me at six. I punched and folded the pillow a few times trying to get comfortable, my head filled with too much stimulus. Sirens echoed somewhere in the city as I closed my eyes. Like every night, my brain switched to autopilot, and I couldn't settle down. I sat up a little, resting my back against the pillows and raked my fingers through my hair. The lights of Times Square flashed inside my head, the kid laughing in the park on a loop inside my ears. And Ethan. And his mouth. And his scent of wood and soap and rain. I blew out a long breath, wishing I hadn't packed away my book.

"Goddammit."

Giving in, I grabbed my phone and opened up the app I'd been avoiding ever since Ethan had mentioned it. Attraction was an idea. An idea that plagued you until you either acted on it or moved on. Maybe seeing him like this, outside of the confines of the office would quell the growing curiosity.

I'd never been so wrong about anything in my entire life.

A simple shot of Ethan's abs filled my screen. His fingers were fisted in what looked like a blanket as he pushed it dangerously low, exposing the smooth, pale skin below his tan line. I stared at the trimmed brown hair that dusted the top of his pelvis, and the ache in my dick became too prominent to ignore. I reached under the sheets and palmed the growing erection inside my boxer briefs. This was *not* the reaction I wanted. Instead of switching out of the app like I should have, I scrolled through his pictures. Bad idea number—I'd lost count. Some of the images were older, and I had to admit, the leaner version of Ethan was just as sexy. He had broad shoulders and a swimmer's body all packaged with a bright smile and the most unique eyes I'd ever seen.

Not happening.

I closed out of the app and tossed my phone, gently this time, onto the side table. Lying back down, I flipped to my right side and then my left about four times. Growling into the void, I fell onto my back and shoved down the sheets. I slipped a hand under the waistband of my underwear and smeared the dot of pre-come leaking from my slit down my shaft with my thumb. A ragged breath escaped my lungs, the first real breath I'd taken all day. I stroked myself hard and steady, thinking about his soft pale skin, that patch of hair, and how it would feel against the tip of my nose, my hip, rubbing against my dick. I forced out all the warnings and the rules and let myself go. This didn't have to mean anything. It was a physical response to a hot picture, and I hadn't gotten laid in over a month. It was about flesh and muscle. I thought about the sharp line of his jaw and how it would taste. I didn't think about his eyes or his smile or his smart mouth, and how I wanted to fill it with my cock or my fingers. My hips jerked as I groaned through clenched teeth, and my orgasm splashed against my stomach. Breathless, I slammed my eyes shut as goose bumps broke out across my skin. The longer I lay there, the harder it was to rationalize away what I'd done.

I'd gotten off thinking about an employee.

About Ethan.

His eyes, his smile, his smart mouth.

Everything I shouldn't want.

Everything I couldn't have.

On my flight home, I told myself I wasn't going to overanalyze what had happened last night. I'd been restless. I'd needed to sleep. An orgasm had gotten the job done.

Ethan made you come.

I pinched the bridge of my nose, hating myself more by the minute. Eventually, I had to get out of the car and go inside. It was my office, after all. This was childish.

"He was just a visual."

A knock on the passenger-side window pulled me from my mental spiral.

"Are you hiding?" Nora asked, holding up a brown bag. "I have food."

I'd texted her before I'd left the airport and asked her to grab some lunch.

I cut the engine and picked up the small bag from the back seat before I got out of the car.

"How was your flight?" she asked as I stepped onto the sidewalk.

"Cramped."

"I don't know why you don't fly first class. It's not like you don't have the money."

"If I flew first class every time I went to New York, I'd be broke."

"It's a tax write-off," she said, and I opened the office door for her.

"Write-off or not, I can think of better things to spend my money on."

As my luck would have it, Ethan was at his desk when we walked into the lobby, his nose buried in a book. It took him a few seconds to look up, and I recognized the familiar cover. *The Secret History.*

"That's my favorite book."

"Yeah?" he asked, staring at me like he'd been caught doing something wrong.

"Yeah."

Ethan's cheeks flushed red, and all I could think about was that patch of hair hiding underneath his gray slacks.

"Well, this is a riveting conversation." Nora sighed. "If either of you plan on eating lunch while it's hot, I'll meet you in the boardroom."

"We have a boardroom?" Ethan asked and I tore my eyes away from his.

"It's more of an empty office," she said and tilted her head. "Come on, or I'll be forced to eat all of this by myself."

"Uh... Alright," Ethan stammered and rubbed the back of his neck as he stood. "Sure... yeah, I'm hungry as hell."

I was the one who jacked off to images of him last night. Why the hell was he being awkward?

"I got you something," I said, once Nora was out of ear shot.

"You did?" I handed him the bag and he pulled out the book. Smirking, he lifted his brows. "You're something else, Anders."

All the guilt and weirdness I'd felt about last night evaporated when he laughed.

"I figured you'd need it. Think of it as a tool," I said.

"A dictionary... Did you get it from the Strand?"

"I did."

"Of course, you did," he said and set it on his desk.

Ethan's eyes trailed down my chest and back up again. "Are you trying to prove a point or something?"

"What do you mean?"

"You're wearing jeans and a t-shirt," he said matter of fact. "To work."

"I didn't have time to change after my flight." I shrugged.

His gaze swept over my chest and arms. "You look normal."

"Thanks?"

He laughed and bit the corner of his bottom lip. I had to force myself to look away.

"We should head back. Nora wasn't kidding. She'll eat all the fries if we don't stop her."

"True..." he said, distracted, and I turned toward the hall. "Hey, Anders?"

"Yeah."

He gave me a crooked smile, but there was something in his expression I couldn't read.

"Normal looks good on you."

Ethan

Nora sat on the edge of my desk, waving her hands, rambling about the difference between sweet potatoes and yams. I'd lost track of what she'd been trying to say a full two minutes ago. I flipped open the dictionary Anders had gotten me, wanting to read the line he'd written on the inside cover again for the thousandth time.

"Your assumptions are your windows on the world. Scrub them off every once in a while, or the light won't come in." Isaac Asimov~

I stared at the page, remembering how different he looked when he'd shown up to the office in dark-washed jeans and a black t-shirt. The shirt looked like it had been tailored to fit his broad chest and biceps. And hell, those biceps. I might've been in shock when he'd first walked in, never having seen him in anything besides his sharp suits and dress clothes, but I could've sworn I'd spotted the tiniest bit of ink peeking out from under his sleeve along the inside of his arm. I'd probably imagined it. Anders and tattoos did not compute. The quote on the front page, written in his perfect script, glared back at me. I'd made another assumption, hadn't I? Why couldn't he have a tattoo? I didn't know much about him. Unfortunately, I didn't think I ever would.

Over the last nine days he'd reverted back to his usual prickly self. His emails had been short and to the point, never venturing outside of work-related territory, even when I tried. He ignored my snarky remarks and sighed whenever I'd said anything unprofessional in front of the other agents. Anders seemed more stressed than usual—tired. I wanted to rewind time and take back my comment about him looking good. Maybe I'd pushed the line too far? I hated myself for caring, hated that I'd let him get into my head at all. But that wasn't true either. I liked that he'd let me in. There had been a spark between us, and as much as I'd been nursing wounds not yet healed, having someone who fired back at me, pushed me, it had been a relief. I wanted mustard yellow beanie Anders back, not this weird robot version. Hell, I'd even take his pretentious pettiness at this point.

"Ethan? You're not paying attention to a word I'm saying, are you?" Nora laughed, and I crinkled my nose like the guilty asshole I was.

"I'm sorry, I spaced out."

"Spaced out... or you're ignoring me?"

"Tomato, to-mah-toe."

She glanced down at the dictionary and I snapped it shut. "I asked about your plans for Thanksgiving?"

I'd rather talk about sweet potatoes.

"I think I'm going to drive down to Bell River. See my folks." I tapped a nervous finger on the arm of my chair. "You?"

"I'm flying out to Seattle tomorrow."

"How come I didn't know you were from Seattle?" I asked.

She smiled with humor in her eyes. "You don't ask a lot of questions." She held up her hands like she was framing a scene. "The strong and silent type."

"Anders thinks I'm nosy."

"I'm offended."

"What do you have to be offended about?" I asked and laughed when she gave me a dirty look.

"You ask Anders questions? And not me?"

Her pouting skills rivaled Wilder.

"Not anymore. He clammed up on me."

"He's been weird, right?" she asked. "Like he looks like he hasn't slept in a week."

"I don't pay much attention, to be honest."

She snorted. "You're a terrible liar."

"Liar? You're high on printer ink."

Nora laughed, her head tipping forward as she covered her mouth with her hand. Eyes wide and shoulders shaking. I loved her laugh. It was full-bodied, but not obnoxious. It vibrated in my chest and made me smile.

"Ethan... be serious. The sexual tension between you two... it stinks up the office."

"You're definitely high. The man is in love with himself. And I..." Nora's smile grew, and I glared at her. "I'm not talking about this."

"Come on..." She leaned over the desk and pushed my shoulder. "It's fun watching you get all squirmy. Look, you're blushing."

"Fuck off."

She gasped, but her smile never faded. "Such language and at work. What would the boss say? Do you think he'd punish you?"

"Oh my God, please go away." My cheeks were on fire. "I have a ton of shit to do before I leave."

"After today, the office is closed until Monday. What could you possibly have to do besides sit here and pine."

"I am not above shoving you off this desk."

She stood and I decided I hated her laugh. "Fine. But, when you and Anders become a thing, I want the record to show I called it first."

"What? You're a lawyer now?"

"I think I'm pretty convincing."

I flipped her off.

"Have a safe trip tomorrow," she said, escaping to her office.

"I hope security randomly searches you at the airport," I hollered as she shut her door.

I heard her laugh, and I might've smiled too.

I hadn't been lying when I'd said I had a bunch of tasks to complete before I left for the day. This job, for the most part, was pretty straightforward. Familiarizing myself with Anders's clients was the hardest part. I was grateful for Kris and her organizational skills. Every client had their own spreadsheet, and when I could, I read through them.

Brushing off Nora and her bullshit, I opened the acquisition files and started to attach them to an email to send to Claire. Even if Nora had a point, Anders had thrown down brick and mortar the minute he'd gotten back from his trip. The line I'd pushed across had been firmly set back into place, and I wasn't sure if I wanted to cross it again. That was a lie too. I missed getting a rise out of him, getting him to give in. He annoyed me and intrigued me, and I wanted more of it. Shit, I needed therapy.

I sent Claire an email and was about to start working on Anders' schedule for after the holiday when my inbox pinged.

FROM: AndersLowe@LoweLitFic.com

TO: EthanCalloway@LoweLitFic.com

DATE: Nov 24 1:20 PM

SUBJECT: Calendar

Ethan,

Please switch the meeting on Monday with Mr. Welles to the noon spot and book a reservation for 12:30 at one of the restaurants on his pre-approved list. It's in his file in case you're unaware. There will be three of us.

Thanks,

Anders~

FROM: EthanCalloway@LoweLitFic.com

TO: AndersLowe@LoweLitFic.com

DATE: Nov 24 1:25 PM

SUBJECT: RE: Calendar

Anders,

Mr. Welles? Really? I live with the guy. And he has a pre-approved list of restaurants? I can't wait to give him hell for that.

What do you want me to do with your appointment at one?

Thanks,

Mr. Calloway (since we're being fancy today.)

P.S. Whatever happened to the Prince of Peasants? I liked that guy.

I stared at my screen trying to talk myself out of sending the email. I could rewrite it and play the role of the good employee.

Screw that.

I hit send and hoped I'd have a job at the end of the day.

FROM: AndersLowe@LoweLitFic.com

TO: EthanCalloway@LoweLitFic.com

DATE: Nov 24 1:33 PM

SUBJECT: RE: Calendar

Ethan,

Cancel my appointment at one and reschedule for Tuesday. Same time slot.

My clients' preferences are important to me. It's my job to know what they want and what they like. As it is yours. Kris set up a list in every client file. Wilder is no exception.

Might I suggest you use the dictionary I've given you to look up the differences between fancy and professional.

Anders~

P.S. He's still sitting on that mushroom in Central Park.

FROM: EthanCalloway@LoweLitFic.com

TO: AndersLowe@LoweLitFic.com

DATE: Nov 24 1:55 PM

SUBJECT: RE: Calendar

Anders,

I've rearranged the appointments and booked a reservation at East End.

I'm well versed in the definitions of both fancy and professional. That being said, I found this little gem that I think you may enjoy.

Word of the day: Narcissist - an individual who admires themselves in a disproportionate and unhealthy way.

What do you think? Ringing any bells?

Ethan~

P.S. Well, tell him to get his ass back to Atlanta. We miss him.

FROM: AndersLowe@LoweLitFic.com

TO: EthanCalloway@LoweLitFic.com

DATE: Nov 24 2:11 PM

SUBJECT: RE: Calendar

Ethan,

I think the word you're looking for is perfectionist (an individual with high standards of themselves and others and rejects anything other than perfection).

I'm glad you're enjoying my gift and putting it to good use. Maybe you could read it over the holiday break? Better start with the word tiresome.

Anders~

P.S. I miss him too.

There it was. A small crack in the wall.

I miss him too.

His quippy little comebacks gave me hope. I picked up my phone from the desk and tapped out a text. I could have just as easily gone back to his office to talk to him. But I didn't want to push my luck, and besides, he was a lot more open when he wasn't face to face.

Me: What are you doing for Thanksgiving?

Anders: Going to my parents'. You?

Me: Same. I leave tomorrow.

I waited and he didn't reply. I chewed on my bottom lip as I typed out my next text. My thumb hovered over the screen. This could be good or bad. Probably bad. I pressed send anyway.

Me: I'm nervous though. My relationship with my parents is... strained.

Anders: Mine too.

Me: I haven't visited since I moved to Denver. The whole me being gay thing isn't their favorite.

Anders: Wow.

Me: Yeah, and they don't know I'm coming home.

Anders: Wait… Do you not talk to them anymore?

Anders: I apologize, I shouldn't pry.

Me: I brought it up. And no not really. I've talked to my mom once or twice since I left for Denver. They don't even know I'm here.

Anders: They think you're still with Chance?

Me: Yeah.

Me: What about you? What's the story with your parents?

I waited and waited, but he didn't reply. Disappointed, I lifted my eyes from the screen and found him standing in front of my desk.

"Hey," I said.

Actually, croaked seemed more accurate. He looked good today; well, he looked good every day. But I liked the green color of his button down. The shade pulled out specks of yellow in his blue eyes.

Anders picked up my copy of *The Secret History* from the desk. "Did you finish?"

I shook my head, staring at his fingers clenched around the spine of the paperback. "Not yet. It's… odd."

His lips raised at the corners, almost a smile, but more reserved as he met my gaze. "*'I believe that it is better to know one book intimately than a hundred superficially.'*"

"That's from the book... in the beginning..."

"Did you know Donna Tart won a Pulitzer?"

"I didn't."

Anders set the book on my desk. "I don't like to talk about myself," he said, abruptly changing the subject. He ran a hand through his hair and swallowed. "You're intrusive."

I couldn't help my smile. "That's a good word."

He smirked. "Thank you."

"It's okay," I said. "If you don't want to talk."

The muscle in his jaw flexed. All of his angles seemed sharper today. "My mother..." He looked down the hall, then back at me. "I'm adopted... And it's a long story, not one I want to have here. Let's just say, my mom isn't thrilled I'm bi, but she 'loves me no matter what.'" He made quotes with his fingers. "And maybe I get my perfectionist standards from her."

"It all makes sense now."

He bit back his smile. "Don't psychoanalyze me."

"I don't even know what that means, maybe I should look it up."

His chuckle warmed my stomach. "Good thing your amazing boss bought you a dictionary."

"So, what are you going to do?" I asked.

"About what?"

"Thanksgiving?"

"What do you mean?" he asked. "I'm going to my parents' house, like I said."

"I know... but will you hash things out with them, or eat turkey and run?"

"It depends on how much alcohol I consume."

"Will you drunk text me? I might need the support. My father doesn't like to look at me."

"I'm sorry," he said, and I believed he was.

He understood what it was like to hide who you were for the fear you might lose the people around you, only to come to the realization you were right to be scared in the first place.

"My mother and I haven't spoken since I was in New York. She sent me a text two days ago asking me to come for Thanksgiving. I almost said no."

"Why didn't you?"

He was quiet and I worried I'd pushed too far. Again. My need to solve the riddle of Anders Lowe was an addiction I could do without.

"It could be worse. My parents accept me. They may want something I might never give them, but at least they accept me." He let out a long breath. "I think that's enough truth for one day." Anders stuffed his hands in his pockets and nodded his head toward the hallway. "I better get back to work."

"Yeah... quit slacking," I said, and he scoffed.

"Slacking isn't even part of my vocabulary."

"It should be." As he turned to leave, I asked, "One more truth?"

"Maybe."

"Do you have a tattoo?"

Anders paused, his lips spreading into a wicked grin.

"Several... in fact."

Anders

Rain fell against the windshield, distorting the image of my parents' house, the rivulets drawing the colors down the glass as I sat in silence inside my car. A blue SUV I didn't recognize was parked in the driveway, and I took a steady breath, preparing myself for whatever I was about to walk into. My mom was notorious for trying to set me up. I didn't think she'd do that given the circumstances of our last conversation. I'd have thought she'd want privacy and family time. Perhaps whoever was in there had been invited as a buffer. An avoidance. I couldn't say I'd be disappointed. I didn't want to get into shit with her today and ruin my dad's favorite holiday. I cut off the engine, grabbed the bottle of wine I'd brought, and my umbrella from the back. The front door opened before I stepped onto the porch, and my father stood in the entryway with a smile on his face, lifting all my apprehension from my shoulders.

"It's good to see you, son," he said and pulled me into a hug.

"Let me get rid of this umbrella and I'll come inside."

"Of course, leave it on the porch and come on in." He lowered his voice to a whisper as he took the bottle of wine from my hand. "Your mom's been fretting all day, don't give her too much trouble, alright?"

A ball of remorse stuck in my throat and all I could manage was a nod.

"Good... I've missed you around here. Sundays aren't the same without you, Andi."

He shut the front door and I cringed.

"Dad... You know I hate that nickname."

"You used to like it."

Used to.

Before Wilder.

I didn't think my dad wanted to hear about how my ex used to call me that when he came.

"I'm too old for nicknames," I said, and he scoffed.

"Since when?" Mom asked as we walked into the kitchen.

She was alone, standing by the stove stirring something. The whole house smelled like poultry spice and apples.

"Since now." I kissed her cheek before taking a look around. The kitchen was open to the living room, and as far as I could tell there was no one here. "Did you invite someone?"

"No, why? Oh... The SUV is new, dear."

"You got a new car?"

My parents shared a look.

"Your mother got into an accident last week."

"An accident." A sharp pain squeezed at my chest. "Mom, are you—"

"I'm fine. Wish I could say the same about the car. Completely totaled." She set the spoon down and wiped her hands on a dish rag hanging from the oven. "You look pale, I'm fine. See."

She twirled in place, making a show of raising her hands up and down.

"You didn't tell me."

"You didn't answer your phone."

Fuck, I was the worst son. The thought of losing my mom made me sick. Especially with the way I'd left things between us.

"I'm sorry," I said, my throat tight as she pulled me into a hug.

"Water under the bridge."

"Did you catch the game this week?" Dad asked and pulled a cutting board from the cabinet. Pointing his knife, he said, "Grab me those tomatoes, would you, son?"

I set the tomatoes onto the cutting board and he got to work slicing them into wedges.

"I didn't catch it, was it a good game?"

"Great game. Close, too. But we pulled it off with a field goal in the end."

I'd never loved football as much as my father had. But I'd always been good about faking it when I needed to. It didn't matter if I loved the game or not, I liked talking to him about something he enjoyed.

"I'm sorry I missed it. One of my clients has season tickets. He's always trying to get me to go with him. We should go to a game or something." I grabbed a slice of tomato and popped it into my mouth.

"Hey, those are for the salad," he said and smiled before stealing a slice for himself.

"Everything will be ready in a few minutes." Mom handed my dad the salad bowl. "Anders, help me set the table?"

"Sure," I said and picked up the small stack of china and silverware she'd laid out.

We only used the china for special occasions. It usually sat in the cupboard in the dining room on display. I loved the nostalgia of it all. I couldn't remember a time we hadn't eaten a Thanksgiving dinner or Christmas dinner on these plates. A thought crept into my head. One I hadn't had in a while. I wondered what my life would've been like if they hadn't adopted me. Wondered what my biological parents were like. Everything would've been different, and most likely not for the better. A sudden wave of gratitude washed over me. I had it pretty damn good. Ethan's father wouldn't even look at him, for Christ's sake.

Ethan.

I hadn't been able to stop myself from thinking about him. I'd tried, unsuccessfully, after New York, to revert back to a professional relationship, but every time I'd look at him, I'd been reminded of how hard

I'd come with his image in my head. Every time he'd throw out a smart-ass remark, or I'd catch him staring at me when we were forced to have lunch together in the boardroom with Nora, I'd told myself it couldn't happen. We couldn't happen. I'd blamed my reasoning on him being an employee, but the excuse had run dry. It was inappropriate and could fuck up the dynamic in the office, but the real reason I'd persuaded myself to keep Ethan at a distance was directly related to Wilder. I'd broken my rules for him and had started something when I shouldn't have. I would be a rebound for Ethan like I had been for Wilder, and I wouldn't be another person's consolation prize. Not again. This time I had to make the right choice for myself. Stop before I got in too deep.

"Ready to eat?"

Dad walked into the dining room holding a platter with a giant turkey on it.

"What the hell? How much does that thing weigh?" I asked.

"Fourteen pounds." Mom handed me a bowl filled with mashed potatoes. "Put that next to your father's plate."

"Mom, fourteen pounds?" I said and set the bowl on the table. "For three people?"

"One day there will be more," she said, and I sighed.

"Sandra..." My father warned. "Remember what we discussed."

"What did you discuss?" I asked as my mother disappeared into the kitchen.

"Nothing. Now... don't look at me like that. I want to have a good dinner without any fighting. Can we do that, please?" Dad walked over to the small wooden hutch he'd converted into a bar a few years ago. "Bourbon?"

"I'll have some wine," I said and tried to snuff out the flicker of irritation building inside my stomach.

He poured a generous amount of red wine into a glass and handed it to me.

"Tell me about work."

And for the next thirty minutes I did just that. I filled the silence with small talk about business, while Mom filled the table with too much food. We ate like we were a party of six instead of three. My dad did a good job as moderator for the most part, but as I took my last bite of pie, the thin ice we'd been walking on cracked.

"Are you seeing anyone?" she asked.

"Let the boy digest before you start your cross examination, Counselor." Dad wiped at his mustache with a napkin. "Or else he's bound to get indigestion from all your poking and prodding."

"It's a simple question," she said, blushing from the half a bottle of chardonnay she'd consumed during dinner.

"It's fine, Dad." I wished I had the benefit of liquid courage like my mom. I wasn't drunk enough for this conversation. "No... I'm not seeing anyone."

My mother's shoulders relaxed, and the flat line of her lips split into a small smile. "That's okay. I'm sure the right girl will come along."

"Or guy," my dad added. Always the diplomat.

She waved him off, pouring herself another glass of wine. "If you can choose between the two, wouldn't the girl be an easier choice."

"Sandra, I think you've had plenty of wine. Come on now... enough of this." Dad took the bottle from her hand, and she had the audacity to look offended.

My fingers gripped the napkin in my hand as I fought off my anger. She'd been drinking all night. This wasn't her. She'd accepted me and loved me. All the reasons I shouldn't snap back piled up like bricks on my shoulders.

"I'm only saying, it's a choice to—"

"That's enough." My dad's hand smacked the table and my mother jumped. I'd never heard him raise his voice in anger at my mom. Not once in my entire life. I hated that I was the one who'd put a wedge between them. "You are determined to drive him away."

"Can we not do this," I said, my voice wavering. "Mom, you know it's not a choice. We've—"

"It *is* Anders. You could *choose* a woman. Marry her. Have children. But you choose to fool around with men too. You're the one making your life harder than it needs to be."

Stunned, I sat there, every word she'd said cutting through all the years of acceptance like a knife.

My dad shook his head, his anger pulsing with every breath he took.

"Do you think I chose you?" he asked my mother. "Do you think I had any control over how I felt about you when I met you in that classroom when we were practically kids? I could have chosen to ignore it. Married someone else. A girl with money. Even if I wasn't attracted to her and could never love her. My parents would have loved that." A tear ran down Mom's cheek and I struggled to breathe. "I could have taken the easy road. But instead, I *fell* in love with you. A farmer's daughter. Not a socialite like my parents had wanted. I fell in love with you, and there was no turning back. That wasn't a choice. And I gather it's the same for our son. It isn't a choice for him either."

Mom wiped at her cheeks, and when she looked at me, it was like she was seeing me for the first time. My eyes stung, but everything my dad had said wrapped around me and held me together.

"I don't try on people like clothes, Mom. It's not about gender. I don't wake up and think, today I'll only look at women. I could avoid men. I did for a long time. And every time I stopped myself from falling for someone because they weren't the traditional idea, I lost a piece of who I am." She lifted her hand from the table like she was about to say something, but I cut her off. "And don't say you want me to be happy because if that were true, you'd lay off. Either accept this is who I am, or don't, but I'm done talking about it." I stood, every muscle in my body pinching with anger. "I'm done."

"Where are you going?" She panicked.

"For a drive."

"Don't," Dad said. "You've been drinking."

"I had two glasses and enough carbs to soak it up. I'll be fine. I need..." I looked at my mom. "I need a minute to process."

"Will you be back?" she asked.

"I don't know." More tears fell down her cheeks and I softened my tone. "I'm not shutting you out."

"You promise?"

"I promise... We could both use some time to think."

"If you head home, let us know you got there safe." My dad stood and glanced at my mom. "I'll walk him out."

I said goodbye to my dad at the front door and he tried to talk me out of leaving one more time.

"I'm sorry I'm leaving a mess."

"Are you talking about your mom, or the dishes?" he asked and managed a small smile.

"Both."

"We'll be fine... Go blow off some steam."

"Love you," I said and grabbed my umbrella. "At least it stopped raining."

He waved at me as I opened my car door and slid inside. I pulled my phone from my back pocket and set it on the dash as I started the car. My dad gave me one last wave before he went inside, and when I lifted my phone, I noticed I had a text message.

Ethan: You drunk yet?

I coughed out a humorless laugh, the entirety of this evening crashing down around me.

Me: I wish.

He responded immediately.

Ethan: Uh-oh...

Me: Understatement. How's your Thanksgiving? I see you made it to Bell River alive.

Ethan: I didn't go. I chickened out.

Me: You did?

Ethan: Yeah.

Me: Are you alone then?

I figured he was with Jax and Wilder, but I wanted to make sure. Even with the fight I'd had with my parents tonight, being alone on a holiday would've been depressing.

Ethan: I am now. Jax and Wilder went over to June and Gwen's for dinner. Apparently, the dinner we had at Jax's mom's this afternoon was "elevensies."

Me: What did Wilder call this dinner then?

Ethan: Supper.

Me: Wilder has a love affair with Tolkien I'll never understand.

Ethan: Are you alone...

Was he flirting again, or worried for me like I'd been for him. I didn't want to rehash everything via text and sent him the simplest answer.

Me: I'm headed to Lullwater. Needing some clarity.

Ethan: Want company?

I typed out a no and then deleted it. Did I want company? Hadn't I literally told myself earlier I wasn't going to do this with him?

Ethan: I can hear you overthinking this from all the way over here.

Nothing had to happen between us. I mean, it was possible for me to be friends with someone I was attracted to.

Me: Meet me at the Hahn Woods entrance.

The park closed at sunset, but I didn't think anyone would care or even see us, for that matter. It was late enough, any stragglers would have left, and I'd been here before at night many times when I'd attended Emory. On the nights I hadn't been able to sleep, or if I'd needed time away from the hectic ebb and flow of the dorms, this had been my sanctuary. I could've always lived at home, but I'd wanted the full college experience. I pulled into a parking spot and shut off the engine. Ethan hadn't taken long, and about ten minutes later, his headlights flooded the tree line. I waited until he got out of his car before I did the same. He smiled at me, lopsided and confident, in faded jeans and a long-sleeved red thermal that hugged the lean muscles of his arms and chest.

"Hey... you keep looking at me like that and I might start thinking you dragged me out here for nefarious activities."

"Nefarious." I chuckled and slipped my hands into my pockets. "I think that might be one of my favorite words."

He nodded his chin toward the trailhead. "Are we hiking or fishing?"

"Hiking. I didn't bring a pole."

"You should've told me, I would have brought Jax's."

"I think I'd prefer walking tonight," I said. "Is that alright with you?"

He smirked and dimples formed in his cheeks. "Hey, I'm here for whatever you want."

"Now that sounds nefarious."

His eyes locked on mine, and in the low light they seemed bottomless.

"Lead the way."

The moon was high in the sky as Ethan walked next to me on the trail, every breath he took expelled from his lips in a thick fog. The cold front that had moved through had brought record low temperatures, and after about ten minutes, my fingertips and nose had gone numb.

"Fuck, it's cold," he said and brought his hands to his mouth as we stopped for a break. He blew a breath against his fist and turned to look at me. "At least I'm wearing a thermal. That sweater you have on looks thin."

"It's adequate enough," I lied. "It's my hands. I think my fingers are officially frozen."

Ethan reached out for my hand, and I pulled away. "Trust me, okay? Curl your hands into fists. But don't punch me." He grinned and wrapped his fingers around my wrists, his gaze holding mine as he lifted both of my hands to his lips, not quite touching them to my skin. He smiled again, and between that and the way his fingers were gripped around my wrist, my cock stiffened inside my jeans. "Don't pull away." He blew his hot breath against my skin until my fingers began to thaw.

"Thanks," I said, and he glanced up at me.

"No problem." Ethan lowered my hands between us, not once dropping my gaze. Warmth gathered under his fingertips and spread up my arm. "Want to keep going?" he asked.

Yes. Keep going.

He let go of my wrists and the loss of his touch cleared my lust-filled brain.

"A little farther. I'm not ready to go home yet."

"Want to talk about it?" he asked as we continued up the trail.

"Are you genuinely asking or just being nice?" I ran my fingers over my wrist where the spark of his touch lingered.

"I wouldn't have asked, Anders. I'm about as genuine as they come."

His dimples reappeared, and I wondered how many people he'd charmed with that smile. How many secrets he'd collected.

"You have a great smile," I said without thinking. His lips twitched, and I swear he puffed out his chest. "Don't let that go to your head. It was only an observation."

"It's okay, Anders... you can like my smile. I like yours too. When you actually have one. It's pretty damn spectacular."

I glanced at him and wished I hadn't. His cheeks were red from the cold, and that damn smile had stretched to his eyes. Now that was a spectacular smile.

"I'm beginning to think you're actually reading the dictionary I gave you."

"I have a large vocabulary... you'd be surprised what you'd find out about people if you actually relaxed once in a while."

"I relax."

He shrugged. "If you say so."

Ignoring him, I pointed to the turn off. "We're here."

"We are?"

There was a break in the tree line that led to a small clearing. Ethan followed behind me until we found the two trees I'd been looking for.

"When I was in college, I used to hang a hammock here and read." I touched the tree with the palm of my hand, remembering all the time I'd spent here. "It's much nicer in the summer."

Ethan stared at my fingers spread against the bark. "What happened tonight at your parents' house?"

"You first. Why didn't you go to Florida?"

He swallowed and kicked the fallen leaves on the ground with the toe of his shoe.

"Fuck, I don't know..." He ran a hand through his hair and looked up at the sky. "I guess I wanted to be with people who make me happy instead of driving six hours to sit in a silent house with people who are disgusted by me and think I'm going to hell."

"They think you're going to hell?"

"My dad sure as shit does. My mom... she used to, but she's come around, I think." He met my eyes. "They tolerate my presence, Anders. And why would I fight for that? Why would I go out of my way to earn their love? They're my fucking parents."

He exhaled, and the air turned white between us, filling the small space. I hadn't realized I'd stepped closer to him.

"You shouldn't have to mend that bridge. That's their job."

"I don't know if they'll ever see it that way." Ethan leaned against a tree. "But it's whatever... What about you? That's why we're out here. What happened?"

I told him everything that had happened at dinner. How everything had seemed good at first, and eventually devolved into my mom drinking too much and telling me how she really felt.

"That's awesome your dad stuck up for you like that," he said. "It's what she needed to hear."

I didn't do this. Have long chats about my private life. It had taken me forever to open up to Wilder. And when everything had fallen apart between us, I'd built my walls even higher. Ethan had found a way to break some of them down. His ability to see through my bullshit probably helped. I shoved my hands into my pockets as a light breeze bit at my fingertips.

"I hope it sank in."

"Are you going back tonight?"

"It's late. I might head home and call her in the morning."

"You should go back to their house," he said and pushed away from the tree. "Don't let her talk herself back into thinking she's right."

177

My situation was salvageable, and I was a dick, sitting here complaining to him when his parents had basically written him off.

"Yeah...you're right. I'll head back."

"You ready to go then?" he asked, and I nodded.

We walked in comfortable silence on the way back to the parking lot. I hit the ignition key on my remote and my car came to life.

"That's obnoxious," Ethan said, giving me a grin. "Let me guess, you have heated seats?"

"I do."

"I hate you even more now." I laughed as he narrowed his eyes without any real ire. "Why the hell do you need a car that fancy?"

"I sometimes have to pick up clients. Again... Mr. Calloway... It's professional, not fancy."

He didn't have a witty comeback lined up, and as the seconds ticked by, the air around us turned to static.

"Thank you," he said, breaking the charged silence, the tone of his voice low and raw. He took a step closer, his eyes landing on my mouth. "For inviting me tonight."

"Thank you." I fixated on the freckle he had under his lower lip. "For showing up."

His gaze trailed up from my mouth to my eyes and his pupils dilated. With barely a foot between us, he wet his lips, and it took every ounce of self-control I had not to reach out and pull him against me. I let out a stuttered breath.

"Goodnight, Ethan."

The line of his jaw was covered in thick stubble, but I didn't miss the way it tensed.

He rolled his full bottom lip through his teeth and nodded. "Yeah, it was." That easygoing grin of his spread across his face as he walked backward toward his car. "I'll see you on Monday."

Ethan

"Don't worry about it. I can cut off the edges and no one will know the difference," Mrs. Stettler said.

Wilder gaped at me, a deep scowl marring his lips. I had to hold back my laugh at the sight of him sweating in the kitchen, apron, and all.

"He'll know," Wilder said and pointed an accusatory finger in my direction.

"I'll never tell a soul." I set the cooler I'd brought in down onto the tile, watching as Jax's mom trimmed the charred crust off the pizza.

He pulled on the string of his apron, tugging it off, and for a second I thought he might cry. "It's fine... it's totally fine. I ruined Jason's favorite pizza and his girlfriend is coming over and—"

"It smells real good, Wilder." Hand on his hip, he scoffed at my attempt to ease his anxiety. "Honestly, who the hell likes crust anyway?"

Mrs. Stettler picked up the burnt pieces and put them into the trash. "Ethan has a point, dear. Jason never finishes his crusts and ends up feeding them to Rosie."

The fluffy mutt herself strutted into the kitchen at the sound of her name. I scratched the back of her head. "Hey, girl."

Rosie stuck her nose into the overflowing garbage can and snatched a piece of the ruined crust, swallowing it like it was the best damn thing she'd ever had.

Wilder laughed and wiped at his eyes. "Well, at least Rosie appreciates my cooking."

"Where are the boys?" Jax's mom set the pizza on the dining table. "Dinner will get cold if they don't hurry."

"They were right behind me on the freeway. They should be here any—"

"Momma," Jax hollered and Gandalf hightailed it through the kitchen, toward the garage door, making Rosie bark. "Can you send Wild out? I need a hand."

"I got it," I offered. "You finish up in here."

Wilder grabbed salad tongs from the drawer. "Thanks."

It smelled like rain as I stepped outside. The sky was heavy, the clouds drooping low enough I thought they might touch the treetops. Jason and Mabel stood by Jax's truck, looking like they were deep into some sort of silent conversation. I waved at Mabel and she gave me a shy smile. She'd gone fishing with us this morning despite the frigid temperature. Jason had smiled more in the last few hours than I could remember him ever smiling before. He'd baited her hook and helped her cast her line. Jax and I had stood back and watched with pride.

"Ethan, can you grab the poles?" Jax asked.

"Sure thing." I playfully shoved Jason in the shoulder. "You ready for this?"

He signed something to Mabel, and she looked at me and nodded.

"I... I think so," Jay said, a nervous smile tugging at the corner of his mouth.

"Aww... listen, Jay, it'll be great. Wilder and your momma are excited to meet her. They made pizza and everything."

"Uh-oh." Jax grimaced. "*They* made it?"

"About that... just eat it and smile, alright. Or you might be sleeping on the couch tonight."

Jaxon laughed at my warning, and Mabel mouthed the word *what*.

Jason signed and spoke at the same time. "My brother's husband cooked the pizza. It might not taste good."

She shrugged and placed a quick kiss on his lips. Jay's eyes went wide, and his face flushed with color as he looked at me and Jax.

"Looks like she didn't come here for the pizza," Jax said to me under his breath.

"Come on," Jay grumbled.

He signed something and he gave us a dirty look before he led her inside.

"I think he heard that."

"I hope so." Jax laughed and shut the gate of the truck. "Just leave those anywhere. I'll put them away later."

I followed Jax through the garage, setting the poles against the wall while he threw his and Jason's gear in the corner. When we walked in, Mrs. Stettler had Mabel wrapped up in a tight hug.

"Alright, Momma, she can't breathe with you squishing her like that." Jason shifted on his feet, his anxiety radiating all around him.

"I'm giving her a proper welcome."

Mrs. Stettler stepped back, and Wilder jumped in, taking his turn to torture the poor girl.

"Wild," Jax admonished. "Let the girl catch her bearings, for Christ's sake."

"Jaxon." Mrs. Stettler paled. "Don't say the Lord's name like that... and on a Sunday?"

I didn't think it was supposed to matter whether you said the Lord's name on a Sunday or a Wednesday, but who the hell was I to judge.

He rubbed the back of his neck. "Sorry, Momma."

"You should be." Mrs. Stettler's eyes glittered as she framed Jason's face with her hands. "She's perfect."

"Figures..." Wilder snorted. "I knew she would like her better than me."

"Are you playing?" Jaxon's mom gave Wilder a look, and honestly, it kind of scared me. "How could you say such a thing?"

"Because it's true."

"I love you like a son."

"You didn't at first," he said, all smiles and smugness. "But I forgive you, Barb."

She swatted him on the ass, and Mabel let out the cutest damn laugh. Soft and quiet. Jason tucked her in beside him with a smile as Wilder lifted his hands and signed.

"What did he just tell her?" Mrs. Stettler asked.

"Welcome to the family," Jason said, his voice thin and unsteady. "H-how... Did you learn that for her?"

"I sure did." Wilder looped his arm around Jax's waist. "I know how it feels to be an outsider. I wanted to make her feel special. But tell her that's literally the only sign I know. I'm useless otherwise."

"You are far from useless, baby," Jax said and kissed him on the temple.

"Gross," I teased. "Don't ruin my appetite, it's bad enough I live here and have to listen to—"

"Who wants pizza?" Wilder clapped his hands.

Jax's mom sighed, mumbling something about God and forgiveness as she led Jason and Mabel to the table.

Thankfully, the rest of the night went as smooth as anyone could have hoped for Jason. Wilder had apologized for the lack of crust, while Jax had assured him it was the best pizza he'd ever eaten, and no tears had been shed. Jason had tried his best to translate for everyone, but about halfway through he'd looked a little helpless. It had been obvious Mabel didn't care about all the chatter going on around her. She'd looked at Jason the entire time like he'd hung the damn moon. I was happy he was happy, and I'd reminded myself to stop worrying about how all of this would turn out for him. Jason had struggles and baggage, but who the hell didn't.

Even sexy suits had baggage, I thought as I placed the last dish into the dishwasher. I hadn't heard from Anders since Thursday, and as much as I wanted to text him to find out how everything had gone with his parents, I'd decided the ball was in his court. He was the one with all the hang ups about appropriate and professional. If he wanted to talk to me, he had to be the one to reach out. This friendship-attraction thing we had confused the hell out of me. There was no doubt in my mind he'd wanted to kiss me in the parking lot the other night after our hike. He was closed off and stuck up, and as much as I shouldn't want him, I did. Boss or not, I wished he had kissed me. He was the exact opposite of Chance. Therefore, he was exactly what I needed.

"What are you over there smirking about?" Wilder asked as he plopped down onto a bar stool.

Your ex.

"Wouldn't you like to know?" I asked, wondering if he'd be pissed about my not-so-suitable-for-work thoughts about Anders.

"I would."

I laughed and wiped my hands on a towel. "She's sweet, right?"

"Who?"

"Mabel."

"Entirely, but back to the issue at hand. The whole I-want-to-go-out-and-do-something-stupid smirk. Who's the lucky guy?"

"You got all of that from one smile?" I asked.

He was way too perceptive sometimes for a guy so self-involved.

Wilder rested his chin in his hands and batted his lashes. Pursing his lips, he whined, "Come on... it's not fair. You and Jax go sweat in the sun all day every Sunday and talk about all the things, while I'm left behind bored and completely uninformed."

"Christ, you're a child sometimes." I shook my head.

"And... your point is?"

"There's nothing to tell. Stop making up shit in that writer's head of yours." Jax walked in, saving me from his husband's inquisition. "Wilder thinks he can read minds."

Jax chuckled and kissed the top of his head. "Stop picking on Ethan."

"Gasp." Wilder shot a well-rehearsed glare in my direction. "You both always gang up on me."

"Such a twink."

"Sterotypist."

"That's not even a thing," I argued and had to pinch the corner of my lip to stop myself from outright laughing at his frustration.

"You two bicker like old ladies." Jax opened up the fridge and took out a beer.

"How was the drive?" I asked Jax, hoping to change the subject.

"Good, I thought Momma was gonna cry after we dropped Mabel off." He took a swig of his beer before he nodded his chin. "I think Mabel's good for Jay."

"What if she breaks his heart?" Wilder asked the question I'd been chewing on since I found out Jason had a girlfriend.

"Then he'll get to experience heartache like the rest of us. It's life, Wild. Heartbreak. It's all sorts of fucking messy." Jax set his beer on the counter and stared over his husband's shoulder, lost in some memory as he spoke. "It's all I ever wanted for him, you know... To experience everything. In whatever way he was able. Jason is a man... I think we all forget that sometimes. If she breaks his heart... he'll heal and work through it like he's had to do his whole life."

"And hey... maybe he'll break her heart," I said and Jax laughed.

"Maybe."

"Speaking of breaking hearts..." Wilder grinned and turned his full attention back on me.

"Nope, not having this conversation with you," I said and headed to my room.

"But you admit there's a conversation to be had?"

"'Night, Stettlers." I smiled at Wilder's sour expression as I shut my bedroom door.

FROM: AndersLowe@LoweLitFic.com

TO: EthanCalloway@LoweLitFic.com

DATE: Nov 30 11:26 AM

SUBJECT: Lunch plans

Ethan,

It seems, unfortunately but not surprising, Wilder is unable to make it to lunch today. Please reschedule for next Monday. I believe the entire day is open. It shouldn't cause any schedule conflicts. Don't worry about calling Working Pictures, I'll let them know it's been rescheduled.

Thanks,

Anders~

P.S. Thanks again for Thursday.

FROM: EthanCalloway@LoweLitFic.com

TO: AndersLowe@LoweLitFic.com

DATE: Nov 30 11:31 AM

SUBJECT: RE: Lunch Plans

Anders,

I'll reschedule the reservation. I guarantee you he canceled because he's sleeping. He was up writing when I left for work. Said he hadn't slept all night. I'd call him a slacker, but I guess writing is kind of his job.

Now that you're free for lunch, feel like sharing a ten-piece nugget?

Ethan~

P.S. No thanks needed. I was happy to be there.

FROM: AndersLowe@LoweLitFic.com

TO: EthanCalloway@LoweLitFic.com

DATE: Nov 30 11:40 AM

SUBJECT: RE: Lunch Plans

Ethan,

As much as I'd love to indulge, I have a better idea, if you're interested in more than nuggets.

Anders~

FROM: EthanCalloway@LoweLitFic.com

TO: AndersLowe@LoweLitFic.com

DATE: Nov 30 11:45 AM

SUBJECT: More than nuggets

Anders,

I can't decide if your last email is some weird form of sexual harassment. I'm going to assume you meant you wanted something better than shitty drive-thru nuggets... like Sal's?

Ethan~

P.S. Just so you know, I wouldn't mind if it was sexual harassment.

FROM: AndersLowe@LoweLitFic.com

TO: EthanCalloway@LoweLitFic.com

DATE: Nov 30 11:51 AM

SUBJECT: RE: More than nuggets

Ethan,

I'm laughing at myself. I figured you'd like to know that. Maybe you can even hear me. No. I assure you that was not some type of come on. And yes, Sal's was what I had in mind.

Word of the day: Chagrin - a feeling of mortification.

P.S. You should mind.

I read his email and decided to ignore the last bit at the end. Tucking my phone in my back pocket as I stood, I focused on the fact that he hadn't shut me out. He'd been in his office all morning, and when he hadn't popped his head out once, not even to say good morning, I figured we'd fallen back into the pattern of one step forward, two steps back. But he'd accepted my invitation to lunch. I'd take that as a win.

On my way to his office, I stopped and knocked on Nora's door. "Come in."

She smiled up at me, her dark hair pinned into a tight bun with a pencil. "What's up?"

"Want to go to Sal's with me and Anders?"

Nora leaned back, a knowing grin sliding across her face. "He invited you to Sal's?"

"Technically, I invited him to McDonald's..." I shrugged. "It's not a big deal."

"Uh-huh."

"Are you coming or not?"

"As fascinating as it would be to watch you two pretend you're not completely attracted to each other, my schedule is full today." She pulled the pencil from her bun and swore as her hair tumbled down over her shoulders. "I'm a mess."

"Anything I can do to help?"

"Bring me back cookies and I'll love you forever."

"Done."

"Enjoy your lunch," she said, implication rounding every syllable.

"Stop it."

She hummed and shooed me with her hand. "Go... and don't forget my cookies."

"She's demanding, isn't she?" Anders asked, the familiar deep tone of his voice sent a wave of goose bumps down my spine as I shut her door.

"How long have you been standing there?"

"Not long," he said, and I couldn't help the way I drank him in. His blond hair was disheveled like he'd been raking his fingers through it all morning. His dark gray sleeves were rolled up to his elbows. Anders was classy even when he was casual. "Ready to go?"

"Yeah," I said and tore my eyes away from his slow smile.

"We should drive, it's too cold to walk."

"In the fancy car?" I asked and he laughed.

"Yes."

"I feel so special."

And shit, I should have. His car smelled like leather and expensive cologne. Unlike my sad excuse for a car that had torn cloth seats and crumbs embedded in the carpet from God knows when.

He stared at me as I took in my surroundings. "It's just a car."

"The fact that you think this is *just a car* proves how entitled you are."

Anders's laugh warmed my stomach. "And arrogant?"

"This car probably cost more than I'll ever make in one year as a nurse," I surmised as he pulled onto the main road. "It's not just a car."

"You're right... And you're not." His jaw flexed as he turned the corner.

"Okay?"

Silent as he made another turn, he pulled up to the curb and parallel parked, sliding between two cars like it was nothing. The entire ride had taken less than three minutes.

"We should have walked," I said. "I feel like we just added a few points to our carbon footprint."

Anders didn't smile, avoiding my eyes, he shut off the engine.

"This car..." he said. "It's a thing. It's metal and leather and nuts and bolts. It's not me."

"I get that—"

"It's expensive and I'm lucky to have it. I know that, Ethan. But I worked for it... for this thing." He turned, his hard edges softening as his eyes trailed over my face "Everything I have I've earned."

"Anders, I..."

I lost my train of thought as his dark blue eyes trailed over my face and landed on my mouth. He was intimidating as much as he was vulnerable. I wanted to hear how he'd earned his way and how he'd made his small empire of books. I wanted to know things I shouldn't. How the hair on his thighs felt. Soft or coarse? How his skin smelled after a day in the sun. After sex. It was Thursday night all over again as Anders leaned in, the scent of his soap saturating the air between us, and I inhaled it, needing whatever he was willing to give.

"Ethan..."

"Yeah."

"We should go inside."

"We should?" I sounded uncertain, and his chuckle broke through my lust-addled brain.

"Well, they won't serve us out here... and I'm supposed to be the entitled one?"

His smart-ass remark was the last splash of cold water I needed.

"And for a second... I thought I liked you."

Chapter 14

Anders

Sal's buzzed with people. The line from the take-out counter was backed-up all the way to the front door when Ethan and I walked in. I inhaled the smell of hamburger grease and fried potatoes. Almost every silver and red booth was filled. Usually I disliked all the people, the lunch rush thrum. If it wasn't for the food and the family that owned the place, I would have never braved all the chaos, but today the chatter was welcome. Anything to block out the noise in my head. Ethan made it difficult for me to think sometimes. I'd almost made a huge mistake, almost gave in and kissed him in the car. Every time he accused me of being entitled or arrogant, I wanted to show him a different side of myself. One I reserved for those I trusted. And I wanted to trust him even if it was reckless to do so. It was reckless to think about all the ways I wanted him. His mouth, his hands, his body. His fucking smile alone tore through my self-preservation, making it too easy for me to rationalize the desire I had for him.

"Mr. Lowe." Rebecca's familiar smile spread across her face as she approached. Wiping her hands on her apron, she grabbed two menus and two rolls of silverware from the plastic bucket sitting on the rickety plywood hostess stand. It wobbled enough, I worried one of these days it would finally collapse. "Your usual booth is taken, but I was about to clean the one next to it."

"That's fine, I can sit anywhere."

"It's no trouble. Especially for my favorite customer," she said. "Follow me."

"Favorite customer?" Ethan smirked, most likely making assumptions about my privilege and entitlement.

"He comes here enough... he deserves a little special treatment." Rebecca gave Ethan a cursory glance. "And who are you?"

"I'm his assistant. My name's Ethan." He held out his hand and she stared at it. Not the least bit impressed. "It's nice to meet you..."

"Rebecca."

Her shrewd green eyes weighed and measured him, and I stood back and enjoyed his discomfort. Everyone I brought to Sal's had to be approved by Rebecca. She was the owner's oldest daughter, and one of the few people I genuinely liked.

"Did Kris go and quit after having that baby?" she asked, pulling a cloth from the pocket of her apron, she wiped down the table.

"No... she's still on maternity leave," I said as I slid into the booth. "She'll be back by the end of January. Sooner if she wants. This guy is a pain in my ass."

"I figured as much."

"Hey, I'm a nice guy," Ethan said and held up his hand like the Boy Scout I had no doubt he'd once been.

"Nice guys usually don't have to declare it." Rebecca gave me a conspiratorial wink. "But time will tell... You boys look over the menu and I'll be back in a minute."

Ethan watched her as she walked toward the counter. "She's a gem."

"Rebecca is hard to know, but once you're in, you're in for life."

Ethan met my eyes and the tug in my stomach returned. "She's basically the female version of you?"

"I'd say I'm loyal... when it's warranted."

"Good to know."

"Are you psychoanalyzing me again?" I asked.

I lowered my gaze to the menu, not actually reading any of the words. There was no need, I'd memorized the entire thing already. But I needed a momentary reprieve from the weight of his perceptive eyes.

"It's possible. The whole keep-your-enemies-close thing."

The smile on his face was lopsided when I glanced up from the menu. His dimples made it impossible to look away.

"Our friendship is a farce then?" I teased and he bit the corner of his lip.

"Totally. I only used you for your fancy car and impeccable taste in dictionaries."

I laughed, full and uninhibited, and realized Ethan had been holding out on me. The smile that graced his lips had changed to something more vivid and beautiful.

He tapped my shoe under the table with his toe. "You should laugh like that more often."

I should've pulled my foot away, but I kept it against his. It was juvenile and unlike me, but I held on to the private moment.

"Why? Because it makes me seem like less of a prick?'

"Because it's sexy."

My body responded to his words. Heat flushed my neck and chest. I was hard for him like a teenager, uncontrollable and needy.

His Adam's apple moved under the smooth skin of his throat as he swallowed. "I know I shouldn't say that, but I think you've figured out by now I don't give a shit about rules."

"You've made that very clear," I said, and tried not to think about how much I wanted my lips on his throat.

"And that bothers you?" he asked, his confidence fading as he picked at the edge of his napkin.

"It should," I exhaled and pulled my foot away from his, even though it was the last thing I wanted to do. But it was the right thing. Sitting up, I pressed my back into the booth. "You should order the number five."

The smile on his face slipped, and he recovered it enough, it almost met his eyes. "Word of the day... deflect."

"Verb."

"Anders's attempts to deflect are both obvious and annoying."

"Thank you, professor, now will you pick something to eat before Rebecca gets back. She hates it when people aren't ready."

"I already decided what I wanted while you were over there *deflecting*."

Irritation pricked at my temples. "What is it you want me to say?"

"That you like me."

His hopeful brown eyes killed me.

"I like you." I spoke with as little emotion as possible, even still, the three words sounded like a declaration.

Ethan placed his elbows on the table and rested his chin in his palm. "And you like that I make you break some of your rules because you're uptight and wish you could let go a little."

"I'm not saying that."

"But you like me?"

"Right now? No. But for the most part, you're tolerable."

"See, that was easy." He leaned back and chuckled.

"Friends... Ethan. We're friends."

"Of course."

His grin said it all. He'd thought he'd won that round. And maybe he had. But Rebecca showed up, pen and pad in hand before I was able to say anything else. "Y'all ready to order?"

"I'll have the number five, with a Coke."

"Me too," Ethan said and handed her his menu.

She gave him an approving smile and promised to get us our order as fast as possible.

"Think she likes me now?" he asked.

"She's like a mother hen. But I think you're safe."

"How did it go with your parents? Did you end up working shit out?"

Ethan threw loaded questions around like they didn't have the power to tear right through me.

"It went as well as it could have," I said as one of the bus boys dropped our Cokes off at the table. "I think my mom has some soul searching to do."

"About your sexuality?"

"About everything," I said. "She's trying. Like every parent, she had hopes and expectations. She's disappointed."

"Disappointed? You're like the most successful person I know."

"She wants grandkids. A white wedding."

"And she can have all of that... even if you marry a man."

"I know this, and you know this. Hell, my dad gets it." I took a deep breath. "She has to figure it out on her own... and I think she will. She needs time to adjust expectations. Reset those factory defaults." Glancing around the busy diner, uncomfortable in my own skin, I avoided his eyes. "Can we talk about anything else?"

"I know I'm pushy as hell and—"

"Here you go, boys," Rebecca said, placing our plates down on the table, effectively interrupting whatever it was Ethan was about to say. "You want a dozen cookies to go?" she asked me like she did every time.

"That would be great, thanks."

"Enjoy," she said and squeezed my shoulder.

"You really have her wrapped around your finger, huh?" Ethan grabbed a fry and popped it in his mouth. He moaned and Jesus Christ, I didn't think I'd ever forget the sound. "These fries are seriously the best."

"And to think you wanted McDonald's."

"Hey, that's all you, you're the one who started it." He smirked and pointed a fry at me. "I haven't gotten rid of that football, you know."

"I kept mine as well."

"Yeah?" he asked, and I fought myself as I admired the easy blush spreading along the arch of his cheekbones.

"It's in my desk drawer back at the office." And because my curiosity would most likely be my undoing, I asked him, "What were you going to say before... about you being pushy as hell, which I agree with, by the way."

He lifted a fry from his plate and shrugged. "I don't know... I guess I like listening to people. To you. I don't mean to pry."

"Maybe you should be a shrink instead of a nurse," I said, and for a second I thought he'd throw a fry at me.

"Hell no. I want to actually spend time with my patients."

And I could see it. He was kind, and like he'd said, he wanted to know people. Really know them. Not the half-ass attempts people, including myself, made every day with our fake smiles and social media status updates. He was genuine while the rest of us were well-thought-out photographs. Props with good lighting. Ethan's smile on its own had the ability to heal. Maybe it had already started to heal me.

"And you want to work with kids?" I asked.

"Yeah... I hope so. I think that's where I could make the most difference."

"I think that's admirable. Wanting to help others."

"You help others, in your own way."

I laughed around a bite of my burger.

"You do," he said earnestly.

I swallowed and shook my head. "I'm a salesman, Ethan. Nothing heroic about that."

"You make books possible. You spread knowledge and stories. You give an escape from all the shit in the world. Sure, you sell books. But books have the ability to change lives too."

I didn't want to love what he'd said, but the heavy beat of my heart knew better.

"When I went to school, I wanted to be a writer... But I realized, quicker than I would have liked, that talent was not something you could learn. I'd wanted to make a difference too... somewhere along the way, though, I got lost."

"I think you make a difference every day. You and Nora... and maybe even Claire." We both laughed. "Y'all give people opportunity. And that's some big shit right there."

"Some big shit," I repeated and barely kept my smile in check. "That's deep, Ethan."

He ignored my jab. "Do you still write?"

"Sometimes," I admitted and immediately wished I hadn't.

"Can I read something of yours?"

"I made a promise to myself when I graduated that I would never subject anyone to my words ever again. My college professors all agreed it was the best idea I'd ever had."

"Don't worry. I'll persuade you eventually."

"Highly unlikely."

We both ate in a comfortable silence, and after a few minutes, I had to force myself not to look across the table. Every time I'd lost the battle, I was met by a pair of caramel eyes staring back at me, too. After the last fry on my plate was gone, Rebecca dropped off the cookies and the check. And I didn't give Ethan a chance to argue when I handed her two twenties.

"Keep the change."

"See you soon and tell Kris to bring me that baby."

"I promise."

Satisfied, she picked up our plates and headed back to the kitchen.

"You didn't have to pay for my lunch," Ethan said, wiping his hands with a napkin.

"It's a business expense. Not a date."

"Wow... I bet you say that to all the boys."

"And girls," I added, and it made him smile.

Making him smile made me want to unlock all the doors I refused to open. I could tell myself he was a temporary employee. That it was okay to cross lines. But he was attached to me in other ways too. If things got messy between us, it could fuck up my relationship with Wilder. And considering our shared past together, Wilder might not appreciate me hooking up with his husband's best friend. Not that he had any right to dictate who I could or couldn't date. But I'd rather not set him off. Wilder's ability to create drama where it didn't need to be was something I didn't like to provoke.

"Ready to go?" I asked and we both slid out of the booth and headed for the front door.

Light snow fell in delicate swirls as we walked outside, leaving a thin layer of frost on the sidewalk and windshield of my car.

"I thought I escaped this shit," Ethan groaned. "We're in Georgia, for crying out loud."

"It's more a rarity here than the norm."

I held my hand out and collected the fine flakes on my skin.

"It's beautiful, right?" he asked. "But when it falls in feet instead of millimeters, it's not so pretty then."

"I imagine that wouldn't be ideal. Especially not for months at a time."

"Tell me about it."

"Do you miss Colorado at all?" I asked as we crossed the street to where I'd parked.

He'd waited until we were inside the car and I'd turned up the heat before he answered. "I miss my life there sometimes. But then I think about it long enough... sift through all the bullshit, and realize I was miserable."

"The bullshit?"

He was quiet for a moment while I pulled onto the main road. The light at the intersection was red, and I was thankful for the few extra seconds. I wanted to know what had happened between him and Chance even though I had no right to the information. But the bits and pieces Nora and Wilder had given me never added up to the destruction of a two-year relationship.

"Chance is good at saving the world, but he's shit at relationships." His mood shifted and he stared out the passenger side window. "I wasn't enough... well, that's how he made me feel most of the time."

I wasn't enough.

Fuck, I could relate. I'd never been able to fill Jax's shoes when it came to Wilder. Years I'd tried, but it had never been enough, and I never would have been. Seeing them together now, as much as it had hurt in the beginning, it was how it should have been all along.

"Not that it helps, but I've been there," I found myself saying.

The light turned green and I pulled forward, ignoring his inquisitive stare. Ethan being Ethan, he couldn't let it go without an explanation.

"Wilder?"

I clenched my jaw and nodded.

"It sucks feeling second best to something... to someone else," he said, and I took my eyes off the road to gauge his expression.

His head was tipped down, and when he turned to look at me, the vulnerability in his eyes made me want to take back every fucking petty thing I'd ever said to him.

We were the same. Mirrored images in history and doubt.

"At least now we know we should hold out for something better this time."

"We definitely deserve better," he said.

Despite my protests I could see myself slowly giving in, trying to be better, to be enough, for him.

FROM: EthanCalloway@LoweLitFic.com

TO: AndersLowe@LoweLitFic.com

DATE: Nov 30 2:03 PM

SUBJECT: New York Plans

Anders,

Robbie forwarded me the dates and confirmation for The Greenwich Hotel. Checking in Dec. 18th and checking out on the 20th. Let me know if you need me to rearrange anything for the Monday after you get back.

Sincerely,

Ethan~

P.S. Thanks again for lunch.

FROM: AndersLowe@LoweLitFic.com

TO: EthanCalloway@LoweLitFic.com

DATE: Nov 30 2:17

SUBJECT: RE: New York Plans

Ethan,

I already blocked out that Monday in case of flight delays. But I do need you to book another room. If possible, for Claire. Robbie will be in Aspen on vacation, and I'll need all the help I can get to move into the new office before Christmas. Poor timing on Robbie's part.

Thanks, Anders~

P.S. Anytime.

FROM: EthanCalloway@LoweLitFic.com

TO: AndersLowe@LoweLitFic.com

DATE: Nov 30 2:26 PM

SUBJECT: New York Plans

Anders,

You're moving the New York office? I feel like, as your assistant, that's some damn pertinent information. Information I should have known about. Do I need to send out an email to your clients and let them know the new address? Claire... you're aware she'll literally do nothing. She'll order you and whoever else around all day and never lift a finger. You should've invited me. I'm really good at lifting things. If you don't believe me, I can demonstrate.

And I think Robbie's timing was perfect... in fact, I bet he planned it that way. He's shady like that.

Sincerely, Ethan~

P.S. Wednesday? Sal's again? I need Rebecca to like me as much as you. My ego is fragile like that.

FROM: AndersLowe@LoweLitFic.com

TO: EthanCalloway@LoweLitFic.com

DATE: Nov 30 2:38 PM

SUBJECT: RE: New York Plans

Ethan,

Robbie has already informed our clients about the move. And I'm informing you now, no need to have a panic attack. We're only moving a block away from the original office. The rent is cheaper.

And you're right about Claire. That does sound like a disaster and a waste of time. I might have to drink my weight in gin to deal with her, and that's even more counterproductive. If you're truly offering, your help would be appreciated. As much as I'd love to watch this demonstration you speak of, I'll take your word for it.

Robbie is an opportunist. It makes him a good agent. So, he is forgiven.

Anders~

P.S. Sal's sounds good, and I'm sorry to have to say this, but Rebecca will never love you as much as she loves me.

FROM: EthanCalloway@LoweLitFic.com

TO: AndersLowe@LoweLitFic.com

DATE: Nov 30 2:49 PM

SUBJECT: RE: New York Plans

Anders,

It's not nice when rich people dangle amazing trips to New York in front of poor folk like me. It's evil and I'm doubting your morals as I type this. I mean, who does that? Evil people, that's who.

Sincerely, Ethan~

P.S. Challenge accepted.

P.P.S. Also, I would pay to see you drink that much gin. I bet you're a fun drunk. The uptight ones always are.

FROM: AndersLowe@LoweLitFic.com

TO: EthanCalloway@LoweLitFic.com

DATE: Nov 30 2:57 PM

SUBJECT: RE: New York Plans

Ethan,

I'm not joking. I never joke about business. I could use the help. As you know, we're only there three days. It wouldn't be much of a trip. I'd pay for your travel, but not for you to watch me get drunk. That's something you have to earn.

Anders~

P.S. It's your ego's funeral.

I didn't even have a chance to close out of my emails before my phone pinged. I laughed when I read Ethan's text.

Ethan: You're fucking serious?

Me: Yes... it's not a gift, it's a business trip.

Ethan: Whatever. I'm so in.

Me: That's a yes then?

Ethan: That's a hell yes.

Me: Then book yourself the room instead of Claire.

Ethan: She won't care?

Me: She'll probably go to Aspen with Robbie.

Ethan: And Nora?

Me: I could ask her if you prefer.

Ethan: Fuck that. I'm going to New York.

Me: For business.

Ethan: Don't be such a killjoy.

Me: Book the room and the flight and send me the invoices.

Ethan: Can I sit next to you on the plane?

Me: Only if you promise not to talk.

Ethan: I love it when you say sweet things to me.

Ethan

Heated fog lingered in the bathroom and clouded the mirror. I grabbed a towel from under the sink and wiped the glass until my reflection no longer looked like I was seeing myself through Coke bottle lenses. I zipped up my jeans and buckled my belt, wishing I hadn't let Wilder talk me into going out for drinks. Clubbing, dancing, crowded bars—not my scene. I preferred the small-town vibes of those hole-in-the-wall pubs with the tacky neon beer signs hanging in their windows. In my humble opinion, sticky floors and pool tables were better than strobe lights and overpriced drinks. But I'd been overruled. I'd at least thought Jax would've been on my side, but apparently Jax liked to dance. This fact had been the nail in the coffin. There was no way in hell I'd miss out on Jax Stettler dancing. This little outing tonight would provide me with enough shit talk for at least a month.

I'd barely finished brushing my teeth when Wilder poked his head into the bathroom.

"Please tell me you're almost ready."

In white skinny jeans and a green sweater, too thin to actually keep him warm, Wilder looked younger than he had less than an hour ago. Dark black curls hung messy over his forehead, and the eyeliner he wore made his eyes look huge.

"I just have to put on a shirt." Wilder full on checked me out, and I rolled my eyes. "Cut it out or I'm gonna tell Jax you think I'm hot."

"Jax thinks you're hot." He shrugged. "And I guess I can see why."

"Geez, thanks... Will you move so I can get dressed?"

"You're wearing those jeans?" he asked. The way he said "those jeans" you'd have thought the pants I had on were covered in shit.

"What's wrong with these jeans?"

Maybe they were slightly baggy and had holes in the knees, but they were comfortable. And if I had to sit in a loud ass club all night against my will, I wanted to be comfortable.

"So many things," he said.

"Not everyone likes to have their balls pinched in skinny jeans. I'm not into the whole pleasure, pain thing."

He finally moved out of the way, only to follow me to my room.

"Go bug your husband."

"He's getting ready."

Wilder helped himself and opened my closet, flipping through the options. He said the word no about ten times before he settled on something. "Yes... this is good." He handed me the black cashmere sweater I'd bought for work. Which, for the record, I'd only bought because it was soft as hell and I had no idea what the fuck cashmere was. "Why do all your jeans have holes in them?"

"Get out."

"I think Jax might have a pair that'll fit you." Wilder stared at my waist. "Maybe not."

"You really know how to boost a man's self-esteem."

Jax lifted shit for a living, it made sense that he'd be bulkier than me. Wilder's appraisal was borderline pissing me off. I was about two seconds away from physically picking his scrawny ass up and removing him from the room myself.

"Oh... these could work." Gleeful, he pulled out a pair of jeans I'd forgotten I owned from the back of my closet. "No holes."

I grabbed them, maybe a little too forcefully from his hand, and he cringed with a squeak.

"Out. I need to get dressed... unless you want to watch? You and Jax into sharing?"

"I'm leaving, asshole." At the door he turned around. "Don't wear your Converse, they're a tad too—"

I took a step toward him and he held up his hands. "I'm leaving."

Laughing, I picked up the sweater and slipped it on. It was snug in all the right places, and I could admit it looked good on me. Reluctantly, I switched my comfortable jeans for the dark-washed, fitted pair, and out of spite, I decided on the worn pair of gray Converse I'd set out earlier. I combed my fingers through my damp hair and threw on some deodorant, trying to make an effort, I even sprayed on some cologne. But it wasn't like I'd hoped to hook-up or anything. It's why I'd invited Nora to come tonight. I needed someone else to suffer by my side. Messing around with a stranger didn't sound appealing to me. And maybe that had something to do with my sexy-as-hell boss I couldn't stop thinking about. I could feel it, the tension between us. The fragile thread frayed more and more each day. I wanted to hold out, wait for the moment it snapped and he'd finally admit he wanted me too.

There was only a little over a week left before I'd be in New York with him. *New York.* Every time I thought about it, I'd get excited all over again like a giddy fucking teenager. I told myself it was because I'd always wanted to go to New York, and that I'd be staying in the nicest hotel I'd ever have the chance to step foot in. All for free. But that tumbling feeling, those damn butterflies in my stomach belonged to Anders. Every email, every text, every lunch we'd shared at Sal's, he'd let me in even more. He'd thrown up blocks from time to time, but I'd knocked them down just as quick as he placed them. He'd said we were friends, and we were, but any idiot could tell he wanted more. If he crossed the line he'd drawn for himself, I'd let him.

"Our ride will be here in five minutes," Wilder shouted.

Grabbing my wallet and phone, I noticed a missed text from Nora.

Nora: How did you talk me into clubbing on a weeknight again?

I chuckled as my fingers tapped across the screen.

Me: You were sad about your breakup last week, and I said I'd be your wingman?

Nora: Lies. I'm your wingman.

Nora: I'm on my way there, please tell me you're not far behind. Nothing says hopeless and desperate like sitting at a table in a club by yourself.

Me: And that's why I invited you.

Nora: Nice. I feel so used.

Me: I'll buy your drinks.

Nora: Deal.

I pocketed my phone and opened my bedroom door.

"You look nice," Jax said, and I had to do a double-take.

He had on tight black jeans and a red Henley that looked a size too small by the way it stretched across his chest. Every dip and divot of his abs were visible under the fabric.

"Close your mouth, I think you're drooling." Wilder grinned. "He's taken."

I gently shoved him in the shoulder. "I'm not used to seeing Jax in anything but paint-stained coveralls and that same pair of sweats he wears around the house. You clean up nice, man."

"Thanks... I feel ridiculous."

"You're beautiful," Wilder said and glanced down at his phone. "The driver is just down the road. We should head outside."

"Let's get this over with," I groaned and shoved my hands in my pockets like a toddler.

"It'll be fun," Wilder assured me as he opened the front door.

Fishing was fun.

Drinking beer and playing pool was fun.

Tonight had headache written all over it.

As predicted, the place was packed when we'd walked in twenty minutes later. The music was loud, and the bass hit inside my chest, making each of my heart beats uneven. Lights flashed, white, purple, pink, and green as we weaved our way toward the corner of the club. The dance floor overflowed with a variety of people. Men and women all with a sheen of sweat on their skin. Everyone looked as if they were having fun, smiling and kissing, and grinding to the rhythm of the music. I guess I could see the appeal, but I'd never tell Wilder.

"See something you like?" he shouted, too close to my ear.

"Not really, no. Ask me again after I've had a few drinks."

His smile widened. "Oh, I will. I might make Jax drag you out there if I have to."

"Where are the tables? Nora texted me and said she found us a spot."

He pointed in the opposite direction of where we were headed and we turned around, walking through the mayhem all over again. The place was huge. Jax had told me on the way here it used to be an old warehouse the owners had converted into a club. Disoriented by the noise, I stayed close to Jax while we made our way through the sea of people, until eventually I spotted Nora sitting at a table sipping from a martini glass.

"She's over there," I said, hopefully loud enough they could hear me.

Nora slid off her stool and threw herself into my arms. Her hands snaking around my waist, she hugged me.

When she pulled away, I laughed. "What was that for?"

"I wanted it to look like we were a couple... see that guy over there." She nodded her head. "Total creeper."

"Most definitely a creeper." The guy stared at us with intense serial killer eyes. "Looks like we saved you from his freezer."

She smacked my chest. "Oh my God, don't scare me."

"It's nice to see you again, outside of the office," Wilder said. "This is my husband, Jax."

"Nice to meet you." Nora gave him a smile as she shook his hand. "Should we get you guys some drinks?"

"I think I might need five."

"How about a shot and beer instead?" she asked me, holding out her hand to grab one of the waitress's attention.

"Shots sound good to me." Jax sat down and pulled Wilder into his lap.

"Now I get why you needed back up," Nora said loud enough only I could hear as Jax leaned in and kissed his husband.

"I have to live with them." I tugged the hem of her shirt between my thumb and finger. "What happened to Business Day Nora? You look cute."

"Why, thank you." She waved her hand down her body and wiggled her hips. "You don't think it's too casual for this place?"

Nora's pale blue sweater and gray skinny jeans looked fine to me. Her heels, though, looked like they'd break her ankle if she wasn't careful.

"That's a question for Wilder... but for what it's worth, I'd make out with you if enough alcohol was consumed."

She held her hand under her chin and batted her eyelashes. "How you flatter me."

"Come on, maybe if we sit down, they'll stop making out."

"I heard that." Wilder slid off his husband's lap and onto the stool next to him while Nora and I took a seat.

And when the waitress made her way over to our table, we ordered two of everything.

"Are you excited for New York?" Nora asked after the waitress had returned and set the last glass on the table.

I threw back a shot and chased it with a swig of beer. Nora laughed as I raised my hand to my chest. The beer hadn't done much to kill the burn of the whiskey.

"I am... I've always wanted to go to Manhattan. Traveling with Anders is a whole different story."

"Anders isn't that bad," Wilder said.

"I tell him this every day," Nora agreed, lifting her glass to her lips.

"I thought you guys were friends now?" Jax asked.

"Oh... they're friends alright." Nora smiled and Wilder's brown eyes met mine.

"What does that mean?" he asked.

"Nothing, ignore her." I kicked her foot under the table, and she punched me in the thigh.

"I think Ethan here has a crush on his boss." Nora grinned over the rim of her martini.

Wilder stared at me, and with the shadows across his face, I couldn't tell if he was pissed or not.

"Anders?" Jax asked and laughed. "Not this again."

"It could work," Wilder said, his tone indifferent. "They're both caretakers."

"It wouldn't bother you?" I asked. "If Anders and I—"

"Like I've said before, it would be interesting, that's for sure, and why should it bother me?" Wilder reached for his husband's hand. "It's not my business who Anders dates."

Jax's brows dipped. "Wait. You're not seriously into Anders? Are you?"

I lifted my beer and avoided direct eye contact. "Maybe."

Jax didn't get a chance to put in his two cents. The music changed to something I thought I recognized, and Wilder jumped off his stool. "We have to dance to this."

"You guys coming?" Jax asked as Wilder dragged him off of his stool.

"Not drunk enough," Nora said and sipped from her glass.

"If you change your mind, see if you can convince Ethan." Jax took his last shot and set it on the table before following Wilder to the dance floor.

"I forgot about Anders and Wilder." Nora winced. "Sorry about that."

"Hey, at least I know now he wouldn't care if anything happened."

"Do you think it will?" she asked, pushing my other shot in front of me.

"Yes... and no. It depends on him. He has the most hang ups."

She nodded as I downed my shot.

"What about Chance?"

"What about him?" I asked and hated the way my heart squeezed at his name.

"Rebounding with the boss is like..." She tapped her finger against her lip. "Basically, shitting where you eat."

"It's a bad idea... yeah, I get it, but what if it's a good idea?" I nudged her with my elbow. "And aren't you the one who reminds me constantly I won't be working there forever?"

"I am... But I like to play devil's advocate when I'm feeling buzzed."

"Asshole."

"Yup," she said and leaned in closer. "I think that chick is checking me out?"

"Yeah? Where?"

"Three o'clock."

"Mine or yours?

"Um... yours, I think. I had two martinis before you got here."

I turned my head to the right, and like she'd said, there was a girl staring over at us.

"The blonde?" I asked and Nora nodded.

"She's cute, right?"

"I mean, maybe... Yeah, sure, for a girl."

She shoved my shoulder. "I think I'm going to go say hi."

"What? You're supposed to keep me company."

"Sorry... I'm going in. Unlike you, I look for rebound sex outside of the workplace." She pulled a strand of her hair behind her ears. "Wish me luck."

"Traitor," I said and laughed when she stumbled off her stool. "Real smooth."

She flipped me off. "You should text Anders and you both can be boring together."

It was kind of late, but I didn't hate the idea. I waited to pull out my phone and watched as Nora made her move. Once it seemed her attention was fully taken, I sent Anders a quick text.

Me: Never use Nora as a wingman.

A few seconds passed before the tell-tale dots appeared.

Anders: Am I supposed to know what that means?

Me: Wilder and Jax dragged me out to a club, and I made Nora go with me.

Anders: You both better not show up hungover tomorrow.

Me: Nothing exciting happens on Fridays. We'll survive.

He didn't respond, and after a couple minutes, I set my phone down. He'd probably gone to bed like the responsible adult he'd claimed to be. Nora had officially disappeared, and I had a feeling Jax and Wilder wouldn't be back anytime soon. Maybe hooking up tonight wasn't such a bad idea after all. Sitting at this table, while my friends were off having fun, solidified me as the loneliest guy in the room—or the lamest, both probably. And even worse, my beer was warm. Luckily, the waitress was nearby. I flagged her down and ordered two more shots of whiskey. After she dropped them off, and the warmth of the alcohol consumed my nerves, I thought about finding my roommates on the dance floor. Dancing in a group of people had to be better than sitting alone like a pathetic weirdo. I grabbed my phone and it vibrated in my hand.

Anders: What club?

I smiled like he'd given me a gift as I stared at my screen.

Me: Masquerade.

Anders: Never been.

Me: Shocker.

He'd gone quiet again, and instead of leaving it, I let the whiskey make my decisions.

Me: You seem off.

Anders: Bad night.

Me: Feel like elaborating?

Anders: Not via text.

Me: I'll step outside and call you.

I made my way through the crowd, getting bumped and groped the entire way. The cold night air was refreshing and cleared my fuzzy head as I stepped outside. I walked a few feet away from the front door and read the string of texts I missed on my way out.

Anders: You don't have to do that.

Anders: That's not what I meant.

Anders: Don't call me. I'm fine.

Anders: Ethan?

My phone rang at the same time I'd tried to pull up his phone number.

"Hey."

"You went outside," he said, his voice gruff and worn.

"I did."

"You never listen."

I could hear the smile in his voice.

223

"You like it when I'm stubborn."

"I don't think *like* would be the word I would choose right now." He let out a long breath. "Go inside."

"What's wrong?"

"Nothing I'm not used to by now."

I looked back at the door as it opened, and a small group of people spilled onto the sidewalk, their laughter loud enough it carried over the music of the club.

"Go inside," he said again with more force.

"Not until you tell me what's up."

"We can talk about it tomorrow."

"You'll avoid and deflect and be a moody bastard."

He laughed, and the sound of it made me dizzy.

"I had a long night... it's not something I want to talk about over the phone while you're standing outside of a club."

Either I was more buzzed than I'd originally thought, or I'd had one of those strobe light-induced seizures, because before I could stop myself I said, "Invite me over."

"Ethan..."

"Say yes."

An eternity could have passed as I waited for him to answer, and when he finally spoke, I heard that fragile thread between us give way.

"Yes."

Ethan

After Anders texted me his address, I'd waited two full minutes, expecting another text telling me not to come. When it never came, I found my way back inside the club to tell my friends I had to leave. Nora and the girl she'd met earlier were at the table with their foreheads close together, laughing. Glancing at the dance floor, I smiled. A good majority of the men had stripped off their shirts, including Jax. Wilder waved me over to the dance floor and I shook my head. The purple light shadowing his features made his pout even more dramatic than usual.

"Thinking about joining them?" Nora asked. She stood next to me, a grin on her face and a drink in her hand. "This is Katie."

I nodded and Katie gave me a little wave. "Nice to meet you."

"Where did you go?"

The truth was on the tip of my tongue. Nora had become one of my best friends, and I told her mostly everything. But Anders was a private person. His life was his, and I had no idea what his invitation meant. I could go over, have a drink, and talk him out of his shit mood. Live off the scraps, the tiny pieces of himself he fed me with every interaction we had. Or maybe he wanted more. *More.* My pulse skyrocketed, stealing my breath. God, I wanted more.

Nora stared at me, worry swimming in her eyes. "Are you alright?"

I took the rope she gave me and held on tight. I cut my hand through my hair and shook my head. "I'm not feeling great. I stepped outside for some air."

"It's hot as hell in here," Katie said. "I can go grab you some water?"

"That's okay, thanks. I think I'm gonna go."

Nora frowned and held the back of her hand to my forehead like my mom used to do. "You feel clammy."

I hated lying to her, especially when her concern wasn't warranted. If I was clammy at all, it was due to my anxiety. I had no idea how tonight would go down, and I hadn't been with anyone since Chance. The thought sobered me, killing my buzz and my confidence.

"You look like you're about to puke. Want me to ride home with you?" Nora pulled out her phone. "I can get us a ride and—"

"No, stay. I'll be okay. I don't want to mess up your night." I smiled at Katie. "I'll grab a ride and see you tomorrow. Will you tell Wilder and Jax for me though? I should get going."

"Are you sure?"

"One-hundred percent."

We said our goodbyes and she promised to tell Jax and Wild I'd left. I wasn't worried about possibly not being home when they got there. My bedroom door was closed, which usually meant I'd gone to bed for the night, and I didn't think they'd barge in to check on me. Especially not after grinding on each other all night in a club. They'd probably come home and screw each other's brains out. Another reason going to Anders's house would be beneficial. No roommate sex noises.

Ten minutes later, I was in the back of an Uber questioning my sanity and way too sober. I wanted Anders. I wanted to erase the shitty feeling inside my chest every time I thought about the two years I'd wasted on Chance. The two years I'd given away to a man who cared passionately about everything else but me. Hell, that wasn't true either. He cared, but not enough. And maybe I hadn't cared enough either. If I had, wouldn't I have waited? But why did I have to be the one who dropped everything for him all the time? Jesus, I was annoying. I let my head fall back against the seat and closed my eyes. My shit train of thought had taken a depressing detour. This was not the mood I'd wanted to channel right before I showed up at Anders's front door. Wasn't I supposed to be the one to cheer him up? Fortunately, I didn't have too much time to wallow in my past. When I opened my eyes, I recognized the neighborhood from last January. All the houses were huge, the lawns well groomed. I thought it was strange that Anders had chosen the suburbs over the city since he lived alone. All that square footage seemed sad with no one to fill it.

The car slowed, and as we pulled into the driveway, I second-guessed myself. Was this a bad idea? What if it ruined our friendship? What if he wasn't into me? Was this like the time I'd been into Jax, and I'd gotten my signals crossed thinking Anders wanted me more than he really did? We rolled to a stop, and I stared at the dark blue front door until the driver glanced over his shoulder.

"Is this not the right address?" he asked.

"No... I mean, yes. Yes. Thank you." I handed him a tip having already paid for the fare when I ordered the ride.

"No problem. Have a good night."

I stepped out of the car and the air nipped at my cheeks. I shoved my hands in my pockets and made my way up the walk, trying to wrangle all of my doubts. Small, lantern-type lights lit the cobblestone sidewalk. Ivy clung to the brick exterior and along the porch railing. The windows were lit with a low yellow light hidden behind the shutter-type blinds. I stepped onto the front porch, my breath puffing out in quick little bursts of fog. Nerves made my fingers tremble as I reached out and rang the bell. Waiting for him, I shook my hands at my sides and inhaled the cold air. The latch from the lock clicked and my chest tightened. I told myself to forget everything I'd worried about. I had no reason to be nervous. Anders was my friend, and it didn't need to be complicated, but when he opened the door, looking beautifully wrecked, all I wanted to do was make shit complicated. His tie was undone, hanging uneven along both sides of his chest, still stuck under the collar of a white button down. Both of his sleeves were rolled up, and he'd untucked his shirt. He held a glass half-filled with ice and an amber-colored liquid I'd assumed was whiskey in one hand, almost dangling it from his fingers, his arm loose at his side.

"Hey." He ran his other hand through his messy hair and stepped to the side. "Come on in."

I heard the door shut behind me as I took in the large living room with its exposed brick walls, high ceilings, and tall windows. The couches looked brand new, but they were the exact same ones from January. His house reminded me of one of those model homes. Everything was picture perfect but void of any real personality.

"Want a drink?" he asked, walking past me, and I inhaled the faint scent of his cologne.

"Sure," I said and followed behind him. "Thanks."

The kitchen was open to the living room, all earth tones and stainless steel. A large, granite-top island with stools on one side acted as the divider. I pulled one out and took a seat.

He held up his glass. "Bourbon?"

"Uh... yeah, alright."

"I have beer if you'd prefer." He grabbed a glass from one of the cabinets, not meeting my eyes.

"Bourbon is fine... no ice, though."

He filled the glass a little less than half full and slid it across the counter, finally giving me his attention. Under the bright kitchen light his eyes almost looked gray. The blue color of his irises faded to a silver star in the middle. All the nerves I'd tried to pocket away scurried across my skin, tingling inside my fingertips as I raised my glass to my lips. I drank the overly sweet drink like a shot, his eyes locked on me the whole time as my heart drummed inside my chest.

"Anders—"

"Ethan—"

He chuckled as we both tried to speak at the same time, and the hard lines of his jaw and shoulders relaxed.

"Sorry, you go ahead," I said, wanting him to make the first move.

He had to decide what he wanted. I'd already made my choice. I wanted whatever he was willing to give.

"I shouldn't have said yes."

I pushed my glass across the counter, and he filled it before filling his too.

"But you did."

He watched me as I finished my second drink, his eyes trailing over my chest and lingering on my mouth.

He exhaled and pulled his tie off, setting it on the counter. Popping the first two buttons of his shirt, he spoke. "I'm not sure why."

You want me too.

"Ouch." I grinned. "I'd like to think I'm pretty good company."

"Sometimes," he said, a small smirk forming before he raised his glass to his lips.

"Do you want to tell me what happened tonight?"

"Not particularly. I'd rather get drunk."

He filled my glass again, and like a good little assistant, I drank it down. If he wanted to get drunk, so be it. When he was ready to talk, I was here for it. All my nervous energy evaporated into the warm fuzzy feeling spreading through my limbs. Anders leaned against the counter behind him, putting more distance between us. His head tilted back, and he closed his eyes allowing me free rein to stare. I fixated on the hollow below his Adam's apple, thoughts about his skin and how it would taste flooded my pulse.

"I stopped by my parents' today," he said and any inappropriate thoughts I'd had flew out the window.

"Yeah?"

"It wasn't bad. My mom is trying."

"But?"

Anders opened his eyes and stared back at me. "I live in this house. Alone. It's fucking ridiculous. And she sees... she sees empty rooms and wants me to fill them with things. With a wife and biological children and pot roasts and..." His voice cracked and he set his glass on the counter. "Fuck, I don't know."

"Are you happy here? In this house?"

"No."

"Can I ask why you bought such a big place then?"

He dropped his eyes to the floor and all the tension returned to his shoulders. "I'd always thought I'd get a place like this with someone. For a while I thought that someone would be Wilder. Obviously, that didn't work out."

"You bought this place for you and—"

"No. I bought it after." He lifted his gaze. "Last fall, actually. It felt like the right thing to do. Like the next step. But now it's this giant fucking reminder of how..." He swallowed and grabbed his glass off the counter. "I'm a morose drunk. I should have warned you."

Reminder of what? Of Wilder? Of what he thought he could have? Questions spun through my booze-soaked brain, but I didn't utter a word as he filled both of our glasses again.

"Drink up," he said, raising his glass like he wanted to say cheers instead.

I tapped the rim of my glass to his and we both swallowed down the bourbon.

"Morose is a good word."

The heat in my veins flushed my cheeks, fueled by the alcohol, and the way his eyes skated over my skin as he walked around the counter.

"I'm glad you approve," he said, and I turned to face him. He stood in front of me, close enough I had to tip my head back to see his eyes. "Sullen doesn't have the right ring to it. It doesn't evoke enough emotion." His lopsided smile was a reward. "I'm glad you're here."

"Me too."

A rush of warmth pooled in my chest and stomach as he brushed his thumb across the curve of my bottom lip. "This freckle does things to me." The rough sound of his voice shot straight to my dick.

"What kind of things?" I asked, my tone equally as hungry as his.

I opened my legs and he stepped between them, pinning my chin in place with his fingers.

"Things I shouldn't want."

I pushed up from the stool and grabbed his hips to stop my hands from shaking. I wanted this too much. Chest to chest, the ragged rhythm of each of his breaths paired together with mine. He slid his hand from my chin to the back of my neck, his grip firm and commanding. I held my breath as he leaned in, afraid he'd pull away at the last minute, that he'd remember all of his rules, and leave me burning from the inside out. But Anders's hold on my neck tightened with resolve as he dipped his head and tasted that small freckle. I exhaled slow and relieved, tugging him closer. He groaned as our hips came together, his body responding to mine, and pulled my lip between his teeth. His hot breath fanned across my lips as he hesitated, the sweet scent filling my lungs.

"Stop thinking so hard," I whispered, and he raised his lips to the corner of my mouth.

"You talk too much," he said, and when I smiled, he gave in.

He kissed me with soft touches that weren't enough, lips moving slow and lazy, cataloging every inch of skin, every taste. It took all of my restraint not to take over, not to push for more. Anders had created all the barriers, and he had to be the one to break through them. Parting my lips, his tongue teased mine and I moaned, my fingers itching with the need to touch him. Unable to resist, I pushed my fingers through his hair and nipped at his lips. A quiet grunt rumbled inside Anders's chest, and he backed me into the counter, stumbling as the stool behind me scratched against the wood floor. He dropped his hands to my waist to steady me, and with one fluid motion he lifted me, landing my ass half on and off the counter in a clash of teeth and tongues. The urgency in his lips alive, feeding off every sensation of taste and skin. Coming up for air, he pulled away, and I could read the vulnerability in his eyes. Before he could say something stupid about being my boss, or how we needed to stop, I kissed the line of his jaw, pulling him in until he tipped his head to the side, and I sucked on his neck hoping I'd leave a mark.

He swore, dragging me almost completely off the counter, and I wrapped my legs around his waist. With my hair twisted in his fingers, I opened for him as his tongue dove into my mouth, desperate and thirsty for more, for me. I unfastened a couple of buttons on his shirt, and when he didn't stop me, I made quick work of the rest. The heat of his skin soaked into my palms as I rested them against his chest. My fingertips explored the flawless muscles of his pecs, the dips of his abs as he explored the curve of my neck with his teeth. I leaned back, wanting to look at him, to see his face, to remind myself this was actually happening. That I was here with him. Anders's cheeks were stained red, his pupils wide, his lips wet as he stared back at me. I lowered my eyes, absorbing as much as I could. His chest moved with every unsteady breath, but he stayed silent under my scrutiny. Every muscle was formed and etched under my touch, and I mapped them with my fingertips until he shivered, until I pushed the fabric of his shirt over his shoulders and it fell to the floor.

"You weren't joking about the tattoos," I said, tracing the letters on his ribs. "Is this Latin?"

"Yes." He rested his hands on the tops of my thighs. "*'I will either find a way or make one.'*"

"Is that what it says?"

"It's an old proverb. I was at Emory when I got it. I might've been drunk."

I laughed trying to picture a much younger and irresponsible version of Anders. "And this?" I ran my fingers over the quote inside of his left bicep. "*'We lived in the blank white spaces at the edges of print.'*"

He touched the tattoo on his right bicep. "*'We lived in the gaps between the stories.'* Those are both from *The Handmaid's Tale* by Margaret Atwood."

I hadn't heard of her or the book, but I kept that to myself not wanting him to think I was stupid or naïve. But I did recognize the quote he had from *The Secret History* inscribed in an elegant-looking script below his left collarbone. *"Beauty is Terror."*

"Even your tattoos are arrogant," I teased.

His laugh was lighter than I'd ever heard it. "Maybe."

Framing my face with his hands, he leaned down and kissed me until I couldn't breathe. My legs wrapped around his waist again, and this time, when he tugged me close, he actually hauled me off the counter, holding my weight with ease as he started down the hall.

"Anders..." I whispered his name against his lips, and he squeezed my ass. "Where are you—"

"Bedroom," he said, and when his mouth crashed into mine, I panicked.

His bedroom.

The same bedroom where he'd found me with Chance in the bathroom. The memory shoved its way into this moment, into this kiss. Chance had no place here tonight.

"No. Not in there... okay?"

Anders searched my eyes. "We don't have to do anything. We shouldn't be doing—"

I kissed him again before he could stop this—before I ruined everything. He pushed my back into the wall, cupping my ass as I rocked into him. His scent, chocolate and spice, crowded around me, drowning me as I buried my nose in his neck. Lost in the pressure of his hands on my body, the heat of his skin, I reached down, and palmed the hard bulge swelling behind the zipper of his slacks.

"Ethan," he hissed, and I lowered my legs, letting him blanket his body over me as my feet hit the floor.

He pinned me to the wall with his hips, grinding his cock along the length of mine. I hadn't been with anyone like this in a while, and the friction, his taste, it brought me too close to the edge. I pushed him away, shoving him across the hallway into the other wall. His hands found their way under my sweater, flesh and nails, his touch against my overheated skin too much to take as our mouths fought for control. My head buzzed with bourbon and ink and Anders.

He pulled my sweater up and I raised my arms as he lifted it over my head. Anders's hands were on my chest, my stomach, as he left wet kisses along my jaw and neck. Inhaling, he skimmed his nose down my throat, his palms seeking as much of my skin as possible as he ran his hands over my abs.

"I want to touch you," he said, his hot breath tickling my ear.

I unbuttoned my jeans and lowered his hand, not giving a fuck about the wet spot on my underwear. He unbuckled his belt, rubbing me in slow strokes with one hand, his lips chasing mine as we both lost our self-control. I pushed his pants down below his hips and rutted against him. His head hit the wall and he grasped my waist, groaning as I pulled my pants down, all my rational thought gone to the feel of his hot skin and hard body. Pre-come leaked from my slit, and I dragged it along the long length of his thick shaft with my thumb. Together we lined up, we matched, his slick velvet skin gliding along mine. Anders's nails dug into my hips, his teeth sinking into my lip as I stroked us both at the same time.

"Fuck..." He pumped into my fist, leaking for me too. "Ethan..."

He raised one of his hands to the back of my neck, pulling his forehead to mine. He gave himself to me. Every wall tumbled, every line crossed as his hips stuttered and his back arched, cock pulsing in my hand as he cried out. His release hot and slippery through my fingers made my orgasm hit that much quicker. We both shuddered, overstimulated as I trailed my thumb through the mess we'd made. He raked his fingers through my hair and pulled me to his mouth. Anders's kiss was rough and wet, claiming and deep like he wanted to climb inside of me and never leave. And when he finally met my gaze again, there was no reluctance. His blue eyes were bright and real. I wanted to believe I could be his to have. That maybe this time I could be enough.

Anders

We were both sticky with mistakes I didn't want to regret the moment my head stopped spinning. Dizzy, I pressed a hand to the wall and let the last few minutes resonate, let the heat of Ethan's skin sink into my pores. I wanted his scent to live inside my lungs. Wood and rain and sex. He circled the pad of his thumb around the head of my cock, and I sucked in a breath, sensitive to the touch. I lowered my hand and trapped his wrist with my fingers.

"Too much?" he asked and gave me a cocky smile.

I wanted to take him to my room and fuck him until he begged me to come.

Too much.

He had no idea.

Drawing in a deep breath, I tried to clear his heady scent from my muddled brain. My efforts in vain, I released his wrist and pulled my pants to my hips. "We should get cleaned up."

He took a step back, his dark eyes losing some of the confidence I admired. Ethan knew what he wanted and took it without offering excuses. I, on the other hand, required a half bottle of booze. My courage was weighted in percent by volume.

"Yeah... probably a good idea," he said, and I didn't miss the anxious way he watched me, most likely waiting for me to shut down.

I didn't blame him. The panic was there, hiding under the surface, dulled by the blush of his cheeks and the afterglow of an orgasm. It scratched at my skin, all the worry and unease of letting someone new into my space, offering him a weapon to use. But then Ethan smiled at me, and I couldn't look away.

"Come on, we can take a quick shower." His perfect smile fell, and the color in his cheeks paled. "Or not." I gave his shoulder a gentle squeeze. "Hey... we don't have to shower together. I don't expect anything if —"

"I know..." He stepped away from my touch and buttoned his pants. "I can clean up in the guest bathroom or whatever."

"Are you sure? You're kind of a mess."

"So are you... it's kind of hot," he said and pressed a quick kiss to my lips. "All I need is a sink and towel and I'm good."

"Luckily, I have both." I leaned down and grabbed his sweater from the floor. "Follow me."

I led us back to my bedroom and opened the door. I was halfway to my bathroom when I realized he wasn't right behind me anymore. Turning, I found him in my doorway, face blank and staring straight through me.

"Ethan?"

He didn't answer, his chest rising and falling in a quick succession. His entire body was rigid with his hands balled into fists at his sides. In the silence, everything clicked into place. Earlier he'd shot me down when I mentioned my bedroom, but I'd figured his resistance had been related to anxiety and not wanting to take things further than he'd been comfortable. And then everything in the hallway about the shower and the guest bathroom. This wasn't about boundaries at all.

"This is about Chance," I said, and he flinched at the name. "Because he fucked you in here."

Ethan's eyes darkened as he glared at me. "Why do you sound pissed?"

I'd blame the bourbon for the anger and disgust welling up inside me, but hadn't I been here before? Playing second chair to another fucking guy. Maybe I was more intoxicated than I'd previously thought because every inch of my skin had turned to ice.

"There's a bathroom at the end of the hall on the left."

I'd kept my tone flat.

Cold.

Composed.

Slamming shut every door I'd opened tonight.

"Anders," he said my name like I owed him something.

And maybe I could have afforded him a little empathy if I hadn't given it all to Wilder. I wouldn't go through this again. I couldn't go through this again.

"I can't... I..."

"It's fine," he said and took his sweater from my hand. "It's late... I should get going. I'll call for a ride."

My anger ebbed as he stood in front of me. Caramel eyes pleading for me not to close down and shut him out, to understand. My arms ached as I held them firm and unmoving at my side, willing myself not to give in again. I'd fucked up enough for one evening.

"I guess I'll see you tomorrow." He turned to leave but I stopped him.

"You guess?"

"You're joking, right?" His jaw clenched and he laughed without humor. "Don't worry, boss, I'll be there to do my job. Unless tonight fucked that up too?"

The taste of his lips, the heat of his release, the pinch of his teeth on my skin, every sound he'd made, all of it twisted and rooted itself inside me, ruining me along with everything else.

"That's up to you."

"It depends on how I feel when I wake up, but I wouldn't fucking count on it." He nodded toward the doorway. "I'll see myself out."

I should've followed him, told him it was too late for him to leave, asked him to stay, but I couldn't move, held back by the promises I'd made to myself and the fear I'd break them all over again.

I'd contemplated not going into work several times. I'd thrown up twice before I managed to swallow down a piece of toast, and once more before I'd gotten into the shower. I hadn't slept for shit after Ethan left. I'd tossed and turned, sweating out the booze and anger until all that had remained were shame and regret. I shouldn't have let him leave like he had. I'd messed up in the first place inviting him over, but I'd let myself give in to my baser needs, consequences be damned. Thank you, Jim Beam. Now I was sitting behind my desk, feeling nauseous as hell, worried I'd not only blown up my entire non-fraternization policy by thinking with my dick, but I'd lost a friend because of it too. It was selfish to want to keep him in any capacity. But I liked Ethan. I liked his snark and his overconfidence. I liked how he listened when he didn't want to and how he put up with my pretentious façades. He was present in everything he did.

Everything.

I tried not to sift too much through the blur of everything that had happened last night, but there was nothing I could do about this incessant loop running havoc through my defenses. *Ethan's lips parting for me, his eyes on mine, swallowing me whole as I came in his hand.* I grit my teeth, wishing away the memory. But it had happened. There wasn't anything to be done about it, and if he did show up today, I'd apologize for letting things get out of hand. He was an employee. A friend. A guy still in love with his ex-boyfriend. He wasn't mine to have.

"You look about as shitty as I feel." Ethan leaned his shoulder against the doorframe, a small, weary smile on his face.

"You showed up."

"I keep my commitments."

"So it seems."

He exhaled and tugged at his tie. "I could do without this shit today."

Despite what he'd said, he looked good. Better than good. The deep red shirt he wore added color to his cheeks. His hair was damp, and I shouldn't have known that he'd smell like wood and rain. Ethan fidgeted as I warred with myself, an apology sitting on the tip of my tongue, but he spoke before I could figure out how to deliver it.

"I'll be at my desk if you need anything. Don't forget you have a lunch meeting today."

I had to fight the urge to tell him to cancel it and ask him to go to Sal's with me. It was better this way. This is how it should be.

"Thanks."

He stared at me, his posture hardened and closed.

"Yeah."

After he left, I tried to distract myself, answering a few emails, my attention span completely annihilated. I closed my eyes and pinched the bridge of my nose. I couldn't fucking pretend like nothing had happened. I owed him at least that much. Decision made, I closed out of the email I'd been working on and opened up a blank one. My fingers flew across the keys, spelling out everything I was too much of a coward to say face to face.

FROM: AndersLowe@LoweLitFic.com

TO: EthanCalloway@LoweLitFic.com

DATE: Dec 11 8:51 AM

SUBJECT: My Apologies

Ethan,

About last night... I could blame the bourbon. I could say I let things get out of hand, that I should have never called you, but I'm done lying to myself—to you. I know what you're going to say. You're not very good at keeping your opinions to yourself, but this can't happen. It's inappropriate, at best. I'm your boss. Not to mention, you're clearly still hung up on him. I'm not a consolation prize.

Regardless, I'm sorry for how I acted and that I let you leave like that after everything.

Sincerely,

Anders~

FROM: EthanCalloway@LoweLitFic.com

TO: AndersLowe@LoweLitFic.com

DATE: Dec 11 9:14 AM

SUBJECT: RE: My Apologies

Anders,

You didn't think it was inappropriate when you had your tongue down my throat, but I digress. As for your accusation, I'm not the only one stuck in the past, but at least I'm not running from it. I can't believe I'm about to say this... Maybe you're right. You shouldn't have called me. Especially if you never intended to own it. Own that you wanted it to happen. Admit that you wanted me.

Not so sincerely,

Yours~

I stared at the word *yours*.

Those five letters held too much power. As much as I wished they were true, wished I could have someone who belonged to me without the weight of a ghost between us, Ethan wasn't mine. If anything, last night proved my feelings for him were reckless.

FROM: AndersLowe@LoweLitFic.com

TO: EthanCalloway@LoweLitFic.com

DATE: Dec 11 9:29 AM

SUBJECT: RE: My Apologies

Ethan,

I wanted it to happen. I wanted you. I wanted you in more ways than I had any right to. But it was a mistake. And maybe you have a few things you need to own up to as well. You're not over Chance. You couldn't stand the idea of being in my room with the ghost of what happened in there with him. I wasn't enough to free you from that memory. And I won't go through that again. I've been second best already one too many times in my life. That being said, I don't want to argue. What happened can't be changed. What's done is done. I messed up and I'm sorry, but I can promise you it will never happen again.

Anders~

FROM: EthanCalloway@LoweLitFic.com

TO: AndersLowe@LoweLitFic.com

DATE: Dec 11 9:43 AM

SUBJECT: RE: My Apologies

Anders,

I'm not Wilder and never will be. I wouldn't drag you along and use you like that. I love that guy, but what he did to you was wrong. And I'm sure you've concocted some excuse about how you both used each other. Save it. I don't want to hear it. I do, however, want to hear about the ways you wanted me, that sounds much more interesting.

But on a more serious note, you're right. Go ahead and clap. I'm not over Chance. And thinking about him last night, thinking about what happened at your place, at that party, fucked me up. But that doesn't diminish what I feel about you. I wanted you. Just you. I didn't want Chance to taint that, and I guess in the end I let him. What I had with him is over. I chose to walk away. I want someone who is willing to choose me. Someone who will make me a priority. Someone who doesn't make me feel second best. Huh… looks like we have that in common.

And for what's it's worth, I wouldn't want to change anything about what happened between us. Well, maybe the way it all exploded right before I left.

I don't want to argue either. I don't want shit to be weird. We're adults, right?

Yours, aka Ethan, aka Not a mistake~

P.S. Don't make promises you can't keep.

I stared at the screen as confusion and irritation and amusement fought for my attention. Confusion winning out in the end.

"Are you having an aneurysm?" Ethan asked as he shut my door.

"Possibly."

He hummed under his breath as he sank into one of the chairs on the other side of my desk. With him this close, I could see the dark circles under his eyes. I'd put those there.

"It was unfair of me to compare you to Wilder. I'm sorry for that… for a lot of things it seems."

"I should have been upfront about the Chance thing." He shrugged. "I guess we both have some baggage to unpack."

"I guess we do..." I hesitated. "I meant what I said, Ethan. I like you... but I can't... I think you need time."

"Thank you for telling me what I need, Anders." He huffed out a laugh. "Christ, you're an asshole."

I leaned back and wiped both of my hands over my face with a groan. "I am. Fuck... I'm such a prick."

"Sex with employees, swearing in the office... oh how the mighty have fallen." His smile reached his eyes, and the anxiety wrapped around my ribs released its grip.

"I thought you said we were going to be adults."

"Overrated." He pinned his bottom lip between his teeth and let the silence percolate between us. Unconsciously, I leaned forward, drawn to him, and he did the same. "How are we supposed to do this?" he asked. "Should I quit?"

"Absolutely not." The thought made me sick to my stomach. I couldn't have him the way I wanted him, but at least we had this. We had Mondays, Wednesdays, and Fridays. Snark and attitude and words of the day.

"No?" He lowered his voice. "You had your dick in my hand last night. I'm not gonna forget that. I don't want to forget that."

"Ethan."

"Anders."

"I should quit."

"What about New York?"

"Fuck, I hate you."

"You couldn't possibly hate me as much as I hate myself right now. But I need you there." *I need you.* "I'll never get everything moved in three days without your help."

Ethan's gaze drifted to my bookshelf. "If I didn't work here... would you let us happen?"

"You're not ready."

"Neither are you." He sighed and picked at the small scratch on the arm of his chair with his thumb. "I'll go to New York, but I think after that I should find another job."

My stomach wrenched and any ease I'd gathered disappeared.

"If that's what you want."

"It's not, but I can't look at you without wanting more. You want to protect yourself. I want to protect myself too."

Everything he'd said was fair. I didn't trust he was over Chance, and I wasn't ready to open myself up for another heartbreak. I couldn't expect him to work here either, not after everything that had happened. And maybe that would be a reprieve for both of us. It had only been five minutes since he'd taken a seat across from me, and I'd struggled to keep my thoughts from wandering where they shouldn't. Thoughts about his reverent fingers on my skin, tracing over the letters of my tattoos, his lips soft and greedy against mine, his teeth on my neck. My cock twitched and I hated myself even more for allowing him to affect me.

"What's a word for rock and a hard place?" I asked and grinned when he laughed.

"Screwed."

Ethan

Two small piles of folded clothes sat neatly on my bed ready to be packed away into my suitcase. I hesitated, staring at them like they had the answer to all the questions running circles in my head. Questions about Anders, about Chance, about where the hell I would find a job less than a month away from classes starting. My last day should have been the morning Anders called what had happened between us a mistake. Evidently, self-preservation wasn't one of my priorities. Anders had locked himself down again. Full-scale, steel enforced, shutdown. Our emails this week—strictly business. We didn't go to Sal's. We didn't talk about anything personal. In fact, we didn't talk at all unless it had to do with work.

Even Claire had noticed his cold behavior and asked what I'd done to piss him off. And Nora. Fuck. She wouldn't leave me alone about it after I'd told her this past Monday I'd decided to quit. Every day had turned into a cross examination. Why was I quitting? Had something happened between me and Anders? Was he the reason I was mopey? Why was he being such an ice princess? The last question had actually made me laugh. And for a moment I'd doubted my decision to quit. I'd wanted to tell her what had happened. I needed help sorting all this shit in my head. Maybe she had an answer I hadn't thought of. But I wouldn't betray his trust. Regardless of how much of an asshole he was. And the worst part? I still wanted him, to have the right to kiss him, to taste him again. That night, his vulnerability, every second he'd given me, I didn't want to forget it. I needed more. I held out hope he'd change his mind, figure out he'd messed up and ask to start over. Completely pathetic. I'd held out hope Chance would figure out I was worth it too. Obviously, that hadn't worked out well for me, and I didn't think waiting around for Anders would either.

I picked up one of the piles and tossed it into my suitcase, wondering if it was too late to back out. As much as I wanted to go to New York, I didn't think sleeping two doors down from Anders and torturing myself for three days would be worth it. Needing a distraction, I picked up my phone to switch on a playlist and found a missed text from Nora.

Nora: Don't quit.

She'd sent me something similar every day since Monday, and I groaned as I sat down on the edge of my bed.

Me: School starts on January 4th. I need to find something closer to campus.

Nora: Then stay until you find something.

Nora: You can tell me anything. You know that. Something happened.

Me: NOTHING HAPPENED!

Nora: You're running. I'm a runner, I can tell.

My mouth was dry, my throat aching with the need to yell, to be angry. To tell her she was right. Something had happened, and it was fucking amazing, but it was all irrelevant because Anders was an idiot and a coward. I kept all of that to myself though.

Me: Nothing happened.

Nora: I'm here, Ethan. Whenever you decide you want to talk.

Nora: Enjoy your trip.

Me: Thanks

Nora: Make sure the pilot isn't drunk.

Me: Jesus.

Nora: Sorry, it's just something I always say. Like have a nice flight.

Me: Charming.

Nora: Mwah.

Tossing my phone onto the bed, I stood and packed the last pile of clothes. Tomorrow I would be in Manhattan, hopefully at some point, standing in Times Square, soaking it all in. I didn't have to let Anders and his stupid perfect tattoos ruin that for me. I'd do my job, help him move shit, and then spend the rest of the day and night exploring one of the greatest cities in the world. With or without him. I set my suitcase on the floor and headed to the bathroom to grab my bag with all my toiletries. Jax was in the kitchen with Wilder preparing dinner. June and Gwen were supposed to come by tonight with their four-month-old daughter Charlotte. And even if I was in a funk about everything else, at least I got to squish a cute baby before I had to go to bed.

"All packed?" Wilder asked after I finished grabbing what I'd need from the bathroom.

I held up the small black bag in my hand. "Almost." He followed me into my room, and I narrowed my eyes. "You're coming to inspect my outfit choices, aren't you?"

He bit the corner of his lip, his smile peeking out the side of his mouth as he shrugged. "You're welcome."

"Wilder... I'm moving files and furniture all day. I don't need to get dressed up for that."

"What about after work? You need to eat," he said, skimming over the shirts in my closet. "And Anders will most likely pick some place nice for you both to go."

"I don't think so."

"You're free to think what you want, but I know Anders..." He kept busy tearing through my closet. "And even if it's a bit odd for me to talk about it with you, it's the truth. He'll want to take you somewhere impressive. Flaunt his good taste. It's his modus operandi."

"His what?" I asked, playfully body-checking him out of my closet. "What the hell are you talking about?"

Wilder pushed his curls out of his eyes and he stared at me like I was missing something. "Listen... I know what this *business* trip is," he said, using finger quotes. "You guys are into each other, hooking-up, whatever. It's cool and totally not my business, but I figured I could give you a few tips."

Nausea rolled around my stomach like I'd swallowed bricks. "W-what... Tips... No—"

He waved his hand and laughed. "Don't look so shy. I honestly don't care. I mean," he whispered. "At first, when you'd mentioned it in the club last week, I had a weird twinge of something. Not jealousy, but like more of a protectiveness thing..."

"Wilder, it's not—"

"Ethan... it's *fine*. Anders is a great guy, and you are too. Jesus knows you've both been fucked over." My eyes widened and I tried to interrupt, to tell him he was way off base, but he mowed right along. "I know, I know. I'm an asshole. I hurt him. I'm aware of how selfish I was. I can't change the past, okay. But I can do something about the future. You two could be perfect for each other... if you're ready."

"Nothing is happening between me and Anders."

"No?"

"No," I lied. "This is an actual business trip. Not some excuse for his modus opera... or whatever the hell you were saying. It's work, Wilder. That's it."

He pressed his lips together and pierced me with dark brown eyes.

"I'm serious," I said, a nervous laugh bubbling up my throat.

Wilder hummed under his breath and clapped me on the shoulder. "Anders doesn't let people in unless he cares about them."

"We're not—"

"That's all I'm going to say."

"Okay."

He nodded once and gave me a sad smile. "Okay."

Everything I wanted to say, all the questions I had stuck in my throat choked me.

"June and Gwen will be here soon. You're joining us for dinner, right? Jax made tacos."

"Tacos sound good."

"Pack that purple long sleeve. It looks nice with your eyes," he said, smiling as he turned to leave.

Anders doesn't let people in unless he cares about them.

God, I hated how much I needed that to be true. Anders had admitted he'd wanted me. But wanting and caring were two different animals. He'd opened up and then shut the door. He'd let me in only to push me out. The back and forth was what killed me. It might've been easier if he'd straight up told me to fuck off. The doorbell rang and saved me from yet another mental digression. I didn't want to think about this shit anymore. I'd made my choice. After this trip, I had one week left at Lowe Literary. I had no idea what I would do once I was gone, but possibility was so much better than regret.

"Are you nervous about starting school?" Gwen asked as June handed me their daughter.

"A little. I feel unprepared," I said and smiled down at the baby in my arms. Charlotte blew spit bubbles and squawked until I ran my fingers through her wiry copper curls. "I have a lot of prerequisites I have to complete before I can start the nursing program."

"Ugh. Don't remind me," June complained. "Anatomy was the fucking worst."

Jax chuckled as he sat down next to Wilder on the couch. "Charlie's first word will be a swear if you're not careful."

"It's Charlotte… thank you very much. We did not approve that nickname, Ethan, just so you know." June leaned over and kissed her daughter's forehead. "She's four months old, I don't have to worry yet, and besides, I don't care what words come out of her mouth. They'll all be beautiful to me."

"Until she's a teenager and talks back," Gwen said, reaching into the diaper bag by her feet. She handed me a white cloth. "Just in case. She's been spitty lately."

"Projectile vomit is what she means," June warned. "Don't sugarcoat it, sweets. Charlotte will end up scaring the poor guy and he'll never want babies of his own."

"I'd never really thought about having kids," I admitted. "I mean, if I found the right guy and everything, I could see it happening. Especially if they turned out to be as cute as Charlie."

"Charlotte," June corrected and Wilder sighed.

"Charlie is a cute name, June. Get over yourself."

"Wilder does have a point."

June glared at me.

"Ethan, I swear to God, if you take their side, I'll never help you with homework."

"Charlotte is great too," I said, with a smile. "Charlie may be a bit too chipper."

"Traitor." Wilder scowled at me as Jax tugged him closer.

"Should we tell them?" he asked.

"Tell us what?" June looked at me and I shook my head.

"Don't look at me. I've got no idea what Jax is talking about."

"We're thinking of adopting," he said, and every face in the room lit up.

"Yeah?" I asked, hoping my shock didn't sound like a disapproval.

Jax and Wilder would be the best parents any kid could have. Jax had basically been a father to Jay, and Wilder had stepped in without any hesitation once he and Jax had gotten back together.

"It might take a little while," he said.

"At least another year," Wilder explained. "We want to make sure Jax's business stays steady and that Jason continues to do well."

"We've started the process, and it looks like we'll have a long road ahead, but we're excited." Jax's smile was all love and hope as he gazed at his husband. "We didn't want to wait to share the news with y'all. You're our family."

"Does your mom know?" I asked.

"Not yet. She's still adjusting to Jay having a girlfriend." He laughed. "When we have more of a timeline, we'll let them both know."

"Wait, Jay has a girlfriend?" Gwen's eyes widened. "How the hell did I miss that?"

"You're always at work," he said.

My phone vibrated in my pocket and I leaned to the side, shifting the baby in my lap as I reached for it.

"Here... I can take her," June offered, and I handed Charlotte back over to her mom.

The conversation buzzed around me in a flurry of white noise as Anders's name blinked on my screen. The tips of my fingers prickled as I opened the text, the same way they would have if I'd slept on my hand funny.

Anders: Are you ready for tomorrow?

Work related. Of course.

Me: As ready as I can be.

Me: You?

I glanced up and found Wilder covertly staring at me while everyone else discussed which adoption agencies were the best.

Anders doesn't let people in unless he cares about them.

He didn't care about me, not enough to actually do anything about it at least. Another text came through and I lowered my eyes to the screen.

Anders: No.

Me: Did I forget to do something?

Anders: Can you talk?

My heart thudded heavy inside my chest as I typed out a response.

Me: You had all week to talk.

Anders: I didn't know what to say.

Me: But you do now?

Anders: Not really, no.

I exhaled a deep breath, and I could feel the eyes of the room on me. When I looked up, everyone had gone quiet.

"Everything okay?" June asked, and I forced a smile.

"Sorry, yeah... just a work thing." I stood and avoided making eye contact with Wilder. "I'll be right back."

Once I was in my room, I leaned against the closed door and called him.

It rang three times before he answered. "I'm sorry."

"For what?"

"Ethan..."

"No... seriously. You'll have to be more specific," I snapped. All the anger I'd let build this week boiled over as I pushed away from the door and paced toward the window, away from listening ears. "Are you sorry about being a bastard all week, or for shutting me out *again* or for making me feel like shit. I thought we were going to be adults about what happened? So please. Tell me... What the hell are you sorry about?"

"All of it. This. Exactly this," he said, and I could hear how tired he was.

I was tired too.

"You're fucking exhausting, Anders."

"I don't want you to quit."

"Because working for you is such a pleasure."

Shit, I sounded like a bratty teenager.

"Give me this weekend. Let me fix this."

That same sliver of hope slid underneath my skin and I wanted to pick it out. Remove it before it could sink too deep this time.

"I was always leaving. This was never supposed to be permanent."

"Give me this weekend," he said again. "And then decide."

I pictured him sitting at his desk, his blue eyes unwavering, his jaw tense and ready with a quick comeback.

"You stopped talking to me."

"I know."

"I'm pissed off."

"I know."

"Stop saying that."

I counted each of his breaths as the silence stretched on.

"It was miserable," he said. "Not talking to you."

I sank down onto my mattress and rested my elbows on my knees. "Nora called you an ice princess."

His soft chuckle rumbled through the phone. "Sounds about right."

"If you want me to stay, you can't give me the cold shoulder whenever you feel like it. I'm not just an employee, Anders. Not anymore. I'm not saying you owe me anything after what happened. But at least treat me like a fucking human being."

"You're right."

"We hooked up, it's not the end of the world."

"It's not."

"For hell's sake, we're friends. Or at least I thought that's what you wanted. Do you even know what that word means? It's a noun."

"I'm aware of the definition."

"Yeah?"

"Two people who have a mutual affection for one another."

"God... mutual affection." I couldn't stop myself from laughing. "Do you ever listen to yourself?"

"What?" he asked, the smile in his voice poured through the phone. "It's the definition. Look it up."

"Can't. I left my dictionary at the office." I bit back my smile. "Why is it I can't stay mad at you?"

"Because we share a mutual affection for one another."

"Yeah... I guess we do." I sat up and stared at the ceiling. "I'll give you this weekend."

"And if I can manage not to fuck it up," he said. "You'll stay until Kris comes back?"

"I'll stay."

His relief was palpable as he let out a deep breath.

"Goodnight, Ethan."

"I'll see you in the morning."

I wanted to let go of the pent-up anxiety and anger I'd held onto, but I couldn't strip down my armor. His avoidance, it had affected me too much, and if I'd learned anything this past week, it was that Anders had the power to hurt me.

Anders

I couldn't tear my eyes away from him. Ethan's smile stretched across his face as he stared out of the cab window, eyes wandering skyward, absorbing as much of the city as he could. To be honest, I'd stared at him the entire flight from Atlanta to JFK. He'd been quiet on the way to the airport with sleepy brown eyes and hair sticking up in the back. Once we'd boarded the plane and took off, he passed out before we'd reached cruising altitude, sleeping until we'd landed a little over two hours later. I'd memorized the lines of his face while he'd slept, the slope of his nose, the shape of his lips with each breath he'd taken and wondered if it was possible to fall for someone in a span of two hours. And now, this smile, it opened him up and I wanted to fall inside, I wanted to find a reason to make him smile like this every day.

This past week I'd done everything I could to push him away. The fear I might've started another one-way relationship had suffocated me. It confused me because the longer I'd shut him out, the more I'd wanted to let him in. The more I'd pushed him away, the harder it had been to stay away. The distance had provided no relief, it had only served to feed my desire to know him, to have him, to call him something other than friend. The night we'd shared together, though brief, had become the pilot light burning in my chest, a constant reminder of him. A reminder of what I'd told myself I'd always wanted, of what I could have if I'd let go of the past. I'd realized this morning, while he'd slept, his head unconsciously on my shoulder, over time he'd somehow managed to sneak his way into my life in a permanent way. I'd come to care for Ethan, and as alarming as that was for me, I was done fighting it. If I ever wanted to move forward and fill those vacant rooms in my house and in my life, I had to let myself trust again. It could be with Ethan, or maybe someone else, but I had to stop closing myself off to the possibility.

Ethan reluctantly turned away from the window and caught me staring at him. "What?"

"You're adorable." His brows dipped into an annoyed little crease and I laughed. "You are. You've got this whole wide-eyed-country-boy-goes-to-the-big-city thing going on. It's cute."

"Wide-eyed country boy," he said, hamming up his southern accent. "I guess I'm happier than a pig in a pickle jar to be here, boss."

"Now you sound ridiculous."

He flipped me off, but his bright smile remained. "I'm allowed to be excited. Atlanta is big, but this place is insane. It's claustrophobic as hell, but I love it."

"If we finish early, we should take a walk to Rockefeller Center. See the tree."

"Holy shit, I didn't even think about that." His dimples popped, and I wished I had the right to pull him closer, to take his hand in mine and kiss him. I scrubbed my hand through my hair to stop myself from giving in. "Your office is that close to Rockefeller?"

"Yeah, the new one is too. Robbie's assistant and one of the other part-time agents rented a moving truck. It's small but should fit everything. They're supposed to meet us at the old office." I checked my watch. "They're probably already there."

"How much longer of a drive is it?" he asked.

"In this traffic? Who knows."

I'd decided we should go straight to the office from the airport to give us the most amount of time. We only had two bags of luggage between us, and instead of going all the way down to Tribeca to check in to the hotel, only to have to turn around and head back up to Midtown, I figured we'd hold on to our bags and keep them in the office while we worked. The plan would give us an opportunity to finish faster, and a chance for me to take Ethan to dinner later. I wanted to show him around the city, and if I had to use efficiency to hide my ulterior motive, so be it.

It took another thirty minutes to arrive at our destination due to an accident on Fifty-Fifth Street. The morning gridlock was a headache, but better than being crammed like a sardine in a can on the subway. Once we'd made it to the office, I'd introduced Ethan to Dereck, Robbie's assistant, and Keith, our part-time agent. The New York branch of Lowe Literary was a fledgling venture, slowly building its client base, but had the opportunity to take off with the right people manning the ship. New York was the center of the publishing world, and as much as I loved Atlanta, after Wilder and I had split, I'd seriously thought about moving here permanently. When going back and forth between Georgia and New York had become too much, I'd gotten lucky and found Robbie through a source at Bartley Press. The thought of moving away from Atlanta and my family, as much as they drove me nuts, wasn't an idea I wanted to entertain if I didn't have to.

With the four of us deciding to skip lunch, we'd been able to load everything up by two-thirty. The long day and lack of food had begun to wear on me, making my head pound and every muscle in my body ache. I considered myself fit. I went to the gym, worked out as much as I had time for, but lifting heavy furniture with guys almost ten years younger than me all day had put a dent in my ego. After we'd sent Dereck and Keith to the overnight parking lot with a promise to meet them at the new office tomorrow morning to unload the truck, I thought about skipping Rockefeller Center and going to the hotel for a nap until Ethan mentioned it again.

"We should grab something to eat on our way over to Rockefeller. Like a hot dog... Oh, or pizza." He grinned and it made me want to give him anything and everything he desired.

"You're doing that cute, excited thing again."

His smile dimmed and he glanced over to where our luggage sat against the wall. Ethan's entire body language had changed. He crossed his arms over his chest, closing in on himself. I wasn't sure if it was what I'd said or that I'd teased him again. I'd promised him and myself I wouldn't fuck everything up this weekend, and it looked as if I'd already started off on the wrong foot.

"Are we leaving those here for now?"

"We could grab them when we're done exploring," I said. "If that's alright with you?"

"Yeah, I don't want to drag that shit around all day."

"I'm sure there's a street vendor or a pizza place somewhere along the way," I offered, trying to win back his good mood.

It worked.

"Yeah, that sounds good." His smile was sheepish as he rubbed his neck. "I'm so hungry I'm starting to get a headache."

"I'm glad I'm not the only one. You guys made me feel old."

"Thirty-six is not old."

"Says the twenty-eight-year-old. I'll be thirty-seven in January."

"Shit, okay." He laughed. "You are old."

I bumped my shoulder into his as I headed for the door. "Let's go get something to eat before I fire you for that comment alone."

His laugh was husky as he held out his hand. "Lead the way."

I locked up the office and we headed down the five flights of stairs to the street entrance. The sky was overcast with the stark gray of winter, but at least there wasn't much wind. Ethan pushed his hands into the pocket of his hoodie and shivered.

"I should've brought the jacket I used to wear in Colorado. I didn't think about how cold it would be here when I packed."

"Walking will keep you warm. Come on."

We made our way down Forty-Seventh Street to Times Square. Ethan was all giddiness and smiles once again as we walked by street performers, the light of the billboards reflecting in his eyes.

"I want to come back here at night," he said, looking up and around and ignoring the swarm of people brushing by. "Fuck, this is cool."

He looked at me, his expression all awe and wonder. With his eyes on mine, the cold air couldn't touch me. We were in this tiny pocket of time and the noise of the city faded. If I wanted this, I had to be the one to reach out and take it. His hand was at his side, only a few inches from mine. We were shoulder to shoulder, the heat of his skin pulling my hand toward his.

"I want to hold your hand."

He swallowed as my finger brushed his thumb and a flash of trepidation darkened his eyes. It lasted maybe a second until his pupils dilated with a longing that mirrored mine.

"Then hold it."

His fingers were warm against my chilled skin as I took his hand. His lips parted with a soft exhale, and the city came to life around us again. Ethan lowered his eyes to our joined hands and furrowed his brows, his posture closing off like it had back at the office when I'd called him cute.

"Friends don't hold hands, Anders."

"I don't want to be friends." My heart pounded, pushing my pulse higher, past the tall buildings and into the gray clouds. Ethan lifted his gaze, uncertain, and I tightened my grip. "I learned something about myself today."

He bit back a smile. "What's that?"

"I like watching you sleep."

A warm blush flooded his cheeks, and he set free that magnificent smile. "You watched me sleep?"

"On the plane. The whole way here."

"That's kind of a strange thing to do," he said, amused.

"I care about you." The admission surprised me, like my heart had taken control and cut off communication with my brain. "And that scares me, but I don't want to miss out on something good because I was too afraid to let go... I need to let go of this shit. I've held onto it for far too long."

"I'm scared too. And not because I'm hung up on Chance." He turned and brought us chest to chest. Every inhale and exhale brought us closer together as he slid his fingers into my other hand—the chaos around us muted by the moment. "*You* scare the shit out of me."

"I want to change that." I released his right hand and trailed my thumb along the length of his jaw, my fingers settling on the nape of his neck. "I asked you for this weekend. But I want more. If you're ready, Ethan... I want you."

"I'm ready... I have been for a while. I can't say I don't have stuff to work through, too, but I want this."

Leaning down, I hesitated, my lips barely brushing his. He didn't tense or pull away, instead he raised his hand and cupped the back of my neck, melding his mouth to mine. I forgot to care about my empty stomach, or the chaos around us. Everything was him, his tongue, his taste, mint and sweet and something other that only belonged to him. The possessive way he twisted his fingers in my hair grounded me, and I pressed my hand to the small of his back. Closing off the last few inches between us, I thought I heard someone whistle, and maybe a few laughs and cat calls, but nothing mattered to me in that moment other than my need to show him I was here, willing to let go for him—for me.

I wasn't sure which one of our stomachs rumbled first, but Ethan laughed and smiled against my skin. "I might be willing to trade you sexual favors later for a slice of pizza right now."

Framing his face with my hands, I gently pulled his bottom lip through my teeth. "I think there's a pizzeria on Forty-Sixth."

Ethan placed a soft kiss to the corner of my mouth and laced his fingers through mine as he pulled away. "Is that close?"

"Not too far."

"Good... feed me. Then I'm all yours."

Ethan's amazement with the city only continued as we checked into the hotel. He took in every detail, from the leather lounge chairs in the lobby, to the art hanging on the walls behind the desk. I was half tempted to cancel the reservation for Ethan's room, but navigating a new relationship was tricky. Everything seemed to be going as I'd hoped, Ethan hadn't let go of my hand except to devour the four slices of pizza he'd ordered. Tired from travel and a busy day, we'd decided to hold off on seeing the tree at Rockefeller until later tonight. And on the cab ride back to the hotel, he'd let me pull him close, tucked under my arm the whole way. But here, with the heat of the fireplace, and the hum of the people around us, the real world made its presence known. I didn't want to rush this. We both had excess baggage, and if this was going to work, we had to find a way to either traverse around the issues or get rid of them altogether. Either way, that wasn't happening in the span of one afternoon.

I handed him his key card. "You're on the same floor as me."

"I know." He smirked. "I was the one who booked the reservations."

"Such a good assistant." I pressed a quick kiss to his lips. "Are you sure you want to be a nurse? I bet I could convince Kris to be a stay-at-home mom."

He rolled his eyes and grabbed his bag. "I don't know how Kris puts up with you five days a week, I can hardly handle three."

"I pay her well," I said with a smug grin and nodded toward the elevators. "Let's take a nap."

"Is that a euphemism?"

"Nice word."

"I'd like to think so." The elevator doors slid open and a couple of people stepped out. Ethan hit the button for the fifth floor once we were inside, and as the door closed, he sidled in next to me. "You know, you could've saved yourself the money and gotten one room."

"I thought about it, but I figured you'd want your space. This is new, and I promised I wouldn't fuck up this weekend. I didn't want to assume."

"When it comes to sex, Anders, always assume the answer is yes."

I tilted his chin with my thumb, grazing my lips along his cheek to the shell of his ear. His fingers curled into the fabric of my jacket as I spoke. "What about showers?"

"Always a yes."

"And naps?" I asked and kissed the freckle on his bottom lip.

"Yes."

The elevator doors opened and a woman with a small child stared at us. Ethan's face flamed red as we stepped into the hallway, his embarrassment another thing to add to the growing list of adorable shit he did.

"Did you see her face?" he asked. "She was offended, right? Or did I imagine that?"

"Do you care if she was offended?"

"Hell no."

"Then don't worry about it." I stopped in front of my door. "Are you coming in?"

He tucked his keycard into his back pocket, a sexy, lopsided smile forming on his lips. "Yeah... I owe you for the pizza, remember."

Anders

Reality hit me as the door of the hotel room clicked shut behind us. There was no pedaling backward, no more walls for me to hide behind. Ethan was here. With me. And I couldn't have been any happier. He walked through the suite, his fingers grazing along the back of the leather sofa, stopping in front of the large window. I unbuttoned my jacket as I watched him. Waited him out. The rustling sound of fabric cut through the silence as I slipped it off and set it on the back of the couch. Ethan looked over his shoulder, a sexy smile curling at the corner of his lips.

"This is how the other half lives?" he teased. "Is my room this nice?"

"I have no idea." I pushed my sleeves to my elbows one at a time. He turned to face me, wetting his lips, and giving me his full attention. "I'm sure if you find it unsatisfactory, other arrangements could be made."

The city painted inside the frame of the window dimmed as the gray sky finally opened. Sleet hit the glass, rivulets of water and ice obscuring the view, leaving Ethan front and center. He abandoned his suitcase, walking toward me with purpose. "I forgot how good you look when you're not wearing all that uptight bullshit."

His hands settled on my hips and I chuckled. "Uptight bullshit?"

"I like you like this. Casual. It's welcoming." Ethan moved his palm over my abdomen up to my chest. "You're more approachable, less... bossy."

"I think you may find my domineering side has its benefits as well."

I brushed my knuckles along the line of his jaw, his caramel eyes soft as he stared up at me. Without asking, I lowered my hands to the hem of his sweatshirt and lifted it. Ethan obeyed, raising his arms as I pulled it over his head and let it fall to the floor. As slow as possible, I peeled off his white cotton undershirt, indulging in his warm skin, my fingertips leaving a wake of goose bumps behind. He didn't speak, letting me take the lead. The tension mounted between us with each rise and fall of his chest. I unbuckled his belt, unsnapped the button on his jeans and unzipped him, his lips parting with a raspy exhale as I dipped my thumb below the waistband of his briefs.

"Take these off," I whispered, and he pulled down his jeans, leaving his underwear in place. "Everything, Ethan. I want you naked."

He complied, his thick cock springing free, heavy between his legs. Perusing his body, my gaze devoured the long length of his limbs, the muscles etched in his arms and legs, the deep V of his hips. Ethan looked more like he'd been carved by water, than chiseled out of stone. Not overly thin or bulky. Perfect. I needed to touch him, ached to taste him, to have him in my mouth. The smirk on his face told me he was well aware of the power he held over me. It didn't deter me, and I lifted my shirt over my head, throwing it toward the couch.

Ethan reached for my hip, bringing us chest to chest. My hands gliding over the curve of his ass, I kneaded the muscle until he rested his forehead against my shoulder with a groan. Spreading his cheeks, I let my fingers slip between his crack and he shuddered, looking at me as he leaned into the touch. His hands on my belt, he deftly unbuckled and unbuttoned me until we were both standing together, vulnerable, and bare. He wrapped his palm around the back of my neck, drawing our mouths together, his tongue sliding alongside mine. Furious and needy, his teeth found my bottom lip, dragging across my flesh as I gripped the base of his cock. He grunted as I jacked him without any finesse, fast and rough, our kiss sloppy and wet until the blunt tips of his fingernails scratched into my skin.

"Shower," I panted into the hollow below his ear, reluctant to pull away.

Ethan followed me into the bedroom, leaving our clothes behind strewn across the floor. I flipped on the bathroom light and let out a deep breath, heeding the repetitive voice in my head. *Slow down. Slow down. Slow down.* If I wasn't careful, I'd give in to all the dirty thoughts roaring through my sex-deprived brain and end up bending him over the tub before the water had a chance to get warm in the shower. As appealing as it was to think about fucking Ethan, I wasn't sure if I was ready for that, if we were ready. In the past, I'd fuck whoever I wanted, no big deal, but I wanted more from him, from this fragile thing we'd decided to build. That didn't mean we couldn't enjoy each other, but the pace I'd wanted to set for us didn't involve sinking myself inside him on day one no matter how much I wanted to. Sometimes I hated my rules. Especially now, as Ethan opened the shower door and leaned in. Turning on the water, his muscles flexed across his back all the way down to his incredible and tempting ass.

"You coming in or watching?" he asked as he stepped into the stream of water. Steam billowed around him as he stroked a slow hand down his cock. "Having you watch me get off could be sexy."

"I'd rather you come in my mouth." I stepped in and shut the door behind me, crowding into his personal space. "But that can wait."

The hot water hit my back as Ethan tugged our hips together, both of us hard and slicked with water. He tangled his fingers into my wet hair, and I held the back of his head, my tongue hungry for him as he kissed me. All these weeks of restrained desire spilled between us, aggressive, our mouths fused and fighting, biting and licking. Coming up for air, I placed quiet kisses on his jaw and neck, noticing the standard hotel sample-sized bottles of soap and shampoo on the recessed shelf in the shower wall. We helped ourselves, the citrus scent clouding around us in the steam. Ethan soaped up his dick, a salacious grin on his face, making it impossible for me to pace this.

"Christ," I groaned, reaching down and taking him in hand, the slippery suds coating my fingers and his skin.

His eyes fluttered shut, his head tipping back as I explored his body, my hands working their way into his hair, over his shoulders, under his arms, and down his back.

"Anders," he whispered my name, his head falling forward to claim my mouth as my fingers brushed the crease of his ass and teased the tempting, tight ring of muscle.

We kissed and touched and tasted each other, both ready to explode with need. And after the last bubble of soap swirled down the drain, my lips followed a long and lazy path down to his body. I raised his arms, dragging the tip of my nose over his clavicle, through the damp hair in the curve of his arm pit, to his taut, dusky nipple. I pinched the nub between my thumb and finger, sucking it into my mouth, and his grip in my hair intensified. My palms rested against his rib cage, sliding to his waist as I kneeled onto the marble floor. The stone surface unforgiving, but the view it afforded me was worth the discomfort. Ethan's fingers raked through my hair, tilting my head back, I gathered every detail. His cheeks red from the heat, his eyes hooded with lust, begged me to relieve him, to put an end to the torture. His lashes, wet from the water, blinked down at me as I circled the pink head of his cock with my tongue.

"Ahh..." he groaned my name through clenched teeth. Pumping his hips, he pushed into the back of my throat.

Gagging, I took a breath, and he held my chin in his hand as I stroked him, easing his thumb into my mouth while water dripped down my cheeks. I opened for him again, let him drive past my lips, let him fuck my mouth. Every one of his ragged breaths encouraged me. Spurred me on. His low moans resonated around us as he used my mouth, bracing himself against the shower wall with the palm of his hand.

"Anders... fuck..."

I grabbed his hips, halting his movement and released him, his pupils blown wide, confusion and fire in his gaze.

"What the hell?" he asked, breathless as I stood.

I could feel the pain, too, my entire body throbbed with it, with need. I yearned to let go, to test him, to see how far he'd let me push him.

"Don't worry, I'm not done with you yet," I said, smiling at his frustration, and shut off the shower. "And don't bother with a towel, just get on the bed."

At first, I thought he'd argue, but to my surprise, Ethan stepped past me and opened the glass door, putting an end to my disbelief as he grabbed a towel off the rack.

"You never listen." I spoke the words as steady as possible, my control slipping, and pulled him to me, discarding the towel onto the floor.

He rattled me, his heat, his touch, his brazen as hell gaze. This pull between us was a tug of war, a tight wire, a balance of power I'd gladly fight for as long as it ended with us both spent and satisfied. As if Ethan could read my mind, he went in for the kill first, our mouths colliding, our hands grasping and pushing. We stumbled into the room, his teeth on my neck, my fingers in his hair. He tried to grind against my hip, seeking friction, the release I'd deprived him of in the shower, and I shoved him onto the bed. On his back, I crawled over him, sinking my hips until our dicks aligned, rubbing against him until we were both desperate and slick with our anticipation. He groaned as my pace slowed again, his fingers digging into my ass cheeks.

"I swear to God, if you stop again. I need to... I'll.... Fuck..." He panted, squirming underneath my weight, and I held his hands above his head. "I don't know what I'll do. But it won't be pretty. Make me come, Anders."

"Since you asked nicely." I smirked, reaching between us, and wrapped my fingers around his cock. "Is this what you need?"

"Yes." His piercing gaze held mine, daring me to stop, daring me to leave him wanting again.

Pumping my hand up and down the length of his cock, I pressed a kiss to his mouth. He lifted his head for more, and I denied him, bringing my lips to his chin, kissing my way down his chest, over the ridges of his abs to his groin. I inhaled his scent, citrus and musk. Thoughts about sinking inside him until we were both sated and sweaty punished me as he brought his legs back toward his chest, putting himself on display for me. I swiped my tongue over his hole, his taint, teasing him a little more before I swallowed his cock. Any hope I'd had that I could drag this out was abandoned when a whimpered *please* uttered past his lips. He cried out and thrust into my mouth over and over again. I breathed through my nose, taking as much of him as I could with each frantic jolt of his hips, moaning as I jacked myself at the same brutal rhythm. Both of his hands knotted in my hair as he arched his back, swearing incoherently, coming in heavy spurts down my throat. His briny taste made my mouth water, and I didn't want to stop until I'd taken every last drop of him for myself.

Ethan sat up and I moved with him, our bodies in sync. I was on my knees, my orgasm building fast, every nerve ending sparking as he covered my hand with his, stroking me in earnest.

"Open your mouth," I said, half out of my mind and half out of breath.

Ethan let me take over again, his eyes locked on mine, and as I held his chin with my left hand, he opened his mouth. I placed the head of my cock on his tongue, gripping his jaw as I came. He closed his lips, smothering me in wet heat and I swore, my legs quaking until he lifted up onto his knees. I cupped his face, dragging us into a deep kiss, memorizing the taste of myself on his tongue.

Ethan was the first to break the kiss, resting his forehead against my shoulder, my fingers toyed with the hair at his nape. His skin was damp from either sweat or residual from the shower, but he was warm and loose as I skated my fingers down his spine.

"I think I'm ready for that nap you promised me," he said and the smile in his voice made my heart squeeze several erratic beats.

Ethan leaned back, and I swept his hair off his forehead to get a better look at his eyes. There were no regrets. No awkward, what the fuck did we do? No judgment. Only light and simple relief.

I held his face and kissed the freckle on his bottom lip. "Me too."

We both got comfortable, under the covers this time, Ethan pressing his back to my chest. My arm draped over his waist, and I tucked him in as close as possible, kissing the slope of his neck. If someone would have told me a month ago I'd feel this content with Ethan lying beside me, I would have told them they were full of shit. He'd dismantled me piece by piece. This was only a beginning, and instead of trying to think of ways to self-sabotage, I wanted to make sure I didn't mess it up. It felt right, having him like this, in my arms. In the silence, the sleet made its presence known again, tinkling against the glass panes of the window, and with the heat of Ethan's body and the steady rhythm of his breathing, I was almost asleep when he spoke.

"Is it weird?" he asked softly. "How right this feels?"

"I was thinking the same thing." Drifting my nose along his neck, he shivered, and closed his hand over mine where it rested against his chest. "Does that scare you at all?"

"I'm not sure." He laughed. "Ask me again when I wake up. I'm still recovering from the best blow job I've ever had."

"Ever?"

"At least the top five."

Smiling, I leaned in and gently bit the lobe of his ear. "Fuck that... you said the best."

"Definitely the best, I'm getting chubbed up thinking about it." I reached down to investigate, and he swatted my hand away. "No way. You're a fucking cock tease, making me beg for it, edging me like the bossy prick you are."

"You seemed to enjoy yourself," I said, and my dick twitched against his ass thinking about his taste again.

"Stop, or we won't nap, and then we won't go out, and I'll miss New York because I was too busy fucking the boss."

"Good thing New York never sleeps," I said, remembering one of the emails he'd sent while I was here last month. "We have time for both."

I think even then I knew I'd give in to him.

Ethan didn't say anything at first, the beat of his heart increasing under the palm of my hand.

He shifted, rolling onto his side, bringing us face to face. "This doesn't scare me."

"No?"

His lips tipped up into a smile as he appraised me, his fingers tracing the curved ink under my left collar bone.

"Nah... this is good. You and me."

"Does that mean we can sleep now? I'm exhausted after giving you the best blow job of your life."

"Figures you'd have zero stamina, old man."

"Old man, huh?"

I caught his lips with mine, grabbing his ass and driving our hips together. His tongue dipped into my mouth, his moan drowning out the sound of the rain, our nap officially on hold. Indefinitely.

Ethan

Sirens blared somewhere in the distance and my eyes opened. The room was dark with muted light peeking through the curtains. I rolled onto my side, the white bedsheets twisting around my waist. Anders was on his back, eyes closed, his lips soft with sleep. A smile slowly crept across my face as I admired the sleek lines of his jaw and the high arches of his cheekbones. I understood now why Anders had watched me sleep on the plane. I had free access to stare. He'd never looked this relaxed, not even after the second orgasm he'd had before we'd both passed out earlier. I lifted myself onto an elbow, reading every line of ink again, looking down at the expanse of his chest, down to where the sheet bunched around his hips, remembering the salty taste of his skin, and the way the hard muscles of his abs felt under my fingertips.

His husky moans and gruff commands were on repeat in my head. I had no idea how much I'd like giving into his demands. We were compatible in a way I couldn't have predicted. Craving his touch, I slid my palm over his warm skin in a slow circuit from his stomach to his chest. Anders exhaled a quiet breath and reached for my hand.

Keeping his eyes closed, he asked, "What time is it?"

I flicked my gaze to the digital clock on the nightstand before shifting in closer to his side. "A little after nine."

He hummed and his eyes opened, revealing the quiet blue irises I couldn't get enough of. "We didn't get much of a nap."

"Whose fault is that?"

Beaming up at me, totally unguarded and unlike Anders, he said, "I take full responsibility for my actions."

I bit the corner of my mouth in an attempt to remain cool and unaffected. I wanted this man. Wholly and inevitably, and maybe it should freak me out, but it didn't. My heart was all over the fucking place. And hell, when he smiled at me like this, there was no way I could resist him. Leaning down, I touched my lips to his and he palmed the back of my head, deepening the kiss as I crawled over his body and straddled his waist.

He kissed the corner of my mouth, brushing his knuckles over the stubble on my chin. "I want to take you out to dinner."

I chuckled against his cheek and sat up. His hands fell to my thighs, the tips of his fingers sweeping over my skin and through the hair on my legs. "Like right now?"

"Yes... *like right now*," he said, his blatant perusal of my body suggested otherwise.

"Hmm." I stroked my cock, slow and deliberate. "Are you sure?"

A dark flash of heat crossed his eyes and my stomach flipped with anticipation. I'd taken the upper hand this time. Or so I'd thought. Quicker than he had any right to be, he sat up and tossed me onto my back, pinning me to the mattress like I didn't weigh close to two-hundred pounds. Anders was taller than me by a few inches, broader, too, but we were matched in strength. I could've easily rolled him onto his back, but I liked having his weight on me, holding me down.

"We're going to dinner," he said, pressing a quick kiss to my forehead. He moved his body with ease to the side of the bed. "What are you in the mood for?"

You.

"I don't care. I'm hungry enough I'd eat anything." My stomach growled as if to prove the point. The mattress shook as he stood and I rolled to my side, staring at his muscular ass as he walked toward the bathroom. "Honestly, I'd rather order in." He switched on the light and turned on the shower. "We can get pizza," I hollered.

He leaned in the doorway, his eyes on my not-so-subtle erection. "We had pizza for lunch."

"And?"

"Get in the shower and I'll take care of that for you." Anders smirked as I sat up.

"Don't look so smug," I said, standing, and made my way to the bathroom. "I'm perfectly capable of rubbing one out while you're being boring in the shower. But I'd like to think of myself as a giving person."

He laughed as I wound my arms around his hips. "When provoked I can be awfully charitable as well."

Weaving my fingers through his hair, I leaned in, dragging my teeth along the curve of his neck. Anders's grip on my hip was almost painful as I nibbled and sucked on his hot skin. With a growl resonating in his chest, Anders's palm found its way between us, taking us both in hand. It only took two to three firm pumps of his fist before we were both panting and needing more. His cock gliding over mine, his breath in my mouth, I didn't care about the city waiting for us beyond this suite, or that my stomach was empty. We were chasing seconds like thieves, stealing time for ourselves, adding up minutes until we had hours of skin and lips. I'd jumped off this cliff with him and I wasn't ready to land.

I grunted, pushing into his hand. "Don't stop."

"Can't," he rasped. "Fuck, you feel too good."

Steam from the shower filled the bathroom while we got lost in the feel of each other. Anders came first, hot against my chest, pulling my bottom lip through his teeth. Not even two second later, I spilled over his hand and dragged my fingers through our mess, needing more of him on my skin. More of us.

He pressed two rough and breathless kisses to my lips and pulled away. "Can I take you to dinner now?"

"Yeah…" I huffed out a laugh and rested my head on his shoulder. "I guess you've earned it."

Thirty minutes later we stood under the hotel awning, hand in hand, waiting for a cab. The sleet had turned to snow, covering the sidewalks in a slick white powder. Cars zoomed by without caution, creating gray slush under their tires. It was after ten o' clock, but the city was wide awake. The heavy flakes falling from the sky added to the static energy around us. I was all smiles, feeling drunk on Anders and orgasms.

"We should take the subway."

Anders brows furrowed, his nose wrinkling like we'd stepped over a sewer grate. "No, thank you."

"I want the full New York experience."

"And you will have it. But without getting robbed or acquiring some random flesh-eating disease."

"You're such a snob," I said, and the doorman snorted. "See... even he thinks so."

Anders tossed the poor guy a dirty look, but the guy smiled back at us like we were the most entertaining thing he'd seen all night. "I'm not a snob because I'd rather ride in a taxi than be stuck in a tunnel covered in piss and rat shit."

I stared at his handsome face in disbelief. "Rat shit?"

"He ain't lying, kid." The doorman nodded. "And it's best not to be on the train late at night anyway."

"Fine... but tomorrow we're taking the subway to the office."

"You're cute when you think you've gotten your way," he said and placed a kiss against my temple. "We can catch the train on the way back from the office. It's too busy in the morning."

"As long as we ride the train at some point, I'm happy."

Anders's lips tilted up into a thoughtful smile. "I like making you happy."

Not sure how to respond with my heart in my throat, I managed to nod. He squeezed my hand and turned to look down the street. I took the moment to breathe and take him in. He had on that same mustard yellow beanie he'd worn in the picture he'd sent me while he was in New York last month. Dressed in jeans, a soft brown sweater, and a thick wool coat, Anders looked like he was born to live in the city and under the tall shadows of skyscrapers. Fashionable even when unintentional in leather boots and a silver watch with more dials than he probably needed or knew what to do with. It would've been easy to feel insecure in my worn jeans and waffle-weave, long-sleeved shirt. My boots were from a secondhand store down in Bell River, and the hoodie I had on was simple and plain. I wasn't shiny and neat. But as the cab pulled up to the curb, Anders turned to look at me, giving me the full force of his smile like I was the only goddamn person in a city filled with millions of people. He opened the cab door and I got in. Anders slid in behind me, and right as he shut the door, the driver pulled out onto the busy street like his ass was on fire. I'd never feared for my life as much as I did in the ten minutes it had taken us to get to the restaurant. Cab drivers were fucking crazy.

Anders pocketed his wallet as we stepped out of the cab and made a run for the front door of the sushi joint, snow collecting on my hoodie. Inside it was warm, and I ran a hand through my wet hair, the chatter in the room at a lower volume than I'd expected. I didn't see any tables, and for a second, I was confused. A tiny woman in a long, black cotton dress, her hair in a messy bun held up with chopsticks, smiled at us as she rounded the corner.

"Be right with you," she sang and moved down the hall.

She slid open a bamboo door and kneeled down to hand over the plates she had in her hand.

"Are the tables in there?" I asked.

"It's hard to explain. You'll see."

The woman made her way back to us and grabbed a couple of menus. "Just you two?"

"Just us," I said, and she waved the menus at us.

"Right back here. It's our last table. You're lucky."

We followed her down the long hall, passing several bamboo doors along the way before stopping at the last one on the right. Anders took off his shoes and I followed his lead, slipping my boots off next to his. She opened the door for us, and it all made sense once I saw the set up inside. There was a low-lying table, with a large hole underneath for our legs. Two black pillows sat on either side in place of chairs. It was like sitting on the ground but not. I chuckled as Anders tried to fit his long legs into the small space. My feet found his under the table as I sat down, and his smile widened.

"This is fun," I said, and the woman set menus in front of us.

"What can I get you to drink?"

"Water and... did you want a beer?" Anders asked and I shrugged.

"Sure."

"Two waters and Sapporo for the both of us if you have it."

She gave Anders a smile as she nodded. "We do. Look over the menu and I'll be right back."

I stared at the menu while Anders stared at me. I'd never had sushi in my life and had no idea what to order.

"The smoked salmon here is amazing," he said, and I almost choked when I saw the price.

I couldn't afford this place. Or that fucking salmon. Did they have a kid's menu?

"Do they have fries?" I asked, only half kidding.

Anders rubbed his sock-covered toe on the back of my calf. "Unfortunately, they do not."

Exhaling, I glanced up from the menu. "Can I be honest?"

"Of course."

"I'm used to cooking my fish, not wrapping it in a weed."

His Adam's apple bobbed as he laughed, the sound of it lifted some of my nervous energy.

"You've never had sushi?" he asked, his incredulity seeping into his lopsided grin.

"Can't say that I have. Can't say I can afford it either." I lowered my eyes to the table, pretending to look at the menu as my face heated.

"Hey," he said. "Look at me."

I rubbed the back of my neck and lifted my gaze.

"Why didn't you tell me you'd never tried it when I suggested it earlier?"

"You looked excited."

"We can go somewhere else. Grab a burger or—"

"No way. We're here and..."

A waitress we hadn't met opened the door and dropped off our drinks. "Are you ready to order?"

"Can we have a few minutes?" Anders asked.

"Take as much time as you need. My name's Amelia, by the way."

After she slid the door shut, Anders reached across the table and brushed a finger over the top of my hand. "This is a date, right?"

I knew where he was going with this line of reasoning and I didn't like it. I didn't want him to have to pay for me.

"Anders, I'm too damn prideful to let you pay because I can't."

"I'm paying because this is a date, and I picked the place. Tomorrow you can pick a place and pay if you want." He'd shut down my argument before I'd even had a chance to start it.

"Good thing you like McDonald's." We smiled at each other and my chest expanded, light and warm. I set the menu down and cracked open my beer "You order for me. I've got no clue what the hell I'm even looking at."

Amelia showed up again a couple of minutes later and Anders rattled off a bunch of nonsense. We went over the plans for tomorrow while we waited for our order. He'd told me a few details about the office space and said if it didn't snow, we should have everything in before noon.

"Robbie can set it up however he wants when he gets back. All I want to do is get the shit inside and get out."

"And then we can go do touristy crap... and take the train."

He sipped from his can of beer and smiled. "And take the fucking train."

Amelia opened the door with full hands and set a few plates of food onto the table. Anders explained to me what everything was. He showed me how to use chopsticks, laughing when I couldn't figure it out and picked up the roll of fish and rice with my fingers.

"I can't take you anywhere," he joked, and pushed a small bowl of soy sauce in my direction. "Dip it in here. It adds flavor."

More plates arrived at different times, some with plain balls of rice and fish on the side, and others with more intricate-looking creations. I was impressed with one of the rolls he'd ordered. It was colored like a rainbow and tasted fucking divine. The sweet sauce it had drizzled over it was probably my favorite part. Everything was tasty and the beer was good. I had no complaints. At least not until Anders tried to get me to eat octopus.

Not in this fucking lifetime.

"Your loss," he said, popping the nasty fucker onto his tongue.

"I can't believe you put that in your mouth." I cringed. "It's like a giant gummy spider."

"I could make a joke about the things we put in our mouths, most notably this evening, but I'm a gentleman."

"Well, I'm not a gentleman. I'd eat ass any day of the week before I ate a fucking eight-legged sea creature."

Anders coughed and I thought the beer he'd swallowed might come out of his nose. "I can't believe you just said that."

I raised my eyebrows, impervious. "It's true."

"You say whatever you want. I wish I was capable of that sometimes."

"You can always be real with me," I said before stuffing my mouth with the most delicious smoked salmon on Earth.

He chewed his food with a contemplative look on his face, and I braced myself for whatever he was about to ask. I used to think Anders was hard to read. But I'd gotten better at figuring out his tells. "Have you talked to your parents at all?"

"That came out of nowhere."

"Christmas is coming up soon, and I was curious about your plans," he said.

"I won't be going home for Christmas, if that's what you're asking." Thinking about my parents and how our relationship had basically become non-existent killed my good mood.

"You still haven't spoken with them?" he pushed, and as much as I didn't want to talk about them, if this was going to be a real relationship, he had to know about all the parts of my life. Even the shitty ones.

"I honestly can't figure out what to say to them. Do I call and act like it hasn't been forever since they've reached out to me? You'd think if they wanted to know about what I was up to they'd call me."

"As much as I have to work out with my mom, I can't imagine never speaking to her again." He tapped his foot against mine. "You deserve better."

"It was good, before I met Chance. Well, not good. But they tried. My dad kicked me out after I told them I was gay. My mom was the one who'd talked him into letting me come back. I miss him sometimes. Missed the way he was with me before... everything. We used to fish every weekend, and in high school he'd gone to every single one of my soccer games. But now he's a stranger. Momma used to cry a lot at night. I had to get out of that house, I couldn't stand feeling like I'd ruined their lives."

"You're not responsible for their happiness." Anders spoke with a familiar sadness. "It's a hard concept. I'm still working on it myself.

"I think having Chance around was a dose of reality for them." My throat was thick as I shook my head. "Fuck it. Right?" I held up my drink. "Here's to shitty parents."

Anders rapped his beer against mine. "And to the sexy as fuck sons they raised."

"Now that's something I can drink to."

He kept his eyes on mine as we swallowed, my heart tripping a beat or two when he licked his lips.

"I don't think we'll make it to Rockefeller Center before they turn off the Christmas tree lights," he said. "But we could go to Times Square if you're up for it."

I'd rather go back to the hotel and get naked.

"I'm up for whatever."

"If it's snowing as heavy as it was earlier, we'll head back. You'll freeze to death in that hoodie."

"And then you'd have no one to give your magical mouth to." I grinned as his cheeks filled with color. "Are you blushing?"

"Decorum..." he said, in his sexy professor voice. "Defined as keeping one's behavior in good taste, or propriety."

"God, I love it when you talk dirty to me."

"Foreplay with words..." he said, reaching across the table and threading his finger through mine. "I think I could get on board with that."

When it came to Anders, I was pretty sure I'd get on board with anything.

Anders

My fingers wrapped around the cold, yet oddly sticky, handrail, and my anxiety spiked as I breathed in the distinct scent of piss and body odor. Wishing I was sitting in the back of a cab, I glanced at Ethan, remembering why I'd braved the subway in the first place. He was preoccupied, with a goofy grin on his face, watching this fragile older woman knit something resembling a stocking. The train wasn't packed, but there were more people surrounding us than I'd prefer. I wanted to ask him what he thought was funny, but I didn't want to interrupt his people watching. It was my favorite thing he did. Ethan absorbed every detail of life. He watched the world without judgment, and I wanted to peek inside his brain and discover his thoughts. Once we'd left the office, he'd chosen for us to take a stroll through Central Park as his first touristy duty of the day. I couldn't get enough of his big, innocent brown eyes as he immersed himself in the city. Every statue and tree and bridge had been a revelation to him. Ethan's ability to tap into the joy of the moment had me falling for him faster than I'd thought possible. Had me rethinking my priorities, wondering, after having him all to myself this weekend, how I'd handle having to go back to reality once we left New York.

We'd stayed up until well past three in the morning last night, both of us starving for touch, memorizing each other's body. Even if I was exhausted today, every second I'd spent with him had been worth it. I didn't want to get used to having him in my bed at night, but it was happening, and returning to my empty house would be that much harder when we got back to Atlanta. The thought tried to dampen my mood, but in true form, Ethan picked up on it and leaned in for a kiss.

"Why are you frowning?" he whispered against my lips. "I promise we can take a taxi to dinner. No more trains."

I held onto the handrail above his head with one hand, and his hip with the other, noticing the elderly woman staring at us. "It's not the train... though, I don't think I'll be able to get this smell out of my coat."

He smiled and pulled me toward him by the lapels, swaying slightly as the train slowed. "You can afford a new coat. Maybe donate this one to someone who doesn't give a shit beyond the fact it'll keep them warm."

"I like it when you put me in my place."

Despite the woman and her nosy glare, I pressed my lips to his again, leaving the real world behind as I closed my eyes. Making out on the subway wasn't something I'd ever thought I'd do, and in all honesty, I wasn't big on blatant, public displays of affection. But as Ethan's mouth opened for me, I couldn't find it in me to give a fuck about my usual hang-ups. The lights in the tunnel flashed through the windows, and when the train finally came to a complete stop, I pulled away.

"This is our station," I said, and he gazed up at me with lust-drunk eyes.

"Good… I need you naked and in bed as soon as possible." He'd spoken loud enough, the lady almost dropped her knitting needle. "I think she heard that."

"I think we scandalized her," I whispered, and he laughed softly as the doors opened to Franklin Street Station.

We stepped out onto the chilly underground platform hand in hand, and followed the small crowd of people to the stairs leading up to street level. It was a short walk back to the hotel, and with the sun out, the temperature wasn't as unbearable. The magical, white winter wonderland from last night and early this morning had vanished, leaving a river of mucky water and gray slush running along the street and gutters. We navigated a few giant puddles as we crossed the street to the hotel entrance. Inside it was overly warm, and I pulled off my knit cap. Ethan chuckled and reached up to fix what I assumed were wayward stands of my hair.

"Thanks," I said, waiting for the familiarity between us to trigger my need for self-preservation, but all I felt was calm. We stepped into the elevator, and I pressed the button for our floor. "Did you enjoy yourself today?"

He leaned into me and I draped my arm over his shoulder. "I did. It's overwhelming... I bet you could walk around the city every day for a year and still find something new to look at."

"I wouldn't want to be here for a full year."

"I think the city suits you," he said as the elevator doors opened and we stepped out and into the hall.

"It has its qualities, but truthfully, I've never felt lonelier than I do when I'm here... this weekend being the one and only exception."

"Because of me?" he asked.

We stopped in front of the door of the suite and I nodded, tugging on the string of his hoodie. Earlier we'd canceled the reservation for his room, this weekend had turned into much more for both of us. "It's given me a different perspective... a city is only as lonely as the person experiencing it."

"Can I ask you something?"

"Anything," I said as I opened the door to our room, and he followed me inside.

He averted his eyes, his playful energy nowhere to be found as he spoke. "What happens when we go back to Atlanta?"

"Is this about work?" I wasn't sure in what context he wanted me to answer. "I told you I want you to stay until Kris comes back. But I don't want you to think you have to because we're together now."

"We're together? Like a couple?" he asked, his smile dawning slow across his handsome face.

"I should hope so." I walked toward him, closing the distance between us in three long strides. "Unless that's not something you want."

He took a hold of my sweater, right above my belly button and pulled me toward him. Rolling his bottom lip through his teeth, his cheeks turned a stunning shade of pink. "I didn't think I would want a boyfriend again... not for a while. But I do... I don't think I could go back to the way things were and not be able to touch you whenever the hell I feel like it."

"On the train I had the same thought. I was anxious about what you wanted from this. From me. But I don't want to rush you into another commitment while you're getting over someone else."

"I won't hurt you like Wilder did." I held his face in my hands, outlining the shape of his lips with my thumb. "I'm here for this, all the way, Anders, as long as you are too."

"I'm all in."

Our lips met with a soft crash of hope and need, and like this, with him in my arms, I let the certainty of his words take root inside me.

I slid my blazer onto the back of my office chair, and sat down, yawning as I rolled up my shirt sleeves to my elbows. Ethan and I had arrived back from New York late last night after our flight had been delayed, and instead of doing the responsible thing, and letting him head home from the airport, I'd invited him to stay the night with me. As drained as I was, I couldn't say I regretted the decision. Waking up to a blow job was better than coffee, in my opinion.

I opened up my laptop and switched it on, the quiet hum a welcoming sound to my inner workaholic. I clicked on the email icon, ready to dive in when someone knocked softly on my office door.

"Come in."

Nora walked in with two large cups of coffee in her hand. "Welcome back."

She set them down on my desk and I gratefully accepted the caffeine. "You're a lifesaver. I'm half asleep."

"Late night?" she asked, lifting her cup to her lips.

"Flight was delayed, we didn't get in until after midnight."

In need of a pick me up, I gulped down the hot liquid and burnt my tongue in the process.

"Is Ethan coming in today?"

"I gave him the day off," I said, avoiding her inquisitive stare. I figured Ethan would tell her about us, and I didn't mind if he did. But I was private and didn't like talking about my sex life. "I think he had a thing today."

"A thing?"

"Yeah."

"What kind of thing?" she asked, and I stared at my computer screen.

"Why would I know what kind of thing?"

"Oh... I don't know. Maybe because he's your *boyfriend.*"

My eyes snapped up to meet her knowing smile. "News travels fast."

"He texted me and told me to bring you coffee. Said you were exhausted this morning when you left... He said, and I quote, *'Will you bring my grumpy boyfriend some coffee on your way in, he's going to need it.'*"

I laughed and leaned back in my chair. "Sounds about right... I figured he'd tell you."

"Even if he didn't, I would have put two and two together. You both were obviously bananas for each other."

"Bananas?"

"Is that too phallic of a descriptor?" she asked, hiding her smile behind the lid of her cup.

I sighed and rubbed my palm over my face. "I should fire you both."

"Hey, I brought you coffee."

"Yes... thank you for that, did you need anything else?"

She sat down in the chair across from me and set her cup on the desk, looking to settle in for a while.

"How was New York?"

"Good."

"For a literary agent, you really need to work on your understanding of imagery." Nora grinned and fidgeted with the end of her side braid. "Did you do anything fun or stay in the hotel the whole time like horny monkeys?"

"Shut the door on your way out," I said, sitting up and focusing on the screen of my laptop.

"Come on... don't ruin my fun. Mr. I-Never-Break-Any-Rules is dating his secretary. This is good stuff, Anders. And my life is boring. I need good stuff."

"Call Ethan. I don't doubt that he would enjoy your inquisition."

"I want to hear it from you."

"Why?" I asked, trying to curb my annoyance.

I knew she wasn't trying to make me uncomfortable, being nosy was part of her personality.

"Because." Her smile dimmed, a small, serious crease forming between her brows. "It's not like it was some big secret, Anders. You were unhappy. In this tragic, lonely sort of way. And you never talk about your life, and I don't know... I want you to be happy. Despite your outwardly grouchy appearance, I consider you a friend."

"My private life is mine, Nora. I've never been a water cooler gossip, nor will I ever be." I blew out a harsh breath and rubbed my fingers across my forehead. Functioning on less than three hours of sleep, I wasn't adequately prepared for this conversation. "I consider you a friend, too, but that doesn't mean I'm comfortable talking about certain things."

"That's fair..." she said, scooting to the edge of her chair, she picked up her coffee cup and took another sip. "He's a good guy."

"I'm aware of that." When she continued to stare, unsatisfied with my answer, I said, "You're worse than my mother. Christ... Okay, I like him. He's honest, and he makes me feel like less of an asshole."

She practically bounced in her seat. "Aw... that's sweet."

"Out."

She giggled as she stood. "We should all go to dinner after the holidays. I met a girl. We can double."

"Double? What are we? Sixteen?"

"Adults double all the time," she argued.

My cell vibrated against the top of my desk, my mother's name flashing across the screen.

"I need to take this," I said. "We can *not* continue this conversation later."

"You should know, I'm going to ask Ethan to set up a night we can get together."

"If you must."

She waved over her shoulder as she turned to leave.

"Hi, Mom," I said, once I'd answered the call.

"Anders, honey. How was New York?"

"It snowed."

"It did! You love snow. Did you get a chance to see the tree this year?"

"I did." Warmth spread through my chest as I remembered the way Ethan's hand had squeezed mine when we'd finally stood in front of the large Christmas tree at Rockefeller Center. His quiet excitement had radiated through him in the most magnificent smile I'd ever seen. "It was lovely."

"I'm glad to hear it. Listen... I called to make sure you're still coming for Christmas Eve dinner this Thursday."

"Of course, Mom. I wouldn't miss it."

"I'm glad... I know we're working through things, and I was nervous you might not want to come over."

"I'm sorry I made you worry," I said. "That was never my intention."

"I know, dear." She cleared her throat. "Do you think... you'll bring anyone with you this year?" she asked like she always did, and I almost said no like I did every other year before.

"Actually, I was thinking of bringing someone, but I have to ask him first."

I'd never invited anyone to my family Christmas dinner. Not once. And maybe it was too soon to meet the parents. But I wanted Ethan there. He leveled me out, made it easier to breathe.

"Sure," she said after a long pause. "Let me know what he says."

I didn't think my mom would have outright said no, or told me that he couldn't come, but there was this tiny speck of fear that worried she might have. "Thanks... I'll let you know."

"Talk soon, love."

The call disconnected and I set my phone on the desk. The more I thought about Ethan sitting next to me at my parents' table, the more I wanted it to happen. My dad would love him, and I'd imagine they'd talk about fishing all night, and maybe my mom would have to adjust her lens to see the potential of this new view, but Ethan's charm would win her over. Maybe it was fast, but it wasn't like I was proposing. It was Christmas and he was my boyfriend. It made sense to bring him to the dinner. I opened up a new email on my laptop and started to type.

FROM: AndersLowe@LoweLitFic.com

TO: hook_and_reelife@bellinx.mail.com

DATE: Dec 21 9:32 AM

SUBJECT: Christmas Eve

Ethan,

I would call, but I hope you're sleeping, and this is too much for a simple text. What would you say if I wanted to invite you to dinner at my parents' house for Christmas Eve? If it makes you uncomfortable, I'll understand. We've only technically known each other a little over a month, not counting the first time we met, and meeting the parents feels big. But it's Christmas, and I would love to have you there with me. Let me know if you have plans already.

Sincerely,

Anders~

P.S. Nora wants details about this past weekend. Please remember when speaking to her I'm still considered her employer, and as your boyfriend, I'd like our sex life to be ours... meaning between you and me. Speaking of which, this morning was spectacular. I'm hoping to return the favor tonight if you're planning on staying over again.

FROM*:* **hook_and_reelife@bellinx.mail.com**

TO: AndersLowe@LoweLitFic.com

DATE: Dec 21 11:41

SUBJECT: RE: Christmas Eve

Anders,

I tried to call just now, but it went to voicemail. I'm assuming you're in a meeting with that new author. I hope you saw the notes I added to his file. He's kind of obnoxious, if you ask me. He can drink tap water like the rest of us peasants. Bottled water should not cost eight dollars. I'm just saying!

As far as Christmas Eve dinner goes, I would love to come with you. But on one condition, you agree to be my plus one for Jax and Wilder's Christmas party on Friday. It's supposed to be small, but knowing Wilder, he'll invite everyone on his contact list. I shouldn't have to suffer through that alone. With that many people we could probably sneak into my bedroom and no one would be the wiser.

And yes, meeting the parents seems kind of huge. I feel kind of honored that you asked. I know things with your parents are strained right now and having me there could make it worse for you. The fact you want me there means a lot.

Hope you're not too tired.

Sincerely,

Yours~

P.S. So what you're saying is... I shouldn't tell her about that thing you did with your tongue. Got it. What about that freckle you have on your right butt cheek? Is that up for discussion? And this morning was fucking amazing. Aggressive Anders is my favorite. Remember that for tonight.

FROM: AndersLowe@LoweLitFic.com

TO: hook_and_reelife@bellinx.mail.com

DATE: Dec 21 12:34 PM

SUBJECT: RE: Christmas Eve

Ethan,

It seems we're playing phone tag today. Are you in the shower? I'm going to pretend that you are. The visual is too tempting to pass up.

I did get your notes, thank you. Nora was able to procure this gourmet water before he arrived. Why did I want to sign him again? His prose stinks of repurposed Salinger. Sometimes I hate my job. I think the lack of sleep is getting to me. And I miss my assistant. He always makes the day go by faster. And for the record, he means a lot to me too.

I can agree to be your plus one for Wilder's party. But maybe make sure he's okay with it. I don't think it would be weird for him, but you never know. Wilder's idiosyncrasies are hard to keep up with.

Call me later if you have a minute. I'd love to hear your voice.

Sincerely,

Anders~

P.S. Any mention of my tongue, butt cheek, or freckle are off limits. And your preference for aggression is noted. Though, I may want to change things up some tonight. To keep things fresh.

Chapter 23

Ethan

"I thought you left already." Anders's face lit up with a smile as he adjusted the strap of his leather laptop bag, allowing me a moment to admire the way it stretched across his broad chest. "Weren't you supposed to leave an hour ago?"

"Had a few things I needed to finish," I said, avoiding his inquisitive gaze.

He rounded the corner of my desk, and I quickly closed the email I'd been reading. Anders glanced at the screen of my computer. "What were you working on?

"Nothing, responding to a few inquiries." And by inquires, I'd meant confirming my purchase of his Christmas present, which I had to pick up on my way home. But he didn't need to know that.

"Anything I need to worry about?"

I shut down my computer and stood. "Nah, not until after the holidays."

Anders surprised me and crowded into my space. Wrapping his arms around my waist, his eyes fell to my mouth. His bold display of affection heated my cheeks. Today was my first day back to work since we returned from New York, and for the most part, besides our occasional flirty email, our relationship at the office had remained business as usual.

"I've been waiting to do this all day," he said, his voice low and hungry as he leaned in.

He pressed a kiss to my lips, and I gripped the strap of his bag, dragging him closer. This kiss was quiet and subdued, and I melted into the soft way his mouth took mine. As he pulled away, he lifted his hand to my face and swept his thumb across my cheek.

"Have dinner with me," he said, his tone almost vulnerable. "We can go out or stay in. I don't have a preference."

"Aren't you sick of me yet?" I asked, mostly in jest, but there was some truth hiding in there somewhere.

We'd spent every night together since our first in New York. But the last three nights had been spent in his bed, both of us staying up way later than we should have, exploring this new thing between us. We'd shared our bodies but not entirely, and as much as I wanted that, wanted to give myself to him, I liked the way he worshiped me without taking, without pushing for more. Like he had to learn every inch of my skin before he could turn to the next page. This was more than a simple physical attraction. The connection we had, the way he'd changed into a different person when it was only me and him. Like I was the only one in on the secret. He'd opened up to me and laughed and released the tight hold he had on himself. He made me feel special in a way I hadn't ever experienced before.

"Is that your polite way of saying you need some space?" he teased, but I heard the truth in his words too. "I've monopolized a lot of your time. I bet you haven't even unpacked your luggage yet."

"I unpacked and did my laundry, thank you very much." I planted a chaste kiss on his lips. "You can have as much of my time as you want. But if space is something you need, tell me, and I'll do the same. Open communication, Anders, it's important. I don't like sitting around, waiting for the other shoe to drop."

"Honesty is essential," he agreed and stole another quick kiss. Pulling away, his eyes widened, and he stepped back, clearing his throat. "We were... Uh, I was just leaving."

Nora snickered and my cheeks heated. "No explanation needed, Mr. Lowe."

"Mr. Lowe?" I snorted and pocketed my embarrassment, figuring Anders must be mortified. "Don't pretend to be a professional."

"Says the man kissing his boss while on the clock," she quipped. "I think it's cute. Aw, and look, Anders is blushing. I never thought I'd see the day."

Anders stunned me again with his flagrant abuse of the rules as he kissed my cheek; leaning in, he whispered,

"Call me when you get home, and we can discuss dinner plans." He dropped his hold on my waist and headed toward the door. "Have a Merry Christmas, Nora."

She pressed her lips together as he squeezed her shoulder, both of us shocked silent as he walked out the front door.

"He didn't even sass or scold me," she whined, plopping her ass on the corner of my desk.

"I think I broke him."

"Thank God, someone needed to." She grinned. "That blush... honestly, it's obscene how adorable you both are."

"Thanks," I said, grabbing my keys from my desk drawer.

She hopped down, and without warning, attacked me with a giant hug. I stumbled back a few steps, gathering my footing, and relaxed into the embrace. "You okay?"

"Yeah." Her voice was muffled against my chest. "I just get emotional around the holidays."

She pulled back and gave me a wet smile, her eyes glittering. "You sure? I mean, you look like you're about to cry."

"Pfft," she said with a dismissive wave of her hand. "I don't cry."

"Sure, and I'm super attracted to women now."

She shoved me in the chest. "I get unreasonably ooey-gooey the week of Christmas. I know. It's gross."

I chuckled and nodded toward the door. "I'm heading out, want me to walk with you to your car?"

"I've got a few more things I have to wrap up before I leave for the airport."

"When are you coming back from Seattle, after the New Year?"

"It depends." She exhaled, tension stealing her easy smile. "My dad had some tests done last week, and he's waiting for the results. He's sick."

"Shit, Nora. I'm—"

"It's okay. We're hoping it's nothing. He had his yearly checkup and had some abnormal labs. They did a biopsy on his liver." Her voice cracked and I moved to hug her, but she held up her hands to stop me. "I can't or I'll break down. One hug is all you get." She huffed out a laugh. "I'd rather think about happy shit. Like Anders having a heart after all."

"I'm not much for prayers, but I'm here. Alright? Call me any time."

I reached out and tucked a strand of her hair behind her ear and she nodded. "Thanks."

"You're the walking definition of positivity, Nora. The universe sees that, sees you."

"Fuck, don't make me cry." She lifted her chin and gave me a strained smile. "Get out of here."

"I can stay a little while—"

"I'm good. I promise."

"Alright... text me though."

"Just don't say anything to Anders until I know more. I might have to stay in Seattle, help my mom if the test results aren't good news, and I don't want to freak him out unnecessarily before Christmas." She gave in and let me tuck her into a small side hug.

"I won't say a word."

"I'll text you. I swear. As soon as I know more."

Nora gave me one more small hug before I left, with another promise she'd be okay. I was halfway to my car when it occurred to me, this might've been the last time I'd get to see her for a while, or ever if she moved back to Seattle permanently. I wanted to turn around and sit with her until she was ready to leave, but she was stubborn, probably more stubborn than Anders sometimes. There wasn't much I could do if she didn't want the company, all I could do was hope selfishly, and for the sake of her family, I'd see her again after the New Year.

Rosie jumped on me as soon as I shut the front door, and I leaned down and kissed the top of her head, her tail wagging back and forth with an easy happiness I envied.

"Hey, girl, get down, baby." She licked my hand and whimpered, trotting next to me as I made my way into the living room.

Wilder was sprawled out on the couch wrapped up in a plush green blanket reading a book. He lifted his gaze momentarily, giving me the briefest of waves. "I ordered pizza if you're hungry. It should be here in an hour."

"I'm not sure what my plans are yet."

Rosie's tail whacked the side of my leg as she nipped at the tips of my fingers.

Without looking up, he said, "I figured as much."

"You figured what?"

He flipped a page.

"Nothing."

I was two seconds away from asking him if something was wrong when Jax and Jason came in through the back door covered in sweat.

"Hey, man." Jax held out his fist and I knocked our knuckles together. "We're taking a break, but you should shoot hoops with us. I set up the net today."

"He has plans," Wilder drawled, keeping his damn eyes on the book in his lap.

I clenched my jaw and Jax looked between the both of us. "You heading to Anders's place again?"

"We're having dinner. Not sure when yet. But I definitely have time for a game."

Jason gave me a big smile. "Really?"

"Yeah... I need to put my bag away real quick and change out of these clothes. I'll meet y'all out there."

Without another glance at Wilder, I headed for my room. I quickly changed out of my dress clothes, swapping them for a comfortable pair of gym shorts before I sent a text to Anders, letting him know I'd be later than I thought.

> Me: Playing basketball with Jay and Jax. Can I pick something up on my way over? I'm thinking around eight.

> Anders: Send me a text when you're on your way and I'll order something.

> Me: Are you ever going to let me buy you dinner?

I laughed when his response came through.

Anders: Maybe next time.

Me: That's what you said last night... and the night before that.

Anders: If it'll make you happy, pick up dinner.

Me: Thai?

Anders: Sure.

Anders: Are you staying over?

Me: Is that an invitation?

Anders: It's more of a request.

Me: Like a bossy request?

Anders: If I say yes, will that get you into my bed tonight?

Me: I believe it will.

Anders: You're staying over.

Me: I'll pack my toothbrush.

Anders: See you at eight.

My stomach was light as I tossed my phone onto my bed and a pang of guilt shot through me. The conversation I'd had with Nora lingered in the back of my mind and sobered me. Life was transitory. One day you're happy, and the next you're waiting on liver biopsy results. I grabbed a t-shirt from my closet and slipped it on. Not in the mood to deal with Wilder, I ignored him as I walked past the couch and opened the sliding glass door to the back porch. It was unseasonably warm, the perfect temperature for an impromptu game of basketball. I smiled listening to Jax and Jay laughing. Two giants colliding, fighting over a ball. Jax pivoted and turned on his heel, and attempted a shot, only to have it swatted down by his brother.

"Foul," I hollered, not knowing what the fuck I was talking about.

Basketball wasn't my sport.

"It was not," Jay yelled, pouting at me like I'd pissed in his chocolate milk.

Jax's head tipped back, and he barked out a laugh. "You gotta watch out for this one, he plays dirty."

"I can see that," I said and caught the ball as Jay threw it to me with more strength than I'd expected.

"Someone's feeling cocky." I dribbled the ball and swore under my breath when I almost lost my hold on it. Jason couldn't contain his laughter. "I didn't know y'all were so competitive."

"Yeah, you did." Jax smirked. "Now shoot the ball or shut up."

"Didn't your momma teach you it's not nice to tell someone to shut up?" I asked with a grin, and failed miserably at my attempt to maneuver around the hulking mass that was Jaxon Stettler.

He easily stole the ball, running up the short driveway and sank it into the net, looking like the Bell River High all-star champion I remembered from so many years ago.

"Well, fuck."

"No swearing on the court, Ethan. It's bad sportsmanship." Jay's brows dipped with concern. "Okay?"

I held up my hands in surrender. "Got it."

Over the next forty minutes, I had my ass handed to me by the Stettler brothers. Exhausted, I was more than ready to quit when Wilder had appeared to tell us the pizza had arrived. Stinking to high heaven, I stripped off my t-shirt and headed inside. Wilder was busy in the kitchen setting plates on the breakfast bar when I walked in and slid the door shut behind me.

"That smells good," Jax said and kissed his husband on the cheek.

"You're sweaty." He cringed. "And not in the good way."

Jason laughed as he sat on one of the stools. "I don't think there is a good way to be sweaty."

Jax and I shared a look and I had to choke back my laugh.

"You should grab a slice, Ethan. You sure as hell worked for it." Jax's grin was evil. Or it looked evil because he was the reason my muscles were on fire.

He and his brother had run circles around me.

"I've got to get in the shower, but thanks."

Purposely avoiding Wilder, I escaped to the bathroom and took a quick shower. The hot water was exactly what I'd needed to unlock my sore muscles. I was refreshed and energized and had just finished getting dressed when there was a knock on my bedroom door.

"It's Jax."

"Come on in."

He opened the door and gave me one of his shy smiles.

"What's up?" I asked and he sat on the edge of my bed.

"Haven't seen much of you lately."

"Did Wilder send you in here?"

"What?" he asked, but I didn't buy it. "Why would he have?"

I dodged direct eye contact and retrieved a small duffle bag from the top of my closet. "He was being weird earlier." I picked up the change of clothes I'd set out for tomorrow and my toiletries and packed them into the bag. "Anders is my boyfriend, if that's going to be a problem, Wilder needs to talk to me. Directly. No middleman."

He cut his fingers through his hair and shrugged. "There's no problem. At least not like you're thinking."

"Then explain it to me, because I'm confused as hell. Wasn't he the one who said Anders and I would be good together?"

"Yeah... When you were ready for another relationship. I guess he's worried about you hurting Anders."

"What the fuck? Why does he think I'd hurt Anders?" I winced. "I didn't mean to raise my voice... I'm sorry. It's frustrating. Why isn't Wilder in here if he's so concerned?"

"He doesn't think it's his place, because of the relationship he had with Anders." Jax grimaced as he said the word *relationship*. "But he told me Anders has always wanted someone he could have a family with, someone who was a hundred percent committed to him."

"And?"

"Are you ready for that? Ready for another commitment? Y'all are moving kinda fast. I thought you came here to do your own thing." His concern twisted in my stomach, making me second-guess myself. "If this is a rebound thing—"

"It's not. I'm not using Anders to get over Chance." As I spoke, the truth of my statement held me steady. "I like him, Jax. A lot. And I have for a while, but we were both too stubborn to do anything about it. New York sort of forced us both to come to terms with what we wanted."

"And what's that?"

"To be together."

Jax's laugh was soft as he scratched his head. "Wilder told me he saw it coming, and I didn't believe him. I couldn't picture it."

"He did?"

"After you started working there... he said something about sexual tension and some other thing about protesting too much, I don't fucking know. I thought he was crazy. But if you're happy, then I'm glad I was wrong. You're like family to me, to us. We don't want to see you get hurt either."

"He's not upset then?"

"Not about you guys being together. Anders bugs the shit out of me, mostly because Wilder cares about him, and wants him to be happy. I'm a jealous asshole when I want to be." He rubbed the back of his neck, uncomfortable. "He was more worried about you needing someone to get over Chance, he didn't want that to be Anders."

"You can tell him to mind his goddamn business."

"I heard that." Wilder opened the door and Rosie jumped on the bed.

"Get down," Jax grabbed her by the collar but she wouldn't budge.

"It's fine," I said and turned my attention to the drama queen standing in my doorway. "You were sitting out there listening? Why doesn't that surprise me?" I stuffed Anders's present in my bag and zipped it closed. "Did you get all the answers you wanted?"

"I should have said something when you got home, but I didn't want to piss you off."

"Why would it piss me off? You were looking out for your friend. It could've been a simple conversation. I'm pissed because you always have to make a fucking production out of everything."

"Hey now." Jax stood and I instantly regretted my words. "He meant well, Ethan."

I didn't think it wise at this moment to tell Jax he was biased. I'd save it for a Sunday fishing trip.

"In the future, Wilder, if you have something to say to me, say it. Don't pussy foot around it and send your poor husband in to do the dirty work."

"Noted." He bit his lip as Jax draped his arm over his shoulder. "Can I ask you a question?"

"Go ahead."

"Are you going to invite him to the Christmas party?"

I smiled, feeling relieved and much calmer than I had been two minutes ago. When it came to Wilder, I never knew what the hell would come out of his mouth.

"I already did. I wanted to ask you first though. Make sure you were okay with it. We didn't want to parade our relationship in front of you if it was going to be a problem."

"Parade that shit in front of me all you want," he said, and I laughed, my aggravation waning under his outrageous smile. He wanted to protect his friend, like I would have for Jax or Jason. "It's not a problem for me at all. Like you said, I need to mind my own business."

Rosie jumped down from the mattress as Jason walked into the room. "Are you gonna give me a ride home soon? I'm tired."

"Yeah, let me grab my keys." Jax leaned down and kissed Wilder on the temple. "I'll be right back, y'all are good then?"

"Yeah," I said. "We're fine."

Once they left, Wilder gave me a cautious smile.

"I'm sorry I butted in."

"Meh... like Jax said, you meant well. I care about Anders too. I get it." I debated on leaving it there or telling him everything on my mind. Wilder stood next to my bed, fiddling with the end of his sleeve, looking nervous. I chose to put him out of his misery. "It was hard at first. Chance meant a lot to me. And I can't lie, I think about our relationship more than I want to admit. But in New York something changed. I didn't want my past to own me, and I think Anders recognized the same thing in himself. I'm not sure how this will turn out, and I can't promise one of us won't get hurt, but I'm not going to worry so much I forget to enjoy what we have. It's new and I want it. It's the only commitment I'm capable of right now, and he knows that."

Wilder's smile was slow to spread across his face as he leaned against the door jamb. "You guys are totally going to get married."

Groaning, I picked up my bag and slung it over my shoulder. "Cut it out. I don't need that kind of pressure."

"Listen, I'm only saying what the universe already knows is true."

I sighed and rubbed a palm over my face. "I'm late."

He stepped to the side and I pushed past him, pulling my car keys from my pocket. "For the record, you're a nosy asshole. And I would have said it earlier, but I'm pretty sure Jax would've hit me."

He crossed his arms, smug as ever. "Probably. Isn't it sexy when he gets all aggro?"

"I'm not answering that." I opened the front door and a light breeze shuffled through my damp hair. Hiking my bag higher onto my shoulder, I turned and found Wilder staring at me, all traces of his humor gone. "Shit... now what's wrong?"

"Nothing, nothing at all." He shooed his hands at me. "I swear... I just wanted to say I'm sorry," he said, his repentance palpable. "Thanks for putting up with my theatrics all the time. You really are like a brother to me and Jax."

"And you're the sister I never wanted... we've been over this."

"And... I hate you again."

"It happens." Laughing, I stepped outside and turned to catch him smiling too. "It's a sibling thing."

"Drive safe," he said, and I waved over my shoulder. "And don't forget the lube."

And now I hated him again too.

Anders

A faint buzzing picked away at the silence, and I rolled over to grab my phone from the bed, closing out of my seven o' clock alarm. I set my cell back on the bedside table, wishing I'd remembered to turn off the daily wake-up call over the holiday break. Ethan shifted next to me, rustling the sheets as he twisted onto his stomach, and tucked his arm under the pillow. The faint, dusky gray morning made it easy to want to stay in bed, having him next to me made it impossible to get out. His hair was sticking out every which way, his face and jaw covered in a day's worth of stubble. Torn between wanting to wake him and letting him sleep, I trailed my fingers gently over his shoulder and down his back. Goose bumps prickled his skin, the fine hairs at the base of his neck reminded me of the peaches that grew in the small orchard my father had planted in the backyard of my family's home when I was younger. I leaned down, brushing my mouth across his skin, and closed my eyes, comparing the warm, downy feel of him against my lips to the fruit I'd spent an entire summer picking, finding him much more appealing. When I raised my head, I'd expected him to be asleep, but I was met with a drowsy grin.

"Do that again," he said, and of course I wouldn't deny him.

I rubbed his shoulders and he groaned, turning his face into the pillow, granting me better access to his sore muscles. Last night, while we attempted to watch a movie, he'd told me about his failure at basketball with Jax and Jay, and I had a feeling he'd be worse for wear this morning.

"We should take a bath," I suggested.

He turned his head to the side as my fingers kneaded into the muscles of his lower back. "I could be down for a bath. Wait, what time is it?"

"A little after seven."

"No bath, more sleep."

"Are you always this monosyllabic in the morning?" I chuckled when he flipped me off.

"Why are you awake?" he asked and rolled onto his back, the sheet falling below his waist.

"I forgot to turn off my alarm."

My eyes roamed over the length of his body, down past the narrowing of his hips, to the pink head of his hard dick. He raised his arms and rested his hands behind his head, smirking as I was distracted by all the lean cut muscle spread out before me. My pulse thrummed, feeding my desire for him. My cock throbbed as I tried to maintain an indifferent tone, loving how it annoyed him when he didn't get the reaction he'd wanted from me.

"I'm going to brush my teeth." His smirk fell into something between a pout and scowl as I got out of bed. "Take a bath with me, your muscles will thank me later."

"Or..." he said, his fingers wrapping around his cock. "You could come back to bed."

His breath hitched as he circled the crown with his thumb and I almost gave in. Almost. Patience was something I prided myself on, delaying my gratification made getting what I wanted that much better.

"I'll be in the bathroom when you're ready."

I didn't wait to see his reaction and walked naked into the bathroom. I turned on the faucet, running my hand under the water until the temperature was right. I plugged the tub and walked over to the sink to brush my teeth. I was almost finished when Ethan strolled in looking like a fucking gift from God, frustrated and naked. He kept his eyes on me as he pulled his toothbrush and toothpaste from the small bag he'd left on the sink last night, and my eyes snagged on the condom peeking out of the side pocket. I rinsed my mouth with water, deciding not to assume he'd packed that for us. It could've been an old condom. I bristled at the thought. It reminded me that Ethan had, in fact, gotten fucked on this very sink. Which he seemed to not have a problem with anymore. I chose to focus on that as I stepped behind him and kissed his neck.

He bent over to rinse his mouth, rubbing his ass against me as I draped my arms around his waist and dragged the palm of my hand over the dips and valleys of his abs.

"And you say I'm the cock tease?"

He grinned and turned in my arms, bringing us chest to chest. "All's fair in war and all that."

"I forget how eloquent you are before the sun has fully risen."

His fingers ran down my stomach and I shuddered. "Words are overrated, especially when you're naked." Ethan brought his mouth to mine, hovering close as he spoke. "And kissing, much better than words."

I threaded my hands through his hair, our mouths coming together with a desperate clash of mint and heat and moans. I pushed him against the counter, claiming it for us, evicting the images that had overstayed their welcome. I wanted to fuck him here, like this, reclaim it, but I didn't want our first time together to be muddled and mixed with the past. Ethan gripped my shaft and I sucked in a breath, a deep groan parting my lips as he cupped my balls with his other hand. I dug my fingers into his hips as he worked me over, already close to coming. Every muscle in my body strained, ready to fall over the ledge until he stopped abruptly.

Breathless and aching, I thought about finishing myself off, but his smile was too much, too proud. He was edging me, giving me a taste of my own medicine.

"The bathtub is getting pretty full over there," he said, laughing as I swore and pushed past him to turn off the water.

Thankfully, the level hadn't risen too high. "Come on," I said as I stepped in and sank down into hot water. "Get in."

Ethan ambled over to the tub and gave me a skeptical look. "I don't think we can both fit in there."

"Trust me. We will."

I sat back as far as I could, making room for him as he got in. The clawfoot tub wasn't huge, but it was big enough for both of us. He sat down between my legs, his back to my chest, a shocked moan spilling past his lips as the hot water enveloped him. With my arms draped around his waist, I pulled him as close as possible.

"I might fall asleep," he said, resting his head on my shoulder. "You know who takes baths at seven in the morning? Old people, Anders."

Laughing, I rubbed my hands down the slick surface of his chest. "I thought it was old people who hurt themselves playing basketball."

"Ha-ha."

He covered my hand with his and I laced our fingers together. We made no effort to move at first, enjoying the warm water. Eventually our hands wandered, touching as much as the small space allowed. Ethan turned, kneeling between my legs, and I massaged the backs of his thighs, my fingers teasing his crack. I spread his ass cheeks and he gripped my shoulders, a desperate sound falling past his lips as my thumb breached his tight hole. Ethan's mouth opened on a quiet gasp, breathing into my mouth with an uncoordinated kiss.

"I need to taste you," I whispered as he nipped at my lips. "Fuck you with my tongue."

He pulled back, his light brown eyes sparking with desire as he swallowed. "I want more than your tongue."

He grasped my chin in his hand and licked into my mouth. We were sloppy, sloshing water as we moved to stand, breaking apart as we stepped out of the tub, not bothering to drain it. He grabbed two towels off the rack and threw one at me. My cock painfully hard as I haphazardly dried off. Leaving the towel on the counter, I followed him into the bedroom. He dragged the soft cotton over his red, heated skin, torturing me.

"I think you're dry enough," I said, and he dropped the towel to the floor.

The room was chilled, but as our bodies came together again, our shared heat warmed our skin. He left a path of kisses below my clavicle. The ink one of his favorite spots. In turn, I lifted his chin with two fingers, and kissed the freckle on his lower lip, loving how he smiled every time I did it. Our cocks glided together as he pressed his hips into mine, the contact sending a cascade of need to the base of my spine. He'd infiltrated every nerve with his claiming touch, his lips fused to mine, my hands bruising his hips.

"Supplies?" he asked, and I nodded toward the bedside table.

His grin dissolved any remaining doubt I might've had. He wanted this as much as I did. He wanted me.

Ethan crawled into the bed and I grabbed a bottle of lube and a condom from the drawer, setting them on the mattress as I sat next to him. He looked at me with hooded eyes, and without saying anything, I heard him.

I trust you. I want this. He leaned into me and I kissed him, his hands holding my face, his tongue diving into my mouth.

"How do you want me?" he asked.

"On your stomach."

He sat back and turned over, leaving himself prone for me as I straddled his legs. Leaning over his body, I ran my nose across the peach fuzz on his neck, smiling like I'd won a fucking prize when he shivered. I kissed his shoulder blades, shifting my body as I made my way down to the pert, round curve of his back side. I separated his cheeks with the palms of my hands, grazing his hole with the pad of a finger, and when he tried to lift his hips, I smacked his ass.

"Christ," he panted, and I did it again. "Fuck..."

I rubbed a soft hand over the red skin, and he squirmed. "Did I hurt you?"

"God, no, but I might come if you do it again."

I placed a light kiss on his lower back, licking and tasting his skin. He opened his legs, exposing himself as I kissed my way up his inner thigh and flicked my tongue over his hole, lapping the rim and loving the way he whimpered as I pushed inside. Ethan's pleading moans filled the room as I fucked him with my tongue, and he unraveled. He'd given me complete control, and I'd never wanted anything more.

I sucked on one of my fingers, wetting it as much as possible before sliding it inside him.

"Yes," he hissed, rutting against the mattress.

I pulled my finger out and reached for the lube. Knocking his legs farther apart with my knee, I popped open the cap and poured out a generous amount. Starting with one finger, I worked him open. Ethan groaned as I slipped in a second finger, crying out and grasping at the sheets when I found his prostate.

"Yes..." He looked at me over his shoulder, his eyes glazed, his neck and face splotched with pink. I spread my fingers and his forehead fell onto the pillow. "Fuck... please."

"I like it when you beg. Tell me what you want."

I pushed in a third finger and he swore again.

"You..." he sputtered. "Fuck. I want you."

I lifted my hand from between his legs and picked up the condom. Quickly tearing it open, I rolled it on and poured more lube in my hand. Ethan watched over his shoulder as I stroked myself with a slick hand. I settled between his legs and pressed the blunt head of my cock against his ass. My mouth was dry, wishing for his lips as I sank inside of him. Inch by inch his body gave way, the tight heat sucking me in until I was completely immersed in everything that was Ethan. I didn't want to move, I wanted to savor the feel of his body wrapped around me for as long as I could.

"It's too much," I breathed and grasped the cheeks of his ass, opening them wide, watching as I pulled out and pushed back in, his body the perfect fit.

He groaned as I restrained his hips with my hands, holding him down as I fucked into him over and over again. He twisted the sheet in his fist, grunting into the mattress. Sweat beaded on his back, the hair at his temples damp as he pushed against my hold, moaning, fighting for control, and stuttering out breathless commands.

"I need to come, Anders... fuck, touch me."

I released his hips and pulled him up onto his knees. He kept his head down, supporting his weight on his forearms as I reached around and grasped his leaking cock. I jacked him, thrusting my hips in rhythm with my hand, and his entire body trembled. Heat covered me, my climax surfacing faster than I wanted, my heart racing inside my chest, chasing some form of release. Ethan's hips jerked, groaning into the pillow as he erupted into my hand. His body pulsated around my cock, and my eyes slammed shut as I let go. My arm wrapped under his waist and I held him while my hips jerked, and my legs trembled. With heavy breaths, I leaned forward, placing a kiss between his shoulder blades, and as I pulled out, he winced.

"Shit. Are you okay?"

"I'm fine," he said, smiling as he rolled onto his side.

My lips eager for his, I gave him a quick kiss before I headed to the bathroom. "I'll be right back."

I discarded the condom in the trash and cleaned up a little, returning to find Ethan completely passed out. His eyes were closed, his lips barely open with the even breath of sleep. I chuckled and tossed the wet washcloth I'd gotten for him onto the towel he'd left on the floor. I debated staying awake, I had a few gifts I had to wrap before we went to my parents' house tonight, but it wasn't even ten yet, and missing out on post-sex snuggles didn't sound the least bit appealing. I set my alarm, not wanting to sleep the day away, and as quiet as possible, I situated myself on the bed, pulling the sheet and duvet over us.

Ethan's eyes blinked open and he smiled. "Hey."

I kissed the deep wrinkle between his brows. "Go back to sleep."

"Bossy time is over," he said, and my lips twitched as he closed his eyes. "You can't tell me what to do."

"Okay."

Ethan inched his way closer and I pressed my lips to his, lingering until he kissed me back.

"Are you sleeping yet?" I asked.

"Yes, can't you tell?"

He grinned against my mouth.

"Kiss me."

Maybe I was tired, or high from sex, or maybe my literary brain had taken over the logical side, but as his eyes opened, the warm color of his irises engulfed me. Inside his eyes I saw hallways, never ending and imperfect. I wanted to get lost in the maze of him and never find my way out as he drifted his lips, slow and sleepy over my mouth. I cupped the side of his face, the prickling bite of his stubble burning my chin as he deepened the kiss. I could do this all day, forgo sleep and food. The outside world was a figment of my imagination when his taste was on my lips. I'd never felt this complete before. Our differences were the missing puzzle pieces, and they filled the holes in my life effortlessly. Instead of dreading what could go wrong like I had with Wilder every second of our relationship, Ethan made me want to go with the flow, wondering instead of worrying.

"Did *you* fall asleep?" he asked, and I opened my eyes.

"Maybe."

He pushed a strand of hair off my forehead. "You checked out mid-kiss."

"I might've been overthinking."

"That's not possible. You never overanalyze." He smirked. "Word of the day, sarcastic. The talent of mocking an individual with irony and whit."

I laughed into the crook of his neck. "I'm quite sure the dictionary does not call it a talent."

He gently pinched my hip. "What were you thinking about?"

"Nothing in particular."

"Did the sex freak you out?" he asked, and I raised my head.

"No... Why? Did it freak you out?"

His mouth curled into a lopsided smile. "Hell no. If I didn't need time to recover, I'd do it again."

"What's your turnaround time, fifteen maybe twenty minutes?" I asked, biting back my smile.

"You wish."

"We'd never leave this room."

"I could live with that." Running his finger over my hip, he said, "Tell me, for real. What were you thinking about?"

"How well we complement each other. I've never had that before."

"Me either."

I kissed his forehead, stalling, trying to talk myself out of full disclosure, knowing I'd never give him anything less than the honesty he deserved. "I told myself to take it slow, but I'm falling for you. And I don't want to run you off."

"After yesterday, we both know my cardio is for shit." He smiled. "I'm not running anywhere. I think I fell for you when you smacked my ass."

"Are you ever serious?" I teased.

"I'm falling for you," he said, leaning up onto one elbow. Looking down, he traced the line of my lips with his thumb. "It would be difficult not to. You're everything I want, Anders. But I moved to Atlanta because I needed to focus on myself, figure out my life."

"I don't want to stop you from doing that."

"I know." He lowered his head to the pillow, bringing us nose to nose. "But part of me feels like you're wasting your time on me. I'm a starving college student, for hell's sake."

"You're not a waste of time, Ethan. You *should* come first for once, it's not a hardship to care about you. It's a privilege."

"God, you say the best shit sometimes."

He rested his forehead to mine and closed his eyes.

"*The best shit*," I smiled. "You have a way with words, I happen to know a few good literary agents if you're interested in a writing career."

"I'm sleeping."

"Oh, I apologize," I whispered, drawing circles on the back of his neck with my fingers, the soft hairs a new favorite. "Ethan?"

"Hmm?"

"Happy Christmas Eve."

Ethan

Holy. Shit.

Anders cut the engine as I stared at the huge ass house through the windshield. It was like a cottage straight out of *Hansel and Gretel* but multiplied by ten. My mouth hung open, gaping like a fresh caught fish. The shutters were a muted shade of blue, the paint looking brand new against the aged stone, and the yard meticulous, with every shrub shaped and pruned to perfection.

"Breathe." Anders smiled at me like I'd lost my mind. "It's just a house."

"I'm sitting in a BMW, in front of a house that could fit five of mine inside of it, with a guy who has on a watch that probably costs as much as my shitty Toyota... brand new. I'm a little overwhelmed."

"First of all, my watch was a gift from my dad, and I seriously doubt it costs as much as a car. Second—"

"A dad who lives in this house could afford a car-watch."

He laughed and reached across the console to squeeze my knee. "Second... My mom was raised on a dairy farm, and even though my dad comes from old money, he's one of the most down-to-Earth people I know."

"I grew up in a double-wide trailer, with moss growing on the fucking shingles, Anders." My face heated with embarrassment. "Down to Earth or not, they're your parents and they'll probably think I'm some backwoods redneck who's nowhere good enough for their son."

"Did you miss the part where I said my mom grew up on a dairy farm? My grandparents wanted my dad to marry money, and he said fuck that and married my mom. Love is more important to them than money."

"And your mom knows you're bringing a guy?"

His chuckle untied the knots in my chest and stomach. "Yes..." Anders raised his hand and grazed his knuckles over my jaw and under my chin. "You don't have to be nervous, even though it's cute as hell."

"Shit... alright. Let's do it."

For once, I was grateful for Wilder and his fashion advice. I'd packed my only pair of jeans without holes and my black sweater for tonight. I couldn't fucking imagine showing up here in a t-shirt and torn denim. I shut the door and met Anders in front of the car. Inhaling a deep breath, I took his offered hand, feeling more centered, the heat of his skin a comfort for my anxiety. When I'd met

Chance's parents, we'd been together a few months. They lived in Bell River, in a house like mine, I'd had no reason to be nervous. All their money had gone to their daughter and her disability. Sometimes I missed them and their easy acceptance of sexuality, more like parents to me than my own. As we stepped onto the porch of Anders's childhood home, I felt anything but welcome. People with this much money had to be out of touch with reality, right? The front door opened before we had a chance to ring the bell, and a man, who I assumed was Anders's dad, greeted us with a toothy grin. "Merry Christmas," he boomed in a warm southern accent. "Come on in. I hope you're hungry because your mother cooked enough food to feed the entire neighborhood."

"And you're surprised?" Anders asked as we stepped inside, and his dad laughed, clapping his son on the shoulder. "At least this year she has an extra mouth to feed."

His dad's light eyes found mine, smiling enough the skin at the corners crinkled. His hair was more salt than pepper, and I liked the way his thick mustache twitched as he smiled. "You must be Ethan."

He held out his meaty hand and I shook it. He wore a simple sweater and slacks, his belly hanging a touch over his belt. I had to admit, he looked less like an astute lawyer than I'd thought he would.

Feeling less intimidated, I ignored my surroundings and focused on his kind eyes. "I am. Thanks for having me over tonight, Mr. Lowe."

He snorted and gave Anders a private smirk. "Call me Harlan. Mr. Lowe is my father and he's a bit of a prick, if you ask me."

I coughed to cover my surprised laugh, and Anders squeezed my hand. "You'll have to excuse my father. He forgets his manners sometimes."

"Manners are overrated," I said, and his dad's smile spread wide.

"I like him already."

"Is Mom in the kitchen?" Anders asked and his dad nodded.

"She's been in there all day." He pointed a thumb over his shoulder. "We should see if she'll actually let us help her this year."

"Every year she insists on making dinner on her own," Anders explained. "She's stubborn."

"Like you?" I asked.

"Worse." He grinned when I swallowed. "You'll be fine."

Christmas music played from a radio somewhere as we walked through the house. The place was incredible, every room decorated to match the cottage style of the home. It was warm and didn't scream "*rich pretentious assholes live here.*" The Christmas tree reached high into the vaulted ceiling, but like everything else, the decorations weren't showy.

"Hanging in there?" Anders asked in a low voice. "You don't seem as nervous."

"I'm good." I gave him a genuine smile, and as we walked into the kitchen, he leaned down to press a soft and short kiss to my lips.

My cheeks were on fire as he pulled away, his mom and dad stared at us with mixed emotions. His dad's beaming smile was a good sign, while his mom's was less enthusiastic, it was polite, nonetheless. She was a small woman with elegant-looking limbs, her salt and pepper hair shining under the kitchen lights. Dressed in expensive-looking black pants and a dark green sweater, she looked nothing like a dairy farmer to me.

Wiping her hand on a towel, she apologized, "I'm sorry, I promise it doesn't always look like this."

"Mom, you don't have to apologize, trust me, Ethan doesn't care." He glanced at me and smiled. "He's nervous too."

I bit the side of my cheek and tightened my grip on his hand. "Thanks."

To my surprise, his mom laughed. "Anders, you're embarrassing the poor man."

Grinning, he was totally at ease. "He has thick skin."

Anders stood tall, our fingers entwined. He was proud of me. Proud of us. I took courage in that.

"Meeting the parents is always nerve wracking," I admitted.

"Don't be nervous," she said as she walked toward us. She gave her son a hug first, and I was glad he hadn't let go of my hand when she hugged me too. "We're happy to have you here."

"Thanks, I'm happy to be here."

The next twenty minutes went smoother than I'd hoped. His mom had refused help as predicted, shooing us into the living room like we were little kids. Anders's dad had given me the "five-cent tour" of the house while my boyfriend tagged along, not letting go of my hand once. I'd started to think he needed the anchor as much as I had. I'd listened to his dad talk about his son's achievements like any proud father would, sprinkling in some embarrassing stories here and there.

"Remember that time you fell out of that peach tree and broke your arm. I thought your mother was going to rip me a new one." His dad sat down on the couch with a long exhale. Anders let go of my hand and walked over to the small bar cart in the corner, while I sat in one of the two chairs by the fireplace. "I planted a few peach trees years ago. Anders used to call it an orchard and insisted on helping me pick the fruit every summer. Even back then you pushed for what you wanted."

"Isn't that what you taught me to do?" Anders asked, handing his father a drink.

"You're damn right I did," he said, smiling, and took a generous sip from his glass.

"Did you want something to drink?" Anders asked me.

"No thanks, I'm good for now." The last thing I needed to do was get a buzz and say something stupid, or worse, drop the f-bomb.

"Have a drink." His dad persisted, lifting his glass. "It's Christmas."

Anders smiled down at me. "Bourbon?"

"Sure," I said not wanting to be rude. "Why not."

Anders had handed me a drink when his mother announced dinner was ready.

"I'll give you a tip," his dad said as we stood. "Take a small portion of everything, that way your plate will look full and my wife won't nag you to take more."

"Good to know," I said as Anders laced his fingers through mine again.

A ham big enough to feed twelve people sat in the middle of the dining room table, surrounded by an excessive amount of side dishes. I was sure they'd have leftovers for a month if the food would even keep that long.

"Have a seat before everything gets cold," his mom insisted and pulled out her chair.

I sat next to Anders and he rested his hand on my knee under the table. His mom gave me a small smile as she placed her napkin in her lap.

"Help yourselves," she said and picked up her plate.

"Sandra, we should probably say grace."

"Since when do we say grace?" Anders laughed as he scooped mashed potatoes onto his dish.

His dad glanced at me and then back at his son.

"Sir, I haven't been inside a church in years," I admitted with a smile. "Don't say grace on my account."

"Well... alright, then. Dig in."

I wasn't sure where to start, but I took Mr. Lowe's advice and got a little of everything. Anders's mom seemed to appreciate it.

"I tend to overdo it on the holidays," she said. "I grew up in a house with more mouths than there was food sometimes."

"I can relate to that." I'd welcomed her honesty. "We didn't have a big family. Just me and my mom and dad.

But times were hard. My momma didn't work, and my dad had a tough time finding jobs for the most part. He and my mom got married right out of high school and had me a year later. College wasn't in the cards for either of them."

"Did you go to school?" she asked right as I took a bite of ham.

I chewed as fast as I could, forgetting to taste as I swallowed. "No, ma'am, not yet. I start at Georgia State in January."

"What do you plan on studying?"

"He's going to be a nurse," Anders answered for me, a proud smile reaching across his lips. "He wants to work with kids."

"Nursing is a fine profession," she said, and from what I could tell, it sounded like she meant it. "Taking care of others... especially kids. I think that's wonderful."

"It took me longer than it should have to figure out what I wanted to do, but better late than never."

"Your parents must be pleased," she said.

My stomach took a nosedive.

"I'd like to think they would be, but we haven't spoken in a while."

His father's perpetual grin faded, his brows dipping with concern. "I'm sorry to hear that."

"May I ask why?"

"Mom." Anders shot a glare in her direction and she paled. "You don't have to answer that, Ethan."

"It's okay." I wanted her to hear it, hear how bad it could be. Maybe then she'd understand how difficult it was for her son that she didn't fully accept his sexuality. "My parents struggled when I came out to them. Kicked me out. We tried to work through it, but when I moved to Denver with my ex, our relationship kind of disintegrated."

Her fork hovered over her green beans, her eyes shining with unshed tears. "They shut out their only son?"

I shrugged, my throat thick as I spoke. "It's like that for a lot of us. Anders is lucky he has parents who accept him for who he truly is."

I didn't miss the small hitch of her breath, or how her worried gaze darted to her son. A purposeful silence settled over the room, and I internally chastised myself for my passive-aggressive remark.

"If you'll excuse me." Anders pushed out of his chair, and I panicked as he stood.

"Hey, I—"

"It's okay." He leaned down to kiss my cheek. "I just need a glass of water."

His mother's eyes tracked him as he left the room.

"Go talk to your son," his dad sighed. "You know you want to."

She stood, setting her napkin on the table, and walked out of the room without another word.

"Ethan..." Harlan gave me a tired smile. "Anders tells me you like to fish."

"Yes, sir."

"Enough with that sir business," he said, his grin reappearing on his face, and shoveled a forkful of sweet potato casserole into his mouth.

We talked about the best fishing holes near Atlanta, his dad asking me awkward questions about what bait and lures I preferred while we waited for Anders and his mom to return. I couldn't eat, my stomach too upset. I hadn't meant to start family drama on Christmas Eve, but I'd opened my big mouth. It pissed me off that she was cavalier about her son's sexuality. She was okay with it as long as he didn't choose a man in the end, or at least that's how I understood it from Anders's point of view.

There was a lull in the conversation, and I jumped at the opportunity. "I'll be right back. I have to use the restroom."

"Of course," he said. "Go ahead."

I found my way to the guest bathroom next to the garage door. The kitchen was empty as I passed by, but I could hear hushed voices coming from the den next to the living room. I wasn't sure what to do. It wasn't my business to interfere, but I wanted to be a support for Anders if he needed it. I lingered in the doorway of the bathroom, deciding I'd rather be a nosy asshole and support my boyfriend than hide in the bathroom when he might need me.

Resolved, I marched through the living room. The door to the den was slightly open, looking in I saw Anders with his arms crossed over his chest, his cheeks wet.

I hesitated, unsure of what to do when I heard his mother's voice. "You care about him. Anders, I can see that."

"But do you accept it?" he asked. "I know the picture in your head and he's not it."

"He can be."

"Mom—"

"I love you, Anders. I don't care if you marry a man or a woman. If you have kids or a dog. It breaks my heart Ethan doesn't talk to his parents. I don't want that to happen to us. I refuse to let that happen to us."

"I don't want you to tolerate my sexuality because you fear losing me. I want you to accept me as I am. No conditions."

"I do." She wrapped her arms around him, pulling him into a hug.

He stood with his arms at side, but slowly gave in and rested his chin on the top of her head as he hugged her back. Guilt stormed through me and I took a step backward.

I shouldn't be here. I should have known Anders would fight for himself.

"I'm proud of you, of everything you are." She inhaled a shaky breath. "That picture in my head doesn't matter. Not anymore."

"Why?" he asked and moved out of the embrace. "Why is it so easy for you to see an alternative now?"

She raised her hand to his cheek, and I told myself to leave. But she said my name and I froze.

"Ethan... You're different with him. I've never seen you like this." She wiped a tear off his cheek and lowered her hand. "You have a big heart... and you've kept it locked up. But not with him. It's easy to see how much you like him. You haven't let go of his hand once unless it was necessary." His laugh was quiet, and she smiled. "You're happy... and that's all I want for you. I've said it before, I know. But I understand now. I understand your happiness has to be on your terms not mine."

Intruding longer than I thought was right, I turned around as Anders pulled his mom in for another hug. I couldn't clear the image of his wet lashes and cheeks from my head as I walked back to the bathroom and shut the door. He was beautiful even when he was breaking. His mom was right. Anders's heart was big, and he wore it on his sleeve for those he deemed worthy. And he'd chosen me.

You're not a waste of time, Ethan.

I stared at myself in the mirror.

You should come first for once, it's not a hardship to care about you.

Feeling empowered by everything that had happened tonight, I pulled my phone out of my back pocket and opened up my text messages. I scrolled down all the way to the bottom and opened up the thread I'd avoided long enough.

Me: Merry Christmas, Mom and Dad.

"Ethan?" Startled, I put my phone away and opened the door. Anders smiled, but it didn't hide the red rings around his eyes. "My dad was worried you drowned. You've been in here so long. Are you feeling sick?"

"I might've been hiding. Family drama gives me hives."

He wrapped me up and I leaned into his chest. "What you said at the table... It hit close to home and I shouldn't have reacted. But I'm glad I did. I think my mom and I are going to be okay."

"Yeah?"

He nodded and kissed my forehead. "Yeah, thanks to you. She said seeing me with you opened her eyes."

"I'm glad I could help but, listen I... um... I have a confession."

"Hopefully, it's nothing too severe. I've reached my drama limit for one night."

"I went to find you and might've heard a few things you and your mom talked about. I'm sorry I eavesdropped, but in my defense, I wanted to make sure you were alright."

"What would you have done if I wasn't?" he asked with the sexy smile I couldn't get enough of.

"I'm not sure." I laughed. "Probably would have barged in and made a fool out of myself."

"How chivalrous of you."

I shoved my palm into his chest, but he captured it with his hand and our lips collided. His mouth was warm, inviting me in and his tongue slid sweetly past my lips.

"We should get back out there," he said, his breath fanning over my cheek. "My mom wants to apologize, and by apologize, I mean force feed you as much pie as humanly possible."

"What kind of pie?"

"Peach."

"Wouldn't you know that's my favorite kind of pie."

"Mine too," he said, his fingers tickling the back of my neck, as he took one more claiming kiss.

Anders

The kitchen had become my sanctuary over the last forty minutes. I preferred to quietly watch from the side lines as Wilder's living room turned into a makeshift dance floor. The Christmas party had started out small, but as the night wore on more people showed up, most of whom I had no acquaintance. Uncomfortable, I sipped from my watered-down gin and tonic, wondering where Ethan had disappeared to. I poured my drink in the sink, resolved to go find him and convince him to bow out a little earlier than we'd planned. From the edge of the room, I spotted my boyfriend by the back door talking with June. Relieved, I stared at him for a few moments, loving the smile stretched across his face, and how he held his stomach when he laughed.

Last night at my parents' house, having him there with me, having my mom finally see how happy I was, he'd taken the weight of the world off my shoulders. My life wasn't hard, but it had always been lonelier than not. And with Ethan, I could easily see the days and months ahead, even the mundane minutes. Breakfast with him before work. Lunch at Sal's. Sleeping in on Saturdays. Showers and baths. Once he started school, I wanted him to study on my couch while I read, tell me everything about what he learned that day. I wanted him to have Sunday brunch at my parents', and maybe take Jay fishing with my dad. All the things I'd never had with anyone else, I wanted to share with him. Even if what we had was new, he felt right. He was the story I chased every time I sat down and put pen to paper. He was my *The End.*

"Wow." Wilder grinned up at me, his eyes rimmed in a deep violet liner. June's daughter wrapped up in his arms, blowing spit bubbles. "If I didn't know you better, I'd think you'd already fallen in love with him."

"I don't know what you're talking about." I glanced back at Ethan and he smiled at me.

For some, love was tabulated in standards and measures of time. To me love was knowledge. And every day I'd spent with Ethan I'd become more aware. Aware of his details. His past, his present, his skin, his smile, his heart, his mind. I wanted to be well versed in all of him.

"Don't be cute. It's obvious how much you like him."

"The baby's getting drool on your sleeve." I warned and held back a laugh when he squeaked, amused by the horrified look on his face.

Wilder shifted the pudgy little human from one arm to the other. "Shit, that's gross."

"Are you supposed to swear in front of your best friend's baby?"

"Fuck... No." He slammed his eyes shut. "Goddammit. I'm going to be a terrible dad."

I reached down and plucked the baby from his arms. "Going to be?"

He wiped the drool off on his jeans and grabbed a napkin from the breakfast bar to wipe Charlotte's mouth. He flicked a quick glance in my direction before averting his eyes. "Yeah, Jax and I have been talking about adoption."

"That's amazing news," I said, my smile widening as Charlotte's fragile finger curled around mine.

"I'm selfish, Anders, you know this. I'm high maintenance with a capital M. I have no idea what the hell I was thinking. I can't be a parent." He held up his arm, pointing at the wet spot the baby had left behind. "This is my future. This and no sleep, shitty diapers and puke that smells like rotten milk. I'm going to be the worst dad that ever was."

"You are selfish. And yes, as your agent I can attest to your needy nature, but that being said, I don't think you'll be the worst dad ever."

Wilder set his hand on his hip and rolled his eyes. "That's supposed to give me confidence to become a parent? Anders... Come on... where's your winning speech? Your can-do attitude?"

Chuckling, I tucked Charlotte against my chest. "I think any parent has fears that they'll screw up. And it's an adjustment, putting yourself second to another person. You'll adapt, especially when it's your own baby. You'll love the hell out of him or her or them. And unlike your parents, you'll never abandon your kid. I was adopted by two terrific people. And they've messed up a ton, trust me, but I was loved. I *am* loved."

Wilder's eyes misted with unshed tears as he stared at the baby in my arms. "It's what I... we want. We want to give a child a home. If I have the chance to give a child a loving home, one like I never had, that's all that matters." His lips twitched. "Even if it means I have to live in sweats for God knows how long and gag over shit... I want to raise a child. I want to give them a good life."

"I have no doubt you and your husband will do everything you can for your child."

"You look good holding a baby," Ethan said, and as I turned to face him, he kissed me. "Doesn't he look good?"

"Not as good as you," I corrected, handing him Charlotte.

She kicked her feet and giggled, more spit bubbles exploding from her pink lips. Ethan kissed her forehead and whispered to her. Mostly gibberish, but the smile on his face was gorgeous.

"You're a natural."

He laughed at my praise.

"Hardly, this little princess is over here all the time. I've had practice."

"You can be my nanny anytime you want." Wilder held out his arms. "I'm going to need the help."

Ethan passed the baby over with one more kiss to her forehead. "I don't know about being a nanny, but I'll babysit for you and Jax whenever."

"I better get this little girl back to her momma." Wilder nodded toward June. "It's getting a little crazy in here."

All three of us looked at the mass of bodies writhing together in the middle of the room.

"Who the hell are all these people?" Ethan asked.

"One of Jax's crew members told one of his buddies there was a party tonight, and word traveled fast and far apparently."

"They look young... or maybe I'm old?" I asked.

"Both." Wilder laughed. "A lot of the guys on his crew are young. I don't think Jax expected all these people. He's not very happy."

"Where's he hiding?" Ethan looked around the room.

"He's outside. I might join him after I drop off this cute little bag of drool."

"I think we're going to take off." Ethan threaded his fingers through mine. "Good luck with all of this. I'll help clean up tomorrow if you need it."

"Thanks."

We said our goodbyes and snaked our way through the small crowd to the front door. Once we were outside, and the noise of the party was behind us, I exhaled a sigh of relief. "Let's never do that again."

Ethan lifted my hand to his lips and kissed my knuckles. "Deal."

We were on the road, halfway to my place when Ethan let go of my hand for the first time. He pulled his phone from his pocket and slid his thumb over the screen. He was silent as he read, his eyes glued to the phone he gripped in his hand. He'd gone completely pale.

"Everything okay?" I asked.

He didn't answer, only turned to stare out the window as a car passed. The headlights illuminated his face and the lone tear running down his cheek.

"Ethan? Do I need to pull over?"

"No, just take me home," he said, his voice thick.

"Alright." Panic sent a jolt to my heart as I thought about who could have texted him. Selfishly, I hoped it wasn't Chance. "I'll turn around when there's a break in the median."

"What? No..." He swallowed and rested his head against the seat. "I mean, take me to your place."

"Okay."

As we drove, the tension rolled off of him, crashing against every surface, cracking at my chest.

"It was my dad." The words were hoarse, scratching past his lips as he spoke. "He replied to my text from last night." Ethan rubbed a hand over the top of his head. "Said I had a lot of nerve texting them. Said I chose to live in sin." His chest moved with fast, angry breaths. "Said the day I left was the day I was no longer welcome in their lives."

"Ethan..." I started to pull over and he shook his head.

"Drive, Anders... just fucking drive, alright?"

I reached across the console and he let me take his hand. "Okay... We're almost home."

My keys clattered against the kitchen counter as I set them down. The warm, white light of the small Christmas tree I'd set up before I'd left for New York seemed too bright as Ethan sank down onto one of the bar stools.

"Want a drink?" I asked, grabbing a glass from the cabinet, and setting it on the counter.

"No." His eyes were vacant pools of amber. "What am I supposed to say to them?"

"Nothing. They don't deserve your words."

"When I was in Bell River with Chance, things weren't right with my parents, I knew that... I did. And when I left for Denver, I knew they didn't want me to. But I didn't know leaving was an answer to some unspoken fucking ultimatum. I've been out for years, Anders. And I thought... Shit. I don't know what I thought."

I rounded the counter and stood behind him. He leaned back and I held him against my chest. "You thought they'd work through it like good parents should."

"I thought at least my mom would be there for me."

He turned on the stool and faced me.

"Would you have left if you knew it would end your relationship with them permanently?" I asked, wiping my thumb over his wet cheek.

"Yes. I can't change who I am. Not for them. Not for anyone."

"I think that's what you should say to them. Even though I don't think they should get any explanation at all. Fuck them, Ethan. Fuck anyone who can't love you without conditions."

Ethan stood and I pulled him into my arms. He burrowed his face into my neck and his hands gripped my sides.

"Thank you," he whispered, his hot breath warming my skin. He lifted his head, his glassy eyes searching my face. "I think the part I hate the most, is even though I hadn't spoken to them, I had hope. I feel so fucking stupid."

Tears fell over his lashes and I caught them with my thumbs as I held his face in my hands. "You're not stupid." I ghosted a gentle kiss across the bow of his lip. "You're not stupid," I repeated the words and watched as they sank in. "They fucked up, not you. Blood is not always binding, Ethan. The people you have in your life who love you, who you surround yourself with, Jax and Wilder, June and Gwen, Nora... me, that's your family. Your family will grow and those people in Bell River, they'll be miserable, because they lost the one good thing they ever had in their lives."

"You're right... and I know that. But it hurts, I guess, that they'd actually throw me away." He turned and kissed the palm of my hand. "I've come this far without them, right? I can keep going."

"You have and you will." I raised his chin. "Don't give them another second, Ethan. Not one more second."

He exhaled and took a step back, reaching into his pocket. At first, I thought he would text them, but instead he pressed his thumb on the screen and said, "Delete." There was a mix of pain and confidence and relief in his gaze when he looked up at me again. "Not one more second." He set his phone on the counter and reached for my hand. "Did I ruin Christmas?"

"No..." I looked at my watch. "And besides, there's only forty minutes left."

His smile almost reached his eyes. "I better hurry up and give you your present then."

"If it's sex, I don't want to hurry. I like taking my time with you."

His chuckle broke through the last vestiges of his dark mood. "It's better than sex."

"That's a tall order."

He tugged on my hand, leading me toward my bedroom. "Trust me."

I watched him for a second, making sure he was fully distracted as he dug through his bag before using the opportunity to get his present from my dresser drawer. I set the small box on the mattress and sat down. Ethan pulled out a plastic bag from his duffle and grinned. His cheeks were dry, and his lashes were only slightly damp. I hated his parents more fervently in that moment than I had merely two minutes ago. Ethan's heart was pure, and open, and I was baffled how anyone could walk away from him. I'd only known him a short while and all I wanted to do was find ways to keep him around for as long as possible.

"I didn't get a chance to wrap it," he said as he stood in front of me. "Close your eyes."

I laughed and stared up at him. "What? Why?"

He narrowed his eyes. "Don't ruin this by being stubborn."

I held up my hands in surrender and closed my eyes.

"I'm going to put it in your lap, but count to three before you open your eyes," he said, and I could hear the smile on his lips.

A light weight landed on my thighs and I counted. "One... two... three."

I opened my eyes and found a copy of *The Secret History* sitting in my lap.

"Turn to the first page."

I did as he asked, and my breath caught in my throat. "Ethan... how—"

"I might've used some work resources. I hope that's okay."

I ran my fingers over the autograph. "She signed her name."

"I know."

"This is too much."

He smiled down at me as he shook his head. "It wasn't. And honestly, I was surprised you didn't already have a signed copy. But then I remembered you're you and you never do anything for yourself. Not really."

I gripped his shirt and pulled him to my lips for a kiss. He tasted like tears and happiness.

"Thank you. I'll cherish this forever."

Ethan sat next to me on the bed, his smile more mischievous than ever. "I got you one more thing."

"Oh?"

He reached into the plastic bag and pulled out a gift certificate to McDonald's.

I took the small plastic card from his hand unable to contain my laughter. "I think I like this better than the book."

"I should think so. That book is incredibly dull."

"What? You never finished it," I accused.

"Exactly, because I was bored as fuck."

"You wound me... I might actually return your present now."

"No way," he said, and practically climbed across me to grab the small box off the mattress. His playfulness was probably my favorite thing about him, it reminded me to not take myself so seriously all the time. "Can I open it?"

"I don't know, can you?"

"Grammar is irrelevant on Christmas."

"Grammar is never irrelevant."

He ignored me and opened the box, his smile cheesy as hell as he stared at the hideous tie inside.

"It's covered in fishhooks," he said.

"And lures."

Ethan pulled the tie out of the box and my pulse tripped. "Wait, what's this?"

He set the tie in his lap and removed the envelope hidden underneath it. He looked at me, then back at the envelope.

"Open it."

Ethan carefully lifted the sealed edge and pulled out the three tickets inside, his eyes as wide as saucers. "Holy shit... Anders, this is..."

"I figured we could take Jay."

He set the tickets down and swallowed. "He'll love this so much..." His voice cracked. "*I* love this."

"Yeah?"

"Fuck yeah. I've always wanted to go deep sea fishing. And Jay will lose his mind when he finds out. I don't even want to know how much this three-day expedition cost you. It's way too much."

"I can afford it."

He placed the tickets in the box and set it aside, his eyes falling to my mouth. "I want to argue about this some more... but I also want you to fuck me."

"Hmm. I'm not sure," I whispered, gliding my fingers over the stubble on his chin. "I think I can be persuaded though."

Ethan had already started to unbutton his shirt. "Right now, I'd do just about anything you asked. It's been a long night and I want it to end with us. I want to remember this moment... and nothing else."

He stripped off his shirt and nipped at my lips as I reached for the tie in his lap.

"I want you to ride me, wearing only this," I said and draped it around his neck.

"Done," he said, tying it around his neck like he would've if he had on a shirt. "Any other requests?"

His cheeks flushed as I stared at him and palmed his cock through his jeans. "I think that's all for now."

"Then let's get started."

Ethan

Running a half-hour behind, it was already fifteen minutes past noon by the time I made it to the office. Feeling frazzled and exhausted had become my new norm. I couldn't believe my first week of school was already over. I set my backpack under my desk and powered up my computer, a wave of bittersweet sadness washing over me. This was my last day at Lowe Literary. After the New Year, Kris had called Anders to tell him she'd decided to come back a week earlier than previously planned. And as much as I didn't think I was capable of juggling a full-time course load and this job, the thought of leaving made my stomach sink. It was nice being able to go to lunch with my boyfriend three days out of the week. After New York, I'd essentially lived at Anders's house, knowing once school started, I'd have to snap back to reality. Having a job that placed me three doors down from my man was a luxury I wasn't quite ready to give up. Instead, I'd have to settle for the Cup and Quill. I'd applied after we'd received the news from Kris, and they'd hired me the same day with an agreement I'd finish up my last week at Lowe. I'd like to think my charm had won them over, but I had a sneaking suspicion they'd hired me because Wilder was with me. He was the patron saint of the fucking coffee shop.

I sat up as the computer screen came to life, the familiar programs popping up one by one. I couldn't shake this shitty feeling, and I would've walked my sappy ass back to Anders's office to make myself feel better, but I remembered he'd had an appointment at noon. My stomach growled as I opened my emails, and I hoped the appointment wouldn't last much longer. Sad and hangry was not a good combination. I opened up a blank email and started typing, even if I wasn't sure he'd see my message until after his meeting was over.

FROM: EthanCalloway@LoweLitFic.com

TO: AndersLowe@LoweLitFic.com

DATE: Jan 8 12:25 PM

SUBJECT: FEED ME

Anders,

Food. Soon.

I'll make it worth your while...

Word of the day: Innuendo - an allusive or suggestive remark.

It's my last day, I think an office BJ is a nice way to send me off, don't you think?

Yours~

P.S. And so there's no confusion, I'll be on my knees for you, sir.

I pressed send, my cheeks aching as I grinned. If only I could see his expression when he read it, hopefully, while still in his meeting. Fuck, I'd bet a million dollars he'd blush, or better yet, get a semi. I was evil. But he loved it.

"Hey, you," Nora said, pulling her purse over her shoulder.

"You heading somewhere?"

"I'm done for the day, figured I'd head home. Are you heading to lunch soon?" She stopped in front of my desk.

"Yeah, I'm waiting for Anders. It's my last lunch date with him for a while."

God, I sounded miserable and clingy.

"Aw... don't look so sad. You'll have lots of dates. You guys are pretty serious, right?"

"We are. I like him a whole hell of a lot." My face heated as she bit back her smile. "It's probably a good thing Kris is taking over again. Space is a good thing. It'll make the time we spend together mean more."

I'd miss seeing him as much, but when I'd been with Chance, I'd thrown myself into him. His life. His job. And it fucked me up. I didn't want to make the same mistake with Anders. Having our own goals was a good thing.

"Doesn't mean it'll make it easier to be apart though." Her smile fell. "I broke things off with Katie on Wednesday."

"Oh man, I'm sorry."

She shrugged it off. "I'm leaving. Might as well end it before either of us gets more attached."

"Still sucks."

"You know what else sucks? Cancer." Tears brimmed along her lashes. "I hate that my dad has to go through this. He's too young, Ethan. Sixty-seven is too young to die."

"He's not going to die," I said, knowing it was a promise I had no right to give.

"He has stage-four liver cancer. I'm not feeling too hopeful."

"Shit, I'm sorry. I shouldn't have said that."

She reached across the desk and messed up my hair, a sad smile moving across her lips. "You're a nice guy, trying to make me feel better like you did over the break. You didn't have to check up on me, but you did. You're one of the good ones. I'm going to miss you."

"Come with us to lunch, or better yet, you're not leaving for another week. We should get together before you fly out."

"I'm going to pass on lunch but thank you. I'm not up for much these days. Besides, goodbyes are the worst."

She tucked a piece of her hair behind her ears. "I'd rather say *see you later* because you never know."

I huffed out a laugh. "Alright."

"See you later?" she said, and I stood.

"Come here."

She pressed her lips together as I pulled her into a hug. She sniffled, and I squeezed her tight. "Tell Anders I'll be by tomorrow to grab the rest of my things."

"I will."

She pulled away and wiped at her eyes. "I better get going."

"See you later, Nora."

Her lips quivered as she smiled and waved her hand. "See ya."

The front door closed, leaving me with an overwhelming ache in my chest. I couldn't even imagine what she must have been going through. My parents had written me off, a fact I'd been struggling with on and off since Christmas, but if my mom or dad had been given a death sentence like Nora's dad had, I'd be devastated. Anders had told me that blood didn't make family, and he was right, but it wasn't easy to wipe away the good memories, despite how fucked up the bad ones were.

"I'll have my assistant call you next week with the details, Mr. Brody." Anders's smooth tone ran up my spine as he walked into the lobby. "Welcome to Lowe Literary."

A man who looked about Anders's age, dressed in a smart suit, walked by my desk. His dark hair fell neatly to one side, his gray eyes almost wolfish when he smiled.

"I'm thrilled to work with you. You're well-loved at Bartley Press, everyone had nothing but nice things to say about you."

Anders pushed his hands in his pockets, glancing at me briefly before he spoke. "Don't believe everything you hear. I'm a hard ass. I expect the best of all my agents and staff."

"He's not joking. He's literally the worst boss," I said, and Anders gave me a private smile.

"Mr. Brody, this is Ethan Calloway, my boyfriend... and ex-assistant. It's his last day."

The man shifted on his feet, his smile less confident. "Nice to meet you."

I held out my hand and he shook it. "You must be the new agent?"

"I am."

"You have big shoes to fill. Nora is the best."

Anders laughed and shot a shut-the-hell-up glare in my direction. Mr. Bossy was back. "I have no doubt you'll do great things here. I'll be in touch."

"Sounds good," he said. "I'm looking forward to it."

Once he disappeared through the front door, I rolled my eyes. "That's who you're hiring? You can't be serious?"

"He comes highly recommended, Ethan. And it's not like I have a lot of time to be picky." Anders wrapped his arms around me. "What are your objections?"

"He's a snob, and kind of a suck up, and way too hot."

He bit the inside of his cheek. "Are you jealous?"

"Not at all. He's hot, but I'm fucking amazing."

"You most certainly are." Anders grazed his lips against mine, slow and soft. "How were your classes?"

I ran my hands over the stiff fabric of his shirt to his neck. "Long. I'm glad the week is over."

He trailed kisses over my jaw, his nose nuzzling right below my ear. He leaned back, his pupils wide, leaving only a sliver of blue behind. "Have you eaten?"

"No. I had my hopes set on Sal's, since it's my last day."

"Sal's is always okay with me. I'll grab my wallet and let Claire and Nora know I'll be back later."

"Nora left for the day. She told me to tell you she'll stop by tomorrow to pick up the rest of her things."

"Thanks. Give me one minute." Anders placed a chaste kiss to my cheek before heading back to his office.

While he was gone, I checked to see if he responded to my email, disappointed he hadn't.

"Ready?" he asked when he returned.

I slid my hand in his. "Let's go."

Sal's, of course, was packed, but our favorite booth was open, and after Rebecca dropped off our drinks, she took our order. We always got the same thing, the number five burger with fries, but she asked us anyway.

"I'll make sure your ticket goes in first." She winked at Anders. "It's good to see you with a smile on your face."

"I smile," he said defensive and I laughed.

Reaching across the table, I tangled our fingers. "Not often enough."

"I like you, Ethan." Rebecca's eyes strayed to our joined hands. "I suspect he does too."

"More than I should," Anders said, and grinned when I frowned.

"I'll be back," she said, giving me my very own Rebecca-approved smile.

She walked off toward the kitchen and I squeezed his hand. "More than you should?"

"I'm going to miss having you around the office."

"I'll miss being there. But this is good." I sat up straight and he let go of my hand. "I haven't felt independent in a long time. This is healthy."

"I agree."

"You do?"

"Ethan, I want you in my life any way I can have you. If it's once a week while you fall asleep studying in my bed, I'll take it. I'm sure there will be days you can meet me for lunch, and there will be weeks where we hardly see each other. I don't ever want you to sacrifice your dreams because you're worried about me. I'm here. For all of it."

"You say the best—"

"Shit... I'm aware." He flashed me a smile and my heart skipped a beat.

It didn't take long for Rebecca to bring us our lunch, and we ate while Anders asked about my courses. This semester wouldn't be a walk in the park by any means, and with the classes I'd signed up for, I was already drowning. I'd picked a few of my pre-requisites for the nursing program, Anatomy, Microbiology, and Nutrition, saving my last slots for my gen-ed requirements. Much to Anders's delight, I'd signed up for a creative writing course, along with a basic English class everyone had to take.

"Will you let me read what you write?" he asked, dipping a fry in the giant bowl of ketchup he'd insisted on having every time we came here.

"Yes... please, Mister Super Smart Literary Agent, read my shit words."

"You should let me read them."

"Why should I? You never let me read your stuff."

"About that. I sent you a file this morning to your personal email. Something I started working on this week, I'm interested to see what you think."

I paused mid-bite. "You did?"

He kept his eyes on his plate and nodded. "It's mostly free association. Thoughts I had to get out. Ideas. Don't get too excited."

"Too fucking late. Anders..." I couldn't stop smiling. "This is big."

"It's nothing." He gave me a dismissive wave. "Don't make it a big deal."

"Hey... look at me." Reluctant blue eyes met mine. "Thank you for trusting me with this."

He was quiet for a few seconds, staring at me, making heat spread up my neck. "My words have always been private... but for some reason, I can't stop myself from wanting to show you everything."

"I'm here," I repeated what he'd said to me earlier. "For it all."

Back at the office, the day was winding down. I'd finished reading what Anders had sent me, and it was as beautiful as it was confusing. His imagery was off the charts. He wrote pages about peaches and summer and skin. The words were seductive and made my pulse race like I had a fever. Goose bumps prickled my neck and arms, his voice in my head, whispering as I read, and hell if it didn't make me hard. I didn't think that was a normal response to reading, but when it came to Anders and the things he did to my body, anything was possible. I was about to pull out my homework in hopes of clearing my mind of my horny thoughts when my email notification pinged.

FROM: AndersLowe@LoweLitFic.com

TO: EthanCalloway@LoweLitFic.com

DATE: Jan 8 4:05 PM

SUBJECT: RE: FEED ME

Mr. Calloway,

If I may, I'd like to have a word with you in my office.

Anders~

P.S. Now.

Grinning, I stood, and closed out of the email. Already worked up from his manuscript, blood flooded my groin as I walked down the hall and past Claire's office. She was busy on a call as usual. I'd almost wished she'd gone home early. I didn't think Anders would be down for screwing around with her here, but he'd surprised me a lot lately. I didn't knock, opening the door and strolling in like always. He kept his gaze glued to his laptop as I shut and locked the door behind me. I recognized the soft music spilling from his speakers. It was the playlist he often listened to while reading submissions. As I approached his desk, he raised his intimidating blue eyes.

"You wanted to see me?" I asked, nervous all of a sudden.

He leaned back in his chair, with his sleeves rolled up to his elbows and a stoic expression, Anders was the embodiment of power.

"Have a seat," he said, and held his hand out to the empty chair.

Screw that.

I bypassed the chair and rounded his desk. "Are you mad I sent that email? I probably should have texted instead of using the company —"

"I'm not mad." He loosened his tie and my dick throbbed behind my zipper. "You locked the door?"

I set my hands on the arms of his chair, leaning down, I smiled against his lips. "I did."

"I can't decide if I want you on your knees or if I want you bent over my desk."

He exhaled a ragged breath as I skated a hand up his thigh. "It's my last day. I get to choose."

I unbuckled his belt as he grabbed the back of my neck and licked my lips. "You can have both if you like."

I lowered myself down onto my knees between his spread legs. "You can fuck me later tonight, right now I want you to use my mouth."

His fingers threaded through my hair as I unzipped him and tugged his pants down enough to free his cock. Over the last few weeks, I'd learned every inch of his body, but I didn't think I'd ever get used to him, to the perfect length of him, the weight of him on my tongue, the way he stretched my lips. His jaw was clenched as he watched me, reverent and needy. I stroked him, up and down, licking him from base to tip. His groans fueled me, his fist twisting tighter in my hair as I took him all the way to the back of my throat. His hips jerked, gagging me, but I breathed through it, wanting it, swallowing as much of him as possible. His moans filled the office, the music not much of a buffer as he fucked my throat. His fingers ran through my hair, while he whispered praise, taking my mouth with rough and delicious pumps of his hips. I never wanted him to stop.

"Yes... Christ... like that...I'm..." he grunted, losing control. "Fuck, I'm—"

His hot release filled my mouth and throat, bitter and perfect. I sucked slow and hard until his legs started to shake, until he begged me to stop. His cheeks were flushed, and his eyes glazed as I stared at him.

"You're sexy when you're wrecked like this," I said, and leaned up to kiss him.

His tongue dipped into my mouth on a moan, and I hoped he could taste himself. Taste the way we fit together.

"You're the only one who's ever made me feel this way," he said, catching his breath.

"That's the orgasm talking."

He held my face in his hands. "You know it's not."

Anders's lips found mine again, his hands falling to my buckle, his fingers breaking through every barrier until the heat of skin was wrapped around me.

You're the only one.

Those four words sowed themselves inside me, closing up old wounds as I lost myself to his touch.

FEBRUARY

FROM: hook_and_reelife@bellinx.mail.com

TO: AndersLowe@LoweLitFic.com

DATE: Feb 5 10:21 AM

SUBJECT: That Professor

Anders,

He's wearing a bowtie again. Why do I find that attractive? It makes it hard to concentrate. Especially when he's talking about the prostate. It should be illegal for professors to talk about ejaculation. Or maybe I'm immature? He literally told the entire room about this study that found men who ejaculate at least twenty-one times a month have a twenty percent less chance of getting prostate cancer. I thought this was anatomy, not sex-ed. Though I think our chances of getting prostate cancer are pretty low. You're welcome.

Yours~

P.S. Thanks for the key. I'm working late at the coffee shop tonight. It will be nice to let myself in without waking you up for once. I guess I could stay at my place, but I feel like your prostate health is more important, don't you?

FROM: AndersLowe@LoweLitFic.com

TO: hook_and_reelife@bellinx.mail.com

DATE: Feb 5 10:40 AM

SUBJECT: RE: That Professor

Ethan,

Is this the same professor you were talking about the other night? Should I feel threatened? I have a few bowties in the closet if you'd like me to wear one, but I refuse to grow a mustache. However, if you feel the need to call me professor from time to time, that's acceptable. And for the record, you are very immature, but it's charming. In regard to the cancer facts, twenty percent doesn't seem like much of a margin, but I'm willing to make the effort just in case. I think we should at least try to be as healthy as possible. It only makes sense.

I wish you were here. Claire had one of her fits and Kris takes it without batting an eyelash. You would have put her in her place.

Word of the day: Longing - unrelenting craving or desire.

I miss your smart mouth.

Sincerely,

Anders~

P.S. You're welcome at my place anytime. As much as you like. Hence the reason I gave you a key. And I would be offended if you didn't wake me. I barely see you as it is, which it now seems could be hazardous to my health and yours.

FROM: hook_and_reelife@bellinx.mail.com

TO: AndersLowe@LoweLitFic.com

DATE: Feb 5 11:04 AM

SUBJECT: RE: That Professor

Professor Lowe,

Threatened? You're sweet when you're jealous.

The mustache guy is my Microbiology teacher, and he is old as fuck and not attractive at all. He's kind of funny though. I think you'd like his corny jokes.

"Boy, you're so hot you denature my proteins." Well, he said girl... but yeah, this works too. And then this one. "I wish I was adenine, then I could get paired with U." And the other day he had on a shirt with I heart Micro written on the front.

Do you think there's bacteria porn?

My anatomy professor, Dr. Michaels, is alright looking. I think it's the bowties honestly, and the fact he makes eye contact with me every time he says semen. I just learned the average load a guy can blow is anywhere from one-and-a-half milliliters to five milliliters. I'd like to think I'm the five ml guy.

I wish I was there too, but not because I want to tell Claire off. I like the coffee shop, but it's too busy sometimes and you're not there.

Word of the day: anticipation - looking forward to and/or being excited about an upcoming event.

I miss you. Just you.

Tonight's not too far away.

Shit. Now he's drawing dicks. I better pay attention.

Yours~

P.S. I'm definitely waking you up, and if you wanted to

wear a bowtie every now and then, I wouldn't mind. Though I prefer you naked.

FROM: AndersLowe@LoweLitFic.com

TO: hook_and_reelife@bellinx.mail.com

DATE: Feb 10 9:03 AM

SUBJECT: V-Day

Ethan,

I'm usually indifferent when it comes to Valentine's Day. But I overheard you talking to June at the coffee shop yesterday at lunch. If it's a day that means something to you, then it means something to me. I want to give you what you want. With your coursework and shifts at the coffee shop, our time is limited, but that doesn't mean we have to spend the time we have locked in my bedroom. I enjoy being wrapped up in you, but it's more than that. I know Sunday afternoons are for Jay, so if you want to celebrate V-day on Saturday, I'd like to take you to dinner. And not Sal's. You get off work at eight that night? I could pick you up. Let me know what you think.

Good luck on your Micro exam today. Don't forget, Mycoplasma genitalium lives in the bladder and waste disposal organs. Look at the root word like I showed you last night and you won't forget it.

Sincerely,

Anders~

FROM: hook_and_reelife@bellinx.mail.com

TO: AndersLowe@LoweLitFic.com

DATE: Feb 10 11:17 AM

SUBJECT: RE: V-Day

Anders,

I got a ninety percent! Hell yes! Thank you for working through those flashcards with me, even though I felt like a dumbass for the majority of the night. Maybe next time I'll make it into a game. Something like strip poker. Every answer I get right I take off an article of clothing. Would you be my study buddy then?

About V-day. It's a stupid, commercial holiday, and normally I don't give a shit. But June was telling me about her plans with Gwen and Charlotte and it sounded kind of fun. But honestly, as long as I'm with you I don't care what we do. And you'll never hear me complain about being locked in your bedroom. Ever. Yes, Sunday afternoons are usually for Jay, but he's celebrating with Mabel. I think they're going to the zoo. So… I'm free all day. Unless we're going to your parents for brunch like usual? You said you want to give me what I want. I want to stay in, never get dressed, and spend as much time as possible with you "wrapped up" in me. Then you can feed me. Take-out. Because the whole never getting dressed thing.

Yours~

P.S. The new girl at the coffee shop picked up my shift tonight... if you want to go out for dinner I wouldn't be opposed.

FROM: AndersLowe@LoweLitFic.com

TO: hook_and_reelife@bellinx.mail.com

DATE: Feb 10 11:42 AM

SUBJECT: RE: V-Day

Ethan,

Ninety percent is very well earned. Congratulations! You are far from a dumbass. And I'd be your study partner regardless of attire or lack thereof, though the incentive may improve your mood. I'll even throw in a blow job if it'll make you focus. Speaking of blow jobs, your V-day plans sound much better than mine. But instead of take-out, I'd like to make you dinner. If it's alright with you, I might put on underwear, for hygienic purposes of course. To answer your question, Sunday brunch is cancelled, my dad is taking my mom away for the weekend. The whole day is ours.

I have to run. Claire is arguing with Kris again.

Sincerely,

Anders~

P.S. Dinner tonight sounds good. Meet me at the office and we'll go to that place you like near Piedmont.

MARCH

FROM: hook_and_reelife@bellinx.mail.com

TO: AndersLowe@LoweLitFic.com

DATE: March 16 10:51 AM

SUBJECT: Random AF

Anders,

Do you like dogs? I never thought about having kids, but I've always wanted a dog. Like a big ass mastiff. Random question, I know. But Dr. Mustache is droning on about ATP and I need a distraction. How's the office? Quiet? I miss having access to your calendar, but not in an overbearing boyfriend kind of way. More like a shit-I-don't-want-to-bother-you-while-you're-in-a-meeting kind of way.

And I didn't forget... I have some time between my lab and creative writing class if you wanted to send me what you wrote last night. I swear you should be teaching my creative writing class. I'd learn more, but I'm much better at the science side of things, even if I find adenosine triphosphate (ATP) boring as fuck.

Anatomy fact of the day - the stapes is the smallest bone in the body.

What's the largest you ask? The femur.

Hope you're still thinking about this morning. Because I am.

Yours~

P.S. Jax texted me. His mom and Jay are coming over for dinner. You should come. Otherwise, you'll have to wait till Friday to see me. Why am I going to school again? Is it too soon to ask you to be my sugar daddy?

FROM: AndersLowe@LoweLitFic.com

TO: hook_and_reelife@bellinx.mail.com

DATE: March 16 11:07 AM

SUBJECT: RE: Random AF

Ethan,

Distraction is probably the opposite of what you need while Dr. Mustache is giving a lecture. But I'll humor you.

I like dogs. Though I think a small dog would be better. Something like a French bulldog. Mastiffs shit like a horse and drool. I have no desire to clean that up. You've never thought about having kids? Some days I think I'd like to have a couple of kids. I know my mom would love that. And other days I think about traveling without having to worry about anyone else, or fucking all day, or sleeping all day, or walking around naked because I can. Kids seem less appealing to me the older I get.

The office is quiet. Claire is out and Mr. Brody has been in and out of meetings all day. He's managed to pick up a few more clients this month. And if you want, I can sync our calendars. It's nosy (very Ethan), but adorable, and then I can keep track of when you have your exams. This way I'll know when NOT to distract you. I need to tweak a few things and then I'll send you the manuscript, but weren't you supposed to send me that poem you were going to turn in today. Did you chicken out?

I don't have any anatomy facts for you. But I do love the word juxtaposition.

What is the smallest muscle in the human body?

Waking up with your lips on me is always incredible.

With love,

Anders~

P.S. I'll head over to your place as soon as I finish up here. My last meeting is at five. But it shouldn't take me long. To answer your question, you're going to school because education is important, and if that means I have to be a sugar daddy, so be it. You already have the key to my house.

FROM: hook_and_reelife@bellinx.mail.com

TO: AndersLowe@LoweLitFic.com

DATE: March 16 11:32 AM

SUBJECT: RE: Random AF

Dearest Sugar Daddy,

I had to look up French bulldogs, and I'm surprised. I pictured you as more of a greyhound kind of guy, very sophisticated. Or I could picture you with a basset hound curled up at your feet while you write the next great American novel in a leather chair, sipping brandy. You have to get a basset hound. Plus, they're good fishing companions. As far as kids go, it's weird. I don't care either way. When it comes to me being a parent, it's hard to say yes or no. My parents fucked up royally. What if I do the same? I feel like I'd give all of myself to the kids I want to work with, and when the day was over, I'd want that time at home to be with my partner. I guess it's hard for me to see it now, my life is too hectic. Maybe one day, maybe not. I mean, fucking all day is kind of nice.

I think it's funny you still call him Mr. Brody. How long does he have to work for you before you'll call him

Donovan?

And I'm ignoring your nosy remark but will say syncing our calendars is a great idea. Don't be surprised if I schedule a few "meetings" for me. Especially during Spring Break. I can't wait to have nothing to do for an entire week. I'm never leaving your house unless I have to, only exceptions being Sunday brunch and fishing with Jay. He's been bringing Mabel a lot. You should come this week. Maybe see if your dad wants to come too. Jay's been asking about the deep-sea trip since New Year's, he's excited, and it'll be good for you guys to get to know each other better. The trip's not until the summer. Lots of opportunity for you and Jay to connect more before then.

Answer:

The stapedius muscle is the smallest, and wouldn't you know, it regulates the vibration of the stapes.

I don't have a favorite word, but I love the way you string sentences together. You make words beautiful.

Yours~

P.S. Dinner isn't until seven, you'll have plenty of time.

P.P.S. I can't believe I'm going to send you this. If you hate it. Keep that shit to yourself.

His eyes like water draw me in, to the river's edge, where I am myself, where I forget to breathe, where I become the thing he covets, where he reels me in, and I become his catch to keep.

FROM: AndersLowe@LoweLitFic.com

TO: hook_and_reelife@bellinx.mail.com

DATE: March 16 11:53 AM

SUBJECT: RE: Random AF

Ethan (My fish),

I think you're quite capable of making words beautiful. If you get anything less than an A, your professor isn't fit to teach. I loved it. Truly. Will you let me read more?

Addressing the rest of your email, I'd like a basset hound, though the image you conjured made me laugh. Besides the brandy, it feels spot on.

You are not your parents. You have way too much love to give. But I agree, eventually your job could make it harder to have the energy you'd need for your own. It's a sacrifice to raise a child, and an admirable one, but that doesn't mean it's for everybody.

I would love to go fishing with you and Jay, thank you for inviting me, and I can assure you my dad will jump at the opportunity. I think he likes you better than me now anyway. And I'll have Kris sync our calendars before she leaves today. By all means, schedule as many "meetings" as you like, though I plan on taking a few days off to spend with you while you're on break.

Thank you for sharing your poem, I know how hard it is to be vulnerable in that way. I'm attaching the manuscript. I'll see you tonight.

With love,

Anders~

P.S. I'll call him Donovan once he proves himself.

FROM: hook_and_reelife@bellinx.mail.com

TO: AndersLowe@LoweLitFic.com

DATE: March 30 7:30 AM

SUBJECT: Lunch

Anders,

I'm free for lunch today if you want to meet at Cup and Quill before my shift starts at one?

Word of the day: Deprived - not seeing my boyfriend for four days.

Yours~

FROM: AndersLowe@LoweLitFic.com

TO: hook_and_reelife@bellinx.mail.com

DATE: March 30 8:45 AM

SUBJECT: Lunch

Ethan,

I'll move my eleven thirty to two. You get off at nine tonight, you should come over. I don't care if you ignore me while you read about cellular biology, I want you there. I need you there. I gave you a key, remember? You should use it more often.

Word of the day: Fulfillment - having your sexy boyfriend's legs on your lap while he studies… and the possibility of morning sex.

With love,

Anders~

FROM: hook_and_reelife@bellinx.mail.com

TO: AndersLowe@LoweLitFic.com

DATE: March 30 8:55 AM

SUBJECT: RE: Lunch

Anders,

I was worried that using the key was too fast. I love that you trusted me enough to give it to me, but at first it felt like too much. But not seeing you fucking sucks. I want to give you your space though. If it's ever too much tell me.

Yours~

FROM: AndersLowe@LoweLitFic.com

TO: hook_and_reelife@bellinx.mail.com

DATE: March 30 9:01 AM

SUBJECT: RE: Lunch

Ethan,

I will always tell you the truth, and the truth is I want you in my space. Our schedules are hard to manage, and seeing you is important to me. You are important to me. I gave you the key so you could have a space in my home. I like watching you study. I like making you dinner. I like taking care of you. And did I mention morning sex?

You're never too much.

With love,

Anders~

FROM: hook_and_reelife@bellinx.mail.com

TO: AndersLowe@LoweLitFic.com

DATE: March 30 9:12 AM

SUBJECT: RE: Lunch

Anders,

I want to take care of you, you're important to me too. Having this conversation via email is probably proof enough we need more time for us. I'll use the key.

I think you sold me with the morning sex.

Yours~

APRIL

FROM: hook_and_reelife@bellinx.mail.com

TO: AndersLowe@LoweLitFic.com

DATE: April 21 11:23 AM

SUBJECT: Mr. Mustache

Anders,

I found out Mr. Mustache is going to be my physiology professor in the fall. I don't think I can handle any more of his jokes. God, listen to this one. "You know what gets on my nerves? Myelin." He's wearing a fucking shirt that says, "Keep Calm and Maintain Homeostasis." Do you think he has sex?

June is going to stop by the coffee shop and help me with my nutrition class. You'll have to start dinner without me.

Yours~

FROM: AndersLowe@LoweLitFic.com

TO: hook_and_reelife@bellinx.mail.com

DATE: April 21 11:38 AM

SUBJECT: RE: Mr. Mustache

Ethan,

Is there not another teacher for physio? And honestly, for all we know, he could be into BDSM. No judgment, but I don't want to think about your professor's sex life.

Why don't you invite June over? I can pick something up on my way home for all of us.

With love,

Anders~

FROM: hook_and_reelife@bellinx.mail.com

TO: AndersLowe@LoweLitFic.com

DATE: April 21 11:40 AM

SUBJECT: RE: Mr. Mustache

Anders,

His class is the only one that fits my schedule, and I will never forgive you for that image. Mr. Mustache in leather and a ball gag. Nope. No, thank you. I should inform you my dick will never get hard again. You might as well find someone else who needs a sugar daddy.

I'll see what June says and get back to you.

Yours~

FROM: hook_and_reelife@bellinx.mail.com

TO: AndersLowe@LoweLitFic.com

DATE: April 21 1:22 PM

SUBJECT: RE: Mr. Mustache

Anders,

June said she's down, she'll have Charlotte because Gwen is at work. I told her that's fine.

I got a seventy-three on my micro quiz. I blame you. BDSM. Ugh.

Yours~

FROM: AndersLowe@LoweLitFic.com

TO: hook_and_reelife@bellinx.mail.com

DATE: April 22 1:41 PM

SUBJECT: Sunday

Ethan,

My mom was wondering if you'd like to invite Jay for brunch this Sunday. I told her I wasn't sure how comfortable Jay would be with that. I know he's met my dad a few times, but if you think it's too much for him, I can tell her no.

Good luck on your nutrition exam.

With love,

Anders~

FROM: hook_and_reelife@bellinx.mail.com

TO: AndersLowe@LoweLitFic.com

DATE: April 22 2:05 PM

SUBJECT: RE: Sunday

Anders,

I think Jay would love that. I'll call Jax and pass it by him first. But I'm sure he'll be okay with it. Jay talks about your dad more than he talks about Mabel lately!

And thanks, I need all the luck I can get. I might actually pass thanks to June.

Yours~

P.S. Will you be around in an hour? I might need to call and vent about this fucking test.

FROM: AndersLowe@LoweLitFic.com

TO: hook_and_reelife@bellinx.mail.com

DATE: April 22 2:09 PM

SUBJECT: RE: Sunday

Ethan,

You will pass this test because you are smart and work your ass off.

Say it out loud three times.

With love,

Anders~

P.S. I always have time for you.

Anders

I glanced at my watch, eager to leave. It was Friday, and the last day of finals week. Ethan had to work till eleven, which would be late for most coffee shops, but Cup and Quill had live music on the weekends and served spiked coffee. I figured I could stop by, surprise him, and have a drink. I couldn't believe it was already May. The thought brought a small smile to my lips as I hurried through an email to Kris. I'd been looking forward to Ethan's summer break. Not that I wasn't immensely proud of him for going after his dreams and working his ass off in all of his classes, but I was excited to have more of his time. These last four months with him, as hectic as they were, had given me a sense of contentment I'd never imagined for myself. I loved how he fit into my family, and how my parents had become a support system for him, taking him in like he was theirs to keep. I loved his relationship with Jay, and how he'd let me be a part of it as well. I loved waking up with Ethan in my arms, staying up late, listening to him rattle off anatomy facts, and even though I'd rather see him more in person, I loved all the emails he'd send me throughout the day. I loved his toothbrush in my bathroom, his smell on my sheets. I loved the way he chewed the top of his pen while he read, and how he bounced his knee, his energy too much to contain at times. I loved how easy it was to love him. And I did, love him. I loved him more than I thought I'd ever be capable of again. I hadn't told him yet, and maybe my reservations stemmed from old insecurities, but he made me want to work through them.

"Hey." Robbie smiled at me as he walked into my office, pulling me from my thoughts. "You got a minute?"

"Sure. Have a seat." I shut my laptop as he lowered himself into the chair with a long exhale. "You seem stressed."

His Adam's apple jumped in his throat, and he rubbed the back of his neck, giving me a weary smile. "I am... I've got to get going if I want to catch my flight, but there's something I have to talk to you about. I wanted to wait until I got back to the city, but I figured you deserve to be told face to face."

He shifted in his seat as I leaned back, my own nerves surfacing as a bead of sweat rolled down the side of his face. "Did something go wrong today? The client seemed happy to sign with us."

"He signed with me."

"Good," I said, confused. Robbie had flown down to meet with a new author at Bartley. The author had plans to move to Manhattan in the fall and wanted an agent close by. "What's the problem?"

"I started my own agency, Anders. I'm leaving Lowe."

"Excuse me?" I sat up, staring at the sheepish fucking look on his face. "You're quitting?"

"It's time. I want to do my own thing. Make my own money." He had the audacity to shrug like what he'd said wasn't a huge betrayal. "I have a big list of clients, and—"

"My clients, Robbie. They signed with Lowe, not you."

"They already said they'd walk with me." He glared and squared his shoulders. "I don't think you want this to get messy. You've worked hard for your rep, I get that. But I did too. The authors I signed are mine."

"Who the fuck do you think sent you those authors?" I clenched my fists and took a calming breath. "Contracts have been signed. If your clients want to walk, then they need to lawyer up, or you need to buy me out. That's how it works. You don't get to come in here and demand shit."

His smug smile faded, his eyes drifting around the room. "Buy you out?"

"Yes. I keep the clients I attained for myself, and the ones you signed, if they wish to leave with you, that's fine, but you have to pay me a commission for the contracts."

"And the author I signed today?" he asked.

"Did he sign a contract with Lowe Literary or a contract with you?"

His posture deflated and he ran a hand through his hair.

"Fuck that, Anders. The well in Atlanta is drying up and you fucking know it. New York has always been your end goal. You do this shit, and no one will work with you when you pull your head out of your ass and move up there." He shoved out of the chair and jabbed his finger in my direction. "Get a fucking lawyer. Waste your goddamn money. I'll be in New York where you should have been years ago, grabbing top talent."

"Plans change, Robbie. I can't leave."

"Bullshit. You won't leave. You've gotten too cozy, feeding off Bartley Press. Atlanta is a sinking ship. Publishing is New York. It always has been." Robbie scrubbed a palm over his forehead. "I didn't want to leave. But I have to do what's best for me."

I lowered my eyes, hurt and anger roaring in my ears. "I'll have my lawyer draft up a contract."

He sighed and I raised my gaze. "I'll buy you out. You keep your clients, and I'll pay you the commission on the ones who want to keep me as their agent."

"I want the numbers by Tuesday, and I'll have the contract ready no later than Friday," I said. "Have a safe flight."

Robbie stood, stunned for a few seconds before storming off. He'd completely screwed me over. I had no doubt a good majority of his clients would walk with him, and honestly, I hoped they would. I'd built my business here. My family was here. Ethan was here. Some of the top agents in the business were based in other states. I'd rather close the New York office than uproot my entire life. Atlanta was my home.

"Anders." Claire stood in the doorway, smoothing her hands down the front of her skirt. "I wanted—"

"Are you leaving too?" I asked more abruptly than she deserved. When she flinched, I shook my head. "I'm sorry. I shouldn't have spoken to you like that."

She cleared her throat and raised her chin, gathering herself. "I'm not going anywhere. I told Robbie he's a snake. I wanted you to know I wasn't aware of his plans."

"You called him a snake?" I probably shouldn't have smiled, but I figured she'd appreciate it. "Thanks for that."

"You taught him everything he knows, basically hand fed him all of those clients. I should have seen it coming." She pushed a lock of her straight blonde hair behind her ear. "If there's anything I can do…"

"I'm not sure what my plan is yet. But I'll keep you in mind."

Claire's icy demeanor melted, and she gave me a small smile. "I'll see you on Monday."

My entire world had been upended in less than ten minutes. Robbie betrayed me, I might end up closing the New York branch, and Claire might actually be a decent human being. Feeling utterly spent, I pulled out my phone and texted the only person I knew could make me feel better.

Me: Anyway, you can fake an illness and come over early? I've had a shit day.

Ethan: I could try. You okay?

Me: I'm not sure.

I huffed out a laugh as my phone rang.

"Hey, what's going on?" he asked, and I could hear the hum of the coffee shop through the phone. Chatter and dishes clanging together.

"It's a long story. Can I stop by?"

"One sec..." The sounds of the shop muted, dull in the background, like he had his hand over the speaker of his phone. "Okay, sorry about that. Nyla said she'll stay till eleven tonight for me, but I'm stuck here till eight."

"You didn't have to—"

"I did. You never ask for anything. When you do, my Spidey senses get all jacked up and I refuse to worry all night."

"And he's annoying when he's worried," a female voice shouted in the background. "You owe me."

"I don't owe her. I picked up her shift last Wednesday." Ethan's laugh stitched itself into my chest. "Want me to pick up dinner on my way over?"

"Sure."

"Any requests?"

"Just you. And food."

"You're okay though?" he asked.

I glanced at my watch. In three hours, Ethan would be on his way to my house.

"I will be."

Heat swarmed my body, my eyes heavy as I tried to open them. Pillowed lips grazed along the stubbled line of my jaw, a pleased hum filling the air, dragging me from sleep. The room was dark, except for the moonlight trickling in through the blinds. Warm, rough hands brushed my chest, and his scent covered me. I lifted my hand, my fingers tangling through his soft hair as the weight of his body anchored me to the mattress. He pressed a kiss to my clavicle, moving up to the curve of my neck and back down to my throat.

"Hi," Ethan whispered, and my eyes found the freckle on his bottom lip. "You fell asleep?"

"Mmm." I traced a line up his neck with the tip of my nose. "What time is it?"

"Eight forty-five," he said, and pulled open the towel around my waist. "I put dinner in the fridge when I found you sound asleep, all wrapped like a present."

I opened my eyes, letting my surroundings sink in. Ethan was completely naked, straddling me.

"I must've dozed off when I got out of the shower," I said and gripped his hips.

He grinned as he stroked his hand down my shaft. "Lucky me."

"I think I'm the lucky one in this scenario." I groaned as he tightened his fist. "Waking up with a hot guy on top of me."

Ethan bent down to kiss me, aligning his cock with mine, dragging up and down my length, my nails digging into his skin as I shuddered. He groaned, moving his body in a measured rhythm, but I needed more. Grabbing his ass, I rutted against him until he moaned. He whispered my name, raising my hand to his mouth, sucking on my fingers. I reached between his legs and teased his hole until his cheeks were flush, his chest spotting with my favorite shade of pink. He leaned over to the nightstand and grabbed a bottle of lube, pouring some into his hand as he settled back onto his knees, hovering over me. Ethan prepped himself, his lip pinned between his teeth as his fingers disappeared inside him. It was the sexiest fucking thing I'd ever seen. I kept my eyes on him, transfixed, until he reached for me, slicking his hand down my cock.

"I need you," he said, and I grasped his hips, rolling him onto his back.

His tongue, tasting like chocolate and coffee, dipped into my mouth. I held his hands to the mattress, and his fingers threaded through mine. Swallowing his desperate gasp, I slipped inside him. We'd both been tested last month, and every time we were like this, fit flawlessly together, without any barriers, I was grateful I'd saved this last piece of myself for him.

Needing the sound of our skin, his breath and grunts, I pushed into him, pounding deep and hard until he fought my grip on his hands, pleading for more. I lowered my mouth to his, kissing him, taking long, slow sips of his lips. He trembled, his entire body shaking with the need for release, and I leaned back, finally letting go of his hands. He stroked himself as I raised his hips, falling into him, I took as much as I could, needing every last second. Ethan's body tensed, his mouth falling open in a silent moan as he came onto his stomach and chest. His orgasm was endless, his body pulsing around me, pushed me over the edge. I let go inside of him, filling his body until there was nothing between us except two hearts, willing and open, and a wholeness I'd never had with anyone else.

"Come here," he whispered, and I leaned down, resting my forehead against his.

His fingers tickled in a zig zag down my spine, scattering goose bumps across my skin. Ethan lifted his chin and caught my lips with his. I held my weight with my forearms as he pressed sweet, lingering kisses to my mouth and neck while my cock softened inside him. Reluctant, I pulled away and rested on my side.

"You're a mess," I said, trailing my knuckles over his cheek.

His smile lit the room. "I don't mind."

I raised up onto an elbow and bent down to kiss him again. He held my face in his hands. "Are you in a better mood?"

The question brought everything crashing back and I tried to hold my smile. "I am."

"Liar." He laughed as he sat up and wiped a hand over his sticky abs. "Let's shower and you can tell me about your shit day."

"I won't argue with that," I conceded, and he grabbed the towel I'd had around my waist earlier and wiped his hand.

I stood and he followed me into the bathroom. Once the water was hot enough, we both got in, and without asking, he knew what I needed. He soaped up my shoulders, using his strong fingers to knead the knotted muscle, and I leaned into his touch. After a couple of minutes, Ethan wrapped his arms around me, pulling my back to his chest.

"Want to talk about it?"

"Not really," I said and smiled when he pinched my hip.

"I skipped out on work, brought you dinner, and woke you up with sex…"

"All things a good boyfriend should do." He pinched me again. "Ow."

"Talk."

I turned to face him, letting the water hit my back.

"Robbie is leaving, starting his own agency."

Ethan's smile waned, his brows dipping with concern. "Shit. You can hire another agent, right? Like you did when Nora left?"

"This is different. He basically ran the New York office. He's taking his clients with him, threatened to take mine too."

"The fuck? Really?"

"I told him to get a lawyer and he folded. He's going to buy me out."

"That's good, right?" Ethan rubbed his hands up my arm. "He won't take your clients?"

"He'll pay me a commission on the clients who choose to leave with him, but that's not the real problem." I wiped a piece of his hair from his forehead. "I'm here, and I have no one in New York. The part-time agent can't handle all of my clients. And it's hard to do it all remotely from Atlanta."

Ethan's posture stiffened. "What does that mean? You have to go to New York?"

"I don't know yet."

He dropped his hands and took a step away from me. "Would you move there? You have clients here. What about your office here and—"

"Hey, I'm not moving to New York, okay?" I searched his gaze. "I'm not going anywhere. If I have to, I'll close the New York branch. I have enough steady work in Atlanta."

"New York is the heart of publishing, Anders." Ethan took another small step backward, the distance falling cold between us despite the hot water streaming against my skin. "You can't close that office. And what about all your clients you have there?"

"I can work remotely as much as possible, maybe hire another agent or two to help. I thought about it a lot after I left the office today. I might sell Robbie a good portion of my client list."

"Fuck Robbie."

"Ethan. I have no choice."

His nostrils flared as he shook his head. "But you do. You could move there. Work your Atlanta clients remotely. Most of your income is from New York. I used to be your assistant, I know what you can and can't afford to lose. You need New York."

"I think I'm the only one who gets to make that choice," I said, and he stared at me, his chest rising and falling with each breath. Did he want me to leave? Losing my clients would be a hard hit, but it wasn't anything I couldn't handle. "I have plenty of clients in Atlanta, I don't need any more money."

"This is your business," he pushed.

"I'm not moving to New York." I reached for his hand, but he pulled away.

"Why?"

"*Because I love you.*" The words dropped out of my mouth, clumsy and vulnerable, and his eyes widened. "I can get more clients, Ethan. It's you I don't want to lose."

"You'd throw all of that away..." He swallowed, his voice thick as he spoke. "For me?"

"Yes. For us." I reached for his hand and this time he let me take it. "I'd choose you every time."

Ethan tugged me to his chest and his hand grasped the back of my neck. "Hell... I love you too."

"Then, kiss me," I said, and his lips lifted into a crooked smile that took my breath away.

Ethan

The lunch rush had quieted down, only a few stragglers lingered, tapping on their laptops. Most of them frequent flyers, Wilder included. He was tucked away in a corner, scowling at his screen. I leaned against the back counter and sighed, staring out the window, anxiety chewing away at my stomach.

"You have got to quit your moping. We got shit to do, Queen." Nyla rolled her eyes as she wiped the counter. "He's been in New York for how many days? Two? And you're acting like he's dead. Come on now." She threw the towel at me and I caught it.

"What if he changes his mind?" Shit, I was being a whiny bitch. I set the towel in the bucket of bleach under the counter. "What if he decides New York is where he needs to be?"

Over the last couple of days, I'd let my fear get the best of me. I'd been down this road a million times with Chance. He'd come home from one of his trips, tell me it would be the last one, only to leave again. Anders had given me zero reason to doubt him. Last week he told me he loved me, told me he'd choose me every time, and I wanted to trust what we had. Trust him. Trust myself. But we'd only been together since December. Two years of history wasn't enough to keep Chance around, what was five months compared to that?

Nyla popped her gum and strummed her long nails against the stainless-steel sink. "Listen. You told him you love him, right?"

"I did."

"He loves you?" I nodded. "Then do what y'all need to do to make it work. If he needs to stay in New York, then go to New York. They have nursing schools there."

"I moved my whole life for my ex. I'm not doing it again."

"Doing what?" Wilder asked, blowing his bangs out of his eyes as he leaned across the counter and grabbed a paper straw.

"Help me." She snapped her fingers. "Tell this boy he's being ridiculous."

"I'm missing something. Clue me in," he said, pushing the straw into his iced coffee.

"It's nothing," I grumbled, shoving a hand through my hair, I pulled out the day-old bagels from the display and set the tray to the side. "Nyla, grab me some of those plastic bags from the back, please."

413

Angry that she'd dragged Wilder into my pity party, I ignored her as she whispered something to him before heading into the kitchen. He sipped from his straw, waiting me out, and after a few seconds of his blatant stare, I caved.

"What?"

"He hates New York."

"I know." I snatched a few bagels from the tray to bring home later. "I'm fine. Nyla is nosy."

"I am not." She dropped the bags I'd asked for in front of me and took off her apron. Hanging it on the wall, she said, "I'll be back in thirty minutes. Try not to run the place into the ground."

Wilder waited until she was gone before he started in on me again. He hopped up onto the counter and I gritted my teeth.

"Get down."

"Nyla lets me sit here."

"Nyla has a crush on you."

"She does?" His lips twitched and he ran a hand through his curls.

"You're married... to a man."

"Hey, everyone likes a little ego boost."

"Your ego is big enough as it is," I said, tossing a few bagels into a bag and then tying it off.

"Fuck, you are cranky." He narrowed his eyes. "When is Anders due back?"

"Friday night." I packaged up the rest of the bagels and set the tray into the sink. Wilder tracked me the entire time. "You're making me nervous."

"The feeling is mutual," he said. "Last I heard, everything was going good with Anders."

"It is."

"Then why are you walking around like a tea kettle ready to blow?"

My phone vibrated in my pocket and I knew it was him without having to check. Sure enough, his name lit up the screen. It was the fourth time he'd texted me today. I wasn't ignoring him to be an asshole. Before he left everything seemed perfect, any worries I had he'd quickly extinguish, but with him away it was easier for me to fall into the dark headspace I'd thought I'd left behind in Colorado.

"Ethan?"

"Sorry, you were saying?" I asked, pushing my phone into my back pocket.

"I know I'm a pain in your ass, and you're closer with Jax. But I'm here if you want to talk. Like I've said before, Anders is the most loyal man I know. If he says he loves you, he loves you and will do everything he can for you."

"That's the thing, though." My throat was thick as I rubbed the sting from my eyes. "What if he stays here for the wrong reasons and resents me for it later? It's why I never stopped Chance from volunteering. I don't ever want to be someone's regret."

"Did you tell Anders that?"

"I wanted to. We don't keep shit from each other. But I want him to make this choice on his own."

"He already made his choice. And it's you. Trust me when I say this, you're worth it, Ethan." I couldn't breathe and I pulled at my collar, the room suddenly too hot. "You are. It took me a long time to learn that for myself. My parents shut me out too. And everything that had happened with Jax. All that time I thought I was the common denominator. I wasn't worthy of love. And it's bullshit. The people who hurt you? That's on them, babe. Your parents... Chance, they don't get to make your choices for you. Don't shut out Anders because they fucked up." The front door opened, and a group of college-aged kids walked in. Wilder hopped down from the counter. "You're worthy of love. Say it a few times. Eventually it will stick."

He gave me a sad smile before he walked over to his table. With my head spinning, I worked through the orders the kids threw at me one by one until they were all happy, sipping their frappes at a table in the middle of the room. Everything Wilder had said was true. I didn't want my parents or my past relationship to ruin what Anders and I were building. There were too many good things, and I needed to focus on that. I'd panicked after he'd left because it all felt too familiar. Which was, like Nyla had said, ridiculous. Anders cared about me. He'd proven that to me time and time again. He'd been there for me every time I needed him, every late night I was stressed over school, and even now, when the company he'd built from nothing was at stake, he'd put me first. I pulled out my phone and read his texts feeling like a grade-A jackass.

> **Anders: It's been crazy around here but wanted to say good morning.**

Anders: Hope your day is going okay. Miss you.

Anders: I ordered a cappuccino from that coffee shop near the hotel that you liked. The city's not the same without you.

Anders: Everything okay?

I chewed my bottom lip, hating myself as I called him.

"Hey," he said, his gruff voice making my stomach flutter. "How's your day?"

"Better now." I leaned against the wall behind the pastry display. "How's the city?"

"Dreadful, as per usual. Nothing new." He chuckled and the sound of it made me smile. "I can't convince you to fly out, can I?"

"I'm already convinced, but I have to pay my bills."

"What's the point of having a sugar daddy if you won't let him pay for everything? By definition, I should be taking you on extravagant trips."

"You have a point... I'll put in my two weeks' notice tonight." I grinned when he laughed, warmth flooding my cheeks. It took one phone call to erase the anxiety I'd been stewing in for two days. I'd never felt like a bigger idiot. "How's it going there?"

"Most of the clients want to stay with Robbie. Which is probably for the best. I can't be as hands-on from Atlanta. I have an interview in a half hour with an agent who used to work for Little Press. She comes highly recommended."

"Did Kassen stay with you or go with Robbie?"

Kassen was Anders's biggest client in New York, and the one he'd been the most worried about.

"He stayed, surprisingly. He's been around awhile. He doesn't need his hand held. Working with him remotely should be easy enough."

I heard sirens in the background, and images of my trip with him flipped like snapshots through my head. I'd loved every minute of our time in the city, and as much as Anders said he hated Manhattan, he'd seemed to enjoy himself. Maybe living in New York wouldn't be such a sacrifice. And Nyla was right. I could go to nursing school anywhere.

"I'd move to New York with you. If you had to."

Anders was quiet as my heart hammered against my chest. If I was worthy of love, he was as well. He'd chosen me, and maybe he needed to hear he was my choice too. No matter what. This wasn't a sacrifice. Being with Anders was all I wanted. The address was inconsequential.

"You would?" he asked, his tone a mix of incredulity and awe.

"Hey, you're not the only one capable of big, romantic gestures."

His soft laugh rumbled through the phone, and I rested my head against the wall, the grin on my face uncontrollably wide.

"Moving to New York is unnecessary, but it's nice to know you'd do that for me."

"I don't want you to regret anything because of me."

It was the one fear I couldn't quite shake.

"My reasons for staying aren't altogether altruistic. I actually like Atlanta. I like being close to my family. And then there's this spectacular guy whom I happen to be in love with. The New York branch is a means to an end, and if I shut it down tomorrow, I wouldn't regret a thing."

"I want to hear more about that guy, I bet he's pretty awesome." I pressed my lips together, holding back my cheesy smile.

"He's the best thing to ever happen to me."

"God, I wish you were here." I glanced toward the door as a couple walked in. "I have to go, there's customers."

"Sleep in my bed tonight," he whispered, catching me off guard.

"What?" I smiled at the couple. "Sorry, I'll be right with you."

The lady gave me a quick nod and looked up at the menu on the wall above the register.

"Sleep in my bed, it's easier for me to picture you there," he said. "When I get home the sheets will smell like you."

"When you get home, I'll be in the sheets waiting for you."

"That's even better."

"Call me tonight when you get back to the hotel?" I asked, turning away from the customers. "I think phone sex is the only way I'll survive until Friday." He laughed and I closed my eyes picturing him, his head tipped back, his lips spreading across his handsome face. "Word of the day: ardor."

"I love you, too. I'll call you tonight."

The call disconnected, and I slipped my phone in my pocket before taking the couple's order. After I finished up, I was back in my head again while I cleaned, but instead of feeling twisted with insecurities, I let myself hear Anders's voice. *I wouldn't regret a thing. I love you, too.* When Nyla finally walked through the front door, I raised my eyes and found Wilder staring at me from across the room. He mouthed the words *You are worthy,* and I smiled.

"You seem better now," Nyla said, tying her apron. "Are you done being stupid?"

"Yeah..." I chuckled as she shoved my shoulder. "I figured some shit out."

"Like?"

I glanced at Wilder as he stood and packed up his bag.

"I'm worthy of love."

She snorted and shook her head. "You're just now figuring that out? Lord, go make some blueberry muffins and come talk to me when you're mature enough for an adult conversation."

"I think I'll take a break instead," I said, untying my apron and hanging it on the wall. "Besides, it's your turn to make the muffins."

"Help me when you get back?" she asked, sounding miserable.

Nyla was too good at her guilt trips. "Yeah."

Before she could con me into doing more of her chores, I headed over to Wilder's table.

"Hey, I wanted to say thanks... for talking me off the ledge earlier."

"I've been on many ledges of my own. I get it." He slung his bag over his shoulder. "Did you talk to him?"

"I did. It was good. Turns out you were right."

"Hmm. Imagine that."

I playfully bumped him with my shoulder. "What you said earlier, I'm close to Jax, but we're close too. Even if you're a pain in my ass."

He held his hand to his heart, and I had to stop myself from rolling my eyes. "I think that's the nicest thing you've ever said to me."

I pulled him into a side hug. "Maybe now you'll stop picking on my wardrobe."

"Sorry, never happening." He shrugged me off. "Speaking of which, I saw these pants and—"

"Stop." I laughed and held up my hands. "I have enough pants."

"A man can never have too many pants." He tugged on the strap of his bag. "I better get going. I promised Mrs. Stettler I'd let her teach me how to make her three-layer strawberry cake. Why I continue to do this to myself I'll never know."

"Because you love her."

"Maybe," he said, a quiet smile curling the corners of his mouth. "Will you be home for dinner?"

"I get off at six, so probably. I might head to Anders's place afterward. Give you and Jax more privacy."

"As nice as that sounds, I'm guessing you need privacy for a video chat with Anders later. I wasn't born yesterday."

Rubbing the back of my neck, my face flushed. "It's a possibility."

Wilder suppressed his smirk and I walked with him to the front door. We stepped out into the humid spring afternoon, the sun beating down onto the asphalt made the temperature warmer than it should have been for early May.

"I'm parked over there," he said, pointing in the opposite direction of where I was headed.

"I'm going to grab a quick sandwich while I have time. I'll see you later." He waved and started to walk away when an idea struck me. "Hey, Wilder," I called out and he turned around.

"What's up?"

"Something Anders and I talked about... I'm thinking I might want to surprise him."

"Okay," he said, drawing out the word.

"Where do you think I could find a basset hound puppy by Friday?"

Ethan

The front door closed, and my eyes opened, the room casted in blue light from the television. I sat up and yawned, kicking out of the blanket, almost falling as I stood. His chuckle made my stomach flip in the best of ways.

"Were you sleeping?" he asked, setting his luggage in the hall as he walked into the living room.

"Just for a second," I lied and looked at the clock on the wall.

The last thing I remembered was the text message I'd gotten from Anders forty minutes ago letting me know he'd landed.

"You didn't have to wait up," he said, but the smile on his face told me he was glad I was awake.

Dressed in a pair of jeans and a simple blue t-shirt, he looked way too hot after spending his day in an airport.

"Hi." His voice was rough and low as he raised his hand to brush back the hair that had fallen over my forehead. "Sorry I'm so late."

"Because you control the airline and the weather," I said. "Besides, it's only eleven, old man. That's not late."

He hummed and lowered his lips to mine for a long overdue kiss. He'd been in New York for a few days, but it had felt like forever. We'd video called each other every night, and even though he'd quelled the majority of my anxiety after I'd spoken to him at work the other day, it was nice to have him in my arms, looking at me like he needed me more than the air he breathed.

"I'm dying for a shower," he said and laced his fingers through mine.

"I won't complain about getting you naked and wet."

He shook his head, a small smile lighting his eyes. "I missed you."

"You can show me how much you missed me in the shower."

"I plan on it."

Anders grabbed his bag from the hallway, and I followed him to the bedroom. While he kicked off his shoes, I made my way into the bathroom and turned on the water. Leaning in the doorway of the bathroom, I admired the muscles of his stomach as he pulled off his shirt, my eyes snagging on the tattoo under his collar bone. I loved that this classically handsome man, with all his propriety, had secrets beneath the surface and I was privy to them.

He shed his jeans and boxer briefs and stared at me. "You have on way too many clothes."

"Sorry, you're distracting as hell," I said, and he walked toward me, every inch of his skin on display.

He helped me take off my shirt and pants. His eyes roamed my naked body with a reverent appraisal, soaking me in heat. He melded his lips to mine, and I raked my fingers through his hair as he cupped my ass. His cock pressed against me, and a deep and desperate gasp fell past his lips. I wanted to skip the shower, I wanted him inside me, filling me, grounding me like only he could.

He pulled away too soon, his lips breaking into a smile as he nodded toward the shower. "Come on."

In the shower, Anders stood under the spray and pulled me to his chest. He held me against him, hot rivulets of water running over our skin. My cheek rested against his neck as I lowered my head and breathed in his familiar, spicy scent.

"I want to ask you something," he said, breaking the silence with a nervous whisper.

For a brief second or two I braced myself. This was it. This was where he told me the trip hadn't gone as planned. That we'd have to move to New York. I could do this for him. I could do this for us. My muscles tense, I looked up at him.

And like he could read my mind, he raised a hand to my face and said, "Hey, it's a good thing." I leaned into his palm. "At least, I hope it is."

I exhaled, relieved, and found my smile. "I keep waiting for the moment where everything goes wrong. And it's stupid because I trust you."

"Old habits die hard," he said and wiped a drop of water from my lip with his thumb. "It's not stupid, Ethan.

It's human. We all have something we need to work through. But we can do that together."

"I want that."

"I want you to move in with me." My limbs were heavy as my eyes widened, and I must have looked as shocked as I felt because he laughed. "I had a feeling this would be your reaction. You took forever to get used to the key."

"Moving in is a big thing, Anders, and I couldn't afford—"

"Stop. Don't think about any of that right now. You practically live here as it is." His blue eyes held mine, hopeful and honest. "I don't want to push you too hard, but I want you here. With me. If you're ready for that. I'm ready, Ethan. I've been ready for you for a while. But I can be patient if that's what you need."

I licked my lips as he stared at me, my heart racing a million miles an hour. Fall semester would be here before I knew it, and I didn't want to fight time and my schedule to see him more than once a week. My life had been on hold long enough. I'd chosen my path, and he wanted to walk alongside me. I'd never had that with Chance. I was always chasing after him, chasing after a life I'd never have. A life Anders wanted to give me. A life I wanted to share with him.

"I'm ready," I said, and as soon as the words left my mouth, the invisible weight on my shoulders lifted. His hands fell to my hips, his smile slowly rising bright like the sun. "But we have to talk about money."

Anders captured my lips in a hungry kiss, effectively shutting me the hell up, and when his fingers brushed the crack of my ass, I figured any budgeting conversations could wait until later. As I'd hoped earlier, the shower hadn't lasted very long. We had four days we needed to catch up on, and by the time we were dried off and tumbling into bed, my body trembled with anticipation. We were a blur of motion, of heat and hands, mouths, and fingers. Anders's damp hair fell over his brow as he positioned himself above me. I trailed my fingers over the tattoo on his ribcage and smiled at the way his skin reacted to my touch with tiny pin pricks. He placed soft kisses on my jaw and buried his face in my neck, sucking on the skin right below my ear. When I shuddered, his smile spread against my skin.

"We can do this every night," he whispered as he made his way down my chest. I threaded my hands through his hair, arching my back as his teeth grazed my nipple.

"And every morning."

He hummed his agreement, running his nose down my groin and inhaled. His tongue licked into the slit on the head of my cock and my fingers twisted deeper in his hair.

"Fuck, you taste good."

Anders took me into his mouth, sheathing me in the wet heat of his tongue, and I swore, clenching my jaw as I tried not to lift my hips. I loved giving him the control he craved. My body his to have. When he came up for air, I released my grip on his hair, rolling to grab the lube from the bedside table.

"Lie on your side," he said and took the bottle from my hands.

He tucked in behind me, his dick nestled against my ass as he kissed my neck and shoulder. I turned my head, watching as his hand skated over my ribs and down to my hip. I raised my knee, kissing him, lightheaded and breathless. The cap of the bottle clicked open and then shut, and when his slick fingers brushed against me, I shivered, hungry for his touch. He slipped inside my body one finger at a time, stretching me, slow and too easy.

I pushed back, needing more, and he stopped. "Hate you."

He bit my shoulder, and with his three fingers deep inside me, I was completely on edge. His chuckle alone would be enough to make me come at this point.

"I think you like it," he said and rubbed the pad of his finger against my prostate.

My head fell forward on a moan, my toes curling at his touch. Pressure and heat began to build under my skin and at the base of my spine. When he pulled his fingers from between my legs, the emptiness consumed me. My face was hot, every muscle in my body ached for more and I cried out with relief as he seated himself inside me. Anders's fingernails dug into my hip, his teeth sinking into my shoulder as he railed into me. My back was sticky with sweat, my hand clutching the sheet, the burn of his body branded me with every full thrust of his hips. The only word in my head, *yours, yours, yours,* echoing louder and louder as my climax neared its peak. I reached for my cock, jacking myself hard and fast as Anders's groans gave way to a strangled gasp. His heat poured into me, and I came with his name on my lips and his mouth on my neck. Out of breath we lay there, tangled and whole.

He kissed me as he pulled out, letting me fall onto my back. I tugged on his lip with my teeth while his fingers sketched lazy circles on my stomach.

"We might need to change the sheets," I said.

"I have another set in the closet." He kissed the tip of my nose, my lips, my forehead. "I can change them if you want to clean up."

"Nah, I kind of like how messy you make me." I nipped his chin. "Is that weird?"

"Only a little," he said and grinned when I wrestled him onto his back.

I hovered over him, my hands on either side of his face. "You love my quirks."

"I love everything about you."

His eyes softened around the edges, his truth bursting inside my chest, flooding my heart, leaving no room for uncertainty. This man was mine.

"I'm confused," Anders said, staring out the windshield. "Why are we at a dog park? I thought we were getting breakfast."

I turned off the engine and internally smiled as I ignored his question. "How come you never told me expensive cars were this fun to drive?"

"Ethan... why are we here?" He scanned the large, open field, his bewilderment more amusing than it should be.

The park wasn't overly crowded, only a dozen or so people were there. The lady I'd purchased the puppy from had agreed to hold on to him until this morning. I could see her sitting on a bench inside the fence, a chubby, floppy-eared puppy scrambling around her feet.

"All will be revealed, but I want to talk to you about something first." I shifted in my seat and faced him, biting back my smile.

It was a rare thing, seeing Anders worried and rattled. He was the definition of composed.

"Talk."

I chuckled and reached across the console and rested my hand on his knee. "I'm moving in."

"Yes. We discussed this last night."

"And last night we didn't talk about money." Anders sighed but I kept going. "I can't afford to pay half of your mortgage, or probably half of your utilities, but—"

"It's insulting, Ethan. I can afford it. You're in school. I want to help you. We're partners, right?"

"Exactly, that's my point. We joke about you being my sugar daddy, but if I move in and don't contribute, the joke becomes a reality."

"Then contribute, you can give me whatever you pay Jax and Wilder toward the bills, and once you have a steady income, we can revisit the topic."

"I'll be in school for at least two years, four if I get my BSN."

"You said you can work as an RN with an Associate's. You'll have a steady income soon enough. I don't give a shit about money. I bought that house hoping I'd get to share it with someone. And now I can. It was an empty shell, and with you it's a home."

My smile stretched across my face. "Well, when you put it that way..."

"What does any of that have to do with a dog park?"

"Not quite there yet," I said, and he narrowed his eyes. "I'll give you what I can toward bills, and you have to let me help with groceries and shit or I'll go crazy."

"Fine."

"Good." I grinned and he laughed.

"Can we circle back to why we're here now?" he asked, and I opened the car door.

"Follow me."

I heard him mutter something under his breath as he got out of the car. He stuffed his hands in his pockets as he walked next to me, and I loved how much being in the dark aggravated the shit out of him. I opened the gate, and a giant fluffy dog jumped on Anders and almost knocked him down. At first, I thought he was pissed, but he pulled his hands from his pockets and scratched the mutt behind its ears.

Once he trotted away, Anders stared at me. "Please tell me you did not get a mastiff."

"I did not get you a mastiff." I pressed my lips together as he fought his smile.

"But you got me a dog?"

"I got *us* a dog." I tried to smile, but cringed at the same time, hoping like hell he wasn't about to freak out. "A basset hound."

He rubbed a palm over his day-old beard and shook his head. "You're serious?"

"Yes."

"Holy shit."

"I didn't want you to be lonely when I started school in the fall. I had no idea you were going to ask me to move in with you. But this is even better," I said, and he blinked at me. "We're partners now, right?" Out of nowhere a wave of emotion hit me, my throat aching as I spoke. "We're family. Every family needs a dog."

He reached up and stroked my bottom lip, his gaze warm as he searched my face. "I couldn't agree more."

He'd barely placed his lips to mine when a howl broke through our bubble. Anders laughed as we both looked down and found our puppy jumping up on his leg. The lady whistled for him as she stood from the bench, but he didn't listen. Anders knelt down, and the white and tan ball of energy licked his hands, his long ears getting in the way of his feet to his own detriment.

"Seems like it's meant to be if you ask me," she said.

Anders' smile was childlike as he lifted his gaze. "He's adorable. What's his name?"

"Didn't pick one yet," she said. "I call him Fatty. But y'all get to name him."

"Fatty?" Anders gave me a look and I smiled. "I think we can think of something more body positive."

She hooted and the puppy barked. "I better get going. I have a puppy I gotta take to Marietta."

"Thanks for bringing him," I said.

"No big deal... but don't forget what I told you about the food, and you have the vaccine information. Don't miss his first appointment."

"Yes, ma'am."

Anders stood as she held out a purple leash and he took it from her hand. "Thank you. We'll take good care of him."

"I'm sure you will."

She bent down to pet the puppy one last time, making sure to remind us again about the vet appointment before she left. Anders and I sat in the grass and the puppy attacked him first, then tumbled into my lap when he stumbled over his feet again.

"He's clumsy as hell. His head's too big for his body," I said, and when the dog looked up at me with sad, droopy eyes, I felt bad. "I think she gave him a complex with that nickname."

"What do you want to name him?" Anders asked, picking the dog up from my lap and kissing him on the nose.

"I have no idea, but you're killing me with how cute you are holding a fucking puppy."

His cheeks pinked as he fiddled with the dog's ears. "What about Hemingway?"

"Of course, you'd want to name him something snooty."

"Ernest Hemingway is one of the greatest writers of all time," he argued.

"Wasn't he into cats, though?"

The dog yawned and rolled over on his back in Anders's lap.

"What about Mack for McDonald's?" he suggested, rubbing the puppy's fat, spotted belly, and as much as I loved the sentiment behind the name, it didn't fit.

"You're adorable."

"I'm serious," he said, his blond hair shuffling in the light breeze. "It's a good, solid name."

"Hank is a solid name."

The puppy yipped and Anders laughed. "I think he likes Hank."

"Do you like it?"

"Hank..." Anders mused and tangled his fingers with mine. "It suits him."

"Hank will be an excellent fisherman."

"I don't know..." he said with a crooked smile. "Hank seems like the type to sleep in and read."

"Why can't he do both?"

"He can."

"Because he's ours."

Anders's eyes got all soft again like they had last night, and I scooted closer to him, needing to feel the weight of his body against me.

"Word of the day..." Anders leaned in to kiss me, hesitating, and my eyes fell to his mouth. "Ours... defined as that which belongs to me and you."

"Our family of three," I said, curling my fingers into the cotton fabric of his t-shirt, pulling him close, I breathed him in, and he kissed me as Hank snuggled across both of our laps.

Epilogue

Anders

Two Years Later

The summer sun poked through the trees, the breeze coming off the lake did little to cool things down. I swallowed the rest of my beer and stood to grab another from the cooler. Ethan smiled at me as he baited his hook, Jason chatting away with a smile on his face while Charlotte tugged on his hand.

"It's just a worm, Charlie. It's not gross," Jay said, and she stuck out her tongue.

Hank had fallen asleep under the picnic table, snoring loud enough he had Sammie giggling while her dad tried to braid her hair.

"Baby, you have to stay still," Jax said, pulling a rubber tie around the bottom of one of her dark brown pigtails.

I sat down and twisted off the cap, smiling at the pudgy-cheeked little girl. She was barely eighteen months old when she'd been placed with Jax and Wilder a year ago, and I couldn't believe how much she'd grown since then.

"You think Hank is funny?" I asked her and she giggled again.

"You should see her with Rosie," he said, finishing off her other pigtail. "She thinks she can ride her like a horse."

I chuckled and set my bottle onto the wooden table. "I think it's a rite of passage for any dog."

"Daddy, swim," she said, and wriggled in his lap.

"Not yet, sweetheart." He glanced over his shoulder at his husband. Wilder was under one of the trees talking with June and Gwen. "We have to wait for Daddy to bring us the sunscreen."

"I can go get it," I offered and Jax shook his head.

"That's alright, he probably got talking and forgot." He stood, holding his daughter in his arms, her big brown eyes wide with excitement. "Should we go get Dad instead of waiting?" Jax nuzzled his nose into her neck and she squealed. "You should come swimming, too."

"Maybe, I think your mom should be here soon with lunch."

"She went all out, I think she thought there would be more people," he said.

"I don't know, between Ethan and Jason, I'm not sure we'll have enough."

"You speak the truth." Sammie wiggled in his arms and he laughed. "I better get her ready to swim before she starts hollering."

Jax retreated to the shade of the trees as Hank yawned under the table and rested his head on my foot. I reached down and scratched his ear, watching as Jax set Sammie down and she ran full force into Wilder's arms. He picked her up and spun her, the baby blue ruffles on her swimsuit fluttering in the wind. It was surreal watching him with her. He'd changed since she'd become part of their family. He hadn't lost his theatrics, but he'd grown, having to put himself second to her needs. It was good for him. Good for her.

"I'm starving," Ethan said, picking up my beer and taking a sip for himself.

He leaned down and I kissed him, the bitter taste of hops lingering on his lips. "Food should be here soon."

He sat down next to me, setting his fishing pole against the table. "After lunch, you should grab a pole and come fish with us."

"I think I will," I said, admiring his sun-kissed cheeks. I rubbed my hand over his shoulder. "You're looking a little pink."

"Yeah, I burn easy." He leaned into me. "It's been a good day so far, though."

"You deserve it, you worked hard."

"I can't believe you put all this together for me," he said. Ethan ran his fingers through my hair. "And I had no idea."

"You were studying for the national board exam. You were distracted."

"I'm so glad it's over," he said and exhaled a relieved sigh. "I almost don't want to go back for my BSN."

"Yes, you do."

He kissed my cheek and laced our fingers together. "Thank you... I don't think I could've done this without you. You pushed me, Anders, gave me hope when all I wanted to do was quit."

"That's what partners do."

"Ugh... when are you two going to bite the bullet and get married already?" Wilder plopped down, bulldozing through our private conversation. "I mean, there's no reason not to."

Ethan kicked him under the table and Hank groaned. "I have an idea, stay out of it. Not everyone wants what you have."

"Wilder is incapable of minding his own business. Shouldn't you be over there with your husband swimming with Sammie?"

"You're almost forty, Anders. It's time to make your little partnership official."

I'd marry Ethan tomorrow if that's what he wanted. We'd talked about marriage a few times, but he was worried about finishing school first.

"We're official." Ethan shot him a dirty look. "We don't need to have some heteronormative piece of paper to tell us we're a forever couple."

"Babe," Jax interrupted, giving me an apologetic smile. "Watch her while I help my mom carry the food from the car."

He set Sammie in Wilder's lap and he squeaked. "She's wet."

"That happens when you get in water." Ethan's sarcastic remark was met with a sardonic smile.

Wilder covered his daughter's ears. "You're in a poopy mood. Isn't this your yay-I'm-a-nurse-now party?"

"Poopy?" I raised my eyebrows.

"Yes, *poopy*. Children are present."

"I'm in a good mood," Ethan said. "I just hate it when you insert your two cents when it's unwarranted."

"Amen." June laughed, taking a seat at the end of the picnic table.

Gwen was right behind her with Charlotte in her arms, and Wilder made room for her, setting Sammie down next to their daughter. The two little girls smiled and chatted at each other, and instead of bickering with my boyfriend, Wilder watched the two with pride. Once Jax and his mom had all the food spread out, Jason and Mabel made their way to the table too. We shoveled food in our mouths like we hadn't eaten in weeks. The heat had zapped my energy, and the fresh sandwiches and cool pasta salad was exactly what I'd needed. After we stuffed our faces, the conversation picked up again. Ethan kept his hand on my thigh the whole time, sneaking kisses when he could.

"I wish your parents were here," Ethan whispered. "It doesn't feel complete without them."

"My mom feels terrible. She said she'll make it up to you when they get back from Italy."

"She doesn't owe me anything. I just wish they could've been here is all. Everyone I love is at this table except for them. They're my family too."

"I know... When they get back, we should do it again. My mom would love that."

"That's too much," he said, but I smiled.

"You're worth it."

His eyes fell to my mouth, and I leaned in to kiss him, not realizing the entire table had gone silent.

"Mabel said y'all are too sweet." Jason grinned at us as we pulled away.

"Thanks," I said and signed at the same time.

"Tell them they need to get married." Wilder spoke as he signed, and Ethan flipped him off.

Mabel laughed, and as she signed Jason translated. "She said that wasn't very nice, Ethan."

Ethan shrugged, a small smile on his face as he signed. "I'm sorry."

"No, you're not." Wilder rolled his eyes and Ethan gave him a cheesy grin.

"How's the film coming along, Wilder?" Mrs. Stettler asked, giving Wilder the attention, he loved, while diverting the conversation away from us.

"I'm going to grab water from the cooler, want one?" Ethan asked me and stood, stretching his long arms over his head.

"Sure," I said, distracted by the muscles of his abs and the way his hip bone disappeared under his swim trunks.

I loved how his shoulders tapered down to slim hips where his swimming trunks sat low enough on his ass, I could see his tan line. While I was busy checking out my boyfriend as he bent down to grab the bottles of water from the cooler, Sammie stole his seat, hanging over the bench to play with Hank.

"Doggie," she said, smiling at him and pulling on his ears.

"Be easy, baby," Jax said, and I sent him a grateful smile.

Ethan handed me a bottle of water and took the seat across from me.

"Thanks," I said and unscrewed the cap.

I took a long sip, and as I set it down, my phone vibrated in my pocket. I chuckled when I saw I had a message from Ethan.

Ethan: We should, you know.

Me: We should what?

Ethan kept his eyes down as he typed under the table.

Ethan: Get married.

I raised my head and found his stunning, caramel eyes staring back at me.

Me: Did you just propose to me via text?

Ethan: I think I might have.

My hands were clammy, and it had nothing to do with the heat. I wanted this, and if he was joking...

Ethan: I want to marry you.

"You're serious?"

Ethan: Marry me, Anders

I exhaled a laugh and ran a hand through my hair as I looked around the table. Everyone was lost in their own bubble, oblivious to my trembling fingers, to the smile I couldn't contain. Surrounded by family, Ethan had given us this private moment. It was perfectly us.

Me: I want to marry you more than I've ever wanted anything.

I glanced up in time to watch his cheeks turn pink.

Ethan: Then marry me.

Me: What's another word for yes?

Ethan: Fuck yes?

I laughed quietly and pressed my foot against his under the table, both of us looking up at the same time, our future starting in that very second as I mouthed the words, Fuck yes.

The End

Playlist

https://open.spotify.com/
playlist/3l5B9JzNqBsJQNkrPht3jm?si=9U3
JIUESRrmkeT_ZEBAfaw&utm_source5=copy-link

If you enjoyed this book, check out *Let There Be Light*.
Available on Amazon.

Acknowledgements

I'm so grateful you chose to pick up this book and read it! It means the world to me! I couldn't have typed THE END without some help from some very amazing friends. Also, it should be noted, I typed these acknowledgments after the editing process, so don't judge the typos and grammar, okay?!

To my beta team and besties: Cornelia, Sammie, Kristy, Ari, Elle, Sheila, Braxton, Rebecca, Bel, Amy, Beth, Jodi, Azeely, Taylor, and Alissa. Y'all hold me accountable and make me a better storyteller. For that I am indebted to you.

To my editors, ladies, as always you are my rock. You are the surgeons of words, getting rid of all my grammatical cellulite. Thank you, thank you, thank you. Don't kill me for writing these after the edit!

To my friends old and new, you know who you are! This year was shit show, and I don't think I would've survived it without you. Marley and Saxon, thank you for our daily talks. The confidence and support you give me is priceless. All of my bookish friends and author friends, Romancelandia feels big and scary sometimes, and having you in my corner, makes the navigation that much easier.

To my darling family, this has been the hardest year we have faced, and yet, we are still breathing. Thank you for letting me escape into my words when I needed to. For understanding mommy needed to sleep after working the night shift at the hospital and writing until 7am some nights, and maybe I should thank Kraft Mac and Cheese while I'm at it. Love you, Wolf. Almost 12 years, half of which I've dedicated myself to this writing gig and you have supported me failure and success.

To the 81,283,098 people who voted for black lives, for love, for human rights, thank you. Thank you for giving me hope again, but also thank you for opening my eyes to what still needs to be done. And to Stacey Abrams, not that you'll ever see this, but you are goals.

Jodi and Beth, I know I gave you shit about Anders and Ethan. I know I didn't think it could work. But without your little push, this book would not be written. Thank you, oodles, and panda hugs for sparking what is hands down my most favorite story I've written.

Ari, my PA and best boo. Thank you for not dying from COVID. I love you. All the pieces and moods and smiles.

Last but not least, to my dedicated and fucking amazing readers. I love you immensely. AJ's Crew, AJ's Biscuits, every single bookstagrammer, FB blogger, all of you who continually support and promote my words, you are **everything**!

I will inevitably have left someone out, and I'll feel guilty as hell, but please know, if you are in my life, you are loved.

SO SO Sincerely,
Amanda

Other Books by A.M. Johnson

Forever Still Series:

Still Life

Still Water

Still Surviving

Avenues Ink Series:

Possession

Kingdom

Poet

Twin Hearts Series:

Let There Be Light

Seven Shades of You

For Him Series:

Love Always, Wild

Not So Sincerely, Yours

The Rulebook Collection

Breakaway

Stand Alone Novels:

Sacred Hart

Erotica:

Beneath the Vine

Made in the USA
Columbia, SC
04 April 2021

35489639R00274